The Invisible Companion

Zhang Kangkang
Translated by Daniel Bryant

New World Press   Beijing, China

First Edition 1996

ISBN 7-80005-299-0
Published by
New World Press
24 Baiwanzhuang Road, Beijing 100037, China

Distributed by
China International Book Trading Corporation
35 Chegongzhuang Xilu, Beijing 100044, China
P.O. Box 399, Beijing, China

Printed in the People's Republic of China

In this novel modernist writing skills are employed to express the complicated inner worlds of the protagonists. The novel aims to explore the relationship between the self and non-self, the link between subconsciousness and behavior.

This story takes place in the 1970s. Xiao Xiao, the heroine, falls in love with Chen Xu, an educated youth from Hangzhou with whom she was sent to the Great Northern Wilderness. Regarding Chen as the embodiment of her ideals, Xiao marries him while still in the countryside and gives birth to his child. However through the mundanities of everyday life, she gradually discovers the ugliness in Chen's soul and this drives her to leave him.

Under immense pressure, Xiao Xiao begins to pursue the type of spiritual life she thinks to be enlightened. But the hypocrisy of reality raises doubts in Xiao Xiao's mind about her own innocence, as well as causing her to question society. Facing the complications of real life, she finally comes to the painful realization that in the past she herself had been as base as Chen Xu.

Xiao Xiao abandons this false loftiness and jettisons her hypocritical, empty ideals. Thus having found her real self, she starts once again on life's lonely road.

1

The sun had set, and now the patient plain had waited a long while beneath a layer of deep purple clouds. Unextinguished sparks of sunlight still shimmered on the tips of the weeds that swept over the low hills. All summer long, night had lingered so in falling; not until it had packed the last pale fireflies into its dark sack and stretched wearily out to rest did the blue sky vanish.

As she squeezed out through the hole on the eastern perimeter, where the earth wall had collapsed, she jammed her tongue tight against her teeth for fear the pounding of her heart should be heard. Her bulging canvas satchel scraped bits of sand from the surface of the wall, grit that in the stillness of the fields fell to earth with all the thunder of bombs dropped during war games with live ammunition. Every hair on her body stood on end, and the two stubby pigtails on her head grew rock hard, threatening to wedge her inside the hole.

She was struck by the bitter tang of the weeds, a grassy smell found only outside the walls. She straightened up and looked out over the vast plain stretching off into the distance like a cloud of thick, drifting smoke. She took a deep breath and let it out slowly, standing still and looking apprehensively all around her.

Where was he?

The evening dew lay cool on the thick grass, which snaked up her calves and tangled itself over her shoes. Her toes began to feel sticky and stiff. Wading for water chestnuts in the winter paddy fields down south, swishing through the thin mud in search of cold, hard lumps. How she had cried when they left the little village, the broad beans sprouting along the paths between the fields, where they had gone to work during her last year of junior high. Beneath her boots now were potato fields. And what was that above her head? Stalks of sorghum? Or corn silks? An endless succession of black nights, just like the endless succession of guard walls; through one after another, but never through the last.

But where was he?

The flashlight had long since grown sweaty in her grip, a stick of freshly washed, purple sugar cane. If she did turn it on, it would only be for a moment. The night was so forbidding and unfamiliar. It had swallowed up the shapes of the trees and the very last streak of sunset. Even the dark blue sky, the silvery stars, the rich green wind, and the mosquitos darting around her were so well hidden that they were invisible, nothing but a buzzing in the air. This was the Great Northern Wastes, a lonely plain where not a single lamplight was to be seen, not a single fisherman's lantern. Only here could there be a night so boundless, a blackness of such infinite extent. It was as resolutely black as the rich earth in early spring, soaked in run-off from the melting snow.

At last she flicked her flashlight on and swept it over the low elm tree above her head.

She shuddered.

A few tangled swaths of wire mesh fencing snaked across the top of the wall. They glimmered silently in the dark, like an immense net cast down from the heavens. At the corners of the earth wall, two ruined watchtowers were dimly visible, facing each other in the distance and blinking furtively, like a pair of prying eyes.

Was it time for their exercise period? Was there a chance that someone would toss a wad of paper at her feet? Perhaps they would just shout slogans, staining the iron bars red with their hot blood. Why were heroes always locked up? You were a hero no matter how you were martyred.

How pious a yearning it had been. It was their hard luck to have been born ten years too late, and now the wire mesh symbolized no more than this simple distinction: one batch after another of city kids replacing the filthy, ragged labour-camp inmates. The ruined earth walls, the watchtowers, the lookout posts, all these reminded them over and over again that this had once been a prison camp, a prison camp, a prison camp...

She broke out in gooseflesh. She had never been outside the walls by herself before, especially not out in the fields, in the whispering wind, with that huge black shape oozing a dank chill, like a tomb, a cage, a pit.

A rustling in the weeds and a man's whisper. "Turn off the flash!"

Two great warm hands embraced her from behind. She smelled something familiar, the sultry smell of a man, blended of sweat and tobacco. She laid her head on that broad shoulder and let out a deep breath. Then she clung to his neck, drew her body up into a ball, and buried herself in his embrace.

He released her at once and spun around, alert as a hunting dog with its ears pricked up. "Listen!" he hissed, "What's that noise?"

It was like the north wind moaning over the bare telephone poles on the vast winter plain, like the distant howling of a wolf heard across the fields as the snow was melting, the swirling, keening lament of a river pouring through a sluice gate or the piping plaints of a flock of injured birds. It was a ragged, intermittent trilling, heard faintly and fitfully inside the wall.

"They're crying," she said. "All the southern girls in our platoon are crying."

"Why?"

"They got some letters from home. The Qiantang River is flooding, and the water is threatening to break into the city. Someone said they'd never see their mothers again. One of them started to cry, then another, and finally they were all crying. A'li cried herself into convulsions."

He interrupted her. "Give me your handkerchief."

"What for?"

"Give it to me."

She pulled out her handkerchief and handed it to him. It was neatly folded and smelled faintly of soap.

He squeezed it once and gave it back to her, with a trace of a smile.

"Well, what do you know! You weren't crying."

"No." She smiled too. "I came out just as they started."

When she was a little girl, she had sometimes sat by herself on her little stool after her mother had gone to work and cried until she got back home. Mama! But she had not even written to her mother since she left home. What could she cry about? Her eyes and nose were numb.

"Did anyone see you leave?" he asked, after a moment.

"No, they were too busy crying."

"What about Guo Chunmei?"

"She didn't cry either. She went to get Dr. Yang. She said she wanted him to give everyone a shot of sedative."

"Hm. Did you bring your towel and toothbrush?"

"Yes, and I've got money and ration coupons."

He was silent. She could hear him cracking his knuckles.

3

"Okay," he said at last. "Let's go."

"Where are we going?"

"Just come with me."

"Are we going to Jiamusi to see a movie, or..."

"I told you, don't ask so many questions." He clasped her waist a little impatiently and gave her a squeeze.

An almost imperceptible path, trod through the weeds by workboots on their way to the fields, led toward the dark, grey road.

She stopped and took hesitant hold of her satchel.

"I have to know," she said.

He yanked up a sprig of grass, broke it in half, and threw it on the ground. Then he growled, "They interrogated me this afternoon, didn't you notice? You should know, you should have known a long time ago where we are going. Back to the South, back to Hangzhou. Where else is there for us to go?"

She gasped. "Back to Hangzhou? But, but I haven't applied for leave!"

"Leave?" He snorted. "What a preposterous idea!"

She shuddered, biting her lip. She was silent for a long time, and then ventured, "But they'll say that we're, that we're deserters!"

"Are you afraid?" In the darkness, two bright sparks flared. "I thought that you would be behind me, even if no one else was." He brushed her aside and headed for the road. "In fact, it wasn't for my own sake that I wanted you to come with me, but for yours. If I went away and left you here alone, you'd have a hard time of it. Deserters? It's not Zhenbao Island.*"

The voice was a little farther away, but his footsteps had halted.

A faint moaning could still be heard from time to time, swirling in the air above the square black walls like a troop of homeless, driven banshees, roaming the unfamiliar land.

That evening a year before, as the 'puffnik', loaded down with baggage and passengers, had swept within those walls, a mournful, battered gong had welcomed them with its raucous bong bong bong, nailing the lid of their box down tight.

She dashed after him and clutched his arm.

Their footsteps whispered away. One could not have told if it was one person walking or two.

* Chinese and the Soviet army had a series of clashes at that frontier island in 1969.

4

She turned and took a quick look back toward the dark shape of the mud wall, surprised to find that she felt no trace of attachment to it. She had lived inside that wall for a whole year, and not once had she dreamed that she might leave. But now, all of a sudden, the two of them had left on the sly, out through the hole in the earth wall that the kids from Hangzhou had named, after an old gate of their hometown, the 'Green Ripple Gate', just blithely walking away from it with their satchels on their backs.

It seemed to be somehow wrong, wrong and unnatural, as though they had things somehow backwards. This road led in the exact opposite direction from their coming to the Farm a year before.

And yet, so long as she was with him, it did not seem so terrible a thing to be a deserter.

The savage night smiled. Her pigtails danced gently on her shoulders.

2

Luck was with them. Not long after they started down the road, two beams of light appeared behind them, coming from the direction of Branch Farm No. 7. A black shape was bouncing along toward them like a giant flea, the motor making a deafening racket.

Chen Xu held his Little Red Book up in the light.

A truck slowed to a halt, rumbling away like steam out of a panful of boiling water. It was what they called a 'puffnik', a kind of combination tractor and truck developed by the Russians.

"Where ya headed? How 'bout a lift?" shouted Chen Xu.

Someone stuck his head out of the cab. It was a large round head, closely cropped, like the green brush of a southern rice paddy in March, when the white plastic film is removed. The corners of the mouth were slightly turned up.

"Over to the kilns to pick up some bricks," answered the driver. His voice was soft and high-pitched, rather childish. Luck was with them. He wouldn't give them any trouble. "Where you guys headed?" he asked.

Chen Xu grabbed the window frame with one hand and stepped up on the running board, shouting, "We're going into town to line up at the Xinhua bookstore. They say there'll be some new books for sale tomorrow."

The truck jumped, and they were on their way. Xiao Xiao jumped too, and was almost knocked down. She tried sitting on the side panel, but it was so low and narrow that she could not keep her seat and had to sit on the floor. The truck plunged to one side and threw her to the left, then back to the right. Her rear end was getting sore from being bounced around, thrown back and forth like a parcel or a rubber ball. The kid driving the truck seemed to think the box was some kind of playing field.

Chen Xu shouted over to her, "You'd better just stand up!"

"How can I stand up?" She arched her back and clung for dear life to the strip of steel running across the front of the bed, but there really was nothing to hang on to or lean against, or even to drape herself over, for that matter. It was a 'tugboat' used for moving grain and fertilizer and not really intended for people to ride in at all. With a loud thud, the truck began to bounce up and down like a heavily laden sampan in a rough sea. Unable to stand up any longer, she lost her footing and was almost knocked off. Chen Xu held her by the waist and shouted into her ear, "Crouch down like me!"

She crouched, keeping her legs wide apart. A cloud of dust and grit hit her in the face so hard that her skin hurt. "It's brick dust; close your eyes!" shouted Chen Xu, holding up her arm with one hand. They must have looked very funny like that. How could the Russians have come up with such a vehicle? When she saw the trapeze act in the Qiqiha'er Circus before the Cultural Revolution, it had made her feel giddy just to watch. It just had to be one of these puffniks; there was one allotted to each company, just like subscriptions to 'Red Flag' magazine.

She closed her eyes. She felt like her skeleton was coming apart joint by joint and her organs changing places. Her ears seemed to have been shredded, and she could not tell if she still had any hair left on her head. The worst of it was that she now had a puffnik driving around in her stomach, which was heaving and ready to split wide open at any moment. From her spine to her shoulder blades, she had been ground into a lump, and her whole body ached and tingled. It seemed to her that if she let go for even an instant, her legs would separate from the rest of her.

"Chen Xu!" she wailed.

Chen Xu thought for a moment and then picked up a piece of brick and lobbed it toward the front of the truck.

There was a loud thump. Her chest was flung forward against the panel, and the truck stopped.

"What's the matter?" The little driver stuck his head out again.

"Better let her sit up in the cab with you. She can't take it back here." Chen Xu stuffed her and her satchel into the cab without waiting for an answer.

"If you can't ride a puffnik you don't really belong on the Farm," muttered the little driver. "Hey! Watch out you don't hit my bird." He stuck one leg out to protect a box under the seat.

"What kind of bird?" Raising birds in a truck?

"I caught it a few days ago while I was ploughing up by the reservoir. It was hurt. I put some mercurochrome on it, but I don't know if I can raise it. If I kept it in the dorm, the guys would have fried it for dinner by now. There are lots of birds out in the fields, all different colours." A trace of fuzz was visible on his face in the light from the head lamps.

Xiao Xiao could not see what colour the bird was; the seat was too high. He was sure taking life easy, driving a truck and raising a bird at the same time!

The truck started up again. It bounced around as much as ever, but now she had something to hang on to, and so her fears vanished. What was it he had just said? Of course, if you hadn't ridden in a puffnik you didn't know what 'bumpy' meant.

"New books? What kind of new books are there nowadays worth lining up at midnight for?" grunted the driver, without looking at her.

If he went on asking questions, their game would be up. Why did Chen Xu have to lie to him? Couldn't he just say, well, what could he have said? That they were going back to Hangzhou? And why did they have to go back to Hangzhou? Why had Political Instructor Yu called Chen Xu in for a talk that afternoon? Did last night's brawl on the farm have anything to do with Chen Xu? He hadn't touched anyone.

The truck gave a sudden lurch and headed off toward the side of the road.

"Shit!" The little driver swore and stepped on the gas, grappling with the steering wheel.

Xiao Xiao could tell he was having a hard time and felt a little sorry for him.

"How long have you been driving a truck?"

"Oh, a week or two, I guess. I was driving an 'East is Red' tractor before."

"My, you've learned fast!"

"Nothing to it! One of the old mechanics says that even a dog could learn to drive if you put steamed buns on the control sticks. It's simple!" He grinned.

He was doing his best to speak with a northeastern accent, but Xiao Xiao recognised the clipped endings of southern speech.

"From Ningpo?"

"Wenzhou. How about you guys?"

"Hangzhou. You must be barely what, sixteen?"

"No, fifteen."

"So young, and serving on the frontier?"

8

"I'm not that young. My dad..." He swallowed the rest of his sentence.

The truck gave a sudden shake, and she was bounced upward. The wheels were vibrating and spinning as though working off some pent-up resentment, flattening it out on the dark road.

What had broken? A window? A thermos? A tile? Or was it that snow-white swan's egg? When she jumped off the brick bed and ran outside, still wrapped up in her quilt, she found the battle already raging in front of the boys' dorm. Shadowy human forms were rolling and thrashing about, curling up into balls, with waving hands and flailing feet, kicking viciously at the darkness—how patient and resilient the darkness seemed. It was as if huge trees had been uprooted by a hurricane, as if an automatic shuttle and a wheel had jammed: moans, calls for help, shouts, curses, they all came crashing hideously down like chunks of earth in a cave-in. Pieces of broken glass were raining crazily all around like dirt flung up by bombs. A cold gleam whizzed by her—they were using spades, mattocks, coal shovels, pickaxes! Someone jumped up on a haystack and then tumbled down screaming, his leg caught by a sharp mattock as though it were a lump of fresh manure. A spade flew through the air and a blossomed cap fell to the ground. She stumbled and touched an arm; something dark and sticky and cold oozed onto her fingers.

"Fighting isn't allowed!" She ran toward them.

"Go back inside!" A hand dragged her roughly away. It was Bubble, Chen Xu's sidekick. There wasn't a single button left on his shirt; a steel grey glint shone in his eyes. "This is militia training." He winked at her.

They had put away their hoes only the day before yesterday. The kids from Hegang and Shuangyashan had gone home. Where was the company commander, Sleepy Liu? Drunk again? Who would come to help? And to help whom? Who was fighting whom?

"Ready to give in your submission to your Master?"

Bubble was kicking at something soft. There was a scream. Why had he put on gym shoes? All summer long he had worn only a pair of slippers. He didn't really have any gym shoes, he had lost them. They had dropped out of the window when their train was leaving for the north. He had got off the train in slippers. In the winter he wore padded boots.

"Hey, Bull! Ready to give in your sbumission to your Master?"

"Don't fight! Why can't you talk it over?" A tall thin boy wearing

9

a dark blue uniform pushed through the crowd. A pair of glasses glinted below his forehead.

"Mind your own business, bookworm. Beat it!" Bubble cocked his head to one side and poked a fist at him.

"Fighting is a sign of ignorance," muttered the boy in blue, going to pick up his glasses. It was Zou Sizhu; he and Chen Xu had come from the same school.

Someone else pushed forward. "Wei Hua!" a girl screamed. Wei Hua, the newly promoted deputy company commander, was from Hegang. His face was badly beaten, one of his lips split in two like a watermelon. Bubble pulled on the bottom of his jacket, whipping it up so that it turned inside out like a sack. Wei Hua's head was caught inside, but his chest and ribs were left completely exposed. Fire hooks and feet pelted his tanned skin.

She shivered and her legs gave way. Her teeth were chattering. She wanted to call Chen Xu. Where was Chen Xu? If this went on, Wei Hua could be beaten to death.

A girl ran up clutching a flowered quilt and spread it clumsily over Wei Hua. A stick hit her on the leg with a crack. It was her friend, Guo Chunmei. What was she doing here? Xiao Xiao ran over and tried to pull her away, but she would not budge.

"That's enough. Stop fighting."

She heard a voice above her head. Chen Xu was standing in the shadows, coolly smoothing down his hair, which was in fact quite neat. Where had he been just now?

He went off to get a cartman so they could take Wei Hua to the Farm hospital in town.

Bull was lying by a haystack, unconscious. And what about that swan's egg? It must have been broken, broken in the fields at noon.

"Here's where I turn off," said the driver all of a sudden.

"What?"

"We're there. Here's where you get off."

The machine shuddered to a halt. Were they in mid-air? At sea? Her head was swimming.

"The Xinhua Bookstore is up at the north end of town. There's a latrine in front," the little driver leaned out and told them. "If you run into a local with a cart, you can hitch another ride."

She had forgotten to thank him. Her face felt a little hot. If she blushed, at least it was covered by the darkness. Chen Xu had come up with that Xinhua bookstore awfully fast; she could not bluff anyone like that. Where had he actually been during the fight? Why didn't he turn up until it was almost over? Why did they have to sneak away from the Farm and go back to Hangzhou in such a rush?

"We covered a good five miles in just over ten minutes." As he watched the puffnik bounce off into the darkness, Chen Xu took the satchel from her shoulder and hefted it.

Just over ten minutes? And yet it felt as though they had made an Atlantic crossing.

3

The moon had squeezed its way out from somewhere or other, a thin crescent like a sickle blade, a grinning spirit with an immensely aloof expression. A few strands of deep blue cloud twined about it, but their attempts at dialogue met with rebuff. And so they fell to earth, shrouding the dimly moonlit land beneath a layer of cryptic night fog. Now the darkness was tempered and the pale light blurred. As the two of them walked along this road rendered uncertain by the moonlight, everything seemed a little unreal, thought Xiao Xiao.

There had been another fight a few days before, in the fields at noon. Where had he been then?

It was too bad that by the time Zou Sizhu had come to tell her to go to the office that afternoon, Instructor Yu had just about finished with his dressing down. And besides, there was a door in the way, and on the door two panes of glass painted over with blue and a board nailed over another so that only one window remained. Most of what they were saying inside was only vaguely audible. She could see Chief Sun with his sleeves rolled up and one foot on an open desk drawer. Bubble was on the floor in a corner of the room, the pistol on Sun's hip almost on a level with his nose. Instructor Yu was leaning back in a leather chair, swinging his legs and smoking. That leather chair had been especially made for him, and he looked very pleased with himself when rocking in it. Bubble was hanging his head, glancing helplessly at Chen Xu, who stood silent and impassive.

Someone flashed by outside the window. A collar faded from washing. The light reflected from his glasses flashed on Xiao Xiao's jacket buttons.

It looked like Zou Sizhu. He had been strolling back and forth outside the window for a little while already.

He had even gone so far as to jump up and look in.

She walked outside. Sure enough, it was him, standing close to the wall. He looked like he had had a fright. Lips trembling, he said, "I was looking for you."

12

When he walked past a girl, he never even glanced at her. If one of the girls got stuck and fell behind while spading, he never took over her row, no matter who she was. None of the girls would help him wash his bedding, but his clothing was always spotless. Wherever he appeared, he was always all by himself. He was the complete opposite of Chen Xu.

"Now, don't get upset when I tell you."

He pushed his glasses farther up his nose. He seemed rather upset himself.

She began to feel anxious. The first time he had come looking for her, years before, he had begun the same way, and then, just as now, his Adam's apple had bobbed up and down and his lips had been stretched tight, as though he were trying to keep a grip on emotions about to explode.

"What is it?"

"Nothing, nothing too important. It's just that Chen Xu has been called in to the office by Instructor Yu and Chief Sun. They're questioning him."

She felt a chill creeping up her back.

Had Instructor Yu come back from his meeting? Questioning him? What about? Strawberry Glen?

A fleeting sensation of shame welled up within her. It was as though a pillow stuffed with secrets had been slit open and all those whispered endearments and promises of undying love had been sent floating about, filling the air like feathers.

"I'm telling you, it's nothing to worry about. It's probably about the brawl," he reassured her, staring at the ground.

She felt her feet stood on firm ground again as she ran swiftly toward the office.

"That brawl last night, did you start it?" bellowed Chief Sun at Chen Xu.

"Your evidence?" replied Chen Xu coolly.

Why did she always remember this part? Even in his sleep tonight Zou Sizhu would never dream that she and Chen Xu were already miles away. Was it really possible that Chen Xu had planned that fight the night before? Out of the question. Even during the violent days of the 'Smash the Four Olds' campaign, early in the Cultural Revolution, he had never hit anyone. Fighting would be all right in a dream. She had even beaten Bull in her dreams. It served him right. Why did he have to snatch her swan's egg!

13

"I dreamed last night that I was looking for Liu the Brute. I went all the way to the summer squash field." There was something a little ridiculous in the way Xiao Xiao said this, walking along beside Chen Xu.

"Why look for him? His brain is pickled."

"In my dream you guys were always fighting, you even had guns. I was terrified. And then a commander came and announced that World War III had broken out."

He grunted absently.

She was walking across a sandy field. The colour of the sand grains kept changing, like iridescent locusts hopping this way and that. She remembered that she had come looking for the company commander, but she could not walk any faster, no matter how she tried.

There was a well ahead of her, with thunderous snoring coming from inside it. Sleepy Liu! She called his name, leaning over the edge of the well. A fight has broken out in the company. Those bums! he yelled from the bottom of the well. Pull me up. She reached for him, but the sides of the well dropped out of sight, coated with fur-like white frost, so she could not reach far enough. There was a crank handle above the well, but it was stuck tight.

She caught sight of a shallow well, with water coming right up to the top. There was moss growing like green felt all around the mouth of the well, and an osmanthus tree on the mound on which it stood. She walked closer, and found that the leaves were covered with icicles. She turned the crank handle and her hand stuck to the metal, taking off a layer of skin. She had never seen such a well. The hole should be plugged up. No wonder Liu the Brute was hiding inside and drinking. She turned the crank again, and this time she brought up a bucket of water.

A young man, stripped to the waist and wearing bright red undershorts, with a bulging pouch between his legs, came up to take a shower. No sooner had he poured the bucket of water over himself than several girls went running off in all directions, screaming, Look out! There's a Chekkie making trouble! Bull hopped down from the ox cart, grabbed him, and started to beat him up, but the young man in the shorts blew some air at Bull, and swarms of purple fleas and lice jumped out of Bull's clothes, each one as big as a frog. The man in the shorts shouted:

14

Northern bumpkins, northern bumpkins,
Fleas and lice as big as pumpkins,
Pour your grub down hollow stumpkins!
Bull chased after him, yelling:
Fuck your mama, Chekkie man,
Shit in the skillet, piss in the pan,
Eat your dinner while you sit on the can!

The other man slid under a black mosquito net. Outside the net the air was thick with mosquitos, lowing like cattle. Bull lifted the net and shook his 'Locomotive' brand spade, shouting, If you southerners have mosquito nets, the mosquitos are just going to bite us instead! Nothing doing! If they bite, they bite everyone the same! The mosquitos were biting her, and she ducked her head and ran. She smelled alcohol; the smell was coming from the summer squash patch.

Commander Liu! she shouted.

Here I am! The voice came from inside a summer squash.

She kicked the summer squash and it split wide open. Liu the Brute was curled up inside the pulp, snoring away. One bright red nose and two plum-coloured eyes. Three red spots and one red triangle. No question about it, it was Liu the Brute.

A fight has broken out in the company, she said.

Don't call it a fight, it's a battle, Liu yawned. Who's fighting who?

She could not remember who it was, probably Ningbo kids against the ones from Hegang, Hangzhou against Mudanjiang, Shanghai against Shuangyashan. It was north against south.

Doesn't matter, grunted Liu. A little drink and everything'll be okay. Go buy a big jug and fill it up with wine.

She hesitated. A big jug? She was afraid she wouldn't be able to carry it.

He leapt from the summer squash with a splat, two sharp red peppers shooting from his bloodshot eyes. Baring his yellow teeth, he yelled, Can't carry it? What do you mean you can't carry it? Is it full of salted cabbage? Pickled cucumbers? It's empty! Why can't you carry it? Stinking little brat! Go remould yourself!

She went off in a huff to remould herself. Someone wearing a green army cap patted her on the shoulder and asked, What's the fundamental political line?

It's cabbage, she answered. People eat it every day, every month, year in and year out.

There were cabbages everywhere, on the ground and up in the air, crawling and rolling, they slid down her throat whole and got caught on her ribs.

"It's true, I can remember my dreams completely the next day," she said, as though to herself. "Sometimes it's clear down to the last little hair. But the me in the dreams isn't very much like the real me. It's like someone else," she insisted. "Really!"

"Hurry up. We have to get to town before dawn if we want to catch the morning train." Chen Xu quickened his pace, adding, over his shoulder, "For some reason, I never dream at night."

Xiao Xiao shook her head. She did not believe him.

He was emphatic. "I never remember having had any dreams the night before. But sometimes I dream in broad daylight, real and unreal all mixed together. And a moment later it's all gone."

"Daydreams? When you're awake?"

"When I'm awake."

They had been fighting off and on for a couple of weeks.

Was it just over buying a meal? Because of that big ox, Bull?

He could have had no nickname more fitting than 'Bull'. Who else had so many bulges all over him, such a rough black beard, or a pair of feet so much like hooves? When he stepped onto one of the ridges between the paddies, it shook as though it were about to collapse. If anyone touched that 'Locomotive' spade of his, the only one of its kind in the company, or if anyone made faces behind Wei Hua's back, he would go for them, bellowing like a bull after a cow in heat. In fact, he was nothing but a squad leader. Four platoons in the company, twelve squad leaders, but ten of them were northern hicks. That was pushing it too damn far. He himself had been a platoon leader for almost a year, and could hardly wait to be promoted to deputy company commander, but who had they gone and chosen upstairs but Wei Hua, a tongue-tied kid from Hegang whose entire vocabulary consisted of 'yup' and 'nope'. He couldn't so much as fart twice in a row if you hit him with a stick. So what if he could split off a piece of frozen manure the size of a table and carry two gunny sacks full of bean seeds? Who was impressed by that, except for Bull? His face was so dark you couldn't have picked it out on a coal heap. Even his teeth were black. But Instructor Yu said his heart was Red. Red heart, loyal heart. A Red fart? Nothing but a turd! To expect him, Chen Xu, a high school graduate and a platoon leader, to take orders from Wei Hua was really turning the world upside down. But Wei Hua was sharp enough to know better than to try bossing him around. It was only that dumb Bull, hanging around Wei like a bodyguard and yapping like a dog with a powerful master.

It was just over buying a meal.

Bull had charged right over as soon as the meal cart arrived. He grabbed a bunch of steamed buns from the basket, raising his arm and lining them right up from shoulder to wrist, six of them. His deeply tanned arms were as thick as the dark seven-ounce rolls, so it looked just like two arms rolled into one. Then he swaggered over to a thicket by the fields, snapped a branch off one of the trees, ran it through all the buns, and stuck it into the ground so that they towered right up like a little hill. After this he picked up his gleaming 'Locomotive' and sauntered over to the serving dish on the cart. He was an irrigation worker, and his spade glistened like tinfoil. There was not a speck of rust on it, and it shone so bright that one could hardly look directly at it. He breathed on the blade, wiped it a few times on his knee, and then, like the ugly customer he was, parted the crowd of people lined up around the cart with the handle and thrust the dazzling blade right under the server's nose, coming within a hair of cutting part of it off.

"Gimme something to eat!" he growled, motioning toward the spade with his chin.

The cook was a friend of Xiao Xiao's. She dodged the tip of the blade and grumbled, "Line up!"

"Who're you telling to line up?" Light glinted off the tip of the spade as he pulled some money out of his pocket and tossed it down on the cart. "Take it and quit stalling!"

He himself had stood there disdainfully, the soles of his feet prickling hot. At the thought of what was going on, all the fury that had been building up inside him for so long began to swirl around like a whirlpool. Who did this guy think he was? They were both registered for a rice ration of 45 lbs.; they were both 'outsiders' with no local backers. Out in this wilderness beyond the ends of the earth, who was going to count for more, himself, Chen Xu, or Bull here?

"Little Calf!" Someone was tapping on a dish.

"Go back to your barn! There's plenty for you there!" Someone sneered.

Bull had been goaded to anger. The steel spade laden with soup went flying. Bubble was promptly tossed into the paddy field, flat on his back in the mud. In no time, Beanpole's face looked like a combination of the two villains from the revolutionary model opera 'Shajiabang', Hu Chuankui on one side and Diao Deyi on the other. The cart tipped over and the girls fled in all directions, pieces of squash flying all over. He himself was the only one to stand his ground, teeth clenched and stamping his foot, tipping the wink to those around him. What about your 'Bear' brand shovels? A bear can climb a tree if it gets mad enough! At this, all the southerners, who had taken as much discrimination as they could endure, and for so long, scrambled to their feet, grabbed whatever tools they could, and spat on them once. A real fight was at hand. In all possibilities, they would have whipped those northern hicks for nothing that day. The northerners didn't know how to give it their all when their blood was up, the way the southerners did. They hadn't been fighting from the tops of their headquarters with real guns a year before, in the days of Red Guard factions 'attacking with words and defending with weapons'. They looked mean up north, but they had a yellow streak deep inside.

But who should come bustling up just at this juncture but Liu the Brute, positively beside himself. One "Oh, shit!" from him and the air was so full of alcohol that people were driven away by the stink. Bull took a bite out of a bun and put in his complaint: "Won't let a man eat. How'm I s'posed to work?"

Just as Liu was about to glare at Chen Xu, Chen glanced sourly at Bull and retorted, "If someone said that dogs laid eggs, would you believe that too?" Liu the Brute got so mad he bared his teeth. So that's how they lost that battle. Just stupid bad luck.

"Us southerners are sharper than these hicks up north," said Chen Xu, out of nowhere. "They're no match for us in a real fight. They may be big, but they're thick as pigs and afraid of dying. Southerners have simply got quicker wits. Did you see how Bubble pulled Wei Hua's jacket over his head the other night and worked him over while he was tangled up in it? Hah! He was really up shit creek!"

Xiao Xiao heard a kind of reckless satisfaction in his voice, and grew concerned.

"Do you think Wei Hua might be crippled? He was beaten so badly."

"Who cares? If he's crippled, we'll see how well he can swing his pickaxe leaning on a crutch. And if they send him back to Hegang, Bull will behave himself." He said it in a nasty tone, the chill coming out between his teeth in a way that made her flesh creep.

She could not see his face clearly in the dark, but she sensed triumph in the swing of his arms, something cagey in his step. Looked like that he had intentionally had Wei Hua beaten. Just to get him sent back to Hegang? So cruel a vengeance. She felt a little chilly and crossed her arms, hugging herself.

"Tell me that you didn't have anything to do with it." She was suddenly frightened at the direction her thoughts were taking. She stopped and grabbed his jacket.

He snickered.

"Tell me! You had nothing to do with it, nothing at all. It was them, Bubble and the others." She hung her head in anxious supplication.

"Them?" he answered impassively. "You don't really think that they would have had the nerve to do it without me, do you?"

She gasped. On the lonely silent plain, a faint tremor echoed through her brain.

"Why? Why did you...?" she murmured.

"Because we had to. We had to show everyone on this farm that we're not going to be pushed around!" His tone was chilling.

Silly girl. Why did you think it was? Not just over buying a meal. Have you forgotten that swan's egg? It was yours, and you are mine.

She slumped to the ground. In the dim moonlight, the wasteland had become even less clearly visible than before. The cracks in the earth opened into a huge black abyss ready to swallow her whole. She clenched her fingers and struggled with held breath.

"Well, this afternoon when they called you in for a talk, why didn't you admit it?"

He did not answer. He felt around in his pocket. A match flared.

"And another thing. You shouldn't have lied to that driver."

She could just barely see him sitting on a greyish log. The log was very long, and raised up above the ground. There was a gurgling noise, and the chill scent of water on the air.

It was a little bridge. A little bridge? They must be almost beyond the boundary of the Farm.

"Why do you have to lie to people?" She kept up her struggle, troubled by his belated confession. She wondered when he had learned to tell lies.

Why? Why? Even you are starting to interrogate me! Don't you think I've been interrogated enough already? In '68, when I was charged with being a 'reactionary student', I was held for interrogation. I was charged with a 'vicious attack on the revolution' and headed for the execution ground. Do you know how I escaped from the jaws of death? A man takes responsibility for himself. I freely admitted those accusations. But someone else wanted me to overturn them. Wanted me to do it for sure, and do it any way I like.

He tossed his cigarette into the water and stood up.

"Haven't you read all those books? Even Chernyshevsky says it: 'There are two kinds of people in the world: cheaters and suckers. If you don't cheat other people, they'll cheat you'. Since I wouldn't admit to planning the fight, Catfish concentrated on asking about the Cultural Revolution. If I'd admitted to it, I wouldn't have got back in the clear as long as I lived. The reason I'm going back to Hangzhou this time is to hunt up the Workers' Propaganda Team and find out once and for all if there's anything in my file. If there isn't, I can come back here and settle with them!"

A gust of wind blew past them, and she shivered. Her eyes blurred. The damp, chill winter fog of the South covered everything. No matter how carefully she walked, she still might bump into a bus. Perhaps, if she turned back, could she still make it in time? The bridge creaked so much she was afraid to walk across it. He was always taking her by surprise, and often she felt that she did not really know him. Had Chernyshevsky really said that?

"So there you have it, clear as can be. Whether you go or not is completely up to you." He scuffed his shoes on the ground. "I guess you think I've gone bad, don't you? I don't have time to discuss it with you now. Anyway, I'm going, no matter what. This little place is no bigger than the bottom of a well. It's enough to drive you stupid, and I won't take it."

She was in a daze. During 'Linking-up', in '66, when the young Red Guards had travelled freely around the country 'exchanging revolutionary experiences', she had seen a kind of streetcar in Shanghai that could be driven from either end, so it didn't have to be turned around. Should she go or not? Even if she went back to the Farm, would she be able to explain things? In the middle of the night...

"I can take you back," he said coolly, as he unbuttoned his jacket and wrapped it around her.

A familiar aroma rose from her neck and surrounded her, caressing the skin of her entire body. One evening late in autumn, he had taken her to find the 'cow shed' where her mother was being held for questioning. To climb over the wall, she had stepped on his chest, his shoulders, his head. The nails on her shoes had left blood stains like azaleas on his collar. He had waited at the gate in the rain one day, dripping wet, holding in his arms a bunch of red azaleas just gathered on South Peak.

"No!" She rested her jaw on that greasy collar and murmured, "I'm not going back!"

4

They had walked for a long time without coming to the highway to Half-way River.

They kept on walking and finally a dim fork appeared. Both roads were very wide, and he did not know which way to turn.

He wondered if he had taken the wrong road. He did not have a watch and could not tell what time it was. Xiao Xiao had a little watch, but it had stopped. The sky still showed no sign of getting light. On a summer night in the Great Northern Wastes, the clouds in the east began rolling up their mosquito netting by one in the morning.

He caught sight of an indistinct black shape off to one side of the road. They had already walked past it, but now something occurred to him and he turned back and swept his flashlight over it. It was a rectangular shed. There was no curtain over the door. It looked deserted.

"Are you tired?" he asked her.

"No, I'm, I'm just cold!" Her teeth were chattering a little, and she had to clench her jaws.

"We'll wait until it starts to get light and we can find out where we are. Then we'll go on," he said. "We can make it in time to catch the train so long as we don't take the wrong road. Late at night the dew forms, and there aren't many mosquitos. It'll be warmer inside the shed than out in the open, anyway."

She nodded. He took her hand and they jumped across the ditch together. There was some straw scattered around the shed, but nothing else on the ground except a cucumber stalk.

"You can rest here for a while." He deftly spread out some straw and had her sit down once he had patted it smooth. Then he turned off the flash and walked over to the doorway.

"What about you?" she asked. Why didn't he sit down with her? Was he angry? He hadn't even given her a kiss. It was so dark, and there wasn't a soul around.

"I'll watch the door from here," he answered. "If I fall asleep too, we could miss the train." What time was it, where were they, that it was so impossible for him to come over and show her a little affection? Better put up with it. If he should just touch her, things might get out of hand.

"Ouch!" She squealed. "Something bit me!"

He came over, shielding the flashlight, and swept it from her wrists to her heels, but found nothing. Nothing but a pair of eyes filled with anticipation, for all their weariness, staring resentfully up at him. His heart skipped a beat.

"Nothing here," he said.

"Nothing." She sighed, a little disappointed.

He bent down and planted a quick kiss on the nape of her neck. He was gone before she could reach out for him. "Better get a little sleep," he whispered.

A stirring in the straw, then silence.

He sat down on a piece of brick in the doorway of the shed, facing the road. A crop was growing low to the ground all along the road, melons perhaps, or else potatoes, the rows stretching far off into the darkness. A bank of thin fog crept silently up from behind him, surrounding the shed and then drifting slowly on. How endless the plain seemed in the quiet of night, how free and ungoverned, so mysterious, so entrancing, and still imbued with all the fascination it had held for him when he had first stepped onto it.

If there were still any unconquered peaks in the world, then he must have been born for the sake of performing wonders that no other man had yet wrought. When he was in the fourth grade, he had swum all alone across the Qiantang River in winter. In the sixth grade, he had led an 'army' of two on a conquest of Thousand Man Cave on South Peak. In the eighth grade, he had taken first prize in the four-hundred meter run at the city-wide high school track and field meet, and second prize in the mathematics competition.

But in 1966, his senior year in high school, all those wonders had been drowned in the sea of red flags flying from the rooftops, along the streets, in front of buses, at the sterns of boats, on tea cup covers, notebooks, towels, sweaters. It was not until he had really made his mark in this scarlet new world that he discovered how cramped and crowded a world it was.

He had opened up the map of China, so long buried beneath Quotation banners and big character posters. There was only one strip of black earth left, atop the comb of the gallant rooster whose shape the map resembled. Perhaps on the sparsely populated Manchurian plain so many thousands of miles away, there might remain an empty corner without the red flag.

It was a stretch of wasteland rich in gifts and promise, for all its primaeval darkness.

Over this thousand year kingdom of ice and snow he would raise the first torch. They would demolish those run-down huts, smash the dirty paddocks and pig pens, and build a new Great Wall in the wilderness. He would be the first.

In all this world, which men had divided up far too minutely, it was only you, the remote Great Northern Wastes, it was only you, your expanse of sky and earth, that could contain his extraordinary ambitions. Every last drop of his blood, every cell, every breath, every beat of his heart, every throb of his nerves, they were all awaiting, day in and day out, a revolution to come, one as overwhelming and exultant as that summer of '66. Impatient and self-confident, he longed for the blasts of wind, longed for the thunder and lightning, longed for the soaring flights, even longed for the annihilation...

And now a whole year had gone by, but had anyone recognised him?

It looked like there was a horse and wagon coming their way, far down the road. Ask directions? No. Had Xiao Xiao fallen asleep? She was so calm, so still.

A black cloud hovered over him, weighing him down, as though patiently, silently, waiting for something.

How much longer was he to keep still?

Had they not passed the boundary of Half-way River yet, after walking for so long?

Five million acres of rich black earth and vast expanses of green water had piled up golden autumn mountains weighing hundreds of thousands of tons. The walls had grown more solid and were whitewashed. They were scattered like mushrooms across the fertile land through which the Half-way River flowed.

Thirty years before, men had brought this wilderness under cultivation. Perhaps even earlier, the footprints of pioneers had come from the South, from the land of the Yellow River.

He was certainly not the first.

In addition to the reservoirs, the wind breaks, the houses, and the fields, which had already divided this stretch of black earth evenly among them and completely filled it in, there were the people who enjoyed the bounty of its fertility. Old and young, women and children, they brought with them all the vices and the bigotry that mankind had bequeathed from generation to generation, and these had combined with the pride and avarice of the residents on this black earth to fill every crack in its desolate spaces.

This frigid outland teemed as unbearably as the tropics. There were no Quotation banners a dozen storeys high here, nor any loudspeaker trucks or Red Guards, but there were even stranger loyalties, even more sensational rumours, even more mindless struggles, even more perverse prostrations, and all these were brazenly remoulding them, their innocent and childish eyes...

Who had told him that they were the masters of a new age, that they would do great things here, that it was a blank sheet of paper on which they would paint the freshest and most beautiful pictures? Who had it been?

He ached inside. Once when he was little, his uncle from Shanghai came to visit them with a camera slung over his arm. Chen Xu wanted to take some pictures himself, and sure enough they let him take quite a few. His uncle went home, but some days later sent them just a few photographs. "Why aren't the ones I took there?" he asked his mother. "Little dummy, there wasn't any film in the camera when you took yours. Understand?"

He bit his lip hard. He was afraid of his silent humiliation, of all the impulses he had contained for so long, of his colossal, crazy courage, his strong but ever cooler emotions, afraid that they would explode without warning, overwhelm the earth, and then turn into an empty cloud of white gas and dissipate. No. He wouldn't take it!

She murmured softly.

They were running hand in hand at top speed across the fields. There was a dense stand of oaks ahead of them, with a dry gully running along the side. The boughs of some willow thickets growing beside the gully arched over it, forming a natural tent. Taking her in his arms, he swept her inside.

There was a thick layer of grass growing on the floor of the gully, scattered with dead brown leaves, all soft and springy. On the bank of the gully behind them grew a network of tiny leaves and crisscrossing vines. Each space in the network was inlaid with a large red jewel, glowing in the dim light. They were heart-shaped, with a sprinkling of

25

tiny flecks on the surface. She touched one very gently, and drops of fresh red blood oozed out. The whole gully was studded with this strange fruit. It was an arbour of red grapes, a mountain of grapes, clouds of grapes, veiling the sky.

Wild strawberries! she said.

Strawberry Glen, he said.

All the world seemed far away. The daily reading of slogan posters, the signal flares, all the rest of it, they had never been, would never be again. The world was so tiny, it amounted to no more than a stretch of grass, a ridge, a dry creek. Nothing was left between heaven and earth but him, and her.

Pillowed on the leaves, the grass, his sturdy arm, she pressed her face to his broad chest and listened to his indistinct murmuring, not hearing any words. There was only his heartbeat and the breeze blowing over the fields. Yes, and the buzz of bees, the song of skylarks, the quiet whisper of the grass. She wished she could turn into a sound herself and melt into the silent symphony of nature. The rich, sweet flavour of ripe strawberries was kissing her forehead and lips. A tenderness she had never known before drifted up from her heels, imperceptibly swelling, spreading, covering all of Strawberry Glen, all the world.

Say yes! he cried, roughly, urgently, his whole body trembling. He squeezed her tightly to him, kissing her passionately. She felt heavy; she was suffocating. He clutched her hands tight. She felt a biting sensation in her palms. The soles of her feet seemed to be on a dry skillet, licked by searing flames and giving off an acrid, penetrating smell. The grass was rolled flat.

A sudden flash of lightning swept over her. She trembled, mortally ashamed. She could smell the fragrance of the weeds and flowers, the alien, compelling bite of a man's sweat. She was pounding on his shoulders with all her strength, and yet at the same time she clung tenaciously to his back. She felt her whole body smeared with sticky, slippery strawberry juice. A sudden wave of disgust welled up within her.

No! She wept from despair, wept painfully and touchingly.

Her tears fell like raindrops onto the sweet moist flowers strewn across the grass.

She rolled over in her sleep.

She was in a park beside the lake. Osmanthus trees, wax plums,

26

camellias, there were flowers blossoming everywhere. She wanted to reach up to the boughs, but she was too small, so she could not reach them no matter how she tried. She jumped and managed to touch the flowers a few times with her fingertips. But just when it seemed she had one, it would look up and rise high above her, letting her tumble back to earth.

I'm not picking you to eat; I want to give you to Mama, she told the flowers.

They turned away and ignored her. How haughty the tall magnolias were, how hypocritical the camellias' smiles; the osmanthus blossoms were devious, the wax plums as cold as ice. They didn't care to make her acquaintance; they yawned listlessly, inhaling all the fallen petals back off the ground.

Little Flower! She heard her mother calling her. Her mother had taken her looking for wild flowers.

They walked along the hills, the plains, the bamboo groves, the streams.

Everywhere there were bonsai pots, plastic flowers. Were all the wildflowers in the South lying crushed beneath the heap of tiles from the old Thunder Peak Pagoda, long since collapsed in ruins? She discovered some miniscule blue flowers in a crevice in the rocks at the base of a hill and ran happily over to them, but they squeezed their way back into the cracks and disappeared.

At last, under the tree at their gate, she found a wisteria blossom that the wind had blown down, like a nestling. She put it in a vase and gave it to her mother.

I'm going, Mother. This city is not ours.

Her mother nodded. The scarlet blossoms of your dreams are far away at the ends of the earth.

The ends of the earth. She walked and walked...

She walked and walked, and caught sight of the ends of the earth, over which the sunset cloud-rack spread in every colour, with wildflowers stitched all over the clouds.

White horse lotus, lavender lilies, yellow poppies, scarlet day lilies, emerald china pinks, sky blue wild roses...

There was no telling who was who; it was simply a rainbow, a rainbow coloured wave.

She rolled around in the flower thickets, sang in the coloured clouds. Pollen was shaken out all over her, covering her hair, her cheeks, her lips.

This was the Great Northern Wastes, where the white clouds lived and the coloured cloud-rack rested. Only in a place undefiled by the corruption of social custom would these blossoms cover the earth for her.

A pair of great hands placed a garland of brilliant flowers around her neck. The stems hung down all around her, and she could no longer see herself. Wave upon wave of fragrance left her dizzy. His hands toyed gently with her hair, his rough fingers like flower stalks, giving off the scent of pollen. She hung the garland up in front of her bunk in the dormitory, and after lights-out it went on shimmering in the darkness like a swarm of many-coloured fireflies.

5

The darkness thinned, wearied, shifted slowly toward the west, and then began to curl up and slip bit by bit into the black crevices in the earth. A large, bright morning star popped through the dense clouds, raising up one corner of their curtain in the east. A faint grey-blue began to spread, as over a marsh on which the ice is about to thaw, concealing some threatening motion.

Now he could see corn growing in one of the fields.

There was a Chinese crabapple tree beside the road.

He went over and picked a few cobs of corn and a double handful of crabapples. He shook Xiao Xiao awake and told her to eat some. The corn was green and so were the crabapples. The corn tasted raw and the crabapples were puckery. She took a bite of each and spat it right out on the ground.

They were cold and hungry.

Then he went over and pulled up a few slender corn stalks. He showed her how to eat them like sugar cane, biting off the rind and sucking on the sweet stem inside. The stems were indeed filled with a sweet juice, but even after eating quite a few, the two of them remained sadly unsatisfied.

They caught sight of a thin wisp of smoke on the other side of the road. It was a fire. If there was a fire, there must be someone tending it, someone they could ask for directions. They walked over. Once past the willow trees growing along the road, they reached a field on the other side, full of green leaves shielding glossy round globes.

A dog came ripping out of the bushes, barking at them. It bared its teeth and looked ready to charge, but only ran around and around their legs without actually biting them.

"Whose dog?" shouted Chen Xu. Where had the dog's master gone?

There was a creaking noise, and a man clambered down from the willow tree overhead. "Hey, what's going on!" he grunted, his nose still stuffy with sleep. He crept along all shrivelled up like a dried

29

eggplant.

"Turnip! Get down!" he said.

He said it as though he were speaking to his grandson. The dog understood and slunk away, tail between its legs.

They looked up and saw a little shanty set high up in a fork of the tree, with a peaked roof thatched with dark straw. It looked like a big birds nest.

"Guarding the melon patch?"

"What's that you say?"

"From the village?" Chen Xu spoke louder.

"No, no, from the Farm. Invalided out."

Xiao Xiao tensed. Not a former inmate? The steel mesh fence. The spots of rust.

Chen Xu relaxed. Just an ex-inmate, an old cob left after the corn was roasted.

"Have a melon? I'll go pick one." The old man started off.

"No, we're cold!"

"Got a fire. Let me roast you up some corn. Want me to go get you a fish? After dark yesterday I caught them with a sow-net; six teats, six fish," he muttered, expressing no interest in where they had come from or where they were going.

"No, don't bother." Chen Xu waved him off and squatted down.

Unease flickered across the old man's face. If they hadn't come for free melons or fish, what were they doing there? It was people who didn't want anything you had to watch out for.

"Got a question for you!" said Chen Xu. "Which way into town?"

"What's that? Have I eaten yet?"

"Are you deaf?" Chen Xu did not know whether to laugh or to cry. He gestured and shouted, "Deaf? How come?"

"Back when they were shooting people, I was stood up alongside. They didn't shoot me, but the noise did something to my ears."

Taken to the execution ground along with people who were going to be shot? Xiao Xiao shuddered.

"What brought you up here?"

"Stole a cow." The old man held up three fingers. "Got three years."

"How long you been here?"

"Since back during the famine down south."

Xiao Xiao tugged on Chen Xu's sleeve, anxious to be on their

30

way.

Chen Xu stayed where he was and asked about the road again.

Now the old man did seem to understand. He pointed off to the right from the intersection.

But Chen Xu still did not move. "Is there a short-cut?" he asked.

"Oh, sure." The old man was getting excited at having people ask his help so politely. He was all ready to take them there himself, and his dog was slinking along close behind. Chen Xu got him out a cigarette. The old man's cheeks started trembling, and his tattered cap fell to the ground.

"Just keep going along this creek and you can't miss it. You'll see a tree..." He coughed quietly, his shoes kicking noisily at the lush leaves.

All of a sudden, everything seemed to glow brightly before Xiao Xiao's eyes.

Huge golden pumpkin flowers floated up out of a jade green field, nodding ponderously and unsteadily in the thin fog. A little polished brass bugle. Play a Young Pioneers song! A sparkling drop of dew rolled around and around the rim of a blossom, but did not fall. Deep in the powdery flowers, happy bees were stirring their thin furry legs. It was breathtaking.

"What a lot of pumpkins!" she exclaimed. How many pumpkins there would be, with so many flowers in this one field. Where would the harvesters put their feet, without any space left for them? They would trip all over the vines.

The old man answered deliberately. "If close to half of them take, we'll be doing all right."

"Close to half? That's crazy. Look how many flowers there are!"

"Lots of flowers all right, but the better part are false flowers."

"Fall flowers?"

"False flowers."

"You mean late blooming flowers?"

Chen Xu interrupted. "False flowers, 'false', as in 'falsehood'."

"Can flowers play false? I've never heard of that."

"Oh well, you take your cucumbers now, your watermelons, your pumpkins, your squash, 'most half their flowers are false. How could all those flowers take? It would wear out the plants, don't you know!" The old man babbled away.

And then there were gourds, winter melons, golden melons, white orchid melons. So, north or south, all the melons and squash in the

31

world took shape among false flowers. Why had she never heard of false flowers in the South? Why did they play false? On any one vine, which were the false flowers and which were real?

She was getting all mixed up. She ripped the yellow pumpkin flower in her hands to shreds and threw it away. She wanted to ask the old man some more questions, but they were already on their way down the little path. The sky was getting light, and they had to hurry on. Chen Xu would not let the old man go any farther with them, and urged Xiao Xiao to walk faster.

"After you pass the ponds, you'll see an old bare tree, and then you'll be on the main road. That's the haunted tree, you know. Not too much farther and you'll come to the big bridge going into town." The old man shouted after them, his voice borne on the wind.

A series of crystal clear ponds had been left behind on the plain, like tangled pieces on a chessboard. They shimmered beyond reeds and cattails higher than a man. On the bank, only partially revived, a jumble of bird tracks was visible. A circle of white foam ringed the shore near the water's edge, piling up in one place and vanishing in another, like bubbles blown by a playful child.

"Don't stop to look!" His pace quickened.

"Aren't those bubbles blown by fish?" she sulked. Falsebubbles? Those golden flowers had left a hard knot tied in her mind.

Bubbles? He said to himself. He sped up and ignored her.

Bubble, bubble. That damned Bubble. Why hadn't he told him to make himself scarce when they did? They were courting disaster by leaving him there. He wouldn't spill the whole business, would he? It wouldn't matter if he talked nonsense; the thing to worry about was if he misread the situation. Bubble knew what was what with Catfish and Susie J. But there was no knowing if Liu the Brute would protect his calves. Liu would be on Bubble's side, that much was certain. If it hadn't been for Bubble, the wall around No.5 would have been reduced to a heap of ashes long since. Bubble had won a lot of credit by saving it from the fire. Liu the Brute had been able to hold his head high around Catfish for weeks on account of it. If Bubble hadn't kept his wits about him in the pinch, all the houses, the granary, the store, the clinic, the grade school, the garage, the barn, the stable, the pig pen, the mill, the bean-curd plant... Maybe they weren't worth much, but could you guys pay for them?

Catfish had really got the shit scared out of him that time. It was three days before he dared raise his voice again, he was so thoroughly buffaloed. That fire was his doing; no wonder he was embarrassed! He never did anything but squawk like a duck and try to pull the wool over people's eyes. He'd had them out in the pitch dark fields twice in three nights looking for signal flares shot off by the Soviet revisionists. And what had they found? Bugger all! A wild duck egg! They were so fed up they got together and agreed to play dumb. You can blow the bugle all night long, but no one is getting up. We can't hear it, can't wake up. What's that? Nothing doing! What do we care if it's a drill?

But that little guy had plenty of rotten tricks up his sleeve and found a way to get the better of them. He had Wei Hua buy a bundle of double-banger fire crackers and light them with a bit of kindling in the room about two in the morning. Wham! Pow! It sounded like the Russkies had driven an APC right into the Farm. The power had been switched off in advance, so everyone tore outside in a panic. Once they had formed up, he marched them over to the mess hall and turned on the lights. And what a sight they were then! There were people with their clothes on inside out, their shoes on the wrong feet, in bare feet. And then he had them go off into the fields looking for signal flares anyway. As if that weren't enough, he himself went back to the dormitory, groping from bunk to bunk, his heart set on finding a foot in the bedding so he would have someone for a big criticism session the next day.

It just happened that there was Bubble, who had been known for thrashing around in his sleep ever since he was a kid. The firecrackers hadn't wakened him, and in his dreams it just seemed to him that the bed had got roomier. He rolled all the way over against the wall, still sleeping like a log. The bed seemed empty when Yu got to it, so he just marched his army happily off to hunt for flares.

And yet it was pure luck that this one guy had slipped through the net, for that was all that saved the baggage and bedding of several hundred people. Bubble was sleeping like a baby when he was aroused by the smell of smoke. His nose was stuffed up and his throat felt raw. He put up with it for a little while, but when he opened his eyes and looked around, there was a pail of charcoal burning furiously nearby. He jumped up and saw that flames were already shooting up from the bedding on the next bunk. In a few more minutes they would have spread to the ceiling.

When the fire was investigated, it turned out to have been started by sparks from the double-bangers. Now Liu the Brute had something to go on. He had been looking after the paddy fields, the stoves, and the cattle, but he couldn't handle Yu Funian, who was such a ready talker. He was already fed up to here with Yu's wasteful, made-up drills. They never turned up so much as a ghost, and then people would be dozing off at work all the next day. Now we'll see if you can take it, Catfish! And so he praised and encouraged Bubble every day in the fields, urging him to keep up the good work.

Bubble wouldn't be hard to turn around; all they had to do was tell him that Wei Hua had cut his pay and toss him a couple of cigarettes. No, they certainly wouldn't let Bubble off.

"Look! A crane!"

Xiao Xiao grabbed his hand in delight.

A large white bird was standing on one long thin leg in the shallows along the edge of the lake. Perfectly motionless, it held the other leg up as it watched the surface of the lake with the utmost patience. It had a long, pointed beak and a bright red cap on its head.

They froze, afraid of startling it.

"It's a crane," whispered Xiao Xiao.

"No, it's a heron. It's waiting for a fish." He corrected her.

And sure enough, it seized a fish. The fish wriggled for dear life, but the heron clenched it firmly in its beak and took off, great wings flapping, body leaning forward, and both long grey legs stuck straight out behind it. Please, Granddad, implored the golden fish, Won't you let me go? I'll grant your every wish!

"Could there be any swans here?" she asked.

"Well, so close to the main road..." He shook his head.

If I could only get another swans egg, she thought.

A white cloud came gliding down to earth from the blue sky, so rich a white that it seemed to glow. It circled above her several times and then glided silently into a clump of reeds in the midst of the paddy fields.

She held her breath. No doubt about it. It was a swan.

"Tell me, why have you come down to the fields?" she asked it.

It did not answer. It was like a snowman piled up on the empty winter threshing ground, mysterious and aloof. In landing on the dark surface of the water, it actually lit up the dense thicket of reeds. Its pure white reflection looked like an ivory statue standing under a crystal cover, sleek and gleaming like snow.

Then a pair of boots tramped over from the path between the

fields and a pair of rough dark hands reached out toward the clump of reeds.

That white cloud floated gently up from the green ripples, leaping up toward the sky like a flash of lightning, a ray of light. It was gone.

And there where it had just been resting, in the midst of the glossy, dark green leaves, there was a swan's egg, like a snowball, like a pure and holy infant deep in innocent slumber, like a flower bud just on the point of bursting into bloom, pink showing through the white, fresh and delicate.

Those dark hands grabbed the egg first. They held it up to a nose set over a long, black moustache. A sniff and a whistle, and the egg went into his own pocket.

"It's mine!" she cried.

"You can come look for the shell beside the stove!" He laughed, spat once, and left without a backward glance.

"Give it back to me!" She chased after him.

"I want to sit down for a minute." She rubbed her eyes and massaged her ankles, scuffing her shoes. "Just a short rest." Her eyes implored him.

He frowned at her. He could not bring himself to refuse, but he felt a little impatient. The morning breeze was blowing in the dense reeds growing in the lake behind her, raising ripples on the water, like a free-spirited village girl, baring her breast and breathing deeply. His look turned gentle and loving.

Springtime in the South was beautiful and bashful, like a southern girl. How slender, how delicate her eyes and limbs were! Whether she was speaking or smiling, her every movement was out of tune with the rough scenery around her. Such tender hands ought to have been indoors, playing a violin or drawing. She was really like a hothouse flower that the wind had happened to blow out into the snow.

And yet, the graceful lines of her body flowed as smoothly as a stream pouring naturally down a mountain. Every drop of its water splashed pure and bright. That natural and unfeigned beauty was forever making him catch his breath in admiration. In fact, it seemed as though both her inner calm and strength of purpose and her evident honesty and charm were actually in a kind of natural agreement with the plains of the Great Northern Wastes.

"Why are you always watching me?"

She was looking at his inverted reflection in the lake, those square cheekbones, that square jaw. He was square all over. She picked up a twig and stirred the water with it. His reflection took on grotesque shapes, but when the water regained its calm, he was still there looking gravely at her.

She could not change him. He was a man and his character was fixed. Actually, if she could, she would rather have liked to change herself a little. When would she finally have ruddy skin and sturdy limbs, like Guo Chunmei?

"Let's hurry. If we keep on just a little farther, we'll be there." He held his hands out to her.

The horizon was streaked with egg-white, with lavender, with orange, silently changing colour as though it were patiently making itself up for a solemn performance. Her kindergarten had held a costume party once, and she had chosen half a watermelon rind, green and striped with black, to wear on her head. She imagined herself as a frog princess. She had wanted to be a frog princess ever since she was little, happy on land or in the water. Perhaps she would be dreaming all her life of turning into a frog princess, her skin patterned in green and black.

"We may be able to see the sunrise!" said Chen Xu.

"Really?" Xiao Xiao had forgotten her hunger and fatigue, as though this night march had been made just for the sake of seeing the sun come up. A Sunrise Terrace? Not quite. This trip would be worth the trouble if they just saw a real sunrise over the plains.

In the thick morning mist, Xiao Xiao caught sight of a bare old oak tree sticking up beside the main road ahead. Lush green weeds and dense trees grew all around it, but it stretched its dead, grey-clad branches up into the air to meet with a strange and savage presence all who passed that way. People said that it had stood like this for decades, neither dead nor alive, neither putting forth new shoots nor falling down. It looked like the back of a hand knotted with blue veins; each gaunt finger seemed to radiate a magic force that controlled the world.

"The haunted tree!" Chen Xu looked up and frowned.

Her scalp tingled. Every time she passed by there on her way into town for something she averted her eyes while still far away, afraid to look at it. She could not tell what sort of fate it was foretelling for her. Once, after the Great Hall at Lingyin Temple had been sealed up, she and some classmates had snuck through a hole in the back gate. They had yelled their heads off in the dark cavernous hall, given nicknames to each of the four fierce statues of the guardian kings, and finally climbed up onto the Buddha's throne and sung 'The White Haired Girl'. But deep in her heart, she had made a wish, a wish that under the Buddha's protection she might still pass the university entrance exams.... After they had walked far beyond it, she stole a look back; it was like a riddle, an old trail leading deep into the mountains, vanishing into the silver fog that heralded the dawn.

They finally caught sight of the edge of town, the bridge over the Half-way River.

The long wooden bridge stretched over the dry river bed. The broad river banks were covered with gravel. The Half-way River oozed its way carefully between the gravel banks like a little runnel after a rain. There was a cow drinking from it, and the water barely covered its hooves. From a distance, there really did not seem to be a river there at all. The Imperial Canal, its banks overgrown with green mulberry leaves and lavender broad-bean blossoms, the coves spread with water chestnut and lotus leaves, leaving only the narrowest of passages between them, through which the oars of awning-shaded boats left chains of emerald eddies. Could this really be called a river? And why, for that matter, did it require so long a bridge?

They made their way through the deserted town of Half-way River. The uniform red brick buildings, the uniform blue windows, the uniformly colourless wooden railings. A few dogs were barking somewhere or other. The shoulder-pole baskets full of glistening amaranth and new greenbeans and fresh-water snails, the counters with piping hot wonton and mixed rice gruel and roast dumplings. The food in the morning market was so good it made your mouth water. All the shops were shuttered. From one end of the street to the other, there was not a single memorial arch, not a single inscribed stone tablet, not a single...

The train station stood by itself at the very east end of the town, a light brown single-storey building, with cracked plastered walls showing the brick beneath. Some people were sprawled asleep at the base of the wall, as though the waiting room were not inside, but on the ground beside the tracks. There was a little flower terrace with a few clumps of cinnabar-coloured yam flowers at the peak of their blowsy glory. The ticket window was shut tight, but the entrance wicket was wide open, so they slipped right on in. They hid behind a large grain storage shed across the tracks, taking bites from a half-ripe muskmelon. The roadbed shuddered. The train had come.

Quarter to four—of all things, there was a clock on the brown wall.

As they climbed aboard the train, Chen Xu cast a quick look over his shoulder along the road leading up to the station, but there was still no one to be seen.

No one after us. And in fact it seemed that there had been no sunrise either.

Was it a cloudy day? Could the colours of sunrise cheat too? Having made it through the whole night, Xiao Xiao now felt a sudden disappointment, a certain dissatisfaction. It was light out; perhaps their disappearance was only now being noticed on the Farm. There was something a little dull about being deserters with no one in pursuit. It would be better if people were chasing them who couldn't catch up. That would make it interesting. What a hullaballoo there must be on the Farm!

There were plenty of seats in the car. Chen Xu chose a couple by the window, looking out on the mismatched grain bins across from the station.

The train started. This little station had just taken it by surprise for a moment.

She was too exhausted to notice more than a white signboard on the railing—there was no platform. As it flashed by, she saw the words 'Half-way River'.

6

Half-way River.

The sky was just starting to get light; the train was astir. People were yelling, We're there! Xiao Xiao pressed her face to the window and looked out, but she could not see anything distinctly. They were there. And where was it they were? She asked people. No one paid any attention to her. The train stopped, and the doors opened, but there was nothing in the way of a platform. They were so high above the roadbed that they had to toss their luggage down to make a stairway. They could hear the crunch of crackers being crushed to powder inside the bags. There was nothing to the station but clouds of dense smoke. She went forward, wiping tears from her eyes, and almost stumbled and fell before she made out the two tractors up ahead, placed side by side to form a stage. The sides had been let down and there were poles lashed at two corners. From a rope strung between the tops of the poles hung a large piece of red cloth with the words: "The Half-way River State Farm Welcomes Urban Young People Coming for Reeducation Among the Poor and Lower-Middle Peasants."

Half-way River? The name struck her as very odd. Half-way River? She was mad. I refuse to be a half-way revolutionary. I'm going back!

The grit kept getting in her eyes, so she did as everyone else and fished a pair of sunglasses out of her satchel. Lots of the boys were putting on the straw hats they had brought from Hangzhou as well. The hats had narrow brims, like the ones worn by spies in the movies. You couldn't wear a wide-brimmed hat on the train, anyway.

A short little guy jumped onto the tractors and then stood up on a bench. They all clapped and shouted slogans. He let them have it right off. All right! Take off them fancy dress hats! Everyone roared with laughter.

These are southern straw hats, not fancy dress hats. Chen Xu shouted.

The little guy got mad. He patted the shiny pistol on his hip and shouted, "I could care what kinda hats they are! You land in a place, you do it their way! An' another thing, you take off all them cap'list sandglasses too, y'hear?"

They were shooed like ducks into a big building surrounded by a wall. There were two long brick beds just inside—someone said you could run the hundred on them. The little guy with the gun cleared his throat and said, "My name's Sun Rujiang. I'm Security Chief."

You could be my 'grand-Sun'! Chen Xu snorted.

What was that? I'm learning northern dialect. Whatcha larnin'? Isn't your name Sun? Sun, grand-Sun, get it? Who do you think you are, insulting the poor and lower-middle peasants? The Poor and Lower-Middle Peasant Sun Ruijiang—hah! Little squirt like you, let's just trim your name down to match and call you Su Ru-J, 'Susie J'!

Hit the sack, hit the sack. We'll see tomorrow. She's learning Shanghai dialect; what a laugh.

Susie J was blowing his stack, yelling outside the door.

What's that you say? A complaint? You'll file a complaint tomorrow? Dare you!

Hear me talkin'? 'Pole! Porky! Angry shouting broke out in the girl's dormitory. Susie J charged into the dorm, pulling off blankets and yelling, Get up, get up, all of you, y'hear...

She climbed aboard a train through the window.

The train set off toward a pure white landscape of ice and snow.

She was riding on the luggage rack. The ceiling above was a rose-coloured sky covered with great scarlet flowers. She picked some and found that they were all damp. She looked up and saw a black star high up in the heavens, blinking its sad eyes and squeezing out great round teardrops one by one, wetting the petals and washing away the pollen inside.

Give me a flower. Give me a flower, said a shrill voice. She looked down and saw a bale of rice straw at the car door, moving toward her like a straw mountain.

Give me a flower, my name is Guo Chunmei.

She watched as someone in a crimson army tunic squeezed out from beneath the mountain of straw. It was a girl with a round face and large eyes who looked like she was game for anything. It turned out that Guo Chunmei was carrying the straw, but the bale was several times bigger than she was. She was carrying more than any of the other girls.

Are you going to the Great Northern Wastes? asked Xiao Xiao.

Yes! My brother is there too. He was in the first group of Young People Supporting the Frontier; his name is Guo Chunjun. The strange thing was that as soon as Guo Chunmei took the flowers, they dried out. She was covered with great scarlet flowers, and the straw had turned to stamens and pistils. They sat on the luggage rack and sang songs. First it was 'Scarlet Plum Blossoms', then 'How Surge the Waves Across the Honghu Lake'. The train was going very fast, so fast that no sooner had they opened their mouths to sing one song than they had finished it.

Later, the train stopped under a huge gateway in a wall. On the far side of the wall there were glistening blocks of ice. Above the gate were written the words 'Guan-Hai-Shan'.

But who is Guan Haishan? She jumped down from the luggage rack and ran outside in spite of herself, dragging Guo Chunmei behind her. As soon as she looked up, she saw Guan Haishan sitting on a silvery white mountain across from them. He was puffing away on a cigarette, so that all the surrounding peaks were shrouded in haze and his own body could only barely be made out. It was long and narrow.

How long Guan Haishan is! she said.

How big Guan Haishan is! she said.

My name isn't Guan Haishan; I'm the Great Wall. As Guan Haishan spoke—how narrow and long he was!—his voice shook some of the scarlet flowers off of Guo Chunmei.

She looked again, more carefully, and it really was the Great Wall after all. It ran coiling across the mountain tops, steep and straight, just like the Great Wall in the movies. She jumped up, and she and Guo Chunmei threw their arms around one another and rolled into a ball.

We have seen the Great Wall! They shouted.

The Great Wall is actually a man!

The Great Wall is actually a dragon!

As their voices died away, the dragon flew up into the air. In the silver light, its grey scales changed to a dark leaf-green. She was astonished, and was just about to touch them when she realised that it wasn't a dragon, but a train, just starting to thunder its way beyond the wall.

Wait for us! They chased after it.

She ran with all her might, but she still could not catch up with the train. When she ran quickly, it went quickly too. When she slowed down, so did it. She called after it. We're going to the Half-way River

State Farm. We aren't half-way revolutionaries.

As soon as she said this, the train let out a strange, shrill, terrifying shriek, and the gold stars on the wheels began to dance. With a great shuddering rumble, it flipped over and the cars came crashing down on her chest.

She opened her eyes.

There were electric power poles like fence posts and little huts like loaves of steamed bread. They went flashing grotesquely by outside the window, while pale clouds and spindly trees whirled above her head.

She realised that she was leaning on Chen Xu's shoulder with one hand pressed against her chest.

"Relax and get some sleep," said Chen Xu, "We have an hour before we get to Jiamusi."

He leaned across and wrapped his jacket carefully around her shoulders like a hoarding, tucking it into the gap around the window.

Wait for me! She chased after it.

The train let out a strange, shrill, terrifying shriek, and the gold stars on the wheels spun around. With a clang and an angry bellow, it spat out a column of smoke and stopped.

They went into the car and found that the luggage rack had come crashing down. All the boxes and suitcases looked like gutted fish and ducks with their entrails spilled out across the floor. Tea cups and cakes had been crushed into candied fruit and the cars themselves were all ellipses and triangles.

All right, who pulled the emergency brake? A conductor with a rum-flower nose marched up to them.

It was me. Chen Xu stood motionless by the door.

She was consumed with curiosity. Do you know where the emergency brake is?

Chen Xu pointed at one of his jacket buttons.

The conductor took the button away, but said, By recklessly pulling the emergency brake, you have wrecked four cars. Are you trying to obstruct the train of our epoch?

She said, You're lying! This is nothing but a spade.

What did you say? The conductor's nose turned white.

It's true. I'm the only one who knows. It's a spade.

Chen Xu said, Hacking someone to death with a spade is just

like peeling a radish.

Guo Chunmei burst into heart-racking robs. All her scarlet flowers had turned white.

My brother is dead, she said. My brother is dead. He was swallowed by the fire. He went to fight the fire.

Chunmei gave her a jar lid and said, This is a little oil lamp my brother left me.

She saw that something was written on the lid: Martyr's Sister Guo Aijun.

Who is Guo Aijun?

It's me! I changed my name. From now on call me Guo Aijun, 'Love the Army'. I'm a martyr's sister.

Guo—Ai—jun, she recited. But as the words came out she realised that she was still saying Guo Chunmei.

She tried again: Guo-Ai-jun.

But what came out was still Guo Chunmei.

She lost her patience and told her, There's no such person as Guo Aijun.

And a martyr's sister wasn't a martyr, either. She threw the little oil lamp out the window. The lamp went out, and all the dry bean stalks caught fire with a roar, lighting up the fields in a sheet of blinding light.

More grain sheds. Every little station, every little village, no matter how remote and deserted, still had to have a few of these self-important watchtowers cobbled together from earth, straw, and old mats all jumbled up and spread over the landscape.

Who knew what was in the rat holes? corn meal? kernel? gaoliang? millet?

For a war? For a political movement? For raising families?

A threshing ground heaped high with golden grain.

The sweat of their spring and summer labours had dried in the sun. The mud rinsed from their calves and the weeds brought under their hoes had enriched each plump rough golden kernel. Rolled smooth as a mirror, and now the final resting place of all that sunlight, the threshing floor cut with its keen sword the umbilical cords linking the wheat the corn the gaoliang with the earth and sent them soaring aloft. The fresh breeze swept away the last moisture remaining in them, like a mother goat licking her kids clean before letting them go off into the world on their own. And now those fresh and sheltered lives burst forth in all their vigour to roll and tumble under the blue sky, turned in one instant to a fragrant rainbow, in the next to a brilliant golden mountain, playful and free spirited, just waiting for those clumsy and unfamiliar hands to thresh them and pour them into sacks.

He had been ordered to supervise the threshing ground, the full winter's supply of grain for food, for seed, for fodder. He marched proudly about his rounds, enjoying this recompense for the year's sweat. He was not easily touched, but there was something fascinating, even moving, in the sight. He had not come to take the same sort of simple joy in a good harvest as the peasants did, but still it pleased and excited him. The threshing floor in autumn had about it a proud air of mastery that awakened his steadily growing sense of self.

As they were coming back from lunch, he caught sight of something in the distance that looked amiss. The long stretch of yellow under the blue sky had suddenly taken on streaks of colour: of red, of green, of black, of white. It was wriggling slowly along, murmuring lazily as it stretched its insatiable belly and reached out with greedy beak to chew up great bites in its quiet, persistent way. Once satisfied, it snorted and scratched, grain sticking to its body, grain trod beneath its feet, grain smeared all about its mouth. It seemed like a great convention of farm animals, with even more mouths than there were kernels of grain.

He exploded in fury at the sight. He picked up a brick and threw it at an old sow. The chickens all scattered, but they had dived back into the pile of grain in a moment, and the sow, being a hardened old pig, didn't so much as twitch. Even the dogs had gotten into the act. They were ploughing furrows through the grain, while the geese strutted and swaggered around the feast. Evidently their owners had done a thorough job of teaching them all their own wiles and persistence in stealing food. Just like their owners, if they couldn't have something for themselves, they would spoil it for others. Here's a whole threshing ground full of state-owned grain, if we can't eat it ourselves, it's nothing to us. We might as well help you shovel it down. Then we can go home for a drink and consider the day well spent!

"Get them out of here!" He roared at his warriors. In a moment, the chickens had taken flight and the dogs run away, and there was no telling fur and feathers from bran and chaff. A dozen young men were left gasping for breath, but no sooner did they lay down their arms than the whole natural banquet party was converging on them from all sides once again, without waiting for invitations to be issued.

44

He went to see the Branch Farm chairman and got his OK to post an order at the entrance to the storehouse. It was also read several times over the P.A. system and was given a lot of attention. But the next day, the birds and beasts were, if anything, even more numerous than before.

Now he did turn nasty. Seething with rage, he lowered the boom. He ordered mass arrests, scorched earth, no quarter. But it was not entirely on account of the grain. It was also intended to demonstrate that he was a city platoon leader after all.

They trussed up all the poultry and hung them from a tree in strings and rows, just like in the roast duck shop in town. The pigs they hogtied and tossed under the tree, like a butcher shop. They were all having a great time at it. It felt good, a little like the 'Smash the Four Olds' campaign. You could work off whatever was bothering you by taking advantage of a chance to smash something to smithereens, to do a real clean sweep, to wreak total ruin. Ecstasy.

When all the livestock had been tied up, they formed a line under the tree and jeered.

"Someone's chicken going to die from overfeeding itself!"

"Someone's duck going to die from hanging!"

"If you don't come get 'em now, they'll be gone!"

Xiao Xiao plucked at his shirt and whispered, "Don't hang them up like that, you could kill them."

That's fine with me. The mess-hall soup is as clear as glass from one meal to the next—you can't find a speck of meat in it.

The old women stood off in the distance, hurling obscenities at them from the street. Come closer? They didn't dare. Go on home? They couldn't stop worrying. All they could do was stamp their feet and glare, until the ground beneath them had been trod down into a mudhole.

Liu the Brute came walking up with a frown on his face. "Better let them go and leave it at that. The little varmints won't dare do it again."

"No!" He was unwavering, exulting in his revenge. Now we'll see who's boss, who's educating who. "Bring in a self-criticism and then you can collect what's yours!" He announced.

Things dragged on into the afternoon, and finally all the bookkeepers and tractor crew bosses and so forth had been forced by the weeping of their wives to bring in their self-criticisms, written out for them by their kids. Their essays hardly made any sense at all, so he

45

sent them back to be corrected, and only after the owners had been sufficiently worn down did he let them cut down their exhausted livestock. By the time darkness fell, there was nothing left but a dozen White Rocks and a spotted sow.

Someone said they belonged to the Security Chief, Sun Rujiang.

Now Chief Sun, great and awesome as he was, had another nickname besides 'Susie J', and this was 'The Rake', and of course his old lady was called 'The Cash Box'. When it came to the management of their household finances, they worked together very smoothly, each bringing out the best in the other. Apparently The Rake was away at a meeting that day and did not hear the news until evening. He came running back and headed straight for the tree, pistol on his hip. First he gave every chicken in the string a good whack and set them all to crowing, to make sure they were still alive. Then he turned around and yelled out of the side of his mouth, "Are you treating the poor and lower-middle peasants like you'd treat capitalist-roaders? Who do you think you are? You..."

He swallowed the rest of his sentence. As Security Chief, he could not help knowing Chen Xu's class background: third generation worker.

Chen said nothing, just eyed Susie J's holster, his greedy little insect eyes. There were steel spikes struck down into the ground beneath his feet, wedged far into the earth and drilling out disdain and disappointment like an oil slick.

The Rake backed down in order to rescue his darling chickens.

And he also hated him from this day forth, on account of his impertinence.

But Chen Xu's own image of the peasants was now smudged and diminished. It could no more be restored than could a mud statue eroded by a storm, once the mud had flowed out all around it.

The grain sheds, the grain sheds dark and golden.

7

Jiamusi!

The crowded, grimy bus made its way along the rough streets, raising a cloud of powdery dust. In the golden light of dawn, everything flashed by in bits of brown and green. It seemed very old; the houses were of some indistinguishable colour, the paving stones worn smooth. But it was obviously still young; an unassimilated mixture of dialects from everywhere in the land was audible inside and outside the bus. It was a small city; there were shops with low doors and windows—the doors so small they seemed meant to let the wind in and keep the people out—and tall smokestacks, something she had not seen for a very long time. And yet perhaps it was not a city at all; there were two-wheeled horse carts rattling past, bringing with them the smell of earth and leeks. Why was it called Jiamusi? What did Jiamusi mean? Was it a Manchu word or from the Hochen dialect? Post Station? Smithy? Korean Cold Noodles? Birchbark Canoe? Fishing Weir? Forest Gate? Fish Skin Drum? Graveyard? She did not know, she had no idea.

The snow raged from the north; the wind blew from the south.

Where had the people here come from? Manchuria and beyond, from every corner of the earth, packing Shandong bedrolls, muffling up sad Tangshan faces, brushing away tears shed on the banks of the Yellow River.

It took them all in, Jiamusi.

They burned over the wastelands, they sowed the fields, built houses, cut trees. They traded with Manchus long since versed in the use of the abacus, with the Hoche, the Oroqen, the Hui people. It was no more than a bead on the Sungari River, anyway. Jiamusi had grown from the sacks the traders had left behind. The sacks were worthless, even though they had once been filled with ginseng, marten pelts, and delicacies from the mountains. When they were empty they became as common as could be.

Xiao Xiao liked the way people from so many places were jumbled together in this one city.

It looked like they were out of danger, and since they still had time before the train going south left in the evening, they strolled around the town.

It turned out the brown was buildings and the green was willow trees.

Through the front windows, she could see people in grass green army jackets and trousers, but without collar or cap insignia. They were packed into little fly-filled restaurants, watering themselves in big gulps from bottles and mugs, faces bright red, laughing or arguing over this and that. White foam and brown liquid leaked from their mouths, oozed down their necks and flooded the tables and the floors.

The brown was beer and the green was city kids.

They were speaking all the dialects the diverse inhabitants of this city found most difficult to understand: Shanghai, Hangzhou, Wenzhou, Ningbo... During the brief slack seasons on the farms, this was the only place they could gather to relax, bringing with them all their news and their nameless frustrations, their praise and contempt for this distant and unfamiliar land.

It seemed friendlier here than on the state farms, at any rate. One might even say that it was easier to get to know than the farms, easier to understand. Jiamusi had become a grass green army camp, an army camp without guns.

It was like a simple and straightforward northerner, accepting these uprooted southern kids with a good-will born of tolerant generosity. To it, this green-clad tumult was no different from the first southern squatters, the gold-panning drifters, the tens of thousands of demobilised soldiers it had known in its short history. They would grow and multiply here, become its masters and its slaves, until they became just a lump on the landscape, a handful of dust.

The breeze blowing through the willows that lined the streets felt hot and cold by turns. Was the sun up north simple and direct, or was it simply weak? It was never able to heat up every corner. The smell of burnt cooking oil shrouding the restaurants, the smell of sweat filling the movie theatre, and the heat rising from the asphalt road were all grimy and vulgar. How self-contradictory a city it was.

She was also disappointed by the Sungari, the Pine Flower River.

The muddy river rolled slowly on. From a distance, it looked like a wide stretch of dead brown grass. No wind and no waves. It seemed to be in no hurry to get anywhere, to be quite bored and lazy. Perhaps it had nowhere to go. The far shore was an unbroken stretch of meadows, brick buildings, grain fields, and woods. It looked as though the Farm itself were there. There was no sign at all of the tall virgin forests that she had imagined, or of the golden pine pollen filling the woods, falling into the fragrant river. No sign at all, neither pine flowers nor forests...

The brown was the river and the green the river banks.

She bent down and scooped up some water in her hands, letting it run out through the cracks between her fingers. A few grains of fine sand were left behind, but there was really nothing to the Sungari River but water. Did you think there was some treasure hidden in it? But wasn't the Qiantang River back home the same? No, not at all! How swiftly it flowed, leaving clams strewn on the sand, and crabs. There were big fish in it, a tidal bore, sailing boats. A bountiful Qiantang River.

"We missed it this year. When the river breaks up next April, we'll come and watch the ice floes for sure." Chen Xu gazed intently at the river and then blurted, "There were three things I wanted to see when I came to Manchuria, and the break-up of the river was number one."

"What were the other two?"

"The blizzards and the marshes."

"What's so worth seeing about the marshes?"

"I don't know." He caught his breath for a moment. "There's something so mysterious and ruthless about them, like an invisible pitfall. No escape, suffocating..."

He said nothing more.

"What's your favourite place in Hangzhou?" she asked, wanting to tell him what she liked.

"Lotus Blossom Pond," he chuckled, "No.19, Lotus Blossom Pond."

"You're awful," she pouted. That hasn't been my home for a long time. "I mean, of the sights around West Lake. My favourite is, is Baoshu Ridge, and Nine Mile Pines, too—there are so many pine trees, and it's so lush and green in the winter."

"If you want to tell me the places you like, just go ahead and tell me," he teased. "What colour don't you like? What places around West Lake don't you like? Go ahead."

She glared at him. Either you won't speak at all, or, when you do, it's like an arrow hitting the bulls-eye. Did I come with you for this? I'll never get free of you as long as I live.

"So, you tell me, is there a colour that you especially like?" she asked in return.

"Black," he said, "Black is the most permanent, the most profound, the truest colour. The earth, the universe, the stars, they're all black."

"Nonsense! What about the sun?"

"Even the sun has black spots, and black holes; and the sun may burn out."

"People!"

"In the end, people turn into black smoke and come puffing out a chimney."

"White!"

"The shadow of white is black."

"Red!"

"Doesn't blood turn black after it clots?"

She had no reply.

"When any pair of colours is mixed together, the result is black, without exception. Red and green, brown and purple, blue and orange. All colours exist in opposition to one another. Black alone rules over all."

Hadn't she seen a black star in a dream? Perhaps even the moon, yes, the moon...

He walked closer. "And then there is your hair. The first time I saw that thick, glossy braid of yours, a thought popped into my head, that it might strangle me, that it contained all my happiness..." He stroked the end of her braid.

She shook her head. A magpie flew over her. Its tail was black.

She did not know where she was.

All she could remember was that they had bought tickets good for only a short distance and boarded a local train headed south. She was exhausted, so tired she could feel herself caving in.

There was a sound walking behind her, taking her with it. It rumbled and clattered and chugged. It was like the puffnik and also like a cradle, and also like the ticking of an old clock, regular and confident. Sometimes it shook her, and sometimes it caressed.

And sometimes the rhythm would suddenly slow down, like the tracks, endlessly extended by the darkness and rolled mercilessly flat. Trembling and fearful and trembling and fearful and...

She was carrying a green mountain on her back, trudging through

50

the paddy fields. The mountain was held up by two canvas shoulder straps, pulled so tight they were half buried in her flesh. She wanted to dump the mountain off her back, but she discovered that it was a sprayer. When its fog fell on the stalk of the barnyard millets, a lot of greenish 'horse nipple' grapes were instantly grown on them. When it fell on the rice sprouts, they turned brown and withered away. In a little while, all that was left in the field was purple grapes, no rice at all. What was the use of keeping on spraying? she wondered, and then walked away.

Guo Chunmei came chasing after her barefoot, shouting, Where are you going?

To Sun Island.

Where's Sun Island?

In Shaoshan.

Why are you going?

To lie in the sun, to get a good tan.

Hmm.

Why are you always grunting like that, like Wei Hua?

You're the only person I have told.

What did you tell me?

I told you that I'm as dark as Wei Hua.

She looked down at herself, a perfectly white reflection in the flooded rice field, like a sheep. She rubbed at that white skin, but she could not rub it off. She looked up and let the sun shine directly in her face. There was a transparent gas rising from the paddy fields all around her, as from a huge steamer basket. Ripples flickered far and wide, their light making her dizzy. After she had stood in the sun and steamed for a while, she took a look at her reflection—still a white sheep. Guo Chunmei reached over with a pair of shears and sheared off a layer of white wool, but there was another layer of white wool beneath it, and when this had all been sheared off, it was still white wool that kept on growing.

She was so upset that she felt like crying, but she couldn't, and besides, she had to go.

Guo Chunmei asked, why are you going?

I'm going there. She held out one finger.

Guo Chunmei said, Can't you hold it a little longer?

No. How can you hold it in when you need to take a leak? You try holding it in! She was a little irritated.

I always hold it in. Stools, too.

51

I had a classmate in grade school who had a disease called precipitant urination just because she had always hold it in.

Don't you know that Instructor Yu often hides in the woods and spies to see who is sneaking breaks from work? If you go for a number one, you can only be a first grade fighter.

She ignored Guo Chunmei. Her belly felt like it was ready to explode. She went for a number one.

No sooner had she pulled her feet out of the mud than she felt a penetrating chill rising up from her feet. A hot wind was blowing in her face, and the dirt on the path along the ditch was hot in some places and cold in others.

The wind was hot, but the ground was cool. The top of her head was hot, but the soles of her feet were cool. She couldn't figure it out. Could it be that there was a torrid Great Northern Waste in the air above this fresh, cool one down below? Below this summer Great Northern Waste, was there a winter one? And in that case, which was the real one?

It seemed as though she had been on a train all her life.

She did not know whether she was going south or north.

Chen Xu patted her on the back and told her to get some more sleep. He was studying the "All-China Timetable." She heard him whisper that they'd be in Shanhaiguan soon. He had a sly and conspiratorial look about him.

They had been lucky. Their tickets had only been checked once, when they boarded the train. She rested her head on his shoulder. It was a wall, safe and reassuring.

Brown? Green? What was it? She could not see clearly.

A stretch of woods, a stretch of gravestones. Someone with light brown hair was sitting on a grave, counting bills. There was writing all over his clothes.

Zdravstvuite, she said, in Russian. Hello.

Have you read "Courage"? I'm Alyosha. He winked and went on counting his bills without stopping.

Wasn't Alyosha a martyr? How could he have come to settle in the Great Northern Wastes? She wanted to ask him, but the questions that came out were, Don't you have a deduction for cotton-clothing fees? Do you get home leaves?

He mumbled a string of Russian. So far as she could tell, he was saying, City kids who come to open up the Far East all get high wages. All the new factories, mines, and farms have cultural palaces and libraries; we can go dancing and see movies. Everyone gets a vacation each year, a trip to the Black Sea coast or the Caucasus...

You have a Revisionist lifestyle. She criticised him.

He could not understand her and shook his head as hard as he could. He answered something, but she could not understand either. Pulling her along by the arm, he walked towards a castle. It turned out that the brown was his hair and the green was the roofs, made of green glazed tiles stuck side by side like books.

Someone wearing a red armband came riding up from behind them on a bicycle, shouting, Come back for the criticism session! Down with the Russkies!

She focussed her eyes on the person beside her and he was not a Russkie after all; he was Chen Xu. The wheels under the bicycle were actually a pair of soft, fluffy balls made of pine flowers, so it could not be made to go very fast no matter how one pedalled. She felt relieved. Chen Xu went over and removed the two pine flower balls, took a sniff, and said, Smells good. The pines have blossomed. This is pine pollen. She took a lick, and a damp pink mark appeared on the brown powder. She sniffed one and grew a golden nose.

The brown was pine pollen, and the green was the pine cones.

Chen Xu remounted the pine flower balls and rode away on the bicycle.He rode once around in a circle and two balls fell off, another circle, and two more. As soon as they fell off, they turned into gold ingots.

Chen Xu gasped in astonishment. Gold ingots are worth a lot of money. We can buy train tickets, even get berths. During 'Smash the Four Olds', I confiscated lots of gold ingots from a capitalist's house. Too bad I didn't keep...

She was crawling like an ant on a pile of gold ingots. There was gold everywhere, so bright that she could not open her eyes. The sun had come up, but it turned out to be a gold ingot too. And then all the gold ingots turned into steamed buns. She was so upset that she felt like crying, but then she noticed a bill stuffed inside one of the buns. Just as she was about to open it up and see how much money was inside, it took off like a magic carpet and flew away to the South, carrying her and Chen Xu.

Thank heavens, they would be in Jinan soon! Jinan, 'South of

53

the Ji'. At last, a place with 'south' in the name. Home couldn't be too far away now.

She and Chen Xu had been thrown off the local train at Dahushan, where their tickets were finally checked. No money to buy your tickets? Off you go! Not even a chance to plead their case or explain that they were city kids sent to the countryside. They had lain low behind a coal heap in Dahushan station most of the night, then hopped a freight, which took them to Tianjin West. There they had made it out of the station by squeezing through a hole in the crumbling wall, along with a bunch of travelling peddlers. They went around to the station entrance, bought platform tickets, and so continued to make their way south in fits and starts by all manner of tricks.

After all, during the preceding year or so, lots of city kids from the South—some of them homesick, some unable to take it up north, and some just bored stiff—had taken their chances, clambering onto coal cars, hiding in toilets, and altering or exchanging tickets. One way or another, a certain number of them had succeeded in getting back to the South for free. What with the great nation-wide Linking-up Movement of only a few years before, their experience with the railways, practical and theoretical alike, already added up to a very rich hoard.

The final outcome was the thing. Out of their combined total savings of sixty-six dollars and eighty-five cents, they had spent altogether a little over ten dollars so far, and they were over half way there already. They had been thrown off the train once at Cangzhou, but now they'd soon be in Jinan. Xiao Xiao had begun to find travelling like this exciting and absorbing. In the repetitive, ceaseless noise of the wheels, she felt a delight like that of an intelligence test, like a game of blindman's buff. She felt as though she were confronting something very large, but very diffuse. The railway police might appear in all their ferocity at any point of the line, in any car. But every spike along the rails seemed to be loosening, so that anyone could squeeze back and forth under the wheels. There were nets everywhere, and holes everywhere in the nets.

Chen Xu told her that Jinan station was very disorganised—we can say we got on at Yucheng and get out of the station by buying a sixty-cent ticket, no problem at all. As long as you believe it's true it will be.

Xiao Xiao felt a little apprehensive. Anyway, no one knew her. Even if they were caught, no one knew her. You didn't even know yourself. You weren't your original self again until you had got off the train and reached your destination.

There was a sheet of white paper stuck up over a door next to the exit wicket. The writing on it was very prominent: Ticket Adjustment.

People were going in and out the door, some wearing red armbands and some not. The people leaving the station this way seemed no fewer than those leaving by the regular wicket.

They walked in. She felt her hair threatening to stand on end. The room was filled with smoke. There was a long desk with people lined up in front of it. The line was moving very quickly. It looked as though one had only to pay a little, more or less, to make up a ticket and everything would be fine.

Finally someone asked, "Where from?"

"Yucheng," answered Chen Xu, with what might generously have been called a Shandong accent.

"Where?" the man asked again. "Speak up."

Xiao Xiao saw that he was a big Shandong guy in a sleeveless undershirt, with scrub-brush eyebrows, a garlic ball nose, and a body stout as the knob on top of a pagoda. What he really looked like was a butcher.

"Yucheng," Chen Xu said again. His Shandong accent lacked something in confidence. It was beginning to slip and slide off to one side.

The big guy winked and looked suspicious. He smirked.

"Why'd ya go?"

"We're at a youth centre."

"Live in Jinan?"

"Uh, no, more south..." Chen Xu was answering in monosyllables, with bits of a Manchurian accent popping into them. The cadences of Shandong dialect had been hammered out over several thousand years, and even a simple 'Hey Pop!' was not to be picked up overnight. How's it, at the Youth Centre? At this rate they would be cornered soon.

The railway man leaned back heavily in his chair, and it creaked. He waved them aside, "Go wait over there. Next!" Rotten Shandong guy.

Carrying their sacks, holding their babies, the line of people diminished one by one. There was a woman in a blue railroad uniform working the abacus. Its hundred and ten beads flew back and forth under her fingers, adding up authority and power.

The big guy finally turned back to them, wiping the sweat from his neck, and asked, in a slightly more friendly tone, "City kids?"

"Yes!" Chen Xu had reverted to his southern accent and looked as though he did not care what happened.

"No ticket? You'll have to pay the fare from where you started." The big guy smiled.

"Do you know where we started?"

"You bet! Obvious, ain't it? Little southern brats from Heilongjiang going back to Shanghai to see their folks, right?"

Xiao Xiao was startled and angry at the way he had exposed their grand strategy, as though he were a grown-up seeing through the transparent ruse of a child.

"Pay up," he said.

Chen Xu hesitated a moment, and then replied, "No money."

"What do you think you're doing, taking off without any money? You expect to take it easy and let the peasants support you? Look, just hand over the money. We know all you city kids' tricks—the soap boxes, the toothpaste tubes, the skin cream jars, the notebooks, the whole works. Hurry up!"

Everyone who snuck onto the trains really did put their money in such hiding places. It was like going underground, passing on secret reports. It dawned on Xiao Xiao that perhaps people all over the world snuck onto trains, so it might be said to have a definite tinge of Internationalism.

"If you don't make up the difference, you'll be locked in there!" The woman with the abacus looked up and gestured out the window.

The holding cells. There was a foul smell. She felt sick.

The big guy rapped his knuckles on the table. "If you don't smarten up, we can search you. That's in the regulations."

Someone interjected from behind them, "Say, Station Master, they're city kids.".

It seemed there ought to be some sort of special policy for city kids.

Xiao Xiao felt humiliated; she hated the station master. Aren't there any city kids in your family? Not an ounce of sympathy...

Chen Xu was holding his satchel down firmly, the veins at his temples twitching.

When Xiao Xiao looked at the woman, her heart skipped a beat. An overseer from one of the old cotton mills where they used little

56

kids as workers? She was afraid of those hands touching her, afraid of...

Then Chen Xu tossed his satchel on the desk and yelled, "Take it!"

T-shirt, trousers, shirt, toothbrush, cup, towel, notebook, sunglasses, timetable, blue-checked plastic wallet.

It's all there, we've given it all to you. Everything we own. Isn't twenty dollars missing? Where did it go? What vampires you trains are!

"Thirty-six dollars and eighty cents." The big guy nodded in satisfaction. "OK, where you going?"

"Hangzhou!" She should have said Guangzhou, Liuzhou, the farther away the better.

The big Shandong guy spent some time carefully sorting out all their bills. The flesh on his stern, mean face curled up and revealed a friendly smile. He said to the woman, "Count their money up carefully, give them two local tickets for Hangzhou, leave them a dollar each to eat on, and count whatever's left toward their trip from the north."

Xiao Xiao could not believe her ears. She could see that Chen Xu was astonished too.

The woman rattled away on the abacus, screeching like a siren, "Jinan to Hangzhou, sixteen sixty each, two is thirty-two twenty, plus two dollars to eat on, leaves a dollar sixty, just enough for tickets from Yucheng to Jinan."

The station master hesitated a moment; then he turned around, raised his heavy eyelids, and asked, "You don't have any more?"

"That's everything. Take it or leave it!" Chen Xu had suddenly grown cocky. "There isn't any more. No, wait a minute. Here!" He patted his hip. "There's a wallet back here. You forgot to check!"

The station master was stung by his prompt ingratitude.

"Deduct another forty cents for administration fees! For the rest, make up their tickets from back in Bozhen as far as fucking Suzhou That's fifteen sixty each. Leaves them three eighty. They can take a boat from there!"

A high degree of accuracy. Added up, the total was still thirty-six eighty.

The stocky station master cleared his throat noisily, his weary peaked eyebrows drooping. The chair creaked as he stood up. He let out a deep breath and walked away, hands folded behind his back. He was intimidating and arrogant, like every station master on their journey, and, like all the others, careless and painstaking at the same time.

"That station master was really all right." Xiao Xiao and Chen Xu had walked out into the plaza in front of the station, still a little shaken. "He was only a little, well, a little rough."

"Actually, they can't search people. He was just trying to scare us." Chen Xu kept looking at the two tickets in his hand, wise after the event.

"But if they did? I couldn't stand it, being treated like a slave," she explained. Then she thought of something else. "Didn't we have more money than that?"

Chen Xu had a satisfied twinkle in his eye. He whispered, "Good thing I took twenty dollars out last night and hid it in one of my shoes. They really stink! What do you say?"

They were standing in a corner of the filthy plaza, feeling, for all their joy and relief, somehow let down. It seemed as though they were not yet entirely awake. Xiao Xiao found the station master's action inexplicable. He had left them almost penniless, and then given them two tickets to their destination. Was he like a school principal? A home-room teacher? An uncle? Now they were past the adventures of the first three-fifths of their journey, and besides, they had tickets for the remainder of the way, so their unique and dangerous journey had practically succeeded, was practically a victory!

She was actually a little sorry, deep down inside. She realised that she had really been hoping that things would not turn out so simple and easy.

And besides, she found that with a ticket in hand, waiting for trains and riding on them was quite dull.

She was piling up building blocks, but they all had odd shapes, and no sooner had she put one on top than another would fall down.

Her father led her into a white house. There was a bed inside, and her mother was lying on the bed wearing a striped dress. Her father put a basket of oranges at the head of the bed. There was a needle in her mother's arm, connected to a flask of saline solution. Her mother asked her father, Why is your face so red? Her father had a thermometer in his mouth and shook his head without saying anything. She herself replied, Father has been sweating because of the heat. Her mother glared at her. Your father has a fever. She shouted, Father told me to say it!

She was kicking a shuttlecock on the playground. Tongtong from upstairs was under a tree, shooting at sparrows with a slingshot. She was helping him by gathering stones. He fired once and a sparrow flew away. He fired again, and another one flew away. Crash! A classroom window opened its big mouth, and flocks of sparrows flew out—pieces of glass. The old gateman grabbed Tongtong by the collar and told him to pay for the window. Tongtong was crying. He hasn't got any money, only a slingshot. Xiao Xiao ran home and told her grandmother, Our teacher is collecting twenty cents from each of us for a movie. Didn't I give it to you yesterday? I lost it.

She was piling up blocks again. She made a long, long train with them, but each wheel was an abacus bead. The train was running in a river. The water was pale green and so clear that the bottom was clearly visible. Schools of minnows were swimming back and forth, blowing bubbles. There was a dense stand of white birch trees growing on the banks, but they had somehow formed strings of mulberries. The river meandered this way and that, covered with green water weeds on whose tips blossomed little golden flowers, and below whose leaves were hanging light pink water chestnuts.

She jumped into the river and began to swim. She could see her reflection in the water. Her tongue had turned a dirty brown. Isn't my tongue pink? she thought. When was it switched for another one? She thought she would go looking for her own tongue.

She swam for a long time and came to an iceberg. She could see a pink stain on it, but no tongue. She came to a black marsh. There was a tongue-shaped mark on the ground, but no tongue. She caught sight of an old, run-down shrine. Chen Xu was standing on the shore beckoning to her. The two of them walked into the shrine, but their way was barred by an old woman holding a large pile of toilet paper in her arms. She forced a piece on Xiao Xiao and then held out her hand and said in a trembling voice, This is a latrine, one cent! Chen Xu gave the paper back to her, saying, We don't have any money! The old woman chased after them, held onto the latrine door, and would not let Xiao Xiao in. She said, Whether you buy any or not, it still costs one cent! Xiao Xiao had to turn her clothes inside out for the old woman, to prove that she really did not have even one cent.

The old woman began to cry. Won't you help a poor lonely old woman? My boy has been sent to the countryside. He runs short every month, so I still have to support him. For one penny he can buy a few kernels of grain.

Xiao Xiao was moved to tears, but she really didn't have any money. That one cent was very important to them both.

The old lady said, Can't you go find some money by wading in the Qiantang River? The name Qiantang means Pool of Money, after all, so the river is full of money.

Xiao Xiao went to wade for money in the Qiantang River. She had never realised just how indispensible money was. She groped around until she found a snail, and then a lotus root, and finally something slippery. When she brought it up out of the water, it turned out to be a goldfish.

Please, Granddad, begged the gold fish, won't you let me go? I'll grant your every wish!

She said, Don't call me Granddad, call me Grandma.

The goldfish brought in a machine and set it running with a flick of its tail. So many train tickets came out that they looked like a long train. She looked up and saw a big beard growing on the goldfish's face. It swam away, waving its tail.

She grabbed a big handful of the tickets and ran from one train car to the next. A ticket was collected at the door to each car. Only when the tickets had been collected did she discover that they were her tongues. She could not understand how she had so many tongues. They rang like copper plates. She had never realised how much she actually liked paper money.

She was terribly tired. The train was going downhill, like a string of loosely made match boxes. It sped down and crashed into a coal heap, the cars breaking up and rolling over, turning into a heap of foam, a heap of shreds, a heap of spindrift...

Saliva had run all the way across her cheek to her ear lobe. Her satchel was damp.

She had actually slept for three hours straight. It was the best and longest sleep she had had since they got on the trains.

Was that a cicada's buzz? Far in the distance she caught sight of an arched stone bridge, plastered boats with awnings. They had crossed the Yangtse; there was a fresh green bamboo grove.

So time was like the train tracks after all, like the wheels, steadily shortening, shrinking the distance between far away places. She had travelled from the north to the south in a dream.

60

8

A stone slab pavement. A pair of unpainted old wooden buckets splashing back and forth and leaving a trail of water. There was a public faucet serving several dozen families at the entrance to the alley.

Brown smoke from the coal briquet stoves shrouded the cotton wadding and diapers draped over bamboo poles slung across the alley from the eaves on either side. Green bean husks had been spread out to dry along the base of the walls. Blackish oilcloth were soaking in a large basin.

In under the diapers and smoke. A narrow, cramped alley.

A low wooden door facing a square well. "Mom!" yelled Chen Xu, pushing open the door. Xiao Xiao followed him in and stood there apprehensively.

Everyone inside froze, chopsticks and bowls in hand, eyeing them fearfully.

"I've come home to do an investigation," he announced. Then he turned back and said, "Xiao Xiao, come on in!"

She was surrounded by eyes, inspecting, suspicious, provoking.

You really are terribly ugly! said the wild ducks. But so long as you don't marry into our clan, it really doesn't matter much to us. The poor little thing! Getting married had never crossed his mind; he was only hoping that they would let him lie down in the clump of reeds and drink a little water from the marsh. That would be enough for him.

"Xiao Xiao travelled back with me. She's come back for a health check. She's got an ulcer." Chen took the satchel from her shoulder and put it on a bench, had her sit down on a bamboo chair, and went to get them some boiled water.

"Didn't you even rate a letter first?" His mother went on staring at Xiao Xiao with narrowed eyes and a forced smile. She was wearing a wide pair of patterned shorts. There was sauce on her hands. She had on a pair of big clogs. It was hard to say whether she looked confused or happy. Her jowls moved woodenly and her open mouth revealed a metal tooth in a stiff and doubtful smile.

"I did write, but I never got any letters back," muttered Chen Xu.

"Your dad's on night shift. He'll be home as soon as he gets a break. Such a long way! How many days and nights were you on the train? Take a nap first, or have a wash-up. Have you eaten? A'lian, go get a couple of snake melons for A'long and his friend."

Her eyes swept over Xiao Xiao's waist. Xiao Xiao felt that nothing Chen Xu's mother had said was addressed to her. It was as though they had come home from a battlefield with no survivors, from Hell itself. Deserters? Xiao Xiao felt uncomfortable. She was not at all taken with his mother's heavy Hangzhou dialect, the way she said 'have a wash-up' instead of 'take a bath'. If only she would never have to call her Mother. A'long? She remembered Chen Xu telling her that he had changed his name during the Cultural Revolution.

She was taken into the kitchen to wash up. With only a single plank partition between her and the front yard, she could hear quite distinctly everything they said. She heard Chen Xu gulping down water and yawning, his mother fanning him noisily with a large fan made of cat-tail leaves.

"Why didn't you come back for New Year's? Last year we pickled two pigs heads in the house and then ate up all the meat! People froze to death in Heilongjiang; did you get chilblains?"

"No, there are brick beds."

"What do you mean, 'brig beds'?"

"You light a fire under the bricks and people sleep on top."

"People sleep like that? I thought you had copper firepots."

"A'long, did you see any wolves?"

"What about bears? Are the bears all blind?"

"They say that when it gets hot, in June, you can go chop a couple of pieces of ice out of the river to nibble on."

But the other ducklings are adorable, said the old mother duck with the red tag on her leg. If you find an eel head, just give it to me.

The door creaked, and someone came into the yard with a heavy tread. Dishes rattled on the table.

"Dad!" She heard Chen Xu's voice. "The Farm is promoting me. They sent me back to take care of some business."

He said it as though it were true, without a moment's hesitation. Xiao Xiao felt hot all over.

"Xiao Xiao'd best stay at our house." He spoke like someone accustomed to having his way. "She broke off relations with her family

62

a long time ago and can't go back. It doesn't matter if she stays here, anyway. In a year or two we're going to..."

Someone cleared his throat thickly.

"Here you are coming back on business and you take and bring her along. As for her staying over here, I don't think it's a very good idea."

His mother took it from there. "You say that in a year of two you're going to, to get... But anyway, as of now, you haven't yet. A girl who isn't properly part of the family, and who has her own home here in Hangzhou, all the neighbours will talk."

The rough voice sounded very grave. "Don't you understand, son? I'm in a Workers' Propaganda Team. I'm out trying to get people to go off to the countryside, and then my own son..."

"People may say you snuck back, or, well, all kinds of ugly things. You're young, you don't understand..."

"That's enough!" Chen Xu slapped the table. "If you won't let her stay here, then I won't stay either. We're leaving right now! I'm sure there's a place for us somewhere in Hangzhou!"

Xiao Xiao hurried clumsily into her clothes and went outside.

Alleys, lanes, weariness, dozing off. There was a little less red paint and a little more dust, but everything was practically the same as when they had left the year before. The buses drove listlessly back and forth, busy and blind. In the past they had carried crowds of young people overjoyed to be leaving for the countryside for ever. But now they were lined with cold, indifferent, uncaring faces. The little shop at the corner had a special counter selling things that young people going to support the frontier would need. Xiao Xiao had come there to buy soap, a flashlight, batteries, an imitation leather suitcase. But now the shopgirl looked at her blankly, locking her smiles, which even before had been pitifully few, inside a shrivelled mouth.

They were squatting by the street, in the shade of a parasol tree.

"Anyway, I'm not going to go look for anyone I know," said Xiao Xiao, hanging her head. How come you're back now? What did you come back for? Has anything gone wrong? "I'd rather, I'd rather go live in the waiting room at the train station."

"I never dreamed they wouldn't let us stay at home. And there isn't anyone at all I can turn to!" Chen Xu scratched his head. "All the people I went to high school with have gone to the countryside, and my comrades-in-arms from the University have been assigned to jobs somewhere else. Kang stayed on at Zhejiang U., but according to his letters, he's living in his office. Say, can't you go look up your old nurse?"

"Her place is only nine meters on a side. They're terribly cramped as it is. In the summer they sleep outside on mats. And besides, she might tell my mother."

Chen Xu said nothing. He was drawing lines on the ground with a matchstick. All of a sudden, he jumped up and grabbed Xiao Xiao's hand. "Of course! Keke's family, at the Provincial Committee residences. The rooms are whoppers, and his mom is very polite to me. They were all set to be kicked out of their house with nothing but the clothes on their backs, but I got them off by putting in a good word with Wang Ge."

Keke and Chen Xu had fought side by side as members of the same faction. Later, Keke had gone in the army. Wang Ge was a rebel boss, famous all over the province. Chen Xu had saved his life. At least this friendship remained. One end of a laboratory balance always pointed up. They were stuck. Might as well give it a try.

Keke's house was on a hillside behind Baoshu Road, a little white foreign-style house.

The steel gate was shut tight. They knocked and yelled. The gate opened a crack. The familiar, pudgy face looked out, but she did not recognise him. An awkward self-introduction, difficulty arousing any interest, working up courage to explain, silence. It was as though they were dunning her. She wanted to get away.

"Come back from Heilongjiang?" she asked again. Half their hope disappeared in that question mark.

"Can't stay with your own folks?" Another question mark. Insufficient cause. Her husband had been a high court judge.

"What about your residence permit? You'd have to apply for a temporary permit. The police come around every two or three days to remind us. They don't let us have any contacts with outsiders. Sometimes they come to check up in the middle of the night."

Period. The gate closed heavily behind them. Even the crack was gone.

They sat for a while on a big stone at the foot of the hill. The stone was very hot; even the stones were inhospitable. Driven off like a flock of sheep, they had lost forever their claim to a place to stay in this city. It had rejected them, forgotten them. Their home! Chen Xu went out into the sun to get them a pair of ice cream bars. She sucked slowly on hers, but just got thirstier and thirstier.

It was always hot here. Although the sun was fierce out in the paddy fields back on the Farm, there was still always a cool breeze. It was a strange feeling. The dormitory on the Farm was also cool, like a cave temple at Ling-yin. On walking in, one's sweat dried. The brick bed wasn't hot in summer, even with a fire, and on it was her very own bedsheet, a white sheet embroidered with flowers.

"I've got it! All we need is to have a key made and we're set!" Chen Xu muttered out of nowhere.

"A key to what?"

"I just remembered. At the back gate of our place there's a storage shed. It belongs to my uncle from Ningbo, but he doesn't stay there much. The roof leaks a little." He slapped Xiao Xiao on the knee. "We'll have the key copied and sneak in at night."

"Well, it does seem a little, you know..." Xiao Xiao caught her breath. Thank Goodness! The duckling breathed a sigh of relief. I'm so ugly that even the hunting dogs don't want to bite me! She could not bear to let him down, so she added, "Won't your family notice?"

"Don't worry!" He planted a quick peck behind her ear and was on his feet and running down the hill at once. The whole pitch of his voice had changed. "Come on with me, we'll get a candle and some mosquito repellant now."

The tram made its way through the teeming bustle of the city. Lakeshore, Magistrate's Lane... A grey building with a spire rose up above the parasol trees, quiet and dignified. A stained glass panel arched up above the cramped round windows, glowing sadly in the evening light and suddenly vanishing. The iron gate was shut, and no one was going in or out. There was no sign on the door, so it seemed like some forgotten ancient site.

"Look!" Xiao Xiao gave Chen Xu a nudge.

She knew that there had formerly been a sign above that gate. The first time she had come here, three years before, she had still been able to make out faint traces of the words, "Purity Hall," which had been chiseled off the concrete. But the place was no longer a 'Purity Hall' for Christian worship. It had become the editorial office of the Red Guard newspaper.

She had come to the office to check up on a manuscript that she had submitted, on the subject of the revolution in education. Her school's mimeographed newsletter wanted to print it, but she had lost her original copy.

The gate was wide open, but there was no one around. The church was gloomy and quiet. It was high noon, and several beams of sunlight shot in through the skylight high above, catching a few columns of randomly drifting dust.

"Is anybody here?" she called, her voice echoing around the vaulted ceiling. Not only was God gone, so were all the people.

"Anybody here?" she called in an even louder voice, to keep her spirits up. She considered leaving, but did not want to. She muttered, "What kind of Red Guard newspaper is this? Have all the Red Guards gone up to heaven for church?"

There was a rustling noise in a pile of big-character posters on the floor beside an old piano in the corner. A head poked out and said with a yawn, "Even God has to sleep. He's been working thirty-six hours straight!"

Well, at least there was someone alive there. Xiao Xiao let out a deep breath. She expected him to clamber to his feet and greet her, but after she had waited a while without any sign of further movement, she stuck her head in and looked. He had gone back to sleep, head resting on the floor.

She was irritated and amused all at the same time, but she also felt a little sorry for him, so she walked out onto the steps and sat down, leaning back against one of the pillars. She would wait until he woke up and then ask him. She waited a long time, and then in a daze felt someone nudging her gently. She opened her eyes and found a tall young man standing in front of her, stretching and asking her with a smile, "Who are you looking for?"

"I'm looking for you!" She was a little exasperated; they were the ones having the big snooze, but they had put her to sleep too. It wasn't a Red Guard paper, it was the Bureaucrat News. "Bureaucrat News, Editorial Desk," she groused.

"Feel free to tell me your business." He gave her his full attention. A red corner was visible in the pocket of his white, short-sleeved shirt.

She told him the title of her manuscript and paid no more attention to him. He walked inside and over to a positively enormous table. After rummaging around on it for a while, he pulled out a manuscript and asked, "This the one?"

She could see quite a few red pencil marks on it, as though it had been edited for publication.

"Hmm. Well it's just that your political check was a little..." His voice trailed off and he swallowed. After a moment's silence, he said very firmly, "We'll use it!"

And a few days later, sure enough, the Red Guard newspaper published her essay.

And a few weeks after this she learned by chance that he was none other than Chen Xu, head of the Propaganda Group of the Red Epoch Society and a polemicist known far and wide throughout the city. She went on receiving the paper, always addressed in the same hand, but she never wrote back to acknowledge it.

Their friendship would have been worth thinking back on, she said to herself, if only for the interesting way in which they had met. How brightly and warmly it had once glowed, even though it had brought some suffering with it. The tram had gone by.

He had known all along that the tram would pass this way. Even before Xiao Xiao reminded him, the dusty cobwebs in his heart had begun to tremble.

The Red Guard newspaper had been driven out right along with God. God had gone back up to heaven after his overthrow, the new-born Red Guards out to the countryside. To each his proper place, Amen. It was just a shame that this church, which had once been the scene of such mighty revolutionary actions, which had given him a Holy Land so rich in glad tidings...

Purity Hall. Ever since she had appeared, ever since she had sat on its steps, his whole heart and mind had been thrown into disarray.

She disappeared out the main gate of the church, a slim and graceful young girl.

He had seen many girls like her, but none who could say "Have all the Red Guards gone up to heaven for church?" None who would sit quietly on the steps and wait for him to wake up, only to say with a pout, "I'm looking for you!"

He took to crawling into the heap of big-character posters every day for his nap.

Whenever he took a nap, he always left the door open, waiting for a gentle voice to come drifting down from the vaulted ceiling.

She did not come back but she did send in a few more manuscripts. He found her address on the back page of these. She did not want rejected manuscripts sent back to her at school.

He went on taking his naps under the posters, but the paper was very thin, and even though he went from a dozen sheets to three dozen, when the season of osmanthus blossom came he caught a cold. At last he understood why it was that he went on enduring his cold, heavy

67

paper blanket, why he had caught the cold. He was forced to face the truth.

As soon as his cold was a little better, he went to look her up at home, going by the address on the manuscripts. She lived in an old two-story brick house, in a little room at the end of a hall. He knocked at the door for a long time, and when it opened, he saw books strewn left and right all over the room. She was buried in a pile of books, with dust all over her hair and on her nose. As neither seemed quite sure of recognising the other, he held his hand out to her. She blushed, and in her confusion knocked over a whole stack of books, which fell with a crash onto his foot. Then he could see that she was putting all the books stacked on the floor and bed into a huge wooden chest.

"My father says that we're going to sell off the books that are feudal, capitalist, or revisionist," She looked heartbroken. "But I can't tell which ones..."

Eugene Onegin, The Iliad, Paradise Lost...

You shouldn't sell a single damn one. He couldn't even find books to borrow. He had stolen a sack of books early in the Cultural Revolution, all Classical Chinese literature.

"Why sell them? Now..."

"My mother is in custody, and what with 'purifying the class ranks', there's no telling but what they might raid our house."

She looked up at him, trusting and sincere, as though they were a pair of old friends. He was touched. It was the first time in his twenty years that he had been so moved. He wanted to take this little girl tightly in his arms and shelter her under the broad eaves of his shoulders from the storms outside, like a tree protecting a tender little flower. No, it was only her, only for her.

What he had achieved already was really far too much. Mass rallies, editorials, a jeep, a telephone. Even the God of the Purity Hall had made way for him, he believed. And yet, in all the great world that he had won in so brief an instant there was no girl like her, one who could read the Latest Directives over the loudspeaker of a public address truck in such perfect Mandarin or play Quotation songs on the old church piano.

The little alleyway where he lived brought together foundry workers, spinning mill workers, sellers of bean-curd jelly, bicycle repairmen, men who pedalled three-wheelers, knife sharpeners. He had been deeply troubled while still very young by the prospect of a life lighting stoves and emptying chamber pots. The girls in the alley were interested in nothing but crocheting needles, glass silk, and salted jujubes.

But he would never offer his devotion to those young ladies who were driven to school every morning in their fathers' cars. Young ladies? They made him sick. What was the proletariat? Was it cars and nannies? Or was it preferential admission by recommendation? He didn't belong to that class. All he had was a school transcript with perfect marks in all his courses and one change of clothes. There would always be a wall between him and girls like them. The only time they would ever weep bitter tears would be at their fathers' funerals.

But this slip of a girl could sit in a cold corner of the church, revising her manuscripts over and over, seemingly endowed with a natural antibody; she was so gentle, but at the same time so stubborn in confronting her adverse fate. She had no sharp corners, and yet her toughness and resilience were evident.

He would love her, love her so much that everyone would envy her. He would tend her like a fruit tree, till she grew strong, with blossoms and honey, with seeds and singing birds. And then, a son!

The lock opened with a click, and they were met by a damp mouldy smell.

They tiptoed gingerly inside and lit their candle. The shed did have a wooden floor. There were piles of odds and ends here and there, and a bamboo couch. Everything was covered with dust. As they went quietly about cleaning the place up, two huge shadows appeared on the candlelit walls, shadows with horns and dishevelled hair, aflicker with claws and fangs.

"Like a monster!" Xiao Xiao almost took fright at her own shadow. She got a grip on herself and chuckled. "Hamlet," she said.

"Quiet!" Chen Xu reminded her in a hushed voice.

In an old trunk, they found a tattered old sheet and some old clothes that still smelled of mothballs. They lit the mosquito repellant coil, and in the wispy shadows of its smoke yet another element was added to the plot. Ghosts moved back and forth on the four walls, sometimes quiet, sometimes dashing fiercely about, then suddenly scattering, and then just as suddenly rematerialising.

She giggled. "Just like a shadow play."

She was entranced with watching her shadow. It was such fun she could not resist speaking again. When she turned around and saw Chen Xu glaring at her, she stuck out her tongue.

Chen Xu drew her to his side, stroked her hair, and whispered in her ear, "The bed is all set up. Be very careful and don't make any noise. I'm going now. Get a good night's sleep. Blow out the candle. If you have to go to the bathroom in the night, there's a hole in the floor over in that corner. After they've all gone out tomorrow, I'll come open the door and let you out."

She said nothing. Their two shadows were quiet.

"Did you hear me?" he asked. "Make sure you lock the door tight from inside."

A strange den of monsters, one shadow left behind, blowing out the candle, then nothing at all, just rats, spiders, who knows, perhaps even snakes and weasels. Perhaps someone had hanged himself from that dark beam, an empty coffin in the parlour of a house nearby...

She threw herself into his arms, clung to his neck, and pressed her face against his chest, murmuring, "I'm scared!"

He looked down, brushing her shoulder with his cheek. He kissed her neck and said, "If I don't go out and lock the door, someone might notice in the morning."

But she held him all the more tightly, begging almost inaudibly, "There are still people sitting in the yard enjoying the evening cool. You can leave a little later, just stay with me..."

She let go of him and deftly spread an old mat from the bamboo bed out on the floor. She knelt on one knee beside him, looking uncertainly up with wide and misty eyes.

In those black pupils there flickered two golden red candles, bright and honest, full of trust and expectation. There was a whole warm inviting world inside them.

Chen Xu seized her roughly and crushed her to his chest. He was not so stupid, after all. He had never wanted to leave, never. In the lamplight, her soft, smooth skin took on a pale golden glow, and her complexion, so white in daylight, a kind of gloss, so soft it was like the surface of a lake in the morning, giving off a light, sweet scent that was suddenly all around him. He could not tell from where this aroma came, but it seemed like a bewitching spirit leading him toward a silent whirlpool, a narrow valley of unfathomed depths, perhaps toward an isle of ecstasy.

He could feel himself melting into a limpid, rippled, lotus pond, bound and enmeshed by that faint and elegant scent. It came from the core of lotus blossoms in bud, from the rich green of the lotus leaves, from the musky black mud beneath his feet, faintly present and caressing his entire body, exciting his every pore. He sucked it in greedily, becoming drowsy, intoxicated, hot. It called up in him a fierce and fiery longing to discharge all his soul and his hot blood in one great downpour, to requite that warm and fragrant earth...

His breathing quickened, his whole body was trembling, some nameless terror, some sudden convulsion, was suffocating him. An infinite sea of pounding waves seemed about to swallow them up, to drown them, to roll them away to some far away and unknown land. Did he really anticipate some other joy in life than this? She alone remained, amid the froth of his ideals and the shreds of his illusions, a flower swaying in the storm, a spark left among the ashes, a ray of light seen in the dark clouds...

Strawberry Glen! That fresh, swelling liquid awaited the plucking, the fire, the storm. She had refused him once, but she would not refuse him again.

He clung tightly to her, a sleek and slippery little fish. Only in that frenzied close combat could he find his help, his refuge. In that magic instant, he felt suddenly confused, uncertain—he no longer recognised himself. In that brief moment, he recapitulated all the history of mankind, passing like a flash of lightning through millenia, back to primaeval ages where to his surprise he met his ancestors. It turned out that his ancestors were not ape-men, but a giant python, a lion, a wild ox, a cricket, or some other living thing whatever it might be. He felt certain that he had died—his soul was soaring, his body empty, his senses demolished, his strength exhausted. And yet he found that he had already revived—revived as by a miracle, restored to life amid that gigantic doubled shadow...

She was walking into a deep, dark cave, with strangely shaped stalactites hanging from the walls. In the distance, an enormous elephant was crouching on a huge boulder.

The elephant rolled her up in its trunk. Hot air was puffing from its nostrils. The trunk seemed to her like a giant python, wrapped around her from head to toe, or like a huge translucent jellyfish covering her completely...

She felt hot and stifled, terribly thirsty. The strange thing was that she was not at all afraid. She wanted to struggle, but her limbs had gone soft and weak.

Say yes! A voice came to her from deep within the cave.

The elephant bore her on its back farther into the cave. It was so

71

sturdy and powerful. She stroked its legs, like giant pillars, embraced it tightly. Carry me away! she said. I want to! she said. I'm yours! she said. I...

She was terribly thirsty. A ball of fire leapt up from the pit of her stomach. She felt no pain, only thirst. Her body began to twitch, to shudder, between pain and pleasure. Her soul no longer belonged to her, nor did her body. There was only it, a dimly discernable form like clouds, like water, like smoke, or fog, gripping her firmly, lashing her, caressing her. She and it were joined into a single indivisible body. She had been divided up and dissolved into numberless shreds impossible to reassemble in their original form. She had almost lost consciousness, but one thing stood out clearly in her mind: she was about to become a true adult, to say farewell to her girlhood forever.

Hold me! She cried. Wax tears dripped slowly from the red candle; the rafters rolled over; the walls wheeled around; the very world itself was coming to an end. She bit at her own hand with all her might.

Her heart was pounding. In the darkness, she could hear a rustling over the broken tiles. A cat meowed a few times, making her hair stand on end. Then it got quiet.

She could not see anything, but there was the sound of even breathing coming from beside her.

She pulled his arm over her, nestled in his embrace, and began to sob quietly.

She walked into a movie theatre. The picture had already started, but she could not see the screen. She looked for her seat. She saw a seat that was folded up and hurried over to it. But just as she was about to sit down, she discovered that it had no bottom, so she had to leave it. There was a door marked 'Emergency Exit' in the wall, but it was locked, and no matter how she tried she could not push it open.

Two points of light were seeping toward her from the distance. She thought they were ushers, and walked toward them, only to find that they were two lanterns. Her grandmother was holding one in each hand and laughing as she approached, reciting, 'The cat is here, the dog is here, and even the silkworm girl is here'.

What about my mother? she asked her grandmother.

Her grandmother blinked and said nothing. She looked at her carefully and discovered that it was her mother after all. Her mother's face was covered with wrinkles, and there were strands of grey hair on her head.

Mother! she cried, but she could not make a sound.

She walked toward her mother, meaning to help her pull out the white hairs. But her mother turned and walked away, walking very quickly. She chased after her, but no matter how fast she walked, she could not catch up. She started to run, but just when she seemed about to catch her, her mother disappeared, vanishing inside a wall covered with wire mesh.

She knocked at the gate, and kicked it, but could not make a sound. There were many doors, but no one would open them. At last she found a door with two red lanterns hanging over it. She forced her way in, but found a man inside, sitting in a leather armchair. He was wearing wire-rimmed glasses and workclothes. He was writing something. She looked at him. He had large eyes and a high forehead, much like herself. She thought he might be her father, but she did not know why he was sitting in an office. Hadn't he long since been chased out to work as a freight handler, carrying coal every day? She edged closer for a look, and it turned out that he was writing out evidence for an investigation, a large page covered in densely written script.

This Chen Xu, well, he was a reactionary student, he has no political future, her father grunted.

I don't want a future, I want love, I want a comrade, she shouted.

Love! How old are you, anyway? You've got your nerve! If you're going to stick with him, don't ever come back! Her father pounded his fist on the table. Get out of here!

I'll get out, all right, but I'm going to stick with him. Tears welled up in her eyes, and she went to look for her mother. It was an old, run-down house with only a cow mooing inside. Her mother was not there.

She put a harmonica, some picture cards, and a doll into her chest, also a photograph of her mother. Someone gave her a residence change certificate, but the other side was a monthly bus pass.

She walked out of the alley carrying her chest. It was very heavy. She lugged it along step by step. No one came to help her. She was the only person on the street.

She was the only person on the wharf.

It turned out she was going by herself to spend the summer vacation at her grandmother's.

From somewhere or other a ball of yarn came rolling along; it had fallen on the ground and just kept on rolling. The core appeared, a small wad of paper, on which was written: If Mother does not come back, no one will be able to open it.

She carried the trunk by herself, surrounded by fog and the fields all wet.

Her mother came chasing after her. She hid behind a telephone pole. Her mother wept into her hands. She stumbled and fell, choking in the dust.

The mat was a little chilly. A lock of hair at her temple was damp.

Grey light filtered through gaps in the planks. The place beside her was empty; Chen Xu had already left.

The outside door was certainly locked.

Then it seemed to her that she was somewhere very, very close to her mother. If she were just to shout, her mother might reply. Perhaps it was only to see her mother that she had come back. She did not blame her mother, she did not blame anyone. She just wanted to have a good cry, head on her mother's knees.

9

He had gone in and out of that big red steel gate for six years. Had his time not been doubled by the Cultural Revolution in his senior year, he should have been chairman of the student body at some university in Peking by now. He was convinced of it.

The gate was shut tight. Over a year before, amid joyful farewell beating of gongs and drums, fluttering reports of glad tidings, scarlet pledges, Quotations from Chairman Mao... They had long since vanished without a trace. On the clumsily whitewashed walls there remained a few traces of large characters: "Down With So-and-so!" "Long Live So-and-so!"

He stopped.

His troops had marched boldly through that gate on their way to the site of gigantic rallies. They sang a song that went:

> We swear we will not rest until
> So-and-so is out,
> So-and-so is out,
> So-and-so is out!

He taught his comrades-in-arms how to work the names of every one of the black leaders from the capitalist headquarters into the song. After all, it was a song that could be repeated and extended without limit, names being added or dropped at will, the lyrics revised or supplemented at any time. Of course, it did require a certain sense of rhythm. Left foot down on 'swear', 'rest', the first 'so', and 'out'; right foot on 'will', 'til', and the second 'so', with a smart stamp of the right foot after 'out', a stamp so solid and ringing that whoever they wanted out would be quaking in his boots thousands of miles away. This song, recreated continually by their genius, added to the ferocity of his troops, until their might commanded respect throughout the city.

He had been twenty years old that year. So shallow and childish an age.

And yet, only in such an age and at such an age could his intellectual and personal qualities have been so happily displayed. Ever since he had walked out that gate, it seemed as though all the gates in the world had been blown shut behind him by a series of successive winds.

He hated that gate. When he walked out of it he had not thought he would ever return.

It was here that he had ridiculed that self-important jerk.

"A left revolutionary may not turn right; he must always turn left!"

The jerk was giving his orders.

"Left face! Left face! Left face! Forward march!"

He had sneered, "Three times left face equals one right face, and no fear of wearing out your shoe heels, either."

So here it was, at the gate of his school, that he had made an enemy. The jerk's dad was a section chief just then awaiting 'integration' with the side of revolution. The son's only ability lay in experimenting with various games of the 'left face' type, but sure enough, eight months later he had become the boss of the school's Revolutionary Committee. Revenge is always exacted. If you're not willing to make a big left face circle under the Chairman's sun, you're doomed to be in trouble.

"Looking for the Workers' Propaganda Team office? It's up on top of the artificial hill. I don't know if there's anyone there." The old man at the reception desk waved them listlessly on.

The pond. Heavy and stagnant, covered with thick green algae, it supported on its surface a few camphor tree leaves and lavender rose petals, just like the marshes up on the Farm.

Across the playing field, the gaping, blasted windows of the classroom building made an ugly face at him.

Cicadas were chirring in the trees, "We're sure, we're sure.." What were they sure of? Were they sure that someone had once drowned in this shallow pond?

Yes. Her name was Shi Laihong. She had taken the leather belt from her waist and beat Mr. Jin with it. With one foot on his back, she had cackled, "Say grandma!" "Say to your Red Guard grandma!" She had failed most of her exams, but when it came to beating people, she knew enough to concentrate on the ankles. Mr. Jin had turned over and rolled into the pond. It was Chen Xu who had snatched the belt out of her hands and thrown it into the water. The pond was clear back then. There had not been so much algae as now, and he had watched the belt slowly sinking, the blood on it floating free little by little.

"You're shielding cow ghosts and snake spirits!" she shrieked.

Perhaps they had become enemies long before. As Progaganda Chief of the Student Association, he had called pointed attention to mistaken characters in her essays more than once, even though she was the first student in the whole school to join the Party as a student member. She could go off at her own expense during vacations to carry out some investigation on Siming Mountain. But he had to rely on hunting for snails during summer vacation and wading for water chestnuts in winter in order to pay his tuition fees. He and she would never comprehend each other; perhaps even tolerance was impossible. He had almost had to quit school in his junior year because he could not afford books. It was Mr. Jin, his teacher, who had come to his house to bring him a scholarship, holding an umbrella shredded by the typhoon and with his trouser legs rolled up.

He had wanted to bring something down, true enough, but not people like Mr. Jin.

He was leader of the majority faction, but somehow power was in the hands of the minority.

He had not saved Mr. Jin. One frosty morning, he had found that pair of worn out shoes, the laces missing, at the edge of the pond.

It was here that his misfortunes had begun. In revenge for the leather belt thrown in the pond, and with the help of the 'left face' heel, he had been sent to the isolation cell on the artificial hill on campus.

When they exposed his 'vicious attack', he felt no desire at all to deny it. Those despairing eyes floating up ever and again from the shallow pond had sobered him. He prepared to pay the price for letting out his abhorence.

It was after he had openly admitted his 'crimes' and was preparing to take his solemn, final leave of this world that he was incomprehensibly and irresistably rescued.

But since they had 'rescued' him, why did he still have this tail he could not get rid of, this wingless rumour that had followed him to the Great Northern Wastes?

"We're sure, we're sure..." droned the cicadas. What were they sure of? Heaven only knew.

That little building on top of the artificial hill was where he had been held in custody.

Xiao Xiao gripped his arm.

"It was here," she whispered, her breath quickening, "It was here..."

Yes, it was here that their common fate had been decided.

The little window faced west. It was on the lowest part of the summit of the hill. There was a sheer stone wall beneath the window, which meant that no one could escape that way unless he were prepared to cripple himself by jumping. This was why the isolation cell was there. But there was a secluded little path running below the window, behind some bamboo, where no one normally came. In his solitude, he had imagined how they could talk without anyone hearing them if she should appear on that little path.

He had sent Zou Sizhu to find her, and Zou had brought back her message, that she wanted to see him. He was beside himself with joy. He drew a map for her. If she managed to get below the window and there was no one around, she was to sing a song. When it first got light in the morning, the layabouts standing guard over him would still be asleep.

He remembered that winter morning, the bright crystal raindrops glimmering on the green bamboo. Through the thin mist he had caught sight of a tiny human form wearing a lavender flowered jacket and blue trousers, with two shoulder-length braids tied with broad ribbons of glass silk. How lovely she had looked in the rainy mist. A small umbrella of light blue plastic, like a sudden glimpse of blue sky, bounced and swayed lightly on her shoulder. She spun the umbrella handle, and all the raindrops on top sprayed out around her, like a fearless acrobat spinning and gliding along a high wire.

"Do not say farewell, with weeping; do not go your way, with tears..."

He heard singing, a graceful voice, clear and sweet, like a distant melody of southern Chinese instruments, drifting through the fine rain. It was like an intangible wraith seen in a dream, entwined about the top of his head. She was standing under a bamboo, looking up, her eyes open wide as though anxiously seeking something. Her thin lips opened and closed as the touching sound of her voice flew from them. But there was something inconsistent between her curious and beautiful expression and the tragic words of her song. To hear her pure and youthful voice singing 'Sister Jiang' made such suffering seem like a source of joy. The way she accepted misfortune with rose petals made it seem as though disaster could be brought to surrender at the feet of an innocent girl.

He trembled deep within. He had never before been so moved by the sound of music. He wanted to jump down from the window and take her tightly into his arms.

"Believe me, I'm for revolution," he said.

"I believe you."

"Revolution isn't a stroll on the Nevsky Prospekt."

"I know."

"If I've made mistakes, you can expose them and criticise me, or make a clean break between us."

"No!" she cried, interrupting him. "I told them that you had never said an unrevolutionary word. I really can't recall anything, no matter..."

He let out a deep breath.

"Oh, do they beat you?" She stood on her toes.

"No. They wouldn't dare."

"Are you scared at night?"

He shook his head.

"Would you like some glutinous rice dumplings? My grandmother brought them back from the country." She pulled two glutinous rice dumplings out of her pocket and held them up, considering how to toss them through the window. She smiled, and so sweetly, for she was still too young to wonder more than if he was afraid in the dark, not realising that daytime was more dangerous. There seemed to be a certain blindness in the courage of her 'prison visit'.

He did not want to disappoint her and he was also eager to have a bite, so he told her to hide the dumplings under some dead leaves in the bamboo grove. He also told her he was looking forward to eating them and would get Zou Sizhu to retrieve them for him. The rain had stopped, and the sky was getting light. Around the campus people could be heard beginning to stir.

"You'd better hurry back. Just bear with it. I'm sure to be out pretty soon."

"How much longer?"

"A month. Well, perhaps two."

She stood there horrified. "That long? What will I do!"

"You should study the 'Communist Manifesto'."

"I'm reading 'Marx's Youth'." She was obviously in no hurry to bring this dangerous meeting to an end. She really did not know what it was to lose one's freedom. She must think it was a kind of game. There were already people awake on the hilltop; it was crazy!

He waved her away with all his might, but she went ahead and tossed a wad of paper right through the barred window into his cell. There was a noise at the lock; someone yelling for people to get up. He stuffed the wad of paper into his shoe and left the window. But for a long, long time he could still hear singing on the path down the mountain, though he could not be sure that it was not the rustling of the bamboo or his imagination. Not until after nightfall, after everyone had gone to bed, did he get that paper wad out and read it by moonlight, a line of delicate script reading, "Love was something sacred to Karl. To him, the words 'I love you' had a special meaning, for included in them was 'forever'."

He loved her. On account of that little blue umbrella in the rain, he would always love her.

"Hey, I asked you something. You're daydreaming again." She gave him a reproving nudge.

"Oh, what is it? What did you ask me?" He struggled free of his thoughts. When he was thinking about something, it was as though he were in a trance.

"I asked you, did you get those two rice dumplings afterwards?"

"Of course. Rice dumplings stuffed with meat. I ate them right up."

He recalled how conscientious his 'guard' Zou Sizhu had been back then.

"Zou Sizhu is really a good sort," she said.

He wished she wouldn't bring up Zou Sizhu just then. The gates of memory were wide open on every side, but not of the slightest use. The gates of life were closed at every turn, but endlessly alluring. Those high school days, when he had sailed so easily before the wind, those glorious days when he was a Red Guard, they were gone forever. They were covered by thick green algae, all their one-time radiance lost. And what he faced now was a blazing hot summer, a long trek without any money to live on, a key, a mat—just for the sake of a certificate, for a swamp whose depth was unknown.

He felt sick.

From the window of the Propaganda Team office came the bold sound of one of the model Peking operas, "My whole body... courage...bravery..."

He stopped in his tracks, took Xiao Xiao's hand, and blurted, "Do you know why I was finally released that year when I was held for investigation?"

"Wasn't it because, because there was insufficient evidence of your 'vicious attack'?"

"No, as soon as they took me in I admitted everything. A man accepts the consequences of his actions." He shook his head with a wry smile. "But in the end they were the ones who had me repudiate the verdict."

"Who?"

"Them." He gestured up toward the top of the hill with his chin, lowering his voice.

"The Workers' Propaganda Team?" Xiao Xiao's eyes opened wide. "Why? Why did they do that?"

"Because they were supporting our faction. If I had been declared a counter-revolutionary, they would have been done for too." He scowled, the trees casting their spotty shadows on his face. "It was a political deal, understand? So long as the defendant didn't admit to anything, they couldn't come to a verdict upstairs, the opposing faction had no way out, and the Propaganda Team would be consistently correct. I was just turned willy-nilly into a bargaining chip, and that's what finally cancelled my arrest."

Xiao Xiao said nothing, just nibbled numbly at the end of a braid, as though she still could not make much sense of all the complexities of those bygone years. She thought for a while, her head bowed, and then murmured to herself, "But, wasn't that the same as the Workers' Propaganda Team having you, having you deceive the Organization?"

The Organization? Well, what was the Organization? But you've finally understood it too. The first time someone tells a lie it isn't that he's forced, but that someone teaches him to do it. Deceived? Who was deceiving whom? Perhaps the whole thing was one huge deception. How many days and nights have passed since I realised it.

And now he was to go cringing to ask them, That lie you had me tell back then, does it still count?

They knocked on the door. The 'model opera' was coming to answer.

10

"Chen Xu! Chen Xu! Wait! Listen to me!" He heard her calling.

Behind him a pair of dainty little feet was following in his footsteps. They staggered along, following him like a shadow.

"Wait for me! Wait a minute, I can't run any farther."

He walked even faster. He heard nothing. Her, car horns, bicycle bells, cicadas, the wind in the trees. Nothing, nothing at all, emptiness, a blank, a vacuum.

Nothing.

How the people had crowded around him when he had come down this street in the old days. How they had welcomed him! The big-character posters he drew up filled a whole three-wheeler, and when they put them up at the headquarters of the Municipal Party Committee, there was not enough wall space in the three successive courtyards, and so they just spread them out on the ground, held down with bricks. All the courtyards were filled with his posters, and when the Secretary of the Municipal Committee came outside, he had to walk all the way around and read every one of them. The big-character poster he wrote out himself, attacking the theory of 'inherited class status', was sent to Provincial Party Headquarters and hung from a fifth-floor window, reaching all the way down to the ground. The people who came to copy it had to climb up onto roofs and into the trees in order to read it. When he spoke in front of the Headquarters, he kicked the microphone over. He didn't need a loudspeaker! Applause rocked the square.

But now, none of the people thronging the streets recognised him. How disdainfully, how distantly they looked at him, avoided him. They swore at him for stepping on their toes in that little bit of sunlight.

It was in that little building on the top of the artificial hill, the place on which he had focused all his hopes while he was still thousands of miles away, that they had actually turned against him. A half hour before, they had answered his request with:

"We are not concerned with young people after they leave school."

"If you have a problem, have the Local Organisation resolve it up there. Have your Farm make out a letter of introduction!"

"Mind your manners! Anyway, we can't issue a certificate!"

"If you are not satisfied, then go to the City Youth Office!"

All those faces he knew so well had suddenly turned aloof and cold. They wore smiles at once cunning and foolish, but their eyes were full of open suspicion, even of gloating satisfaction. How did it all change? All their earnest instruction two years before, their elicitation, persuasion and encouragement had now evaporated and turned into a complete rejection. It didn't make sense. If this was what the world was really like, it was too ruthless. No. Better said, politics was too sordid. When they needed you, you were sent up into the clouds like a rainbow; when they didn't need you, or needed something else, they demanded your life in return. You lay in the palm of their hands, like a tiny little pawn, a thin little poker card. In order to win a play for them, you had to lie, to deny, to subvert justice; but once the situation changed and there was something new at stake, they would wash their hands of you!

It had never crossed his mind that the 'left face-ists' might be in power at the school. They had set up a real ring-a-ding proletarian revolutionary faction. He had flown high and far away, and there had been a rout along the whole front. High School No.22 had long since ceased to be his sphere of influence. The artificial hill had been taken over and occupied by others.

Was this revolution?

Pawn. Poker card. Red Guard boss. Farm worker. Group Leader, Red Epoch Society Propaganda Group. Drifter. Half-way River. Wretch. Wheels. Spades. Twenty dollars under the sole of my shoe. Catfish...

"Chen Xu, wait for me."

It was a voice that seemed to come from some place he had

never been, or from a place that he had left long ago. At the very least, his soul, his legless, wingless soul, had left his cold body and was drifting all alone in space. His soul knew neither hope nor reason, only despair and disgust.

He squeezed into a thicket by the lake. He did not know what it was. He just wanted to hide, to find refuge, to get away from people, to be by himself. He threw himself down on the damp ground, gripping the black roots. The leaves began to shake. He battered the trunk with his head. Something rattled; perhaps it was the branches, perhaps his teeth.

He would now be an ordinary, helpless, filthy farmhand, suffering, getting through life by bearing insults without complaint, insignificant, exploited, spending the rest of his life under the thumb of those country hyenas.

He was pinching the ants as they crawled by, savagely squeezing them to paste one by one.

The sun was grey.

A lake of lead, a lake of blood, a lake of skeletons.

Talent, good fortune, all buried in the marshlands at the edge of the earth.

A piece of tarpaulin that someone had discarded, nothing but garbage now that the sky had cleared, a world of garbage.

He didn't want a soul. His soul brought him pain. All he wanted was a well-liked body with which to lord it over the mass of men.

But his body swarmed with worms; they were wriggling about in his tangled guts.

A pair of gentle hands smoothed his brow and a soft voice whispered in his ear, "Chen Xu, what's wrong?"

"Don't get upset; try to calm down."

"You said we'd have to stick it out."

She wiped the sweat from his brow for him with her handkerchief.

He leapt to his feet, cracking his head against a tree branch as he did so. His face contorted from the pain, and his anger erupted.

He shoved her away.

"Go away!" he yelled. "Why are you always following me around? Get lost! Beat it!"

She shrank before his senseless outburst. She stood there

paralysed, uncertain how to comfort him.

He grabbed a handful of leaves, tore them to shreds, and threw them on the ground, doggedly stamping at them with the tip of his foot until they were a black pulp buried in the mud. Then he cleared his throat violently, spat out a wad of mucus, said something inaudible in a hoarse voice, and burst out of the thicket, ripping the branches from his path.

He strode swiftly away, his fists clenched tight. He could have pulverised the hypocritical sunlight.

He just missed being hit by a black car.

The driver slammed on his brakes, then stuck his head out the window and yelled, "Hey you! Wake up!"

"Wake up yourself!" Chen Xu snarled back.

Someone stuck his head out the back window to see who had the nerve to yell at his driver. Was there anyone in Hangzhou these days who didn't recognise his car?

The man in the car took off his sunglasses.

Chen Xu came to his senses at once. As he got a grip on himself, a wave of joy swept over him, but he put on a frown, folded his arms over his chest, and asked coolly, "Don't you recognise me?"

They looked at each other for a moment, and then the other man exclaimed, "Hey! It's Chen Xu!" The car door popped open, and a chubby figure rolled out.

It was Wang Ge. He had been on the Standing Committee of the Provincial Workers' Representative Assembly and the number one man in a big factory after they seized power. During the armed struggles, he had been confined on the roof of a two story building and it was Chen Xu who had found a way to toss a rope and some buns up to him, so that he could make his escape. Theirs was no ordinary friendship, for it was based on Chen's having saved his life. The day that Chen Xu boarded his train for the frontier, Wang Ge had hurried over to see him off. He had given Chen Xu an old thousand-watt electric stove and slapped him on the back as he said, "You may be working on the northern front and I on the southern, but our hearts are united!"

"What brings you back? A promotion? Why haven't you come to see me? Have you forgotten your own brother?" Wang looked him over, eyes narrowed. Behind his suspicious look lay a surmise that Chen Xu was concealing the news that he had shot to the top like a helicopter.

Chen Xu quickly tucked all his fury and frustration away out of sight and said, with an easy-going smile, "Us educated young people are strangers in a strange land up there. The locals don't take to outsiders, so we can't make progress with every step, and even now we're still trying to gain control. It's nothing like your solid position down here. Anyway, now that I've been hanging in there for a year, the Farm officials have figured out what I'm worth, so they're having me start out as Deputy Chairman of the Farm's Revolutionary Committee."

Just then he caught sight of Xiao Xiao standing under a tree not far away, watching him with an odd look in her eyes.

He sighed and continued, "There's just one thing left. For some reason I still need a political check on account of that time I spent in detention. So I came back for a certificate. But you know, those lazy bums up at the High School Workers' Propaganda Team, they..."

"Oh, that's nothing, you just leave it to me. Consider it settled!" Wang Ge, having suddenly realised the problem, patted his chest. "Why didn't you let me know sooner?"

"Chairman Wang, we're going to be late," cooed a young woman, sticking her face outside. "Are we going now?"

"OK, let's leave it at this. Come and see me when you've got some time. I'll take you up to Wind Screen Hill for a jaunt. The air is nice and cool up in the hills. Oh, I forgot to tell you. I've moved over to head the Worker Transportation Section at the Provincial Revolutionary Committee. My phone number is 22347." He held a plump hand out to Chen Xu and called into the car, "Liu Yin, the next time that Comrade Chen Xu here comes to see me, send him right in."

Liu Yin? A very familiar name. Chen Xu paused a moment. He caught a glimpse of a head of thick black hair, and the door closed. The car swaggered off, puffing dirty exhaust around Chen Xu's jacket, acrid with sweat. He closed his eyes and took an indescribable bitterness into the very bottom of his heart.

He watched in silence as his mighty comrade-in-arms drove away. He was mulling something over, and his pained expression gradually relaxed. He was committing a phone number to memory. His eyes glowed.

His soul itself had returned. His indomitable life had once again escaped from the jaws of death. That tiny but infinite space—a man's heart—swelled with shouts of exultation.

He turned around, but Xiao Xiao had vanished.

11

Xiao Xiao was often awakened in the middle of the night by the inexplicable beating of a gong out on the street. The first time, she thought it was the signal for a military drill. She rolled over and jumped up to fold her bedding. The bamboo couch creaked. It was damp and sticky. The street lamps cast their faint light through gaps in the board walls and onto the floor. Squeaking little black shapes scuttled away and disappeared, dragging their thin tails behind them. She remembered where she was. How strange was this homeland that she and her companions had dreamed of night after night from so many thousands of miles away.

She was afraid to roll over, afraid to move at all, lest the darkness around her should become even more sinister in response or some monster should emerge from a corner. She set her mind to fixing the direction of the gong, wondering if some Latest Directive had been announced. Chen Xu had not stayed with her again, nor did she dare let him. And besides, she had been rather angry with him for several days because of the enormous lie he had told Fatso Wang right before her eyes. Promoted to deputy chairman of a Revolutionary Committee indeed—what nerve! It made her so mad she walked out on him, and when he caught up with her they had a big fight over it right on the street corner.

She lay in the pit-like storage shed, only half awake, but with her eyes open, thinking over her troubles. Perhaps the cavemen had lived like this. Neither dirt nor ugliness was visible in such darkness, so the cavemen didn't need to tell lies. But what about lizards? Cuttlefish? Was it in order to survive? Or...?

Deep inside, she felt that Chen Xu was becoming more distant from her day by day. For all their intimacy, something lay between them, and as soon as they relaxed their hold they became two quite distinct people. He was a many-sided prism, and it took all of her strength to see through him. But he was forever reading her thoughts with the greatest of ease. Even if she did see through him once in a while, on looking inward, she could not see through herself. She was shocked and confused. She did not really know him, and sometimes she even got a little bit fed up with him. When he came closer, he seemed all the farther away. She did not know which was the real him. And yet the strange thing was that in the end she was always talked around by him, always forgave him, sympathized with and admired him.

He loved her. She knew it. She needed his love in that frozen land. And she loved him, needed to love him, among that lonely multitude.

He had been running off each day since that encounter with the car, but she would not go with him, no matter what. She had got a good look at the girl sitting next to Fatso Wang, a girl named Liu Yin, who had been a junior in their high school. She was known to all as "No. 5"—she thought she looked like Qin Yi, the star of a movie about a girl who played No.5 on a basketball team. Liu Yin and Xiao Xiao had both been in the school's drama troupe. Xiao Xiao had never dreamed that Liu Yin not only would not have gone to the countryside, but would even have become Wang Ge's 'secretary', and she was rather upset. Anyway, nothing was going smoothly. What with ten dollars handed over to Chen Xu's mother for food, and more gone for candles and bus fares, their twenty dollars went on shrinking day by day, even though they had given up ice cream bars. Each day that Chen Xu didn't get his certificate was another day they couldn't leave Hangzhou. But where would they get the money to go back?

Today was the third time that Chen Xu had gone off to H.S.22 to visit the Workers' Propaganda Team. He said that he had heard from Wang Ge that the Team had agreed to issue him his certificate. But Fatso Wang had not made a very good impression on Xiao Xiao. Chen Xu had gone off in high spirits, leaving her with a heap of worm-eaten baby green beans.

She was shelling the beans. There was no place for her to go during the day anyway. The big-character posters on the streets were practically all the same, and as for reading, there was hardly a book in his family's house.

An aluminum pan sat on the briquet stove, with rice and water in it. Chen Xu's mother had assigned Xiao Xiao her duties first thing in the morning, just like a member of the old leisure class. But at least they hadn't discovered the secret of the storage shed, thank Heaven! If she had to shell beans and cook rice, it was no great matter.

That summer vacation long ago, when the typhoon blew for days, she could not go out at all. Her mother had her and her little sister hold a bean-shelling contest. Whoever won got to tell a story.

She had told one about the happy prince, and another about the little mermaid. They were stories her mother had told her. She told them to her sister.

They threw the bean pods into the big puddle outside, and a great fleet of ships set sail. She recited a poem she had written: "The street lamps have come on. I am going home with Mother."

Mother!

She still had not seen her mother. Chen Xu was dead set against going to look for her. He said it would be a compromise. But if she didn't see her, how would she find out why her mother hadn't written?

Perhaps she could go to a street that her mother passed by every day and catch just a glimpse of her from a distance.

"The rice is burning!" A rough voice exploded over her head. Footsteps thundered through the door, shaking the very rafters. She ran over to the stove, took the lid off the pot, and was met by the acrid smell of scorched rice.

"If you're going to cook the rice, then pay attention to it. Don't just wander around here like a zombie all day," muttered the voice, guzzling from a tea-pot filled with boiled drinking water. She worked at a neighbourhood-run paper box factory that was almost on their doorstep, so she could come home whenever she got a break.

"If you don't keep house, you don't have any idea how expensive things are!" Xiao Xiao's future mother-in-law rattled the tea-pot against the lid of the water vat. She knew that Chen Xu's mother did not like her at all. The two of them had nothing to chat about, and she would not curry favour.

"When rice is scorched, it helps to put in a few green onions," Xiao Xiao ventured, feeling very hard done by. She had never cooked at home, because her grandmother was there. If the rice got scorched when her grandmother was out, there were green onions. Her mother had taught her this. Her mother often scorched the rice too.

But her attempt to patch things up only sent Chen Xu's mother into a rage. She picked up the pan and flung it on the floor, yelling, "Pah! Little slut! Don't tell me how to run my house! You squawk an awful lot for a hen that hasn't laid any eggs!"

Xiao Xiao was so startled that she flushed a bright red. It's not you I'm marrying! Wasn't it on account of Chen Xu that she had broken with her own family? She gulped, and said as calmly as she could, "Mrs. Chen, if you're unhappy with me..."

She was cut off by a torrent of abuse.

"Here I was, thinking we had ghosts, what with all that racket out in back! And what do you know it turns out we're keeping a little slut who's got her hooks in my A'long. Far be it from me to be unhappy with anyone!"

She was so shocked she just stared straight ahead. All of her resentment was choked off, for she could tell from what Mrs. Chen said that their whole family had probably known all about the secret of the storage shed early on, but had gone on playing deaf and dumb for days in order to avoid embarrassment. She hung her head. The bean husks at her feet danced like a crowd of green imps.

And then he flew over the hedge and escaped. All the little birds in the bushes took fright and flew away. It's because I'm so ugly, thought the little duckling. And so he closed his eyes and kept on running. He ran all the way to a marsh where some wild ducks lived. He hid there the whole night, he was so weary and miserable.

Chen Xu walked in, grinning from ear to ear.

"Look!" He held a piece of paper up in front of Xiao Xiao. There was a bright red official seal at the top. "I won!" He clasped his hands behind his back and paced back and forth. Then he snapped his fingers. "From now on everything starts as of July 23, 1970!"

He was oblivious to the atmosphere in the room, and beamed as he held up the sheet of paper and read it aloud, all the way through. It said something about his role in the Cultural Revolution having been that of a solid revolutionary and recommended that his organization give him a responsible position.

"In the end, it all comes down to power," he concluded. "One phone call from Wang Ge and the Propaganda Team was eating out of my hand. Everything's fine now. I can leave in just a few days—we're going back home!"

"In a few days?" Xiao Xiao was stunned.

"Why not? The train fare? Wang Ge says he'll lend it to us."

"No, no, it's nothing." She put him off and stole over to the door. In that instant her earlier decision came surging back, now firm and unyielding. She would definitely go, even if it were only for a single glimpse from a distance, a few seconds. Then she could hop on the train without a backward look and return to that distant land.

The street lamps have come on. I am going home with Mother. She was writing a poem, writing it as she walked along.

She was still a very little girl, with two red stripes pinned to her sleeves. She was skipping along beside her mother. Under the street lamps, a long thin shadow stuck out behind her mother, like a polliwog with its little tail waving back and forth.

The broad avenue was like a sheet of paper. If what was written on it today was no good, tomorrow it could be turned over and rewritten. The long alley was like a pencil. When the end was reached, poems and songs would flow from the tip all by themselves.

Each and every day, she and her mother crossed the boulevard and walked down the narrow lane. Under the street lamp, her shadow was like a bamboo shoot; in the blink of an eye it had grown several feet. The bamboo shoot became a bamboo; her mother had lost her tail. The little tail had turned into a frog princess.

She paced back and forth by a telephone pole. There was a slogan posted on the pole, but the street lamps had not come on yet, so she could not see what was written on it. She paced off the road, calculating the exact moment when her mother would pass by on her way home from work. She paced it off again and again, but she could never get it right. It was not that her pace was off, but that the pavement was too rough.

There was a dense fog. The sun was like an orange balloon; there was no telling whether it was rising or setting, whether it was dawn or dusk.

Liu the Brute came by, driving a herd of cattle. He spat on the ground and swore. You mothers!

It is forbidden to swear at mothers. She spat on the ground too.

She saw someone watering flowers, and went over for a closer look, but it was not her mother.

She saw someone correcting homework papers and went over for a closer look, but it was not her mother.

She saw a tractor driving ponderously down the highway, making almost no progress even after a long time. There was someone sitting up on the tractor, tying a whisk broom. On looking more closely, she could see white hairs amid the black and a kind of light in the wrinkles around the smile. Mother! she cried. No wonder you're so late, you came by tractor. Her mother got off and walked ponderously up, like a tractor herself, her feet mounted on treads.

Her mother said, You're always making a racket outside the

classroom window. I'm trying to teach, and you're being really naughty.

She said, When I grow up, I'm going to be a singer.

Her mother replied, Frog princesses have awful voices. You'd better be a doctor.

She got mad. She ditched her mother and walked off by herself, flying over the ground.

She was reciting a poem on stage:

> By the shore of the deep blue sea,
> There lived an old man and his wife...

The audience clapped and shouted her name. She wanted to recite another poem and grabbed the microphone. She would not get off the stage; she wanted to do the whole performance all by herself. Her mother came and carried her off. She beat on her mother's shoulders and bit her fingers.

An enormous windmill was shredding the wind into pieces like puffs of cloud, sending them dancing all over the sky.

There was a river flowing up a mountain.

The sky gradually got dark. She was anxious from waiting so long. Her neck ached, and she was terribly thirsty.

Mother, she wanted to cry, but no sound would come out. Mother. She discovered that the switch on her throat had not been turned on. Mother. She could no longer find the key.

A letter came floating along the river. She looked at it, and it was from Chen Xu. He had gone to Yenan for the Great Linking-up. He was not in Hangzhou at all.

In the letter, Chen Xu asked, Do you want your mother or do you want me?

She said, I want my mommy.

Her mother's hair was completely white. The spots on her face looked like the sesame seeds on a flatcake. Wrinkles had climbed all over her forehead like earthworms. Her mother had become an old woman.

The click of footsteps. Her mother walked by, bone weary.

Mother! she burst out in a ringing voice, as resonant as a bullfrog.

Dear little flower, it's you. You've come back.

Mother! It's me. I've come back.

You've made Mama wait so long. I knew you'd come back.

Why didn't you write to me, Mother?

You didn't write to me either, did you?

Dad doesn't want me any more. I'm not your daughter any more.

Silly baby. He was just mad. Don't pay any attention to him.

Forgive me, Mother. How I've missed you!

Mama didn't write you because she was afraid of getting you in trouble. I was released from custody and allowed to come back home, but it was a case of the internal handling of a contradiction with a class enemy, and I am still suspected of being a traitor. I'm sorry for all the trouble I've caused you.

Traitors all part their hair that way. You aren't a traitor.

Silly baby. The street lamps have come on. Come home with me.

No, I'm leaving, on tomorrow's train. There's something wrong with the street lamps. Don't blame me, I miss you. Next time, next time, I'll...

She was positive that her mother's troubled look, as it swept over her hairline, was as warm and limpid, held her as closely to its heart as the two rays of light she had seen during so many black nights.

Her mother asked, Do you need anything?

She thought for a long while and then asked, Do you have any money?

Her mother opened up her pockets and ransacked her old worn-out grey purse, but only found a penny. She blew on it, and the coin turned into a balloon.

Mother—

She chased after her like a madwoman, throwing her arms around her mother's waist, shaking her and calling her, pounding on her. But she did not move an inch. That thin, hard back calmly and quietly let her howl her heart out.

She discovered that she was clinging to a telephone pole with the crook of her arm. The rough old wooden shaft was covered with damp moss.

The street lamps have come on.

The lamps were black. In the black lamplight, a thin human form was waving back and forth, like a little polliwog pulling its tail along after it.

The balloon rose up into the air high above. Among the boundless clouds, a school of little black polliwogs sailed away with the waves, bobbing up and down.

12

He had been wearing a straw rope around his waist all this time. At first there had been a shirt tucked under it, later a dark blue jacket, and now that autumn was past, it was black wads of cotton padding showing through holes in brown cloth. A straw rope was very efficient, a hell of a lot more convenient than buttons. He had several tied over each shoe, top to sole. They prevented slipping even in rain or snow. He only had one button left to his name, the one on his fly. Without a button there, the prisoner was likely to give the turnkey the slip while he was off somewhere having a smoke. The icy wind poured in as though it were having a frozen woman, any way it liked. Those buttons had been stripped from an army overcoat that Bubble had tossed down to him from the luggage rack of the train that brought them up to 'support the frontier'. But now they had all been ripped off him by those bastards. What were they going to do, eat them like candied beans? Hope they choke!

The rope had been twisted for him by Old Bian, back when they were carrying rice straw in the paddy fields. Brothers in adversity. A smile on that big mouth and a chuckled "Been hiding my light under a bushel!" A steel sickle was tucked under the rope. The blade rubbed against his waist, while the handle slid back and forth on his leg, giving him a cocky look. Had it been a pistol, no telling but he might have plugged a few of them. As his worn-out gloves swept back and forth in front of him, they revealed a row of black fingernails.

He could see only his fingernails, sitting there like a row of flies. He could not see how long his hair had grown. It was only the restlessly moving lice that reminded him of the tropical forest growing on his scalp. Lice had proven their great utility back in the days of Hitler. They could breed bacteria and spread them all around to really mow people down. Anyway, there was no mirror, so he did not know how he looked. That was because this place, like all detention centres and isolation cells, accepted responsibility only for the washing of brains. They had soy sauce soup—'clear as far as the eye can see', shared buns as hard as a fortress wall, and snored on plank beds along with hardened criminals of the worst sort. He felt a stranger to himself; he was not even sure that he still existed.

And so one morning he had jumped up from the pile of straw before anyone else, knelt on the ground, and set to work with all his might, sharpening his sickle. His grinding sounded much like the rats busy at night at the ends of the bed. He ground up a glistening bubble and an acrid cloud that stank of stale sweat. The one thing he couldn't get was what he was after. When he held the gleaming blade up level with his eyes and sought to capture his dancing reflection, the skinheads sacked out on the planks all around his kneeling figure burst out laughing.

"Want a mirror? Why don't you just piss on the ground?"

"I say, Chen Xu, you talk a pretty piece, but what about working?"

"You'd better just slit your throat and hold your head up for a look!"

He wasn't going to waste his time arguing with them, a pool of filth. It drew mosquitos, long-tailed maggots.

"What you fucking in for?"

"Doing ideological work."

"Doing it to who?"

"Li'l Shanghai gal."

"Get it done?"

"Yeah."

"So then she turned you in?"

"Naw, I put her on the garbage crew."

"So how'd they get you?"

"Dog dug a dead baby out of the snow."

"What about you?"

"Sold some grain."

"Whose grain?"

"Mess hall's."

"How much you make?"

"Cartload of wood."

"What you do with the wood?"

"Took it to town."

"What you get for it in town?"

"My boy's a truck driver now."

Shit! To think that he had fallen so low that he was mixed up on the same brick bed with these dungheap maggots.

He couldn't hold it any longer, he had to take a leak. Off to the latrine, a few planks, creaking and swaying. Up onto the overhanging cliff, facing the abyss. He took a deep breath of cold air and looked down for that one remaining black button. There was his ashen face reflected in a pool of filthy water. The shaggy cheeks were like the moss-grown bark on the shady side of a tree, packing up all his former proud defiance and revealing a nose like a stubby mushroom, a picture of hard luck. He raised his foot and kicked the board down the cliff, and in that moment of anger his last button disappeared.

"Come with us!"

"Where to?"

"Farm Headquarters!"

"What for?"

"You'll find out when we get there!"

"Who do you think you are?"

"Political Work Unit."

"I'm not going!"

"You don't go peaceable we'll have to tie you up!"

"Try it!"

"Try resisting arrest!"

"Where's your warrant?"

"Judicial process was quashed a long time ago; we've got a seal."

"This is a frame-up!"

"Come on, the government frame someone? Relax!"

"What are you after?"

"You went absent from the Farm for a month without leave; what sort of reward do you expect?"

"I went back to do an investigation."

"An investigation of who?"

"Myself. I wasn't a reactionary student, I was a Red Guard leader. I've got proof."

"Save your breath. Let's go!"

"If you won't listen to reason, I'll lodge a complaint with the Party Central Committee!"

"Well now, why don t you just wait until we get back from our three months' investigation trip to West Lake and then send in your complaint!"

By the time Xiao Xiao could scream, he had been bundled into a jeep.

Frost formed before the season for dew had come, and before

frost would have formed down south, snow had whitewashed even the sun, while heaven and earth shivered in the freezing cold.

Before he knew it, he had been held in that inhuman hole for two months.

How much longer would he have to stay there? All through the endless winter, days, weeks, months...

He lined up to go cut beanstalks with his sickle, which might not reflect his face but which was still the sharpest of all. A crowd of convicts, neither quite brown nor quite green, wriggling around in the knee-deep snow. All those gold, brass beans had to be dug out of the snow, cut down, and stacked in rows to be hauled back by cart. Shoes freezing cold, gloves freezing, blood freezing; shoes wet, gloves wet, bones wet. The ox groaned with hunger, chewing the bean stalks and refusing to move, but the people had to bend over and stick their butts up in the air in spite of their hunger, up toward that blank white sky. There were no whips, to be sure, but there were vulturish eyes raking them from behind. He swung his sickle in a frenzy, hacking and pulling away, little caring if the brittle pods popped open and sent the beans flying into the snow. It was fine with him if they turned into silver beans, water beans, and vanished at once. If they were pressed for oil or ground up for bean curd, who'd ever be able to lay eyes on them? Even the bean cake left over from boiling them would never turn up any place where he could nibble on it. What's the point of digging you out? Might as well scatter them over the fields, let them have a nice sleep tucked under the snow, save sowing them in the spring.

"Watch out kid, Vulture's coming around," Bian wheezed as he hurried over. The poor sod. One morning early in the year he had opened the nozzle of a diesel oil tank so he could wash his hands, but the oil was frozen and when he left he had not screwed the nozzle tight. Come noon and the oil melted and poured out, eight tons of it gone to the last drop. Of course that finished him as a tractor driver, and now he was sure to get two or three years for 'sabotaging production'. When he saw those thick guileless lips, Chen Xu felt numb all over.

"What's your hurry? Wait till threshing time, then you'll see something." Those thick lips whispered close by his ear, suddenly stabbing out like a blade. "I can stuff up the intake eight or ten times in one day."

'Vulture' was bellowing from behind them, "It looks like snow today. Another snowfall and the beans will be ruined. I'm going up to

No.7 to borrow a tractor from their garage so we can get them all baled and taken in before dark. Bian, you see too it that everybody works right along, and no quitting before I get back, hear that?"

He got into the truck and drove off into the wind.

The layers of beans were stacked up like a wall. Grab a few bundles, brush off the snow, clear a patch of black earth, scrape the golden beans off the stalks with the tip of a shoe, a big bunch at a time. Then light the bean stalks and roast the beans on the blade of a sickle until they turn nice and toasty. Delicious.

"Who's got a light?"

There was no response. In the isolation cells, matches were isolated too. The furnace for the heated wall was outside and no candles were issued to use when the electricity was out. But the previous month, when they were storing cabbage in the cellars, they had seen some lanterns downstairs. There was something itchy in the way the flames in them flickered. "Squad leader, a report! The lantern is out; we need a match." "Squad leader, a report! The one you gave us didn't light." You had to have a light under your bushel to sneak a match, too. Once you got one, you hid it in a hollow reed under your bedding, where even Sherlock Holmes couldn't find it. That one was kept for smoking. Any day they were sent to load trucks or something they could always pick up a few cigarette butts, no problem. They scrounged one each, then shook the tobacco out and rolled a strip of newspaper with a twist at each end, like a little locusts leg. One puff each, a deep breath—that felt good!

But where could he get a light out here in the snow? Magnifying glass? Rubbing cotton threads together? Forget it. Better just huddle together here out of the wind and leave it at that.

Something small and grey came whizzing out of the bean stalks and beat a quick retreat, leaving behind a trail of little footprints like flower petals on the snow. Rabbit? Badger? Field mouse? You all have thick fur to keep out the cold. Even you beans have pods. And what about us? The vast sky, the darkened land; ordered around as they please.

Had Wei Hua's injuries really done any permanent damage? If he got a medical discharge and went back to Hegang, it would work out just right, since the deputy troop-leader's position would then come vacant.

Who could fill that spot?

Instructor Yu had finally been made acting Chairman of the

Branch Farm, so what about the vacant deputy instructor's slot?

Why had Guo Chunmei taken up pig raising? Piggery on a grand scale. And she had been named a pace-setter in the 'Study and Application of Chairman Mao's Works in a Living Way' by the Youth Affairs Office. The day they got back to the Farm, he had seen her pushing a wheelbarrow in front of the barn. She had gone right by, pretending not to see him. She had big blue patches on the knees of her work pants; looked just like a mask. There was so much fodder loaded onto her wheelbarrow it was on the verge of spilling. A pace-setter? She probably wanted to become some kind of official. But she didn't seem all that ambitious.

He'd write another letter to the Provincial Youth Affairs Office. How could he send it off?

Someone nudged his foot. Snickering broke out all around him.

"Look at that one. She's built like a potato."

"Look at the guy—thin as a straw."

There were two black shapes far away across the snow, poking intently on the ground. Then they straightened up and continued along a furrow, looking for something. One tall and one short; one fat and one thin. The village idiots from the settlement nearby, come to glean on the State Farm fields. Little was harvested on state fields, and much was left. Gleaning on them could support a family.

"They're a pair, aren't they?" said someone, squinting and gulping.

"A pair? One tall and the other short, how do they do it?"

"Don't you worry, as long as they match up in the middle they're in business!"

"Match up in the middle? Ha! Fucking clever!"

"Who'll give us a little Shandong fast clapper song to pass the time?"

"A clapper song you want? Okay, listen up:

> Dongligeding,
> Dongligedong,
> Gather round and hear me sing,
> A jolly tale but not too long,
> The leader of a bandit ring,
> The bold and stalwart Wu Erlang,
> Dongligeding,
> Dongligedong,

He had what it takes, and that's the thing,
Balls so big and a dong so long,
Dongligeding,
Dongligedong..."

"Get to work!" yelled Bian.

Beneath the snow lay the restless earth, giving off its rank muddy smell every day, every night, hour by hour and minute by minute, below the coarse pellets of snow. Could he keep his desire in check? It was the snow that did it. Her skin was like snow, exquisitely wrought. No, he must not think of her. She was not an object of desire, she was a pure white cloud, a cloud appearing in his dreams. To think of her with watering mouth was a sin.

It got dark. The beans stretched far into the distance. It was like a night march along the sleepers of a railway line. Even though they were invisible, they went on step after step and never ended. The grey clouds sank lower and ended by spreading out over the fields as a clinging layer of fog. But through the brownish dusk, one almost imperceptible little steel file after another reached out and began to rasp at faces, necks, the telephone poles.

"The wind..." he muttered.

"The wind? What about it? Wait till the real cold weather comes. You go to take a leak and all the way down to the bottom there's one pillar of piss and shit after another, just like in those postcards of, what's that place? You know, like the country around Guilin. And that wind's noisy too. It can choke you and leave you frozen on top of a mountain of ice like the frontier guards in the Pamir Mountains in that spy movie."

The cliff? His brows twitched and his heart skipped a beat. How much longer were they going to stay there? An eagle feeding on a corpse, a bear in a tree trunk. The blade of his sickle suddenly flashed with a cold light, leaping away like a swimming snake. Bits of snow flew about, withered leaves tumbled to the ground. His frozen shoes melted, his steel-sheathed spine softened, his bones dried; it was a fire so hot he broke out in a sweat.

He had made it. He threw his sickle as far as he could. He was the first one to reach the end of the field.

There was a little path running along the edge of the field. It led to the village.

He looked behind him and spat disdainfully.

100

Someone was tramping toward him, the breeze blowing ripples over the fine fur on the turned-up earflaps of his cap. It was a hunter with a heavy, long-necked bird hanging from the double-barreled shotgun on his shoulder.

"Wild duck?" He stuck his neck out too.

"No, goose."

Geese loved grain. Hunters made a point of waiting in the grain fields after frost in autumn. Autumn geese were plump and juicy.

"How 'bout selling it?"

"For what?"

It was a holdover from tribal ages, barter. Anyway, he had no money. What did he have? Fountain pen, nail clippers... Don't want them? If you don't want them, I haven't got anything else. Oh, wait a minute, I've got a pair of dogskin kneepads; you can tie them tight or loose, nice and warm. I'll take them off for you. Cold? I don't care. Once I'm full I won't be cold any more.

The trade was quite direct: something for running on the ground in return for something that flew in the air. Oh yes, Uncle Poor-and-Lower-Middle-Peasant, give me a match too. We'll eat it while it's still fresh. Vulture isn't back yet; it's a chance in a million. Don't worry, this isn't the 'hundred chicken feast' in the model opera, where they get ambushed in the middle of their celebration. Thanks. In a second we'll go on stage to play! What are you all standing around staring at? Take some bean stalks, set them alight, thaw out the ground, add some melted snow, and make a lump of mud. Now smear it over the feathers and watch me cook you up some 'beggars chicken'.

What's beggars chicken? One of the great delicacies of West Lake. Even another Smash the Four Olds couldn't touch it. It's a revolutionary dish just made for 'remembering former sufferings amid our present plenty'. Beggars, tramps, people without anything, proletarians, just like us. How could beggars eat chicken? They probably got infected with capitalist ideas. Never mind, eat first and criticise after. You smear it with mud and roast it in a fire, and it tastes so good you'll never want to be anything but a beggar as long as you live. Never heard of it? Well, there's lots of things you guys haven't heard of up north here. All you know is stewed pork and noodles.

Faster! Can't you see those lights up the road, shining like a wolf's eyes? It's the Vulture's tractor on the way back. Light the fire! Never mind, he's still miles away; it will take him two or three weeds to get here, and that's enough. He won't find so much as a goose feather left. More fire! It has to get so hot that the mud crackles. Don't worry. The headlamps won't pick you out, and even if Vulture sees the fire, we can say a peasant dropped a cigarette butt.

It's ready; I think it's ready, you can smell it and see the fat sizzling and running out. Don't grab, don't grab, a leg each for me and Bian and you can divide up the rest. Too tough to chew? Are your jaws frozen? Well, it is a little underdone. Anyway, there isn't time. How could the tractor move so fast? There's still a good three minutes before it gets here. I'll tear off this piece of meat, swallow it; the best flavour comes from cracking the bones, too bad too bad. Can't chew it, just can't chew it. Swallow it anyway; even if it comes out the same way it went in, at least Vulture won't get to eat it. This is what you call 'beggars goose', unity of the proletariat north and south. Ack, goose feather stuck in my throat, itches so much I could fly. If I really could it would be great. If I could be something, be a goose. Stinks? Of course it does, don't be afraid to eat it all, even the intestines, and what's in them, too. We're beggars, poor and lower-middle peasants, even goose shit tastes good to us. Like to roast me a fucking Vulture, that's what I'd like.

"Chen Xu!" A voice crashed into the firelight like a battered gong.

"What is it?" He was jolted to his senses. The fire was out. There were just the two headlamp beams closing in like ghouls.

"You motherfucker. Say, Present!" Vulture's face was grim in the light.

"Present! What do you want?"

"Look at your row of beanstalks. What kind of shitty work do you call that?"

The tractor was snorting as though it had been thrown into convulsions by the sight. The row of beans behind him twisted this way and that in the light of the headlamps, plants that he had missed poking up here and there.

"You pull those up by hand. You're not going back until they're all out."

"I can't see them in the dark," he said grimly. His blood was crackling as it froze. His guts were as empty as a desert. His face had long since gone numb, the wind was rasping at his icicle bones, his hair was frozen stiff.

"Can or can't, do it anyway."

"I've already been working more than twelve hours."

"Sixteen hours won't kill you."

"Can't you treat us like human beings?"

"This is what reform by labour is all about; give me your sickle. Did you hear me? Give me that sickle!"

A flash of light and his sickle went flying away. Leaping the horizontal bar! The side horse! The swing! The flying trapeze! The curved silver hook flew unerringly toward that monster eye. Pop went the pod, golden beans flying in all directions, pitch blackness. Perhaps it would be half a century before that other eye would finally force itself open, all atremble. A single murky patch on the black earth, where the light of only one eye illuminated one black corner.

"This is insubordination, boy! Take him in custody, handcuff him!"

At some point the straw rope had broken, and the sharp steel files chafed his skin, scraping off a layer of skin, cutting away a piece of flesh, filing through a muscle. A hole had been gouged in his heart, and it dripped red blood. So this was where the pain came from. On what ridge, in what furrow, on what patch of snow had that rope been left, his last defence?

Why was it so light? Was there a fire? What was that on the horizon? A blood-shot eye? A wheel of fire of Prince Ne'zha? A bright red meatball? A sesame fritter? It was the moon at its full. How could the moon be so red? He had never seen such a blood-red moon.

At the intersection leading to the Farm's detention unit, he saw in the moonlight a little tree that had kept its leaves, stretching its radiant scarlet branches out over the shining snow.

Xiao Xiao! He cried out deep inside. He closed his eyes and walked past, teeth clenched. Droplets of ice spattered over his frozen chest. That soft, moist mouth, her warm skin, the fragrant nape of her neck, they held an eternal and unique fascination. Perhaps he would have to spend his whole life in this dump. Even if he were released, he would turn into just another dirt clod here, freezing, then thawing, then freezing once again. Harvest after the frost, sow after the thaw. But he would never let any one else get to her! He knew he could make a nest for himself! For her, with her...

He shuddered, startled by his train of thought. The bonds on his wrists burned like fire.

13

One by one the summer wildflowers withered and vanished from the clumps of weeds, while day by day the meadows faded, grew sparse and bare. The hopeless, moaning willows revealed the bald old ravens' nests among their boughs, and the gloomy ditches fell silent, their singing sealed within lips of ice. Flocks of geese honked and wailed their mournful way south. Rows of stacked corn, not yet dragged back to the threshing ground, were dusted with snow. Once the sun came out, clear teardrops dripped noisily from their silks.

Then, suddenly, all anyone could talk about was the Autumn Festival. The full moon of the eighth lunar month was close at hand.

Xiao Xiao was baffled. It made no more sense than celebrating New Years in the middle of summer.

It had snowed, frozen over. How could they celebrate the Autumn Festival now?

But this much was a fact: There was a perfectly round moon in the sky, a moon so round that it might have come rolling down on them at any moment.

And this too was a fact: They slaughtered a pig for the company mess hall and sold everyone a serving of fried pork and leeks. The leeks were as coarse as southern wild rice stems and sliced crosswise like razor clam meat. Trouble was, one bite and your mouth went numb. Fried pork and leeks? Ridiculous. Even if you could fry leeks with meat, these thick yellowish northern leeks, compared to long green southern shallots, were just as tough and unpleasant as the northern hicks. How could you enjoy pork with leeks? Their bite drowned out the taste of the meat. She pushed her plate aside and glowered at it, appetite gone. Of course you could pick out the pieces of meat, but somehow, after she had gone so long without it, meat tasted flat and stale, its flavour drowned in grease.

She was not hungry. They were also issued one watermelon and a few crabapples each. The watermelon was about the size of a ball used in shotput, and frosted with white. And there were two mooncakes, hard as planks.

And an even more indisputable fact: They did not have to go to political study class on the evening of the Festival.

Everyone's faces glowed like the moon. But the moon itself seemed to have taken on a greenish tinge, to have gone mouldy.

She sat there absorbed in the moon cakes and the melon. Eventually, she got two sheets of writing paper out from under the tablecloth. She wrapped up the moon cakes and put them in a manila folder. Then she climbed up on the brick bed and put the folder on the storage rack. But on second thought, this didn't seem too secure, so she got it back down and just held it in her hands, uncertain what to do with it.

Rats ran wild in the dormitory. Once, in the middle of the night, a girl from Hegang had leapt screaming out of bed and gone thrashing around on the floor. They all woke up in a fright and turned on their flashlights. One of her toes was gone. After this, the girls had to sleep with a clean pair of work shoes on. Sometimes, when they got up in the morning, there'd be only one outdoors shoe left beside the bed, the other one having been carted off by some rat to serve as a cradle for its young. Even the bedding was full of rat droppings, and there was no telling but what one day a nest of pink little baby rats would turn up. The ceiling was even worse, haunted by rats dashing back and forth all night long.

One afternoon, as they were setting off for work, Bubble and Beanpole very carefully handed her something soft wrapped in paper, telling her to eat it before it got cold. She thought it was roast corn or a baked potato, but when she opened it and took a look, she was so startled that she threw the thing as far away as she could. It was a bright red headless rat, giving off a strange smell. As soon as it hit the ground, poor Bubble took to his heels. He came back carrying his precious delicacy, which he had rescued from a clump of weeds. His mouth was watering. "You ought to try it, then you'd know how tasty they are. In Canton during Linking-up, I saw snake restaurants and rat restaurants, I'm not kidding! Honest! Besides, there's nothing else good to eat around here."

Eat rat? She'd rather starve!

Even if you ate rats three times a day, you'd never run out of them. Chen Xu had made up a little poem: "Manchuria boasts of three delights: Rats and fleas and no-see'um bites." Chen Xu, do you miss me? "She can't even bear to eat an old moon cake, must be keeping it to feed the rats!" Someone clapped at her from the other bed. You know who I'm keeping it for! Finally she put it in her aluminum mess kit and heaved a sigh of relief. She could take it to him the next time she went to visit.

"Have you gone deaf, Xiao?" Someone was calling from the doorway. "Instructor Yu wants you to come to the office."

She looked up, a little flustered. She had never been called to the office by Yu Funian before.

Was it because of that page from her diary? She had written in her diary that she did not understand why Chen Xu had been sent to the brig. She had written in her diary that she missed him, loved him. But how had that page happened to fall out on the floor while she was away from the dormitory, and how had it then been handed over to Yu Funian?

The company had held a criticism session on account of that page, although she had not been mentioned by name.

Even Liu the Brute had spoken at that meeting. He pulled a notebook from his pocket with a great flourish, opened it up and placed it on the table. There had been furtive smiles from the people in the front rows—they said later that the pages were completely blank. Liu looked at the notebook for a long time, and then spoke to the following effect:

"Back when we was young folks, all we thought about was clearing the land and growing food. We didn't have no time for all this snow and flowers stuff. When a guy in the land-clearing crew got a letter from his girl, he'd post it right up on the notice board for everybody to see. That's right, and when a girl down at the clothing and bedding factory got a letter from a fellow in the crew, she'd read it to everyone. There weren't nothing in them letters but 'couragement for the land clearing. That's what we called rev'lutionary room ants...'"

And after the meeting, Guo Chunmei had posted that page up on the political criticism bulletin board in the dormitory, where it had lingered on for two months.

Guo Chunmei was still mad at her. She knew it. It was because Wei Hua had been hurt in the fight that night. Guo Chunmei associated her with Chen Xu. After Wei Hua left, Chunmei moved to the other bed, her face veiled by a layer of frost. She had wanted to strike up a conversation with her several times, but before she could open her mouth, her lips were frozen by a cold blast from across the way.

The little duckling sat in the corner of the wall, feeling terrible.

106

He felt a strange yearning to go down to the water and play. They don't understand me, said the duckling.

Everyone in the dormitory looked at her with eyes that showed traces of shock, of concern, and of gloating over her fall. She deflected them all off her back. Two whole months had gone by since Chen Xu had been sent to the Farm's detention unit, and she had lived under those eyes the whole time. She had long since become accustomed to her solitude. Cooking, getting water, coming back from work, in political study class... No one ever spoke to her, not even those few who had been her good friends before. They too considered her running away to Hangzhou with Chen Xu without a word to have been an unforgivable betrayal of their friendship. She would not beg for anything.

But not to have betrayed them would have been to betray Chen Xu, to betray her love. The perfect choice would have been to betray herself.

She walked out, head held high.

Maybe there was some news about Chen Xu. Would they let her take something to him? She had done so once and got a dressing-down from someone in the Political Work Unit.

Could it be about the letter she had sent to the Provincial Youth Office? That had been Zou Sizhu's idea. More than a month had gone by, but there had been no sign of a response.

Her heart was pounding, slowly and heavily.

Just as she stepped into hallway of the Branch Farm office, she saw the door down at the turning of the hall open and someone slip inside. She didn't know where Instructor Yu was, and thought she would ask whoever had just gone in. But when she got to the door, she heard voices inside. She could not decide whether to go in or not, so she looked in through a gap in the blue paint on the window. Someone was standing with his back to her. Instructor Yu was sitting at his desk smoking. There was a wad of bills on the table, which the other person pushed over to him before saying something in a low voice and ducking back out.

He left so quickly that she did not see who he was—he looked like a city kid. She knocked on the door and went in. Where the pile of money had been a moment ago there was a green army cap. Instructor Yu kept his cap on all year round. Now, a small scar was visible above his temple.

He invited her to take a seat and asked if she had eaten her moon cake.

Chen Xu had given Yu Funian the nickname 'Catfish', because he was sticky and slimy at the same time.

"The letter you sent to the Provincial Youth Office has been sent back down to us," he said with a smile. He pulled open a drawer and took out a letter, which he shook at her. "You have the courage to report to higher authorities. Good for you."

She felt a little relieved. It looked as though Yu was going to be quite reasonable. There seemed to be admiration in his smile, even satisfaction. There was no knowing if it was real or false, just like those big white teeth.

He exhaled a cloud of smoke and rapped on the letter with his knuckles. Then he blinked rapidly, his drab eyes looking directly at her calf.

"Nevertheless, the next time you report to the higher authorities, you must do so on the basis of the facts. It was the Farm's Political Work Unit that decided that Chen Xu should be suspended and undergo self-examination. There was no question of a frame-up on our part. Of course we understand that so far as his leaving the Farm without permission and planning the fight are concerned, you were simply misled." He nodded indulgently, as though the letter did not bother to him at all.

Xiao Xiao tried to explain. "We went back in order to find out what the verdict was on his role during the Cultural Revolution."

"We don't pay that much attention to what people did during the Cultural Revolution. Everybody says they were on the Rebel side now. I do too, for that matter." He seemed to be getting a little impatient. "As for the way Chen Xu has behaved since he came to the Farm, don't you find it rather dangerous?"

She hung her head. Dangerous? She had never felt really secure since she was born. Dangerous? What did that mean?

"Very dangerous." He nodded decisively. "I called you over today to alert you. Even if Chen Xu is released from detention and does come back, he will have to take his remoulding seriously from now on. If you don't draw a clear line between yourself and him in good time, well, it's completely..."

"Come back? When is he coming back?" She interrupted him.

He smiled noncommittally and went on speaking, but she heard no more of what he said.

Was there really money under that cap? What sort of money

was it? If it was public funds, why did he have to cover it up? Why? Draw a clear line? Between herself and whom? Now that things had gone so far, was it still possible to do so clearly? Remoulding? Remould oneself and not the rest of the world? For how much longer? Would it never end?

"All right, go on home and think things over carefully." He stood up at last. "If you can rein in your horse before you go over the cliff, you can still be a good comrade, you know."

He patted her lightly on the shoulder, leaving his hand on her for just a moment before taking it away. She shuddered and shrank from his touch. His hand glided down and reached for the cap on the table. But just as he was about to touch it, he recoiled and, with a quick glance at her, smoothed down his hair instead.

Xiao Xiao pulled the door shut with a bang and left.

A dark cloud came sailing swiftly toward her, like a bird, beating its wings and taking hold of that round globe. A great heavy shadow fell, its shape uncertain and changing. The huge bird flew on, but now the moon's pale white light was darker than before, as though rough spots of mould had appeared on that frigid silver orb, spots that dodged about here and there. She wondered if poor Wu Gang, the man in the moon, was standing beneath the cassia tree up there, forever trying to wipe those spots away and never succeeding.

When she was young, she had envied the moon goddess, Chang'e, for living in such an otherworldly place and being able to look down on all the great mountain peaks of Earth. But now she felt a little sorry for her, up there with only a rabbit for company. No doubt Chen Xu could see this same moon, though probably through iron bars. Only the moon could see him and her at the same time. If she could talk with it...

She heard footsteps running up from behind her. She looked back and saw a pair of glasses flashing in the light. It was Zou Sizhu.

"How come you're here too?" She asked.

"Enjoying the moon." He frowned. "I hear Catfish called you in for a talk."

"That letter was sent back." She was puzzled. Had he been waiting for her? "The letter to the Youth Office."

"Was there any comment from higher up?" he asked.

She shook her head. Even if there had been, Catfish would never have let her see it.

"What did he have to say?"

"He, well, he told me that I should draw a clear line between myself and Chen Xu." She told Zou Sizhu all about this, the only thing she could remember. She need not hide anything from him; there was no reason to hold anything back. He might well be the only real friend she had left. She could tell him everything she felt.

He was pacing back and forth on the snowy ground. He remained silent for a moment and then said, "From the looks of it, the Provincial Youth Office must have instructed the Farm to handle the case in an appropriate way. The reason why they clapped him in the brig in the first place was to teach him a lesson, to break his spirit. And since he went south for a vacation on the pretense of carrying out an investigation, they could... So, it looks like Chen Xu will be back pretty soon."

"Really?" Xiao Xiao bit her lips.

He averted his face, and the moon cast the shadow of the ear flap on his cap across his shoulder. For some reason he looked unhappy. He stammered, "Yes, I think so."

"Very soon?"

"Not necessarily, but it shouldn't be too long either, perhaps by New Years."

The moon shone down, a brilliant white; the specks of mould on it had somehow been swept away. Near and far, buildings and fields were bathed in the clear moonlight. The thin snow looked like jade, and the moon itself like snow. Now the black night was clear and friendly. Even the strands of wire atop the walls looked like dew-touched spider webs in the woods, sparkling and bright.

It moved silently forward and embraced her, kissed her forehead and her lips, caressed all her body, gentle as water and yet with the intoxicating aroma of cassia wine.

It wandered across the boundless heavens without restraint. How free it was, and how solitary; how beautiful it was, and how sad. Whom was it pursuing in its endless revolutions, for whom was it longing? Where was its beloved? Was it the earth? The sun? Or was it some other star far away in some unreachable galaxy?

"Is there anything else?" She asked. She was beginning to feel hungry.

"That Catfish is no good." He clenched his teeth for a moment and then growled, "Be careful!"

"I know." She nodded. "Don't worry. I'm going now."

He seemed a little ill at ease. Rubbing his hands, he stammered,

"I, I wanted to talk with you about something."

Xiao Xiao smiled. Talk? Aren't we talking right now? How odd; why don't you say it? Why wait for me? What is it you want to say?

She could see on the lenses of his glasses two great round moons shedding their mild and melancholy light.

"No, it's nothing." He suddenly puckered his lips. His Adam's apple bobbed once and he broke off. "It wasn't anything in particular. I just wanted to say you should find a way to get some time off and go see Chen Xu, take him a little something."

"I went, but the people from the Political Work Unit at the Farm Office absolutely refused to let me see him." She threw him a look that expressed her gratitude even as it begged his help. He squatted down, picked up a twig, and began drawing on the ground.

"Behind the paper factory chimney there's a row of old storehouses. They have to pass them every day going to and from work."

She could no longer hear his voice. A figure like a shimmering osmanthus tree hurried into the distance along the wide road.

Across the vast expanse of the heavens moved the unhurried moon, without a single star in sight.

A green army cap was hopping about on the ground like a frog. She kept trying to catch hold of it, so that she could turn it over and see what was inside, but she couldn't. Then the cap stopped of its own accord and turned itself over with a smile, but it was empty; there was nothing inside, just the smiling face of Instructor Yu.

A boy said to Yu, you've had my copy of "Crime and Punishment" for several hundred months; it's time you returned it to me.

Yu laughed out loud and took off his hat. Inside, there were packages of tea, wine bottles, canned goods. He said, Don't you know I like scented tea? I don't drink green tea.

The boy took out a wad of bills and put them in the hat. There was also a medical discharge.

Instructor Yu nodded and turned the cap over.

The sky was very bright. It was definitely night, but it was as bright as day.

She saw a round moon in the sky. It remained perfectly stationary and was still there when day broke. It was still there the next day. It was there every day. It was always just as round, just as bright. And it always gave off the same heavy scent of sweet osmanthus.

Apparently, every day was going to be the Autumn Festival from now on, she thought. She was delighted—no more political study classes every day.

Her mother had brought her home some moon cakes. They were filled with nuts, with candied roses, with bean paste, with sweet osmanthus flavoured rock candy. Her favourite was moon cakes filled with ham in spiced salt, with a thin crust, sweet and salty at the same time. She took a bite, bit off a crescent moon, then a half moon, then a waning moon.

She wrote her mother a letter. On the last evening of the lunar year, I shall be looking at the moon, and so will you. It's the same moon in north and south, so we will be together. Chen Xu said. On the last evening? That would be a new moon.

All of a sudden, there were many moons in the sky.

Chen Xu was gone. She ran off to look for him. She wanted to tell him that since there were so many moons of course there was one for everyone. Everyone had a moon. Everyone could celebrate the Autumn Festival whenever they wanted to.

She ran and ran. She ran by a mountain. It was very steep. She wanted to run right up it. Otherwise the moon would fall down the mountain.

There was a crowd of people on the mountainside digging manure.

Someone yelled, Come see the iron girl! Quick, come see the iron girl!

She saw Guo Chunmei, stripped down to a sleeveless undershirt, digging manure. Her chest was a flat as a man's. She was swinging an enormous pickaxe; it was the size of a ploughshare. Xiao Xiao reached out to pick it up, but it weighed a ton and she couldn't budge it. And yet Chunmei just touched it and a lump of frozen manure the size of a jeep split open with a thud.

Your pickaxe is great. She admired it.

The old labour camp inmate from the smithy stuck up a grimy thumb and said, Her pickaxe was specially made. Weighs nine and a half pounds.

You're so strong. She could scarcely believe it. She touched Guo Chunmei's pickaxe, then her hands. She discovered that they were made of steel. So were her feet, and her hair was made of strands of wire, her eyes from two steel bullets.

112

Have you really turned into a iron girl? She was surprised and frightened. She went on, It's no good to be an iron girl. You could rust, or corrode.

I'm covered with a coat of paint, answered Guo Chunmei. She was sitting under a street lamp reading a book. The book was painted red. The people who walked past the lamp were all spattered with red. When they met anyone, they said, It's Guo Chunmei's paint. She's studying Chairman Mao's works under the street lamp.

She went back to the girls' dormitory and found that Guo Chunmei had moved to the other bed. She asked Chunmei, Why aren't you sleeping beside me any more? Are you still angry? Guo Chunmei replied coldly, I have to go take the pigs for their midnight pee. I take the little piggies to the potty.

Guo Chunmei tucked a book with a red cover under her arm and left, pushing a wheelbarrow.

Instructor Yu was taking a squad of people for a run.

He shouted commands, and the squad ran around in circles outside the door of the branch farm office.

Chen Xu led everyone in a cheer:

> One, two, three, four;
> Running circles 'round the door;
> Our man Yu sure has the knack,
> To rise in life by the inside track!

Hoo! They all roared with laughter.

Have you come back? She asked Chen Xu. Let's go home. Home? Chen Xu ran away again. I'm at home all over the world.

She chased after him. Somehow or other she ended up on the moon.

There was a osmanthus tree on the moon. Someone was chopping it down. He would take a chop, and some flowers would fall. Another chop, more flowers. When she looked at him, he turned out to be Zou Sizhu.

She said, Hey, what did you want to tell me?

Zou Sizhu shook his head gravely.

She said, Go ahead and say it. Chen Xu isn't here.

He pointed to the moon. He seemed to be saying, It's too bright here.

Let's go to the dark side of the moon, he said.

They walked around to the back of the moon, but there were stars there, stars everywhere. Zou Sizhu sighed again and bent near

113

her ear. He said something, but she could not hear what it was.

What is it you want to say? She raised her voice.

He said nothing more, but leaned closer and planted a quick kiss on her cheek. She flinched and fended him off, only to find that she was hanging on Chen Xu's neck. Chen Xu was sitting on a large bed eating a moon cake. At the head of the bed were two plump round pillows.

14

On the afternoon of the day they began the threshing, she heard someone shouting, Chen Xu is back. He was brought back in custody by people from the Political Work Unit. They're having him participate in labour here in the company. When the bearer of the news noticed that Xiao Xiao was present, he broke off and swallowed the rest of his story. But his hearers offered no response beyond a chorus of grunts, as though there could have been no better place for Chen Xu to return to than the company. It was an event of no significance.

But she didn't see him report for work. Were they having him work alone under guard? She was a little worried. She didn't see him in the mess hall either, when they got off work and went in to dinner. After standing in line for a while, she got her usual steamed bun and potato soup. But as she left the mess hall, she saw Bubble leaning against the wall holding two big mess kits. He came over to her, saying in a low voice as he walked, "He'll be waiting for you, eight o'clock, after the study session, at the 'Green Ripple Gate'."

"There's nothing wrong, is there?" Her heart was racing, and it was all she could do not to throw down her food and go to him at once.

"No. He didn't break any laws. Being sent to the brig is just like being made to stand in a corner and take a scolding."

"Why didn't he come to dinner?"

"I came to buy it for him. He didn't want to come, didn't want to see all those people. And then there was you. When you see him, you probably won't recognise him."

It was dull and grey outside the Green Ripple Gate at night, dimly lit by the newly installed mercury vapour lamps visible inside the wall and by their reflection off the snow. But even so she started when she first caught sight of him.

His cheek bones stuck out like rocky crags over a bristly stubble that looked like dry pine needles. His eyes, which had been so fine and prominent, were sunken, with dark shadows under them. A straw rope circled his waist over a tattered jacket, with nothing under it...

They looked at one another in silence.

He was standing, slightly bent forward and with his arms folded across his chest. He looked cold, but he wasn't moving. His lips and brows seemed to be locked shut and pulled taut.

She trembled. Her knees felt weak, but at the same time so heavy that they could not move her. She just managed to take a few steps. He ought to have held out his arms...

"Don't come any closer!" He growled.

Was that him? His voice was so hoarse, like a hunting dog worsted by a pack of wolves.

She stood still, unable to get a sound out of her throat. She had imagined their reunion so many hundreds of times in her dreams, out on the snowy fields, and it wasn't supposed to be like this. What's wrong with you, Chen Xu? I'm Xiao Xiao, your Xiao Xiao, who's been waiting for you to come back. Why don't you say something? I have so much to tell you. I went to Headquarters to see you, I waited on the highway for you to get off work, to catch a glimpse of you from far away. It was such a gloomy little corner. You couldn't have seen me. The moon cake I took for you, I still haven't been able to bring myself to eat it.

Tears welled up in her eyes. She felt dizzy.

"Don't come any closer," he repeated, clenching his jaw. "I want to ask you something first. If you agree to it, we will never, ever part. If you don't, I'll leave now, and we will never, ever see each other again. I won't get you involved, and you won't have to feel sorry for me. And don't give me any of your bogeyman stories either. There is only one way left for me now!"

She gaped, struck speechless by this announcement.

She had never dreamed that things could take such a serious turn, so serious that they were confronting a choice that could mean their separation for ever.

Go ahead. I'll agree to anything you ask.

"I've seen through this dump. There's nothing for me here. I'm leaving. I'll find some place, there must be some place in the world where I can make a success of my life. I'll go back and see Wang Ge. I can resettle in a village in Zhejiang, in Hainan, in Xinjiang, Inner Mongolia. There must be someplace where they need me. I have the ability, I'll make it some day." He was babbling, stamping his feet on the snowy ground. Then he reached out and seized her muffler, roaring

116

at the top of his lungs, "Come with me! Be my wife! Be the mother of my sons! Be..."

He pushed her away and staggered back a step, his face contorted, staring at her with the look of a madman. Then he gave a sudden cackle. "You've been mine since long ago, mine, and you know it. Where could you run off to, thank you for coming to say goodbye, I'm going wandering, drifting..."

Drifting? Hitching the trains? What about residence permits? Fighting over work points and private plots in a village every day? In the Tianshan Mountains? On the steppes? A rubber plantation? The pressure would be the same wherever they went.

She snapped out of it.

"Will you go with me or not. Yes or no!" he yelled.

Now she was calm and firm. Her mind was clear, but her blood raced.

"No!" she said. Her high thin voice whirled on the wind.

Chen Xu stood there transfixed. Then he fell backwards with a thud onto the snowy ground.

But he did not even try to pick himself up and leave. He thrashed about, but weakly, like a baby abandoned in the fields. Normally, the first thing an inmate did on his release was clean up and change clothes, but he was still a mess. He must have been steeped in despair and resentment. Perhaps he would just as soon have gone on sinking, swallowed up by that vast desert, that heavy night, silently buried under the endless ice and snow. To leave would mean destruction; losing her would mean destruction just the same. Who could save him, a young man who had once offered himself to the Great Northern Wastes, full of hope.

"No!" she cried. She was seized by a strange terror; her heart was splitting apart. But from its torn edges there poured forth a great warm flood of tenderness like a vast swirling fog, swallowing her up and bearing her soul lightly up into an indistinct and unfamiliar realm.

She knelt down, knelt in the snow beside him, reaching around behind him to lift up his loosened ear flaps and spoke clearly and distinctly. "I accept, but we won't go anywhere. We'll be married tomorrow."

He trembled all over. After a moment, he snorted, "Are you crazy?"

"Not at all. I've been thinking it over since long before you came back. To go anywhere without a residence permit is a blind alley. If we had a home, we could close the door and lock all our problems outside. No matter what, it would be a hundred times better than going back to Hangzhou to depend on other people, begging for their scraps. I know that I am yours, that only I understand how much you've suffered, and that's why I will never part from you so long as we live."

She could not go on. Hot tears poured from her eyes and turned instantly to strings of frozen pearls on her chest.

He threw his arms roughly around her, buried his head in the curve of her neck, and began to sob. His stiff cotton jacket crackled in the night air like blocks of ice in the river during the spring thaw.

On the vast snow-covered plain, a wheelless cart was sinking into the snowdrifts.

The driver of the cart was an old grey wolf, barking like a dog.

In the snow lay a cartman with a straw rope around his waist and no buttons on his jacket.

People were walking slowly past him in a line, pressing their palms together and singing softly:

> Out on the vast and grassy plain,
> The roads so long they reach the sky,
> The driver of a cart lies down
> On the grassy plain, about to die.

She broke into the line, shouting at them, He's going to die! Why don't you help him?

No one answered her.

She wanted to pick him up on her back, but he was too heavy.

Church bells sounded in the distance.

Someone said, Hurry, the time for your wedding has come.

She said, The Four Olds were smashed long ago. What do you mean, wedding? I'm going to get married on the road.

She picked up a canvas bag and got ready to leave on her travels, but the bag had been chewed up by rats and all her things fell out.

Then she realised they had not registered their marriage.

But everyone at the neighbourhood registry office had gone to a movie.

She saw from looking in a shop window along the street that she was still no taller than a table, her hair tied up in bows.

Her father rapped on the desk with his knuckles. Why did you get only four points? Get out of here!

She was wearing a green checked dress, catching dragonflies in

118

the grass. Someone walked by and said to her, Aren't you having a revolutionary wedding ceremony over there? What are you doing, playing outside?

Her heart skipped a beat. She could not for the life of her recall who it was she was going to marry.

She remembered that according to the Marriage Law one had to be fifty years old to get married, but she was only fifteen. She wanted to run away, but a wedding sedan chair was approaching, along with a band of musicians. She watched the bride get out of the chair and bow in front of a picture of Chairman Mao. Someone pulled the red cloth off the bride's head, and it wasn't her after all, but Guo Chunmei. Chunmei picked up a bucket of paint and looked all around for her groom. Everyone helped her look and they found a cartman buried in the snow with a pigtail showing. When they pulled him out he turned out to be a girl.

She's a girl. What kind of marriage is this? shouted Xiao Xiao at Guo Chunmei.

Aren't you getting married too? Chunmei looked fierce.

No, I'm not, explained Xiao Xiao. She looked at herself and indeed there was no red cloth on her head. She sighed with relief.

15

It was a clear winter night. Cold stars were stuck all over the deep blue sky like frozen snowflakes. The air was crisp and fresh, with an occasional whiff of burnt straw drifting languidly around the low cottages with their red-tiled roofs. The wind was tired from raging all day, and now the remote village was quiet. A little after eight o'clock, a patter of rapid footsteps beat a tattoo across the snow toward the south end of the family quarters.

Past the one-room tiled houses, between the piles of straw, avoiding the wellhouse, skirting Crow the squad-leader's vicious dog. Don't make a sound, we're almost there, someone whispered, looking back. The figure in the middle had the turned-up ends of braids visible beneath her scarf. It was Xiao Xiao, carrying her wash basin and tooth brush.

She stumbled along, overwhelmed by excitement and joy.

She seemed destined for a life filled with risks and obstacles of every kind. Was she not about to repeat her secret life in the storage shed in Hangzhou the previous summer? To repeat the courageous accomplishments of underground Party work? Why did her father have to have been in the Communist underground? He seemed to have handed down to her all the things that he had left unfinished. Chen Xu seemed destined for a life mixed up with detention cells, a life of hard luck. And she was destined to go visiting and running hither and thither. She seemed both compelled and happy to do so. She had just turned twenty.

Twenty years old. By rights, she ought to have been taking piano lessons at a conservatory or sketching on a lawn.

Three days before, she and Chen Xu had gone to see Susie J about a letter of introduction so that they could go to Farm Headquarters and register their marriage. The official seal was in the charge of the Security Chief. Chen Xu was very apprehensive before they went, since it amounted to giving Susie J an opportunity for revenge. But without a letter of introduction from the Branch Farm, even if they went right to Headquarters it would be a waste of time.

They walked into the office feeling as though they were going to execution. Susie J was busy rolling himself a flared cigarette in the local style. Before he had heard them out, his grin had already reached one ear, and his eyes were bulging like a frog's. After a long time, he snickered and yelled, "You? Get hitched? I'll be bitched! Look at you! You're just out of the brig, beautiful dreamer." Chen Xu was gripping Xiao Xiao's two frail hands so tightly that they hurt. He opened his mouth and then closed it, swallowing violently and grinding his teeth.

Humiliated as she was, Xiao Xiao tried to put their case: confinement at Farm Headquarters was not the same as a criminal conviction; even criminals were allowed to marry once their sentence had been discharged, after all; and besides, the minimum legal ages for marriage were eighteen for women and twenty for men.

Before she could finish, Susie J cut her off. "You're up here to build the frontier, not to share a bed. You'd better just wait!" Chen Xu yanked her away and stormed out of the office.

"You should have argued it out with him," she grumbled at Chen Xu.

"It would have been useless." Chen gestured in dismissal. "The more you begged him the better he'd like it. Give him a little power, and he does as he pleases! I knew all along it wouldn't work!"

"Now what will we do?"

"There may be a way yet. Bubble has told me about something."

"What is it?"

"I can't tell you now. In a couple of days, if we can bring it off, everything will work out fine."

He sounded very confident, and his eyes flashed. He had been unusually calm ever since that night at the Green Ripple Gate, when he had gone so crazy and Xiao Xiao had suggested they get married.

Three days had passed. He had made good on his promise. This was a top-secret revolutionary act; even Xiao Xiao did not know where she was being taken, like a hostage.

They stopped in front of a wooden door at the west end of a row of cottages.

Chen Xu took out a key and opened the lock. All of a sudden, the little duckling noticed that one of the hinges on the door was already loose and the door was crooked, so he could squeeze into the room through the crack. And so he squeezed in. The room was pitch dark, but there was a breath of warmth.

121

"Watch your step! The door to the inner room is on your right," Bubble warned her.

She almost tripped over the threshold, but she saw a faint glow shining through the crack around the door. The door opened, and there was an oil lamp burning on the edge of a brick bed. The flame flickered like the budding of a little golden flower.

Their luggage, their trunks, everything was strewn about the brick bed. Bubble walked up, bowed deeply in front of Xiao Xiao, and said, with a cheeky grin, "The bridal chamber. Ready for your inspection, ma'am."

Xiao Xiao blushed instantly, as she realised what he meant. Her vision clouded, and it was some time before she got a grip on herself, rubbed her eyes, and took a good look around the place.

How small a little cottage it was! The big brick bed took up four fifths of the room, leaving only a passageway a few feet wide from door to window. And the window was tiny and low, the cracks around it stuffed tight with bits of old newspaper. The brick bed had a dark plastic sheet spread over it. There did not even seem to be a mat. Except for their two bedrolls and satchels, the room was completely bare. She could hear a coal fire crackling in the furnace in the outer room, which was connected to their hollow heated wall, and the wall itself was rumbling. Even the ceiling was roaring. It was like a huge balloon filled with hydrogen, or like a rocket after ignition, about to blast off for its journey into space, or like a long train passing by her door, the sparks visible as they burst over the tracks.

Xiao Xiao fell for the place at once. Just because it was so small, because there was nothing in it, and because it had appeared so suddenly. It was like a miracle, like a little cabin in the woods in a fairy tale. They would fill its cramped but unlimited space with their love and hope. It would be a fortress, a palace, belonging to them alone, existing only for them. From now on, from now on, all those risks, all those misfortunes, those solitudes, those hardships, would all be far, far away from them. In the midst of the surging waves, a sampan had come floating to them. Out of the broad sea, an island of refuge had arisen.

"Well, doesn't it look like the Decembrists' place of exile in Siberia!" Chen Xu chuckled self-mockingly, leaning against the door frame. "Shoot first and report later. If worse comes to worst and I do another three months in the brig, I'll still have a rear base area when I get out."

Bubble was sitting on the edge of the bed swinging his legs back and forth. "You guys are in luck. There was an ex-labour camp inmate living here, but he was just sent home. So the place came vacant and was still locked up. I saw it a few days ago and it got me to thinking." He made a face. "Chen Xu was saying he wanted to get married, and I thought this place would be just the thing. Settle in here for a few days and we'll see what happens. By the time the officials find out about it, they'll figure that the rice is already cooked and that it could be a bad influence if you don't get married, so everything will work out fine. Convinced? We'll see how things go for a few days, then we can come over and celebrate properly, candy and all. Relax—marriage isn't illegal, after all!"

"Why do they have to make things so tough for us city kids?" fumed Beanpole, who had popped in too. "If we want to go back to the South, we can't. But if we want to settle down here, they won't let us do that either. What do they expect us to do?"

The furnace began to rumble again, a hurricane blowing through a narrow gorge, a speedboat cutting through the waves, a passionate piano sonata, the joyous thundering of hooves. She felt a sudden rush of courage. In this little cottage, there would be no more boring daily readings, no more tiresome criticism sessions, no shouting, no exposing of errors, no whistle-blowing, no green army caps. Nothing but two frozen hearts warming each other by the furnace.

She did not know when the others had taken their leave. The oil lamp burned low. In the darkness, she could see that tall form, those subtle eyes igniting, heating her to the boiling point. The furnace had ceased to sing its tune. The night was so still that only their breathing remained. It was like a rare and magic dream, a flower-strewn meadow blooming the whole year round in the midst of a realm of snow and ice.

"Xiao Xiao..." Chen Xu held her tightly in his arms, pressing her face against his chest, carrying her slowly over to the edge of the brick bed and rocking her gently back and forth. He went on for a long time, murmuring something. His embrace was broad and strong. It was worth being a woman to lie in such arms. It was like pressing against the deck of a boat, against the feel of the water. A frog princess crouched on a broad thick lily pad. She would not seek land again. So long as the river in her heart did not run dry, whatever it flowed past would revive and germinate.

She walked into a palace made of snow and ice.

The palace windows were hung with silver curtains weighed down with tassels like hoarfrost, glimmering in the light.

She was wearing a silver gown with a train and holding a bunch of pale green snowball flowers with six-cornered petals. There were doors everywhere. She walked out one door and in another. None of the doors had locks.

Rippling laughter came from the windows, against which crowds of flat white noses and flat black eyes were pressed. Human figures flashed by.

She walked over, but all the eyes and noses had vanished.

A pack of barking dogs was following her, nipping at her cuffs. She bent down and picked up a rock, and the dogs ran away.

She was walking proudly along the road, head high and chest out.

The road was lined with people packed as tightly as passengers on a train. She had to walk by them all. They were arguing bitterly. Lightning shot from their eyes, and it began to hail.

The hail knocked sheets of paper down onto the ground. She picked some up and they turned out to be marriage certificates. There were no names or dates on them, so it was not even clear who was marrying whom. She was about to write in her own name when the paper fell to pieces.

Chen Xu walked up with their work basket and said, I'm off to nip some coal.

She followed Chen Xu into a cottage. Inside, the towel looked like a thin sheet of ice, the tooth paste tube looked like an ice cream bar, and the soap had grown white fuzz, like a lump of ice cream. The rice in the pot was frozen hard, and frost was so thick in the corners of the ceiling that it looked like a crevasse in the snow.

She and Chen Xu had a contest putting on their shoes. Their boots were so stiff it was like putting on skis.

She and Chen Xu had a contest getting out of bed. They could have ice skated on the top of the brick bed, all the way onto the floor. There were ice rinks inside and outside the door.

She and Chen Xu played at making snowmen. The snow was like dry sand. They made a three-cornered pagoda, a fat-bellied snow Bodhisattva.

She asked Chen Xu, Where are we?

Chen Xu had the twin bar badge of a Young Pioneer class leader pinned on his sleeve. He said, Winter Camp.

They rubbed snow over their bodies, giggling.

There were people swimming in a hole in the ice. She went looking for her swimsuit, but she could not find it anywhere.

The last month of the lunar year, the very coldest season, had come to frozen Half-way River. And yet the snow and ice were all but tramped to water by people's feet.

It was all the work of the peasant women from the area around the Branch Farm, who had braved the wind and cold, not thinking three miles too distant, to come for a look at the bold city kids who had moved in together without having registered their marriage. By having a look they meant just standing well away from the house, pointing and waving their hands, and letting their imaginations run wild. There was a certain amount of astonishment and a certain amount of indignation; a few parts contempt mixed with a few parts envy.

Unfortunately, because the frost was so thick on the little north window, nothing inside could be made out. The window in the front door had been replaced with a piece of wood, the strips of old newspaper around it fluttering in the wind, so nothing could be seen through it either. There were no 'double happiness' signs on the walls, and still less were there any Shanghai candy wrappers littering the floor. At lunch time, the air was clear above their chimney. When it got dark, there was not even a light bulb in there, just a dull red flame, flickering bashfully and pulling all their whispered words up to the slumbering head of the brick bed, locking all the secrets of the little cottage inside for its own enjoyment.

Their curious, well-meaning visitors were naturally quite let down. And more than let down, they were also a little peeved. Those two little southerners must be crazy. Who ever heard of such a marriage?

Nowadays, the State Farm was all city kids, and the children of the people looking after them were not grown up yet either. So, except for a few people who had been away from the area as vagrants, they could go all their lives without seeing a marriage. And even if there had been one, they would not have been allowed to hold a big banquet with lots of pork and wine. They could only bow and applaud, and the bride, instead of being all dressed up in red and green, would just recite from the Quotations. What was there to see in that?

When there had been marriages in the village of Koreans nearby, the bride used to wear a pink satin skirt and white open-work gloves,

125

and they had a troupe of women singing and dancing behind the oxcart, dancing from one village to another, singing from dusk to dawn. But even this went when they 'Smashed the Four Olds', so what was there left to see at a wedding?

Who would ever have imagined that this pair of southern swallows would pop up and make themselves a nest without so much as a by your leave, just building it on a fuel pile, on a sandbank. This was plum new and unheard-of. She must be quite the little hussy, to just move in and set up housekeeping without even getting married. Taking in a man like that—well, they've been going together openly for over a year, why didn't you people over at the Farm give them a licence?

They felt both doubtful and sympathetic, but either way, they did not know what to call something like this, for the concept of 'living together' was still not part of the rich lexicon of the Great Northern Wastes. And so, the local people high and low were thrown into a state of shock and uncertainty. Discussion was universal; there was extensive cudgeling of brains. In the midst of the discussions there were fights, and after the fights they still did not know what to do. They seemed to grasp it, but they could not. There were no grounds for approving it, but they couldn't very well just throw them out. After three days, it seemed that they would have to give their tacit consent, like it or not. And yet this tacit consent had latent in it various counter-strategies, useless though these remained in spite of all the brain-cudgeling that had gone into them.

Overnight, Xiao Xiao had become the absolute centre of attention on the Half-way River State Farm.

Being so much in the public eye, she felt very exhilarated and excited, very brave and proud.

When she went with Chen Xu to the mess hall to eat (their cooking stove had not been built in yet, and the Security Chief had long since confiscated the electric stove brought from Hangzhou), and they had to walk along the slippery ice slope in front of the well house, she clung tightly to his arm.

When she went off to work with Chen Xu and they passed by all the people standing in the doorways to watch them, she held her head up high like an empress and purposely took off her face mask to let them have a good look. Her feet crunched along over the snow with a proud step. Something she had harboured in her heart for a very long time had come bursting out, like an oil well blowout. It did not seem to be the fact of getting married itself. What was it then? She could not say.

No sooner did they get home from having dinner at the mess hall on the evening of their fourth day there—they had just lit the lamp, and Chen Xu was still getting the fire started—when the door was yanked open and in came a blast of cold wind tinged with alcohol. Liu the Brute ducked inside, arms folded.

"Came to look in on you. How you doing?" he said in a noisy whisper. In the dim light of the oil lamp, his normally tense face seemed quite relaxed. He rubbed his permanently bloodshot eyes and took a turn around the inner and outer rooms. Finally, he sat down on the edge of the brick bed and pulled himself onto it, crossing his legs and tucking the sole of each of his cotton snow boots under the opposite ankle. Then he got out a little black sack and a piece of white paper. He took a pinch of loose tobacco, spread it along the paper, licked the edges, and with a roll of his fingers whipped the paper around like a windrower, turning it into a flared tube in a blink of the eye.

"Say, Cherr," he said as he bit off the narrow end and spat it on the floor. He struck a match and took a puff. His expression very serious, he cleared his throat and said, "Write a report for me, and I'll issue you two a light bulb."

Xiao Xiao and Chen Xu were dumbfounded.

Issue them a light bulb? A light bulb? Really? A light bulb was even more important than a marriage certificate. There wasn't a hallway, not a latrine on the whole Farm with a light in it. Had all the workers in the light bulb factory been sent to the brig? Liu, we leave the getting of a light bulb to you—you won't cheat us, will you? We never dreamed you could be so kind.

"Say, you got a rolling pin?" He added.

Xiao Xiao shook her head.

"How about a flour board? A wok lid? A water vat? A work basket?"

Water pot, paring knife, spatula, bowls and spoons, rice, soybean oil, whatever it was, they didn't have it. Why hadn't they thought of any of this before they moved in?

Liu tossed the butt into a corner, spat on the floor, slipped off the brick bed, and muttered, as he walked toward the door, "Settle down and make yourselves to home. I'll go have a word with Yu and Sun later. It's a good thing for you to want to settle down here with us. From now on, you'll belong here, but..."

As he reached the door, he turned back and gestured toward the furnace. "It's that thing. Make sure you take care. You're in more danger of suffocating than freezing. I'll get a plasterer over one of these days to patch it up."

He left, thoroughly satisfied.

Liu the Brute genuinely accepted what they had done, according to his own lights and with a pleasure that could not have been foreseen. Not only had he not given them a hard time, what he meant had been: So long as you take to the people here and are willing to stay... Liu the Brute would be happy about it!

And Chen Xu really did bring home a 25 watt light bulb the next day.

As Xiao Xiao came home from work that day, she could see the line of seven lighted windows along the last row of thatched cottages in the family quarters far away. She was puzzled at first, for she could not pick out their window, the one that had been dark before. She was like a blind man whose sight has suddenly been restored; the first person he fails to recognise is himself.

She pulled the door open and there in the centre of the room hung an electric light. She looked into the light, and the brick bed was covered with burnished beetles, light reflecting in all directions from their carapaces. She squinted. The whole room looked unfamiliar. It came to her that ever since they had moved in, there had been a kind of terrible shame concealed in the darkness of the cottage, a shame that had made her happiness even more intent on covering the bitter shadows. And all at once it had smiled, confident and clear. The light gleamed, began to shimmer, and in its open smile the cottage suddenly became proper and hospitable.

She saw that there were people sitting all along the edge of the brick bed. Yes, all the southern kids in the company had come. There were also people sitting all over the bedding up on the bed. Whoever comes here is a customer, and I have to be pleasant to him; I greet all comers with a smile, and once out of sight out of mind. When the customer leaves...

Chen Xu gestured with his lips toward the brick bed.

There was a low table there, suited for use on the bed. It had not been painted, and there were some scratches on the legs. The surface was uneven, and some candy was gathered in the recessed parts. The air was thick with cigarette smoke.

"We are presenting you with this little table," said Bubble, adopting the serious air of a master of ceremonies, "as a token of our best wishes."

"Where did it come from?" she asked. It must have been stolen somewhere, right? It was very suspicious; it looked like it had once been a picture frame, or was it a wok lid? Why ask?

"It's recycled," chuckled Bubble, patting his stomach.

This was the only gift she had received, and the only piece of furniture in the cottage. In fact it was just some boards nailed together. Cover it with a clear plastic cloth, with a picture underneath, and it would look quite nice. What picture should it be? Lu Xun? The White-haired Girl? It would be fine even without any decoration, more natural, like the streaked walls of the cottage, the rough ceiling. It would go well with them. Yes, there was something rustic about it. She reached out and stroked the table top, and it swayed back and forth with a creak.

"It will be perfect for drinking". Chen Xu leaned to one side and looked at it. "It's drunk before it even starts."

She liked it. She had a table at last. In all the year and a half since she had come to the farm, this was the first table of her own she had had. She wouldn't have to write her diary on the trunk or the edge of the bed any more. She could stick her legs comfortably under the table and keep them there just as long as she pleased.

"In a couple of days I'll go again and get you a wok lid." said Bubble.

"You ought to put a picture up on your wall. They have some at the shop, Li Tiemei, the Red Detachment..."

"They look awful!"

"Better than nothing."

"If you string a rope along the heated wall, you can dry your clothes."

"Dry out your shoe soles."

"Getting married is a good idea. You can stay up and listen to the radio as late as you like."

"Do you have an alarm clock? Watch out you aren't late."

"There's a loudspeaker outside."

"Chen Xu, we'll come over here to cook up a little something, eh?"

"We'll help you steal some fuel. There are plenty of fuel piles."

"My mother sent some glutinous rice. We can come over and cook rice gruel."

"Say, bride! What are you thinking about? Come on, make your three bows..."

Xiao Xiao concealed her confusion and smiled quietly. She should make herself as happy as possible. She had discovered that she was not really relaxed at all, nor even all that happy. There seemed to be something at the back of her mind. There were two people who had not come to see them. One was Zou Sizhu, and the other was Guo Chunmei.

"Where is Guo Chunmei, gone off to give another talk on her 'study and application'?" she asked.

"She's looking for a pig. A spotted piglet went missing. She even skipped dinner."

She hung her head. Yes, Guo Chunmei had gone looking for a lost pig, while she herself...

The furnace was rumbling. The frost in the corners of the room was starting to melt and ooze down the walls. Pop! A bit of mud dropped onto the brick bed. It was dirt from above the ceiling. Could a house melt and cave in? It was liable to vanish like a lump of frost in the sun or a clay figurine in water. It was that much more like a dream, so lifelike and yet so dubious. She took off her heavy coat and leaned back against the heated wall, the hot bricks baking her through her sweater. She felt as though the heat would little by little bake her dry, like an electric current. She sat up. Her spine was uncomfortably numb. The light was very bright. All the people in the room, she herself, looked much more real than ever before, and yet she felt somehow confused. There was something... Was she actually far away now from the ideal she had dreamed of, or was she close? How had she happened to walk into such a cramped, run-down cottage?

There was a knock at the door. She went to answer it and found the Branch Farm messenger standing there. He handed her a piece of paper and said in a loud, unpleasant voice, "Instructor Yu says you can go to Farm Headquarters and register!"

It was a letter of introduction. With the help of the light coming from inside, she read the words, "Chen Xu, male, 24; Xiao Xiao, female, 20."

Xiao Xiao read it through several times and then stared out the pitch black window. Suddenly her eyes were abrim with tears.

16

The wind screamed all the way from the North Pole, growing in violence with its passage over the frozen Siberian steppes. It howled across the slumbering Amur River, whipping up blizzards and attacking at will the tottering telephone poles of the Three Rivers Plain, forcing a lament from their trembling gossamer lines, which seemed to be cut into a thousand pieces, only to squeeze a thousand times back out through the blinding snow.

Sometimes a great curtain of snow, packed with pellets like grains of sand, would blot out the long snaky roads and blanket the country near and far with a single stroke, whipping about as though it harboured some long deliberated malice or some vengeance long foreborne. Heaven and earth were instantly blurred and darkened. Snow-bright lance in hand, the storm charged astride the wind, and the heavens vanished in the streaming silver tassels of its white horse. And then the horse would leap miles across the earth, curvetting in the air and shaking its long white coat until the earth too vanished.

A blizzard! A stern and irresistable white-robed demon king.

It came, and brought with it all the cruelty and fear of winter.

And when it came, it packed the sun and moon smoothly into its pockets. All along the way, it smashed dead trees and flattened the withered grass, sparing not the smallest nook or cranny. All things groveled at its feet, trembling in obeisance. To destroy was its satisfaction and to tread into the ground its joy. And when it went, it left behind an insane, bloodcurdling laugh, and corpses, buried in the snow.

Perhaps this was something that had happened long, long ago. The old labour camp inmate at the vegetable patch had told her that back in the old days people had frozen to death every year, and that when it thawed in April they had come slipping out into the roadside ditches with merry smiles in their white, wide open eyes.

This was something that had happened long ago. Now the storm only scratched with its cold, hard claws at the rickety wooden door of

131

their run-down cottage, moaning as it filed a few dry flakes of snow from cracks around the door, which there had not yet been time to seal completely.

It had been locked outside, outside the little cottage.

The people inside seemed entirely untroubled, quite undisturbed by the sound of the snowstorms. They simply gave themselves up to snuggling close together. Under the dim lamp one sturdy hand and one slender hand held up two corners of the same book.

Having a light bulb did not necessarily mean having light. This was a time when the electricity went off almost every evening. It seemed to be on solar power, as the bulb would sometimes choose to light up while they were eating lunch.

By the light of an oil lamp, they read "Wild Grass" and Fedeyev's "The Young Guard." The lamp was dim, and it was hard to make out the words on the pages. If they squeezed closer, the hair on their temples would catch fire with a hiss and a scorched smell. For some reason, Xiao Xiao insisted they read the "Communist Manifesto" too.

"'In place of the old bourgeois society, with its classes and class antagonisms, we shall have a collective body'," Xiao Xiao recited, following the text with her finger, "'in which the free development of each is the condition for the free development of all'."

She put the book down and asked, all wide-eyed, "What does 'collective body' mean?"

"The disappearance of the state, of course!"

"If there were no state, then people would be able to leave the country whenever they liked, right?"

"If there were no state, what country would there be to leave?" He laughed and laid a finger on the tip of her nose. "The main point here is that there would be no oppression."

"If there were no oppression, then would people have complete freedom?"

"Something like that." He yawned. "When one group of people oppresses another, the oppressors themselves are not free, since they are hindered by the oppressed. Only when there is equality for everyone in the world can human society be free and rational. Anyway, never mind. Don't go chewing over these points of doctrine; it's useless!"

If she were allowed to develop freely, she'd be a poet for sure, or a painter.

"'In this way arose Feudal Socialism: half lamentation, half lampoon...' Say, what about Feudal Socialism? I never heard of that.

Is that the same as social imperialism? Is it social feudalism?"

She thought this was a very interesting question, but when she heard no answer, she turned around and found Chen Xu leaning comfortably against the heated wall. He had fallen asleep. He was snoring softly and the collar of his padded jacket was open, one hand still resting on her waist.

She put down her book and pulled his coat around him. The room was too cold not to wear a coat, but too hot with one on. She lifted his arm, and the corner of a book slipped out with a rustle, stuck underneath him. She picked it up and took a look. It was a tattered old book. The cover was missing, and the lines ran from top to bottom in the old-fashioned way. She stared at it. It looked like a foreign novel. She felt a momentary pang and sighed.

He was tired. All the men in the company had been working day in and day out in an mass battle to thresh the grain. When it blew up a blizzard, the pitchforks were twice as hard to move. No, he didn't like the book she had just been reading. He didn't. If he had liked it he would not have yawned. Don't go chewing over those points of doctrine; it's useless. Then what was useful? He had stayed up all night to read a borrowed copy of "Spartacus" straight through. No, he was tired, and the lamp was too dim. It shrank and shivered from the chill.

She looked at her watch. It was only eight-thirty.

It had been dark for a long time, so long that it seemed to be past midnight. It got dark very early, as though the sun had remembered having left its door unlocked and had hurried back home after completing only half its course. There was nothing visible in the long nights but the endless winter, black as pitch.

For the time being, they had very little to do in the way of household chores. They ate in the mess hall, since for one thing they had nothing to cook and for another they had no lid for their built-in wok, and this meant that they could not steam anything. It was only now that she had her own home that she realized that having a lid for the wok was more important than having the wok itself. Bubble had managed to come up with a wooden lid for them, a vat lid from somewhere or other with a crack in it two fingers wide. When they cooked pot-stickers, the stove smoked and half the steam escaped. The pot-stickers came out half cooked and half raw, not a one of them managing to get wholly done. Actually, Xiao Xiao loved making pot-stickers: mixing up the corn flour, letting it rise on the brick bed, kneading it (which did not require any particular skill), heating up some

133

water in the wok, rolling the damp yellow mass into balls, pressing them flat, and tossing them onto the sides of the wok with a slap. Once they were firmly stuck, everything was set. And if they did slide down toward the water, that was fun too, scooping them up and flipping them over, just like playing a game. She had done it as part of a New Years programme in junior high, and only two years before, in Hangzhou, she had loved sticking up big character posters. When Chen Xu came home from work in the evening and asked, "What's for dinner?" she replied at once, "Pot-stickers." Even if they were only half-cooked, the toasty brown crust had a mouth-watering aroma. Spreading some bean curd dregs over the crust, she put them on a very hot fire to heat up, until the crust turned black and so tough that it made their jaws ache. Chen Xu finally protested, and so they switched to making noodles (steamed yeast buns were out of the question). This blackened the wok, and the dirt on the ceiling, once it was warmed by the steam, came pattering down, substituting for pepper where it got through the crack in the lid. At last, Chen Xu volunteered to undertake pancakes, but in a matter of days, half a pound of oil had gone up in smoke and their pipe dream of cooking for themselves had burst at last.

Eating in the mess hall was fine with them. The rice was cold, and so was everything else, but it did save work.

Now that they had some time, they could do a little reading, write in their diaries, sing songs. Xiao Xiao worked out a schedule for the two of them, a study plan. On odd-numbered days they studied theory, on even-numbered days, they read novels. Those 'feudal/capitalist/revisionist' novels were like hazelnuts under the snow. It looked as though there were none, but a little poking around would always turn up one or two.

It often seemed to her that the wind god raging over the plains outside was actually listening through the windows as she recited poetry and Chen Xu talked. It envied them, and that was why it rattled their doors and windows so, trying to force or squeeze its way in. The thin grey threads that hung in festoons from the ceiling would begin to sway for no reason at all. What was that if not the breathing of the wind?

Often she put down her book and gazed at their window, so small, and still without a curtain. As evening fell, the glass, swept clean by the daytime sunlight, would once again sprout its tufts of frost, like an ornate crystal screen, shutting the cottage off from the world outside.

And when she opened her eyes in the morning, she could see in the glimmer of its silver light the Snow Queen flying toward her in a sleigh drawn by eleven horses.

Her imagination soared above the plain. This was the happiest moment of her day.

The southern kids in the company often crunched their way across the snow to drop in, bringing the cold with them. Their cloth snow boots, clogged with snow and dirt, left grime all over the floor. They played feverish poker games, chatted about everything under the sun, and told ghost stories they had heard as children, or strange tales of things that had happened to them during the days of the Great Linking-up. If all else failed, they reminisced about the small-stoned peaches of Hangzhou, the torreya nuts, the stinking fermented bean curd, and what not.

Then, someone turned up a flour sack full of sunflower seeds and soy beans. They roasted these in the tarnished wok and everyone grabbed a share. Then they sat down in a row along the edge of the brick bed, busily cracking them. The crunching noise sounded like hay mowing or the sifting of fertilizer pellets. No one spoke. They cracked seeds single-mindedly, as though it were a race, and soon the shells had filled up the narrow passage beside the bed like drifting snow.

"Why do the locals call sunflower seeds Russkers?" she asked. She did not like cracking sunflower seeds all that much.

"The Russkies used to crack them between their teeth, piles of them at a time," answered Chen Xu. "That's where the name started."

"Why do they call eating them cracking?" Bubble put in, grinning through the husks. "Sounds crackpot to me!"

While they were cracking the seeds, someone suggested telling stories, and they all wanted Chen Xu to tell one, a long one, something exciting. Chen Xu was happy to oblige, much more enthusiastic than he was about reading. He gave a gripping rendition of "Around the World in Eighty Days," which even Xiao Xiao had not heard before. She had read all of Jules Verne's books except this one.

They all went on cracking seeds without let-up while they listened. Xiao Xiao gradually came to feel that the story did gain in atmosphere from being set off by the faint crackling sound. In the little town where her grandmother lived, they put up a stage for operas at New Year's and the audience ate nothing but pumpkin seeds, listening to the opera to the accompaniment of the cracking husks. It made the plays seem crisp and tasty to watch. So Xiao Xiao ate the Russkers too. The ones here were large and plump. If they were cooked just right, they turned crisp, tasty, and rich. Once started on them, it was impossible to stop; the more you ate the better they tasted. So she sat on the brick bed cracking Russkers with the rest of them. If she didn't have any for one evening, she felt as though she had failed to do something, and the story didn't make much sense.

Chen Xu really did have a knack for story-telling, adapting his voice to the different characters and imitating them to the life. The sounds of the sea and the desert too he could do so well one seemed to be right there. At one moment he was gagging as though he were drowning; the next, his mouth was watering over a sumptuous feast. When his large hands gestured in the air, he seemed to be pulling on an invisible cord tied to your heart, making it jump up and down with his grey eyes.

This serial was performed night after night. The nights became shorter and so too did the winter. The nights grew warm, and so did the winter. Not until she had completed, to her great relief, that trip around the world did she realise how long it had been since she had read a book.

Sweeping up the husks that littered the floor, she felt like her insides were stuffed with feathers and insects, floating and scrambling about. It was unbearable. Fed up, she complained to Chen Xu with a pout, "It's all your fault for inviting those people over!"

And then there was all the smoke that filled the room. She had to breathe it all the time.

Xiao Xiao did not know what to do. She had her little house now, but it did not belong to her.

Chen Xu said nothing. She added, "And they don't talk about anything interesting."

He drawled, "What is there interesting nowadays?"

She said nothing, and he added, "It's cold in the company dorm. They don't care about anyone there. People like Beanpole have had it rough."

She swept the shells into the firebox. Beanpole? There was nothing she could say. In Hangzhou, 'to have it rough' meant 'poor'. Poor Beanpole.

Beanpole was a loyal fan of Chen Xu's and never missed an episode. When he came, he just sat down at the end of the brick bed and listened quietly, neither laughing nor interrupting. He never took off his shoes. His trouser legs were thin, tight, much patched, and cut off short. They were pulled on over thick long-johns, which bulged and showed through in a large patch. Once, Xiao Xiao was trying to knit herself a pair of woolen socks, but she could not get them started. After she had fiddled with them several times, Beanpole reached over and said, "Here, let me do it." And it turned out that he knew how to knit. First he knit a sole, and then he extended it upward and even added one stripe each in grey and blue. There were lots of guests that evening, and there was no place to sit on the edge of the brick bed. Chen Xu invited Beanpole to get up on the bed, but he steadfastly refused. Finally, someone untied his shoelaces for him, and Xiao Xiao discovered that he had no socks on under his cotton-lined straw snow-boots, only a strip of cloth to wrap his feet with.

"If you can knit, why don't you knit a pair of socks for yourself?" She could not conceal her surprise.

He hung his head, stroking his feet and stammering something.

Later, she found out that he had a step-mother. His father had been a KMT soldier and now worked in a neighbourhood workshop. Out of Beanpole's monthly wages of thirty-two dollars, he had to send ten dollars back home every month.

When the pair of socks was finished, she had Chen Xu give them to Beanpole.

He was very good with his hands. He could do plastering and carpentry, and knew how to fix chains and enamel basins. Whenever he was fixing something for someone else, his flat face would glow pink, and his flat nose would turn up.

Xiao Xiao wished that everything in the house was broken, so that she could have him fix it all. But since they had neither tools nor materials, all he could do was cut people's hair, fix fuses for them, and the like.

And so the cottage became a temporary work shed, barber shop, and mess hall.

When the Russkers had finally all been cracked and interest in the roast beans had paled, the cottage was suddenly deserted. Chen Xu was no longer telling stories, but when he picked up a book his heart was not in it.

The blizzards that Chen Xu had liked so much kept on swaggering across the plains, but he and they seemed to have lost interest in one another.

She heard someone knocking at the door and went to answer it, but there was no one there, only dancing snowflakes that stung like hailstones when they touched her hands.

She heard someone knocking at the door and went to answer it, but there was no one there, only a line of footprints, going past her door and vanishing into the storm.

She heard someone knocking at the door and went to answer it. She could see a human figure through the crack around the outer door. She pushed on the door, but it would not open. Water was oozing down the door, dripping onto the ground and freezing into an ice doorsill. She got an axe to cut through it, sending chips of ice flying into the air in all directions like fireworks. When the doorsill had vanished in this display, the person outside walked in wearing wire-rimmed glasses. He took them off. It was Zou Sizhu.

She was curious about the glasses and was about to touch them, but Zou cried, They're made of ice; if you touch them they'll melt.

Chen Xu came out from the inside room, his face like a corn husk, and said, without looking up, There's no chair in my house.

I come to pick up a book. Zou Sizhu looked at her.

Don't bother lending us books from now on. We have our own books. Chen Xu pointed to the hollow wall, which had been scraped out. All the shelves inside were filled with books.

If you put books in there, they may get burned. Zou Sizhu reached out to take one. I left a fountain pen next to the wall furnace once and it melted.

Mind your own business, yelled Chen Xu. What we do is none of your concern!

Zou Sizhu turned and left. She chased after him. A trail of footprints led into the storm as far as the fuel pile and then vanished.

She heard someone knocking at the door. It was the middle of the night and pitch dark. She nudged Chen Xu and said, Listen!

A thief. Chen Xu sat up and got into his clothes. Get up quick and man the battle stations.

She tried to ask Chen Xu what a thief would come to their place to steal. Chen Xu ignored her. At this moment they heard a slight noise at the inner door.

Chen Xu declared, The thief is already inside. We'll have to fight it out. I'll charge out before he can come in. You follow me. What can we use as a weapon?

She found a pair of scissors and clutched them tightly, her heart pounding.

Chen Xu whispered to her through clenched teeth not to turn on the light, so they could take the thief by surprise. He threw open the door and charged out, Xiao Xiao charging after him for all she was worth. No sooner did they get into the outer room than they tripped over something, and when they took a look, it turned out to be the rope they used to tie the outer door shut, firmly fastened to the stove. The door was shut and there was no one outside.

The axe that always leaned up against the door had slid down onto the floor. That was what it was!

17

One day, just as it was getting dark, Bubble came running in, panting for breath and holding both arms over the front of his greasy, stained jacket. He had a bulging bundle of some sort thrashing about underneath. Once through the door, he relaxed his grip, and of all things a little white chicken with a scarlet comb popped out of his clothes, hopping and bouncing across the floor, no more than six inches high. It flapped its wings and squirted out a little puddle of chicken shit.

"If you keep it, by June it will be laying eggs," said Bubble.

Xiao Xiao's brows shot up in surprise. Raising a chicken had never crossed her mind.

"Let's just kill it and have a good meal," said Chen Xu, rubbing his hands together.

"Now that you're settled, why not raise a chicken?" said Bubble, offering them the benefit of his advice. "You won't find so much as egg drop soup in the mess hall."

"Where did it come from?" asked Xiao Xiao, suddenly feeling a bit uneasy.

"I found it," answered Bubble, a little awkwardly. "Anyway, it's a chicken."

The chicken had moulted, it weighed close to a pound. Had he really just found it? If they kept it until it started laying eggs, they could hatch a flock of chickens, have salted eggs, soy sauce eggs, chicken to eat every month.

She did not pursue the question. What she was worried about now was where they would keep it and how they would raise it. When her mother was in custody, they had relied on the four setting hens that her little sister raised to supplement their income of eight dollars a month each.

It strutted around the room with measured steps and then was up on the stove counter with a single leap.

"Better clip its wings and make a pen for it outside the back window with some twigs, so it can't fly away. Then it will be able to exercise without getting lost." Now Chen Xu was interested.

"Where to get twigs?" asked Xiao Xiao. Spring had come, and the fence around their vegetable garden had yet to appear.

"Well, then, let's tether it to the tree out in front."

"It's not a dog!" exploded Bubble. "Besides, I think that fancy chickens must really be shy. Otherwise, you tell me why over at the chicken farm they're all kept indoors, with electric lights! If they see strangers, they won't lay."

Fortunately, Beanpole came by. He said that the simplest thing would be to get together some broken bricks and make a shelter out of them. That would work fine. Bricks were ready-made; you just went over to the pig pen by the barn at night and took a few. And so, the next day there was a little chicken house in front of Xiao Xiao's door.

"Remember, you absolutely mustn't let it run free, and watch out that no one steals it." Bubble kept reminding them over and over. While he obviously had their interests very much at heart, he was also acting a little fishy.

Now that there was a chicken house out in front, it seemed a little more like a home to Xiao Xiao.

Occasional flakes of snow were still drifting about in the sunlight, leaving damp marks where they landed on people's clothing. Although the winter wind still cut to the bone as it howled across the plains, it was a wind that 'froze people, but not the ground', as the saying went. The fields of melting snow and thawing earth looked like pits etched by acid, like wasps nests clustered in the crooks of the trees, where spots and streaks appeared in the gaps steamed open by the warmth underground. By noon, the sodden black earth began to swell. It was completely saturated and began to drain off in all directions, running down the ditches and dripping noisily from the eaves of the houses, as though the world were weeping for joy.

At the head of every brick bed there crouched an old hen. The local people called them brooders. They sat patiently and conscientiously on their eggs day in and day out, working their magic inside the shells.

Now that she had a home, Xiao Xiao realised that spring actually came from within a brooder's eggs.

She did as the peasant women who lived nearby. She collected a few frozen Chinese cabbage stalks from around the pig sty, broke them up on a board, added some grits brought back from the mess hall, put them into a chipped bowl, placed it very politely in the chicken's residence, and invited it to dine.

For the first few days, it clucked and muttered as it stuck its beak out the door into the light to pick up pieces of food. But a few days later, she did not see it when she opened the door. Its nest was pitch dark inside, with nothing visible but a tipped-over bowl by the door and some frozen pieces of food.

She was sure the chicken had frozen to death and went to call Chen Xu.

"If it's frozen, we'll eat it," Chen Xu made right for the chicken's little nest, stuck an arm inside, and then whipped it back out with a red mark on his hand.

He yanked the chicken outside. Its snow white feathers had turned a dirty grey, and it looked like a convict kept in a grimy cell for a long time, crushed and weak, but spiteful. She crouched down and stroked it, but it ignored her.

"Now that we've had it for a while, has it gained weight or lost?" Chen Xu raised its wings and shook his head, his mouth watering.

For the rest of that day, all visitors to the house were taken to the chicken's nest to gauge its weight. Most of the boys said it was heavier; most of the girls, lighter. Never mind whether it had gained or lost. At this rate, when would it ever start laying eggs?

"It seems to me," muttered Chen Xu, "We might as well eat it right away."

"Eat! Eat! Eat! All you can think of is eating!" Xiao Xiao blew up at him. "The nest is too dark and cold. It can't see!"

She decided to give it back its freedom and not pay any more attention to Bubble's advice. One afternoon, she let it out to sun itself, but it just lay there on the ground without moving a muscle, neither running away nor jumping up into the air. It was as calm as a brooder, but even smaller than when it first arrived. It just happened that the barn boss's wife was passing by, and when she saw how the sickly little thing was crouching by their door, she came over to see if she could offer any advice. She looked and looked at it, and then exploded in amazement. "Why, Heavenly Mother! Isn't this a chicken from the chicken house? Look at the mark on its head where the feathers have been snipped away!"

Xiao Xiao stood there stunned, her mouth opening and closing, hanging her head as her face turned red and white by turns. "Who's chicken, it's going to die from over-feeding itself! Who's duck, it's going to be drowned here!" Not even a year and a half. Just squeeze into that dark little nest and be done with it. She ran a few steps, slammed the door, threw herself onto the brick bed, and had a good cry. She did not go to work that afternoon, she was so furious with Bubble.

Once the crowd had dispersed, she ducked outside. The chicken's eyes were rolled back and its feet were stiffening in the sunlight. She found a spade and buried it in a hole next to the garden. Before covering it with earth, she spread an old rag over it. The funeral concluded, she scraped some cinders and refuse over the spot so that no one would notice anything special about it.

When she was in the fourth grade, her class had raised two Plymouth Rocks in the schoolyard in order to help areas hit by natural disasters, but the chickens got sick and died when they were half grown. With her in the lead, some of the girls dug a hole with a stick under a fig tree, put down a piece of wood, and wrapped those pretty feathers up in layer after layer of fig leaves. Then they covered them with two magazine covers that had been used as book jackets, as solemn as if they were burying treasure. Finally, in imitation of grown-up rituals, they burned some note paper in front of the mound and then went home, their minds at rest. But when they got to school the next morning, they found the little mound broken wide open, and the leaves swirling about in the wind. The dead chickens had flown away without wings. The girls were all so frightened they stood trembling at a distance, wondering whether the chickens were alive or had turned into ghosts. In the midst of their panic, a chicken foot dropped down on them from the sky, and the boys came running up to report that they had found a pile of chicken bones in the old gatekeeper's garbage. She stood nervously up on tiptoe and looked in. There, sticking up out of old Uncle A'you's pan, lay a mottled chicken leg. They raged with righteous indignation.

At least Chen Xu hadn't got off work yet. If he started asking questions, she'd say it ran away. Nothing else would make him give up on it.

She felt a little better, both because she had made some small amends for its misfortune and because her first attempt to raise a chicken had failed. She wasn't an old peasant; she shouldn't be raising a chicken anyway! It was precisely because she hadn't become a peasant that she hadn't been able to keep their ill-gotten chicken. A good thing it had died; she was happier now that it had. Who said you weren't keeping a house if you didn't raise chickens?

The air was getting warmer day by day. Long soft whip in hand, it drove people out into the fields, drove them to their labours. Off on the horizon, they were burning over the fields, the tongues of flame licking passionately at the riven bosom of the black earth. The air was filled with the sour smell of horse manure, and, reunited with the roads at last, the tractors' ploughshares were nibbling at the traces of their old love-bites. And to the resonant neighing of horses and the rumbling lowing of cattle, the wheels of the old cartmen, set to itching by the steam rising from the sun-lit ground, rolled by like clockwork all day long, rattling over an oily earth.

When they met her on the road, the women from the family quarters smiled and greeted Xiao Xiao even while they were still far away.

"Xiao! Have you got your fence up yet?"

"Say, Xiao! Plant a little spinach around your house. It'll be ready to eat in ten days."

"If you want to put some soya paste out in the sun to ferment, just come over to our place and get a few beans."

"Plant some chives, Xiao; you'll have more than you can eat."

They called her Xiao. She did not know whether they meant her first name or her last. Anyway, women up in Manchuria did not care much for two syllable names and cut them down to one. So they called their third son 'Three', instead of 'Threesie'. Or else they stretched out the sound, calling Chen Xu 'Cherr'. It sounded very friendly and familiar. As for the business about the little chicken, they had long since forgotten it.

The two of them did have some seeds, but no trace of a fence. The wide stretches of ground in front of and behind the cottages were divided up by invisible boundary markers extending from the door and window of each, but if you didn't put up a fence of reeds or willow twigs or something, your neighbours' chicks would be coming over to peck at your cabbage sprouts, and your own squash vines would be running over next door to grow, and how would things ever get straightened out then? The residents were all permanent workers or poor and lower-middle peasants, so they had got their materials together the preceding autumn. But Chen Xu and Xiao Xiao were a pair of city kids without a thing to their names. Now, in their dire straits they awoke to the error of their ways. All those little stalks of straw and bits of broken brick had been the basic guarantees that one could hold one's head up like a real human being. This was what matter and spirit were

144

really all about.

All through the long winter they had been yearning for the end of the cold weather. But now the spring breezes had finally returned, bringing in tow a great raft of unthought-of garden chores and dumping them on the doorstep.

She liked watching Chen Xu and Beanpole spading the soil. They would dig up a big clod of black earth, turn it over, and break it up, loose and glistening in the sunlight. Chewing on a walnut, its fragrance filling the mouth, an exquisite, crisp taste. Farmers down South would never work the earth like this. There, they used a rake with four sharp steel tines, digging into the roots and rubble, the thin, lean soil packed with the filth from a thousand years of Yangtse sediment. They couldn't use a spade; it might bend. But the earth here was porous, rich, full. It seemed as though it would produce a good harvest without even sowing. Sometimes they turned up a lump of frozen soil, and then Beanpole would patiently plane it down with the tip of his shovel, as though he were sharpening a pencil, shaving off one curl after another. It was pure and unadulterated, except for the splinters of ice glittering in the sunlight. The earth here was open and friendly.

And in this piece of earth they buried pieces of potato, sowed sunflowers, scattered spinach seed, planted early and late beans, just as everybody else did. The fences had been taken care of for them by their neighbours on either side, two rows of reeds enclosing their vegetable garden between them. All they had to do was install a gate at the back and the job would be done. Chen Xu said, "A fence in time saves mine!" He was not grateful in the slightest for the kindness of their two neighbours. After ten days, everything except tobacco that should have been in the ground was. There was still an empty space left for cucumber, tomato, and eggplant seedlings. Somewhere or other, Beanpole had come up with some pea seed, which he called, after the Hangzhou fashion, 'pease'. He said that in autumn they would be eating 'pease porridge sweet'. Their little vegetable garden had a bit of everything in it, like an old-style herbal medicine shop.

Xiao Xiao kept back a few seeds of each kind of bean they had planted and carried them rattling around in her pockets. During rest breaks in the fields, she got them out and admired them. Each one was shiny and firm, with a natural gloss as though it had been glazed. She took an inexpressible pleasure in playing with them. "Wailing and whispering interweave, like pearls large and small cascading onto a jade platter", as the T'ang poet Bai Juyi had written in his "Song of the

Lute Player." Someone helped her out by explaining what each one was. The biggest ones, with a few spots at the end, were called 'horseshoe beans'; they were pretty, but no good to eat. The long narrow ones with a black patch at the end were called 'white-eyed magpies'. The ones with lavender and yellow marks on a white body were 'sparrow eggs'; they produced a long broad bean, both pretty to look at and delicious to eat. And there were 'August Rush' and 'Old Beauty' and so many others; there was no end to them. If you were to string them together in a chain, without repeating any kind, they would be even prettier than pearls! She had seen a dance when she was in the ninth grade, but there would be no dances any more. Where had the lavender wreath in her mother's wedding picture gone?

One morning, bright and early, Chen Xu shook her awake. He was waving a handful of green seedlings and stroking her face. He shouted, "We've got some, we've got some! Get up quick!"

What did they have? "Cucumber seedlings, squash seedlings. They're left over from the neighbours, a whole bunch, enough for us to do some planting!"

The kind of cucumber and squash that put out false flowers? She was awake in an instant and sat up. Why did they play false? On any one vine, which were the false flowers and which were real? She would plant some and find out.

They quickly ridged up the earth in an empty part of their garden. Chen Xu dug the earth into hills, while she planted the furry little seedlings one by one in the loose, fragrant soil. Then she doused them with a little water and carefully tucked them in. Soon they had planted several dozen.

She crouched beside them, absorbed in the sight.

"Why don't tomatoes and peppers have false flowers?" She ventured, turning to look at Chen Xu.

"Still haven't got it? Pumpkins have male and female flowers."

"But are the false flowers the male ones or the female?"

"Well, I suppose they're the females."

"You're wrong! It must be the males. The male flowers don't form fruit, they just bloom and then wither away. It's because they get people's hopes up for nothing that the farmers call them false flowers."

Chen Xu was taking the question seriously. "The male flowers? You're too clever by half. The male flowers aren't supposed to bear fruit. They bloom just in order to supply the female flowers with pollen. What's false about that?"

She said nothing. She was beginning to feel a little confused. Perhaps it really wasn't the male flowers. There was no little knob at the base of the male flowers, which made it obvious that they wouldn't bear fruit. So they could hardly be accused of lying. For something to be a lie it had to be intentional, and this wasn't the case with the flowers. They did not know the meaning of falsehood. It was people's fault for assuming that every flower should bear fruit.

"Well then, what do you think false flowers are?" She asked.

"They're the female flowers that wilt and die off without forming a fruit. They're the ones..."

She broke in on him, raising her voice. "That's because they didn't get any pollen. Is that their fault? Maybe there isn't enough nourishment to go around. That's why there aren't more fruits on each vine."

"Well, this much is clear. They're flowers that ought to form fruit but don't, and so they let people down," he persisted.

"Well that's because the vine cheated the flowers. It's not their fault." She was on the verge of losing her temper.

"Yes, there's something in what you say." He nodded with a chuckle and picked up the hoe and bucket to go back inside. "Let's wait for the flowers to bloom and then we'll see. No point in talking in the abstract."

She followed him back. She really ought to go ask someone whether the false flowers were the males or the females. Apparently either could be, and yet neither really was. It was a real riddle.

The vegetable garden turned out to be harder to conquer than an enemy pillbox. They were so sleepy they were nodding off at work if they so much as closed their eyes. They were late getting to work and often didn't even have time for meals. Sun, moon, and stars ran off their tracks. By the time Chen Xu remembered they wanted to see the Sungari River break-up, people said that the river had been thawed for days. What was more, all the cabbage seeds that they had sowed two weeks before finally poked their green heads through the surface with a vengeance, threw open their mouths, and demanded water. But to water them was to invite a wolf into the parlour, to bring forth a dense carpet of weeds. Hoe them today and they'd be back tomorrow. An endless supply of tomorrows loomed large before them. But if you just took it easy and let them go, there were so many eyes and mouths ready to erupt. "Xiao! Your vegetable garden..." A vegetable garden was a landlord's wife, demanding service. So this was the taste of service. Lili had stayed in the city rather than coming to the countryside. She had married a company commander in the local army district. When she had her baby, she even got a nanny.

The people in charge of the mess hall had ordered them to stop eating there. A young couple like you turned so lazy; aren't you afraid that people will laugh at you? What did you get married for? Doesn't marriage mean cooking for yourselves and sleeping on the same bed? Liu the Brute allocated a load of straw for them to cook with, but it was mixed up with bits of ice, so cooking with it was like fumigating for mosquitos. Smoke swirled all about Xiao Xiao and filled her eyes with tears.

She let her tears, blended of weariness and a sense of undeserved rebuke, flow freely down her cheeks. It was weeping in the midst of a downpour, sweating in a swimming pool. Often she made no attempt at all to avoid the biting smoke, but just let it swirl around her head. It squeezed her so hard that everything before her eyes was blurred and vague. Only after it had squeezed out streams of bitter water did she feel somewhat relieved.

"Have you been crying?" Chen Xu looked at her carefully as he picked up his chopsticks.

"No, I just got smoke in my eyes," she said, trying to sound indifferent.

All her old dreams of love and the future were simply dissolved in those daily multiplying cabbage stalks. Her spirit seemed to have been sucked out by those tender green leaves and turned into fertilizer for the vegetable garden. Each morning, as she woke up in a stupor, she was mystified as to how she could have found herself in such a place.

Xiao Xiao lost weight.

To their surprise, the Branch Farm started selling piglets again. At fifty cents a pound, a piglet was quite cheap, ten bucks or so. By autumn, there would be a fat two hundred pound porker you could either eat or sell for cash. And if a married couple didn't buy a piglet to raise? Every housewife on the Farm would be talking about you behind your back; see if they wouldn't!

And on top of that, the Farm made new allotments of private plot land. Three shares for one person, six for two. Rows five hundred yards long, exactly six of them, just waiting for people to go dig out the corn stubble. Plant them with soy beans and corn, and in the autumn there would be feed for pigs and chickens. What could be wrong with

148

that? Don't you want to plant your six shares? Every housewife on the Branch Farm would laugh you to scorn!

You could not not buy a pig; nor could you not plant your private plot.

Although she had Chen Xu, and Chen Xu had Bubble and Beanpole, the seedlings in their garden still did not do as well as other people's, nor was their piglet as sturdy. Despite his promises that Xiao Xiao would have pork kidney soup and pork liver to eat at the end of year, Chen Xu simply would not go to the mess hall to scrounge after vegetable scraps when the feeding trough was empty.

Xiao Xiao picked up the work basket with a sigh and went outside.

A flock of geese flew over, coming from the South.

In the twilight, the poplar groves were veiled in a grey mist that drifted and dissipated as it rose. On the tree-tops squatted the slowly setting sun, weary from the day's toil and dragging all his unfinished chores down after him. The sunlit warmth carried aloft on the drifting dust settled quietly back to earth, and on the air the fresh, moist scent of growing plants, mixed with the smell of the soil, pushed in on her from all sides. She felt a little dizzy. At the edge of the woods, among the dead weeds along the margins of the fields, she could see clump after clump of new green borne up out of the resurrected earth and blinking curious eyes.

Little herbs, did springtime awaken you? Or did you awaken springtime?

"Let's go 'tread the green'!" said her mother. All along the Su Causeway by West Lake there are cats-ear buds and Boltonia and shepherds purse, excellent stuffings for wonton, as delicious as can be. Let's see who can pick the first king-size shepherds purse...

Here, speedwell and endive and pigweed were thrown into a steamer, but only to fill a rusty wok and be cooked to a paste to pour into the pig's trough. Little herbs, little herbs...

Her basket was cumbersome, though empty. She stood there in a daze and then squatted down.

The loudspeaker beside the road came on. A clear female voice was reading a report on 'study and application'. There seemed to be a familiar name in it, slipping by her ears. She stood up and listened carefully. The voice was repeating it over and over again in the dusky evening air—it was Guo Chunmei; it was a speech on her 'study and application' work read by Guo Chunmei at a regional meeting.

The voice said, She had volunteered to take on the job of fattening up two hundred piglets. In a single day she moved over two tons of fodder, cleaned the pigsty six times, made twenty trips hauling the water cart, and carried bales of straw. And she had invented a foot bath to go between the pig barn and the feeding area, to keep the pigs' feet sanitary. She had also found a way to fry potatoes and add them to the fodder so that the pigs were gaining a pound and a half a day.

Xiao Xiao bent down and dug for all she was worth.

The voice said, She would rather be cut off from her mother for a lifetime than from the Party for a day.

The voice said, She wanted always to shoulder the heaviest burdens and to eliminate imperialism, revisionism, and reaction.

The voice said, She struggled against the 'philosophy of survival' and would struggle to the death against selfishness.

The voice said, She would raise pigs on a grand scale for the sake of revolution, to the last drops of her blood and sweat.

The wind was cold. Xiao Xiao shivered.

She too was developing pork production. For whom? But how pleasant it is to swim in the water! said the duckling. To plunge your head under water and dive right down to the bottom—what fun! She too was developing pork production. For whom?

The rich, biting smell of the herbs in her basket stirred up a kind of melancholy within her. Strands of guilt, of shame, of resentment eddied about in the dusky light. What are you actually doing? What kind of person are you? Aren't you trying to make progress any more? Have you degenerated? Is it vulgarity? Selfishness? Weakness? You're finished!

She fell backward onto the ground. Her basket flipped over, and all the herbs spilled out.

There were little yellow flowers blooming all over the lawn.

She was carrying a flower basket to pick flowers. The basket was made of bamboo. There was a book in it.

She sat on a hillside, reading. The words on the pages were gigantic, like slogans painted on a wall. She could finish the book as fast as she could turn the pages, but she did not know what it was about.

There was a letter stuck in between the pages. It was a rose. She took a sniff and noticed that the flower had no stamens. Chen Xu walked up, took the flower, and stuck it in the mud, saying, This is a broad bean flower; let's plant broad beans.

Her beans grew with great speed, like bamboo shoots, leaping up into the wind. They were even taller than sunflowers. They formed large pods like bananas, with beans inside as white as silkworms. She asked Chen Xu about them, and he said, They aren't broad beans, they're arhat beans.

She swallowed the arhat beans, thinking that she would probably turn right into an arhat. Arhats lived on cabbage and potatoes. She looked down and discovered that she had become very fat. Her stomach stuck out like an arhat's. Chen Xu patted her and said, It must be a boy! She felt a little sick to her stomach and threw up. When she had finished, her stomach shrivelled up. She went out to feed the pig, carrying a pan of swill.

A black spotted piglet was running in circles around the brick pig pen, barking like a dog. She poured corn mush into the worn-out wash basin and the piglet finished it off with a few grunts. Curling its lips, it went around rooting and licking at the walls, and in a moment it had swallowed a brick. What an appetite! An old housewife with a scarf around her head said, Feed it more! She poured in another pan full of mush, and it too was soon gone, another ladle full, and that was gone. She pried the piglet's mouth open and discovered a black and bottomless pit inside, one that would never fill up no matter how much you put into it. She fed it nothing more and left it to go swallow bricks, but it knocked the basin over and pushed at the walls until they began to rock back and forth. She beat it with a branch, and it grabbed the branch in its mouth and almost jumped over the wall. It began to squeal and hunch up its neck, flapping its big ears back and forth. It looked very fierce.

Was it a pig or a dog? She wanted to take a close look. Someone said, Why not sell the pig to me? I can use it to guard my house.

Chen Xu muttered in her ear, There's cinnabar growing in that pig's stomach. Don't be in a hurry to sell it off. No wonder the pig is so strange, it's got cinnabar inside.

She could not remember what cinnabar was. Then she heard the loudspeaker announcing that the Farm's propaganda art troupe had come to put on a show. Just as she was starting back, someone called her.

A girl was walking up the road, with a long braid trailing behind her and a slightly upturned face that caught the sun and gleamed brightly. The girl looked a little like herself. After thinking a moment,

151

she realised that it was Yu Di, the lead singer from the art troupe.

She whipped into hiding behind the pigpen.

Yu Di was holding a set of bamboo clappers strung on a red cord and singing as she walked along:

Learn from Dazhai, that's the way
To make our dreams come true some day!
Ai Hey Ai Hey Ai Hey Hey!

She covered her ears and shouted, What kind of Shaoxing opera is that you're singing? It sounds awful.

Yu Di ignored her and went on singing for a long time, always to the same refrain—Ai Hey Ai Hey Yo! The clappers stopped and Yu Di said, This is a Manchurian Duet.

And what about your partner? she asked. It's obviously a solo.

No, it's a monodrama. There's only one role. Yu Di pulled up one foot, bending her leg like a crane standing in the water. It's also called a one man show.

She wanted very much to learn from Yu Di how to do a one man show, so she climbed up on stage with her. Skylarks were singing above her, and a violin could be heard among the clouds.

Yu Di squeezed into a crack and disappeared. She clambered up a flight of stairs. The stage began to rock back and forth, as though it were about to collapse. She screamed and fell off.

18

Summer, the season of beauty and plenty, roamed the wide fields with satisfaction. But the tree roots and the earth chafed its bare feet, as clover and cocklebur grew more prickly under the fierce sun. Summer hurried away, ripping its glorious raiment to shreds, the bare soles of its feet covered with bleeding scratches. Summer had been parched and now it turned to sere and yellow autumn.

The harvesting of the paddies had left clumps of rice stubble six inches high, which the first frosts turned to a field of cotton, gleaming a dazzling white. When a puff of wind happened to touch one of the dandelions left on the paths between the fields, the seeds drifted away like snow crystals. And in the hollows of the fields one could see stalks of straw sealed under thin ice like specimens under glass.

Autumn was weariness, too.

Chen Xu was sitting on a pile of straw and smoking during a rest break, mulling over everything that was bothering him.

The threshing was not under way yet, so work had not been too heavy for the preceding few days, just stacking the harvested grain and carting it back to the threshing ground. He liked working with a pitchfork, thrusting it savagely into a few sheaves and then tossing them easily away, as though he were tossing away some of his troubles. It was relaxing. With a little skill, he could conserve his strength for work around the house.

The corn and soya beans in their private plot were almost all harvested, but they still did not have enough fuel straw ready to last them through the winter. The weeds along the road had been baled and stood up on end. They all belonged to someone, so he would have to go up to the reservoir to cut reeds, a round trip of six or seven miles. The firebox under the brick bed had to be scraped out and the heated wall emptied, and the northern window would have to be completely sealed over and all the cracks around the southern window filled up. The cabbage and potatoes had to go into the cellar; the carrots had to be covered in sand. There was no end of chores to do, and no sooner was one finished than the next was waiting. It was more like doing one's own funeral than getting a den ready to hibernate through the winter. Everything had to be done just so.

He was fed up to here. He knew that he was just doing all these stupid, trivial household chores mechanically and helplessly.

To give him his due, he was completely uninterested in them all. When his disgust came on him, he really felt like taking all the pots and pans and so forth and smashing them to smithereens. It was all for the sake of pleasing Xiao Xiao, of satisfying her, that he forced his bleary eyes open at first light and went out to their private plot, that after dark he went off weary and aching to the well to get water.

Xiao Xiao went through water like a pipe with no faucet at the end. Whoosh! And the barrel was empty. She could not overcome her unfortunate attachment to cleanliness. She continued to wash her face three times a day, to take a sponge bath every three days, to wash each load of laundry until the rinse water came out crystal clear. Xiao Xiao would do anything for him. Each month, when the Branch Farm sold meat, she saved it all for him, but she never took pity on his water carrying. He did not even have a shoulder pole. It was one bucket in each hand and off all the way to their door without stopping. Then she would smile, and two satisfied dimples would surface, like whirlpools, on her pale face; just a flash and they were gone.

He would do anything for her, all the same. During the summer she had grown very tan and lean, but over the past few months her face and body had suddenly 'risen' like a lump of bread dough. She was so plump and soft that her skin held the impression of a finger. She was forever looking in the mirror. He was afraid to say it: that isn't fat, it's fluid. Practically all pregnant women 'expanded when heated and contracted when cooled' like this.

That unknown little being was like a silent engine driving him frantically back and forth between fields and home. In order to prepare for its arrival, he was instinctively gathering material for his nest, like a fox or a swallow. He realised that he was ridiculous, that he was both anxious and discouraged. In fact he was entirely unprepared, both materially and psychologically, to settle down there and live out his days in peace, providing for his descendants. It had only been in order to recover from the inner wounds dealt him that he had taken shelter from the elements in this little den and drawn from her affection the courage to go on living. And yet, in throwing him that lifeline, she had bound him with it, and bound herself as well. He had taken her prisoner,

154

and also himself. Two defeated warriors, they had won the fruits of victory all the same, even without meaning to do so. The day he learned she was pregnant, he felt the world go pitch black before his eyes and his insides fill with vinegar. He even seemed to show the symptoms of pregnancy himself; he almost vomited from nausea. Those fruits did not seem radiant to him, but were rather a wave of fear, and then a wave of sorrow.

He couldn't even look after himself. How could he possibly be a father?

Xiao Xiao spent an entire day lying silently in bed, her delicate body shuddering beneath the covers. He picked her up in his arms and stroked her black hair. She looked at him with imploring eyes and his heart trembled within him. Those limpid eyes shone with pure innocence. They were still only the eyes of a child, and yet they now were to become those of an impatient mother. He understood her plea; the great brick bed had misinterpreted their passion.

And so at length they decided to make the trip to the hospital in Jiamusi. But they were too late. The doctor told them that after seven weeks such an operation could no longer be performed. He looked at them suspiciously. Since it's a first pregnancy, why...?

As summer turned to autumn, Xiao Xiao's slender body gradually began to fill out. In the still of the night, if he put his ear gently to her abdomen, he could hear the sounds within her womb, faint but distinct, the mysterious tread of footsteps walking toward him, heard as though deep within the earth or drifting across the sea, crossing endless mountains and rivers. This tread was rapping at the gate of human life, and their whole cottage, their whole brick bed, seemed to shake and sway on its account. It was so ordinary, and yet so magnificent, a life in the act of creating itself, and at the same time conferring upon him a responsibility that he could not escape. He was suddenly moved. He stroked it gently as he grew drowsy; in the faint light of dawn, he quietly watched it. That daily waxing moon too could breathe, evenly and contentedly, softly rising and falling in his embrace.

And so Xiao Xiao came to seem even more entrancing in his eyes.

Their early married life had been sweet as honey. Although that honey had been infused with fatigue and pain, their warm brick bed had comforted him in recompense. The long nights were like a playing field, giving you one opportunity after another, letting you run endless vigorous laps. These sprints, these bursts of energy, could be endlessly repeated, and yet never grew wearisome. In those frenzied combats you hurled the warhead of your life; in that eternally unceasing warfare, you discharged all your passions and desire. You longed for night, for the exhilaration it brought your soul, for making you forget yourself; you feared the night, for it turned you into an rabid beast, sinking exhausted into sweet death at break of day.

During the first weeks of their marriage, he scarcely slept for nights on end. Xiao Xiao's smooth skin and sleek hair gave off an intoxicating fragrance. At first, she was bashful and reserved, but later she became more tender and seductive. Her own desires were awakened, and she too was bound up in their love. The flames of her passion were kindled, and she too raged like fire. She never put him off; she was like a vase of lush roses, always fresh and always sweet. He desired her fragrance as though he were drawing in with it the sweet dew of life itself, and in those frenzied instants he would feel as though he and she were merged forever in a single body that could never again be sundered. And then he would scream, "I want you until I die!"

And this was the price of that oblivion, very tangibly moving and growing in its mother's womb. This was the price of that love, a blind and uninvited creature.

He puffed greedily on his cigarette. The sky was clear and still, the blue horizon so close he could almost touch it and yet as far away as the ends of the earth. He had chosen his straw heap well; it kept the wind off, and people too. He pulled out another cigarette and lit it from the butt of the one he had been smoking.

Xiao Xiao didn't like him to smoke.

But he liked smoking. He could think of nothing else he did like.

He knew that he liked tobacco not just because he liked its bite, pricking his throat, his lungs, and his brain, exciting and numbing him at the same time. It was also because he liked the way the brown ends turned black amid the spark, and how the white smoke came from the black ash, like a cloud, drifting slowly through the air, drifting away and vanishing without a trace, its essence taken into his breast and turned into energy that circulated throughout his vitals. Liu Bang, founder of the Han dynasty, Li Shimin, founder of the T'ang, Julius Caesar, Peter the Great... Although they had gone like the ashes and smoke, their great strategies and campaigns, their grand achievements, would last forever and never fade.

Someone came over and sat down next to him, wearing clothes that smelled of mothballs.

He looked around, saw that it was Zou Sizhu, and moved over, trying to ignore him. He did not like being interrupted now, while he was thinking.

Zou Sizhu stuck out a hand and said, "How about one for me?"

"One what?"

"A cigarette."

He was astonished. When did the bookworm take up smoking? He took another look at Zou. There really was something odd about him. He was dressed in fresh clothes, the tip of his nose was red, he was shaking a little, and his lips were trembling.

"What's with you, anyway?" He tossed him the pack.

Zou Sizhu swallowed hard, raised his eyebrows, looked all around, and then said in a hushed voice. "Look, if I tell you something, can you keep it an absolute secret?"

"What is it? Come on, you goofball, let's have it!"

"You mustn't go spreading it around."

"Sure, sure. Some kind of super big news?"

"I'll say, the biggest in the world." He got even more mysterious, cupping his hands around his mouth and whispering in Chen's ear. "I got a letter from Hangzhou saying that Number Two's been killed in a plane crash. An attempted..."

"What Number Two? What are you talking about? Isn't Liu the Brute Number Two?"

"No, it's Lin..."

"Baldy?" He leapt to his feet. "Really?"

Zou Sizhu rubbed his eyes. The smoke was making him cough.

"It's all over Hangzhou. It must be true. It's only here, where things are so tight, that word hasn't got in."

Chen Xu just stood there, the breeze tossing his capstrings.

Zou Sizhu gave him a nudge. "The whistle's blown; let's get back to work. I just wanted to have a cigarette to celebrate, to mark the occasion. There are bound to be political changes in China now. When contradictions reach their height, they reverse direction. We're over the hump. Since you've found out about it early, you can think things out in advance. Didn't they accuse you of being against Lin when we were back in school? Now you can make a come-back. Only..."

He ditched Zou Sizhu and ran for the oxcart, coming within a hair of tripping in the stubble. He felt like shouting at the top of his lungs, like lighting a fire on top of the straw heap, like flinging his arms around that stolid black ox. All of a sudden there stretched across the azure sky a thick, dragon-shaped cloud, its silver scales leaping and writhing, ready to soar, to rise high above...

Comrade Chen Xu, isn't it true that you were already denouncing Baldy Lin three years ago? asked Susie J, standing up very respectfully.

That's right. He didn't look like a good man to me. He had the eyes of a thief or a rat; there was evil written all over his face. He sat in that black leather chair in the office, smoking ostentatiously. In order to bring about his careerist goal of seizing control of the Party, he got up a personality cult and advocated a totally reactionary theory of human genius. Way back during the Cultural Revolution, I pointed out that such theories were contrary to Marxism.

So, could you please tell us a little about how you were able to recognise him as a double-dealing counter-revolutionary? Instructor Yu personally poured him a cup of hot water and added a pinch of flowered tea leaves. You're the anti-Lin Biao hero of the Branch Farm now; no, of the whole Farm, the whole District, a great revolutionary soldier boldly emerged from the ranks of the urban educated youth, an outstanding representative of the study and application of Chairman Mao's works in a living way. In the past we were stupidly blind to your worth. Please accept our sincere and humble apologies now. We will support your 'induction into the Party on the battlefront' with the greatest possible speed and spread the news of your heroic deeds throughout the whole structure of the State Farm...

"What's the matter with you? Can't you see the cart is full? Get off!"

Someone was yelling at him.

"Who threw away this cigarette butt? You fucking tired of living? Look, you piss in the wind, if I hadn't spotted it, the whole straw heap would have gone up in smoke!"

Liu the Brute came tearing out of the threshing ground, swearing a blue streak.

The wind was sighing, but the sun shone bright on the withered weeds.

19

This was their third winter in the Great Northern Wastes.

A few snowfalls turned the farm into a solitary island in the midst of the vast frozen plain, hemmed in by the sweep of the snow, across which the wind combed long low ripples that stretched all the way to the horizon.

Every house had a little square of black earth in front, swept absolutely clean. And each black square extended a black path toward the wellhouse in the centre of the family quarters. All the black lines and squares joined together and formed the temporary winter communications network, cramped and strict. Like the cords binding up a criminal in the old time, they bound the farm into abject, frozen submission.

Each time he went to the wellhouse to draw water, he sensed this same unpleasant bondage.

The pump had been out of order for several days, so he had to go to the well at the company quarters. The wellhead there was now surrounded by a slippery but exquisitely wrought bank of ice. A wet hand would freeze to the crank handle instantly, taking off a piece of skin. Warm air rose from the well, but a cylinder of thick ice had formed around the shaft like a huge slick seamless steel pipe reaching deep into the earth. Nothing could be seen but a grim grey light, no water at all. A little carelessness, and one might well slide all the way down that slippery tube and end up in the Ice Palace. People who came to draw water would toss the ice-caked bucket clattering down the well with the greatest caution. After endless squeaking and whirling of the windlass, there would finally come a thud, which meant that the bucket had reached bottom. The well gave the impression that it contained no water, only ice. But after the windlass had groaned and creaked for a long time, up would come a full bucket of water at last, blinking its impassive eye.

Each time he went to draw water, it seemed to him as though he were standing in the midst of a hope that was equally fathomless even while it lay within his grasp.

And yet, time slipped by, no one came to see him. No reporters, no one from the Farm's Political Work Unit, not even Catfish.

He tried sending a short note to Wang Ge, asking him to write back and let him know how things stood in Hangzhou. It just might be that if Wang could fix things up, his persecuted comrade-in-arms could make a comeback and be transferred home to Hangzhou.

But the days passed without any sign of news.

He was puzzled and discouraged. He waited quietly for a miracle to occur, but the miracle was playing hide-and-go-seek with him. All that came was a third snowfall, freezing clouds, and winter crows. It was snowing again; would there be work in the afternoon? Perhaps he should go see the Branch Farm officials on his own and have a talk with them.

He had filled his buckets and lugged them down the mountain of ice, holding his breath. As he was gasping for air, he heard a voice from the little black square in front of the company dormitory shouting, "No work this afternoon. There's a criticism session."

His heart skipped a beat, and he asked, "What's it about?"

"Well, it's a criticism session, so it must be something big!" The other person shrugged and went off toward the girls' dormitory.

He went home and told Xiao Xiao, "This is one session we're going to!"

"What's it about?" Xiao Xiao wanted to stay home and make herself some sour cabbage. She had developed a great appetite lately.

"I'm not sure, not sure at all," he said to himself. He did not want to mention ahead of time just what it was that he could not say for sure. He wanted to keep all his imagined miracles inside.

Someone had written in bold white chalk on the blackboard at the entrance to the men's dormitory: Resolutely Criticise all Political Swindlers of the Liu Shaoqi Ilk!

Ilk? What ilk? How come it's all pinned on the Right? Swindlers? More swindlers? His heart sank. He hadn't read a paper in days. Where had this new twist come from?

Fresh new slogans were pasted up on the battered walls of the men's dorm. The place was packed, and as usual the boys had taken their shoes off and were sitting on their bedrolls up on the brick bed, while the girls sat along the edge. When the girls came for a meeting, the boys just smoked and kept quiet. As soon as he sat down, several cigarettes were tossed over to him.

"The meeting is called to order." Catfish walked in with an army overcoat thrown over his shoulders, stamping the snow from his boots. He stood in the centre of the room, cleared his throat, and spoke to the following effect: "Today we want to criticise a little more severely those swindlers of the Liu Shaoqi ilk and the reactionary theories of those counter-revolutionary careerists and plotters. We must get at the truth, link those above with those below, and completely eradicate his pernicious influence from the minds, souls, and blood of everyone!"

Chen Xu's look swept across the people sitting on the two brick beds, their indifferent, mystified eyes looking this way and that.

"As we all know, that guy slandered the movement to send educated young people 'up to the mountains and down to the villages' as 'labour reform in disguise'. As we understand the situation, there are also a very few people in our own company who are spreading this sort of counter-revolutionary idea and wearing the same britches as the careerists. We're going to drag them out into the open where everyone can see them."

The deterrent force in his ringing voice fell on each of them like a rain of arrows.

The room was silent for a moment. The fire stopped crackling and began to sputter. The air, thick with smoke and the smell of sweat and dirty socks, was suddenly heavy.

Someone in the corner burst out, "It's Chen Xu! After Chen Xu came back from the brig, he called the rustication of young people 'labour reform in disguise'!"

He shuddered. He could not see who had spoken. Who was it? Bull? Monkey? Guo Chunmei? No, it wasn't Bull. Bull had been behaving himself ever since Wei Hua left. Shit. When had he said that, and to whom?

"Chen Xu!" Catfish spoke sternly. "Stand up!"

He stood slowly up on the brick bed. He was reminded of his height; his head almost hit the low ceiling. He looked like a monument after all, towering over a square. Desperately suppressed smiles flitted across the panic-stricken faces at his feet. He must look very funny. He wasn't confessing, he was reviewing his troops, looking out on the view, enjoying...

"Come down to the front and face criticism!" He heard Catfish shout. "You must carry out a thorough-going criticism of your crimes!"

You smiling tiger, showing your true colours at last. A shameless surprise attack. Why had he chosen him of all people to make an

161

example of?

"I don't think that he meant it like that," faltered a weak voice. It was Zou Sizhu. That bookworm.

Under the cold, dim light and before the clouded gaze of the crowd, he raised his head proudly. Of course he had said that; he had no intention of denying it, of trying to get out of it. He would be as frank and open as he had been that other time. No one but him, Chen Xu, had foreseen what was afoot a year before Baldy Lin's blown up or had shown such vision by saying that. But heaven only knew how they had happened to meet up on the same plank bridge. What sort of joke was Fate playing on him, putting a man of his insight, his genius, in the dock?

Black snow came whipping down.

A black sky, a black earth, black faces, black shoe laces, a black fire in the furnace.

Black sickles stacked in a corner of the room.

If you were to plunge one of those sickles into a shameless heart, black blood would flow out and black bones be revealed inside.

"Come down from the bed! Did you hear me? Get down!" The voice was shouting again.

So he slipped his feet loosely into his shoes and stepped down onto the floor, scratching his head and wearing an enigmatic smile. He spoke slowly. "I did say 'labour reform in disguise'. I was referring to serving time in the brig, referring to myself, and how it served me right to be suspended and investigated. So it was also a kind of self-criticism, right? At that time, I had never heard of the Vice Chief Commander using a reactionary expression like that. If he said it, why didn't anybody notice? Our Great Leader didn't notice it either. According to the chronological sequence of events, it must have been me who said it first. Our Great Leader teaches us that we should seek truth from facts. So, if it's a question of pernicious influence, you never know, perhaps he was affected by my bad example."

Silence. And then, people began to giggle, and finally they exploded with laughter.

20

The snow was unusually heavy that winter, coming in one blizzard after another until it lay a good foot thick on the roofs. After each snowfall, the paths would be dug out, but the network of black lines was no longer visible, only passageways with walls of white snow half the height of a man. They left people feeling as though they were at the front line and going around in circles through the long narrow tunnels.

The storms cut off all road and rail transport. No shipments of coal could get in, and the straw heaps were buried by the snow, so that they could not scratch out anything to burn. In no time, every one of the hundred-odd furnaces for heating the brick beds in the company dormitory was out of fuel. People curled up on the beds, bundled into every stitch of clothing and bedding they owned and still so cold that their teeth were chattering. The Branch Farm officials were all at their wits' ends, wondering if their hundreds of city kids would be able to make it through the winter or not. Just as they were really starting to stew in their own juices, an urgent message was wired in from Farm Headquarters: Three months vacation for the whole Farm, with travel expenses and wages left up to each individual.

A wave of joy swept over the Farm. Travel expenses? Wages? Who cares! Just so we can go home.

In the space of three days, all the city kids were gone without a trace: back to Hegang, to Jiamusi, to Harbin, Tianjin, Hangzhou, Ningbo, Wenzhou; by cart, by wagon, on foot.

Xiao Xiao could not leave. She couldn't figure out when her baby was due. Even the Branch Farm doctor, Dr. Yang, could not say for sure, and she was afraid to take the least chance of its being born on the road. And besides, she did not want to go spend her lying-in month with Chen Xu's family.

"Things will be better, now that they've all gone. The fuel situation won't be so tight," Chen Xu reassured her.

Bubble and Beanpole had gone too; except for Guo Chunmei

and her pigs, everyone had gone.

The cottage, which for a while had been as busy as a tea house, was quiet at last.

The women left on the Branch Farm were all put to work together in the root cellars, storing the cabbage, while the men were out transporting manure. They went to work at ten in the morning and got off at two in the afternoon, as these were the only hours when there was sufficient daylight. Since this was the only work they did all day, they did not need to eat as much as usual, and so every household switched to having just two meals a day. Xiao Xiao felt ravenous by noon. The other women were sneaking breaks to cut the hearts out of a few yellowish cabbages with their sickles and nibble them like rabbits, smacking their lips with satisfaction. Mouth watering, Xiao Xiao broke off a piece and tried it, but it was so raw and cold that it made her tongue go numb, and she spat it right out. In grade school, they had raised a pair of Angora rabbits, feeding them vegetable leaves and bean curd dregs. Someone laughed at her and handed her a partly peeled carrot. It was sweet and crisp. At first she was embarrassed, but then she saw that everyone was eating them, white radishes and red ones, the peels littering the ground. They would have eaten the potatoes too, had they been good to eat. Someone told her, If you don't eat, you're just throwing away your chance. And so whenever they got a break, she would go up to a little hole at the end of the cellar and get out a carrot. It really began to seem as though she were only going to work for the sake of eating carrots. How much more simple than ever before the nature and goals of life had grown. And often, after they had packed some boxes of cabbages, peeled a few carrots, and swept up the leaves and peelings, the sky, visible through the ventilation shaft, would turn murky. Someone would say, Looks like snow again; we'd better hurry back. And so they would clamber huffing and puffing up the ladder, leaving all the rest of the work to the ex-labour camp inmate in charge of the cellar.

It had never occurred to Xiao Xiao that this snowbound winter could be got through so easily. Each day she walked out into the shimmering snow after a very late breakfast, as though she were walking into one of those beautiful sunlit deserts she had seen in books. She squeezed her way along the snow trenches, squinting against the light, until she came to a 'wellhead' with warm air rising from it. She might have been embarking on a voyage to the centre of the earth. The glittering snow palace dissolved into a hellish darkness. It was a dream, an entirely empty but lifelike dream. So long as you stayed in that dream, thinking nothing, saying nothing, just mechanically snapping off the rotten cabbage stalks and nibbling on raw carrots, the time would pass by as though on wings, with all the mindless acuity of sleep, until the colour of the sky met that of the earth. Then you moved your body to the surface to find the silver land of snow transformed into a dream of black. All you had to do was walk home, not too slow and not too fast, lie down on the brick bed, and the dream would continue unbroken.

Xiao Xiao had grown very fond of sleep. There was plenty of time now, but she did not feel like reading, or like anything else, for that matter. She knew that her body was getting more awkward by the day, and that this was numbing her mind, as though by pressure on a nerve somewhere. She felt lazy and hungry, and just muddled along, taking things easy. It seemed as though the attachment of another creature to her body had left her no longer master of herself. That creature would bite her in the midst of her reveries and speak to her in her dreams at night. It forced her to place everything she had at its disposal, to be driven by it. Her own life had been split in two, and the half given to it was active and curious, while that given her was uncertain and confused. She could no longer find herself and she did not have the energy to look. This could happen once to anyone, to anyone at all, she reassured herself.

And then the Spring Festival was almost upon them. They were given a five day holiday for the Festival. Five days; just think of it!

They got ready for the lunar New Year. Chen Xu struck a deal with a local peasant for ten eggs and ten pieces of frozen bean curd, and got someone to buy them a rolling pin in town. The Branch Farm sold some meat, so they could make stuffed dumplings.

On the afternoon of the thirtieth, Chen Xu came home from work, opened the outer door, and said in a hushed voice,

"Say, Xiao Xiao, I just heard someone say that Beanpole is back."

Xiao Xiao frowned. "That's crazy!"

Chen Xu looked serious. "No, it's true. They say he was caught first thing this morning, trying to steal a goose over at the barn. You run over to the company dormitory. I've got to go scare up some straw for the stove. People will have made off with it all if I don't move fast. Ask him over for New Years Eve dinner. And be careful when you're walking!"

Xiao Xiao tied a scarf over her head and put on her thick brown coat, which was so huge she could have hidden a three-year-old inside without anyone noticing. As she walked along, she kept wondering to herself, with New Years so close, why would Beanpole come back?

The company dormitory was almost half-buried in snow. There was no smoke coming from the chimney, which looked more like a giant icicle. An iceberg of wash water and urine stood outside the door, and, sure enough, a line of footprints made its uncertain way into the men's dormitory across the crust of snow long since formed on the ice.

She circled carefully around to the door and knocked, but there was no answer. She gave the door a slight push, and it swung open with a creak.

She could see someone sitting in a stupor on the brick bed, wearing cloth snow boots and a dogskin cap. There was an enamelled cup in front of him and a lighted cigarette in his hand. He was taking a puff on the cigarette and then a drink from the cup. There was an overpowering stench of tobacco and alcohol in the room. She could tell from those cut-off overalls that it was Beanpole.

For a moment, she could not get a word out. Drinking without any food to go with it, just a cigarette, was called a 'dry pull'. Only real locals drank like that.

Beanpole did not even look up. He choked and began to cough, his eyes red and bloodshot. He was a lot thinner, which made his nose a little more prominent.

Xiao Xiao could feel the cold cutting to her bones. Her hands and feet were freezing. She looked all around. The huge brick bed was bare. It was like a freezer or a cold storage cellar. There wasn't a trace of heat or of anything that might be burned. Tears welled up in her eyes. She walked slowly up behind him, reached out, and held down the enamelled cup, saying quietly, "Come home with me."

Behind them the dormitory door banged as it was blown open by the wind and then whipped shut again.

Their dinner was very simple: fried pork with cabbage, scrambled eggs with day lily, stewed pork and potato, and shredded pork with bean curd.

When the plates were put on the table, Beanpole stared nervously at the bowl of bean curd, muttering, "Bean curd. Bean curd. You don't get bean curd till you're dead."

Chen Xu slapped him on the back.

"Never mind where we are. If we don't eat the bean curd, what will we eat? During the Battle of Sangkumryung Mountain in the

Korean War they even drank piss, didn't they?"

Chen Xu poured himself and Beanpole each a little rice wine. It cost a dollar a bottle. Xiao Xiao had got it herself at the store, making an exception because it was New Years.

Beanpole flatly refused to take off his shoes and get up on the brick bed. He just sat on the edge with his patched snow boots drawn up beneath him. He drank silently, hanging his head and saying nothing.

Chen Xu seemed a little irritated. He gulped down a cup of wine and growled, "What's wrong with you, 'Pole? Why didn't you come here as soon as you got back? If something's bothering you, just tell me about it. Aren't we all family here?"

"I," Beanpole stammered woodenly, "I was meaning to come see you, but it makes me feel worse. You got a home, you got a wife. But I don't, I don't have nothing at all no more."

He threw himself back against the heated wall and began to sob like a child. The black patch on the shoulder of his brown padded coat quivered. Xiao Xiao tensed and asked softly, "Does A'cai know you've come back?"

He shook his head.

Chen Xu pulled his head up. "Doesn't she want you any more?"

"She..." Beanpole was sobbing so hard he could scarcely speak. "She's marrying someone in the Xiaoshan Militia, so she can get transferred home. She told me that I was just a farm hand and the farthest I'd ever get was into the tractor crew, driving a combine."

"That slut!" swore Chen Xu. "Wait till she gets back!"

Beanpole shook his head anxiously.

"It isn't her fault, it's mine, for being so worthless. I went to see the head of the tractor crew, gave him two cartons of cigarettes, and not so much as a bubble to show for it. No girl would look twice at me. Don't give her a hard time."

Chen Xu rapped his chopsticks on the table. "So, you should have waited until after the Spring Festival and then come back. It's not easy to get home, and the dormitory's so cold..."

Beanpole stared silently up at the ceiling and faltered, "Spring Festival? What Spring Festival? When I got home and couldn't hand over any money for food, the way my step-mother looked at me... At the dinner table, I didn't dare take anything but rice."

"What about your dad?"

"He kept bawling me out too; he says I'm hopeless. It was my own idea, coming back here."

He had stopped sobbing and picked up the bottle. He started drinking straight from it in big gulps, until he had drunk practically half. Eyes starting out of his head, Chen Xu snatched it away from him and yelled, "You'll kill yourself like that!"

"Yeah, guess 'will. Wha's so hot 'bout living? You're alive, so you're 'live, dead, you're dead, all 's same, lemme drink, I feel s'cold inside..."

He was mumbling incoherently, rocking back and forth where he sat, leaning against the heated wall.

"Go home, can' g'home, st' here, don' treacha like hum' bein', stole 'goose, well, I'w's hungry! Now e'rbody'll think'm really dirt, how long've I gotta hol' out 'fore, 's no fun, livin', leas' when'r dead..."

Chen Xu kept his hand firmly on the bottle.

"Then what about me? I'm alive, aren't I? How do I stand compared with you? I've been criticised up one side and down the other, but I've gone right on living just fine, haven't I?"

Beanpole shook his head, rubbed his eyes, and managed to drag himself off the brick bed.

"You, you got'y'r ticket an' I go' mine. You can talk an' write, you gotta mom an' dad, a wife, sump'n' t' look for'd to. My mom's dead, I'm gonna go fin' m' mom. In m' trunk there's still three cakes 'soap an' new pair 'shoes..."

"Don't, don't go!" Xiao Xiao was on the point of getting down from the bed to stop him, but she was not in time. "Where are you going? It's so cold in the dorm, you'll freeze." She was thinking they should keep 'Pole to stay over with them, but before she could say so he had staggered over to the door, pulled it open, and lumbered outside.

The door swung back and forth, and a freezing blast of air blew in.

They could hear the scattered popping of firecrackers.

"No point in trying to keep him. Better let him go." Chen Xu sighed, leaning against the door. "He's pretty low. He may feel better after he's walked around for a while."

They hurried through their New Year's meal, which now seemed even less appetising. They listened to the radio for a while and cracked some melon seeds, as there was nothing else to do. Although Chen Xu had still not written his self-criticism for saying 'labour reform in disguise', it was not a good idea to dampen their spirits on the last day of the year. A little after eight, Xiao Xiao had him go to the company dormitory to see if Beanpole was back yet. She was still worried.

Chen Xu was gone for a long time, and when he did get home, there were bits of wood in his hair. He held his hand out for her to see. There was a cut on his palm. He said, "Beanpole was by himself in the dormitory, chopping up the wooden frame around the brick bed. I wanted him to come back with me, but he said he wouldn't, no matter what. I helped him split wood for a while so he could get the stove going. Whew! Was that wood split by human hands in the first place? It was hard as coffin boards. Beanpole practically went crazy, hacking off a piece with every swing of his pickaxe. Anyway, now that he's back in the dormitory, he should be okay."

"He won't freeze, will he?" Xiao Xiao was still a little worried. "Why did he say he had three cakes of soap in his trunk just before he left?"

"He was drunk." Chen Xu yawned. "First thing tomorrow I'll go back and invite him over for stuffed dumplings, Okay?"

No one came to visit them. All the families were probably busy stuffing dumplings at that hour. When they had made enough to cover their whole brick bed, they took them outside to freeze. They froze into little silver dollars, hard as rocks and making a clatter if they were thrown on the ground. Afterward, they were tumbled into flour sacks, and when the sacks were full they were hung up under the eaves. Then on the first, fifth, fifteenth, and twenty-fifth people ate these 'five day dumplings', enough to last a whole month. All their happiness for the year was swallowed whole.

Xiao Xiao and Chen Xu stuffed dumplings too. Chen Xu said that he could roll the skins himself, but the 'wafers' he pulled off were all different sizes, and the ones that didn't stick to the board stuck to his hands. He kept on rolling them until he had worked up a sweat. The dumplings Xiao Xiao had stuffed lay squatting there like toads. She giggled at the sight.

"We should have made wonton instead," she said. "Wonton taste better than dumplings."

No good. That might mean we'd be "wantin" all year.

"At home, we made glutinous-rice dumplings for New Years, with meat or sweet bean paste inside and hung up from a pole to dry." Chen Xu smacked his lips and gulped. "And we had sweet dumplings too."

At her grandmother's now, that could be called a real New Years. On the last night of the year, they steamed sweet-smelling new taro roots in the wok. The grown-ups rolled little pearl-like 'good luck balls'.

To eat them brought a whole year of good luck. And there was eight treasures rice, thousand layer dumplings, pork cooked in soy sauce, ham, fish dumplings like snow balls in broth... And when you woke up on New Years Day, you would pull a red packet of New Years money out from under your pillow, and at the head of the bed a pair of red corduroy shoes...

"What do people up here eat for New Years?" she asked, talking to herself.

"High class stuff. Probably just glazed potatoes, or else stir-fried meat."

"What are glazed potatoes?"

"You steam potatoes, then put them into an oiled wok with sugar in it. You stir them around and when you lift them out, each piece pulls threads of sugar with it, like magic."

"Why do they want to pull out threads of sugar?"

"I don't know. Probably because they don't have silkworms up here."

"Do they taste good?"

"Let's try making some tomorrow and see. It's easy!"

"Okay. I want to try them."

"Whatever else you want to eat, I'll find a way."

She wanted to eat pork liver, kidneys, tripe. If that little piglet were alive... Too bad they had sold it long ago. She wanted to eat fish: hairtail, yellow croaker, eel, soft-shelled turtles... And she wanted to eat new taro roots, to scrape caltrops with her teeth; and glutinous rice candy, lotus root, water chestnuts. Like the lines in the model opera: Three meals a day with fish and shrimp, healthy and strong, mount your horses and gallop south to kill the enemy...

All of a sudden, her eyes filled with tears. Why had she wanted to stay here to have the baby? Why hadn't she gone home like everyone else? Perhaps she would never eat any of those delicious things again. She wasn't from the Great Northern Wastes; those were the things she had grown up on. She would never, ever, get used to glazed potatoes and stir-fried pork with scallions. No amount of 'remoulding' would ever do it. She would rather give up everything and go back to settle in a village in the south. She and the Great Northern Wastes were opposed to one another at every turn. Why did she want to give birth to a little native of the Northern Wastes?

"Why so quiet?" asked Chen Xu, looking at her.

She remained silent.

170

"Houses are cold down south. A new-born baby can catch the flu easy," he said.

"Beanpole just wanted to come back," he added.

"Since we don't have to go to work tomorrow, we can sleep in until ten," he murmured with a smile. "Well, let's turn on the radio and see what's on the New Years program..."

She threw herself into his arms and began to sob.

"What's wrong? What's..." Chen Xu was a little alarmed. He kept nudging her. "Does your tummy hurt?"

She shook her head silently. A freezing wave of despair rose from the soles of her feet. She did not know why she had begun to cry either; there was something inexplicable about it.

"I, I can't stop worrying about Beanpole..." she choked out after a long time. She had finally come up with a reason.

The sky did not grow light until very late. There were a few cold pops from firecrackers, then silence.

A dog was yapping somewhere off in the distance. It did not sound at all like a New Year's greeting. And there was the blowing of the wind, 'model operas', and children's laughter, just as jarring and repetitious as usual. It did not seem like the beginning of a year. The sun has risen, the sun has risen, ya yo ya, The sun, its light spreads a thousand miles, a thousand miles it spreads... Above and below for a thousand years, suffering hardship and suffering pain, but today we have finally seen the sun, today we have finally seen the sun... Xiao Xiao lay awake in bed for a while. Then she shook Chen Xu's arm.

"Let's get up early and steam the dumplings. Go invite Beanpole over."

Chen Xu stretched and muttered, "How come it doesn't seem like a new year at all since we're not at home in Hangzhou?"

They got up and washed their faces. Xiao Xiao started heating water to steam the dumplings, while Chen Xu put on his lined coat to go over to the troop and fetch Beanpole.

As soon as he got outside, he turned back and rapped on the door, calling to her. "Say! Come out and look. See all the lanterns!"

Xiao Xiao went outside and, sure enough, every single house had a big red paper lantern hanging up on a pole in front. Streamers hung down from them like horses' tails, rustling in the wind. Joining together, they formed a sea of lanterns covering the whole area... More lines from the model opera:

Mother I drink your wine at parting and it fills me with courage, Strength here I raise the red lantern let its light shine far and The red lantern is our heirloom...

"Say, what's that?" Her attention was caught by the distant scaffolding of the observation tower, which was built up out of round poles and stood about a dozen meters high. There was something that looked rather like a dark human figure at the top.

"There's someone up there." Chen Xu nodded.

"Why would anyone climb up there on New Year's Day?"

"After living on this farm, just to cast his eyes over the whole wide world, I suppose."

"Could he be hanging up a lantern?"

"Doesn't look like it. I don't see anything red. It doesn't look...".

"He's probably going to set off some firecrackers. No one would climb up there just as a joke."

Just as she fell silent, Chen Xu gasped, his face suddenly grave. He was silent for a moment, his lips trembling. Then, with a muttered "It's 'Pole," he broke into a run toward the tower.

'Pole? How could it be Beanpole? What was he doing up there?

She squinted and looked up toward the tower again. Whoever he was, he was still leaning as motionless as a stake against the railing at the top, gazing silently toward the south as though he had something on his mind. Her heart began to race—he really did look a little like 'Pole, the way the ear-flaps on his cap stood up. Come down right now! What are you doing up there? "'Pole!" She shouted. "'Pole..." She waved at him with all her might. "Faster, Chen Xu!" Her voice cracked. She clutched her hands over her heart. Fear and despair swept over her.

She could see Chen Xu approaching the tower. Just as he took hold of the wooden ladder, the figure at the top climbed quickly over the railing. He seemed to stand still for just a moment on the narrow ledge outside the railing, to hesitate for just a moment longer. She had the feeling that he was waving to her. She shut her eyes tight.

A white birch coffin hitched to the tow hook of a tractor.

A little old man with a flat face was pounding his head against the coffin lid, kneading splinters off the lid with his fingers, his face covered with tears. A'gen, forgive me, your dad let you down...

Why are you crying? I've been transferred to the tractor crew, said a voice from inside.

172

The old man went on pounding on the coffin, making the boards thump.

The lid was knocked off. Inside there were three bars of soap, a brand new pair of shoes, and lots of old clothing, every piece of it patched.

The old man wept as he held the clothes. He recognised every piece and pointed here and there on them as though he were telling the story behind every patch.

A'gen, he began to howl again, You never had a good meal in your whole life, never had any new clothes. You had it hard all your life, and now you've died hard too...

All of a sudden, Beanpole arrived from the fields, carrying a sack of peas and shouting, Pease porridge sweet, three pence a bowl.

The old man was following Instructor Yu, crying as he ran, Give me back my son. Hold a memorial service for him!

Instructor Yu's face was like a block of ice. He said, What do you mean! Hold a memorial service for a suicide? You're lucky we're not holding a criticism session!

The old man knelt down, beating his forehead on the ground. Please, please, let me take his ashes back home, don't bury him here in this strange place.

Out of the question. He belonged to the Great Northern Wastes while he was alive, and he'll be a ghost here now that he's dead, shouted Guo Chunmei into a bullhorn. We belong to the Great Northern Wastes in death as in life.

Chen Xu brought a steel plate, a bucket of gasoline, and a bottle of corn liquor. He poured the liquor over the coffin, then drenched it in kerosene and got ready to light it. He was by himself. The place was deserted, now that the city kids had all gone home.

He said, I'll help you with the cremation. Let A'gen go home. If he's buried up here, his spirit will find no peace.

Susie J pulled out his pistol and said to Chen Xu, Are you trying to make trouble? Watch out you don't get thrown in the slammer again!

The old man was tugging at Chief Sun's trouser leg, begging him, Let A'gen come home; poor, poor...

Chief Sun slapped the coffin and yelled, You just remember your place, you old KMT man!

The old man collapsed on the ground, buried in snow up to his waist.

Beanpole hopped down from a combine, his face chalk white.

She asked him, Why did you kill yourself? Don't you know that to commit suicide is to cut yourself off from the masses? He replied wearily, I didn't die. I went to repair the machines.

She placed a wreath on the coffin.

The wreath melted; it was made of snow. Flake after flake, like tree leaves.

Endless, infinite leaves, falling from the sky.

The coffin was covered with wreathes.

A truck came bouncing up. The side-panels had been lowered.

The old man threw himself onto the coffin as though he wanted to jump inside. Some people dragged him off. The coffin was hoisted up into the air and then laid on the truck. The truck drove away.

Chen Xu was tied to a little tree with a leather belt.

She pulled out a wad of money and gave it to Beanpole's father. He was foaming at the mouth, sitting on the snow-covered ground, ceaselessly scraping at the snow with his hands and calling A'gen's name.

There was a fresh black grave in the white snow.

Clusters of yellow gourd flowers were blooming all over the grave.

She was walking across a marsh. There were graves everywhere. They weren't graves, they were ornamental knobs from the tops of pagodas.

A'gen was sitting on one of the knobs crying, Pease porridge sweet...

She felt a colt kicking inside her belly. She was wearing a huge robe. She fell down, down into the marsh. The robe floated to the surface.

21

The tenth of January.

Xiao Xiao was awakened by a slight pain while it was still dark. Something seemed to be moving inside her abdomen, bending back and forth, quietly stretching out and then contracting violently, mild one moment and severe the next. The pain continued, neither getting worse nor going away, like a patient visitor knocking persistently at the door.

She opened her eyes in the faint light and her heart began to pound so loud that she could hear it, quick and uneven.

Was it time? Could it be a miscarriage?

How could it be so soon? Dr. Yang had said the end of the month at the earliest.

She had gone back to work on the sixth day after New Years. The work had not been tiring, just sorting cabbages in the storage cellar. But there had been a strong wind the day before, and she had worked up a sweat walking against it.

Perhaps she had worn herself out over the past few days looking after Beanpole's funeral and taking care of his father, who had come up from Hangzhou. Her back had started to ache.

Was a backache a sign of impending birth? She had gone into Jiamusi with Chen Xu a month before for a prenatal checkup. The doctor had said that the foetus was in an awkward position, lying crosswise, and that if it didn't right itself before delivery, it could be dangerous. He had emphasised that she should go into hospital at the first sign of labour pains.

Anyway, a belly-ache wasn't a good sign, no matter what. They were almost forty miles from Jiamusi and a dozen from the Farm hospital. If...

She shuddered.

"Chen Xu..." She shook him.

"Wake up," she said.

Chen Xu rolled over and mumbled something.

"Hey! I think I may be..." She whispered. "It's starting."

"Oh. It's starting." He echoed her, eyes still closed.

"Really!"

"Really what? What's starting?" He opened his eyes.

"What's starting? What do you think!" Xiao Xiao lost her temper. "Here we are, my stomach hurting, and you..."

At last he was awake. He sat up. "I'll run get the doctor. You wait here." He got out of bed, dressed, and ran out the door without bothering to put on his cap.

Xiao Xiao dozed off for a while. After a long time, she sensed that someone was standing by the bed and smelled the aroma of a medicine kit. She could tell from his voice that it was Dr. Yang, the branch farm doctor. He had been in the army before, and then more than ten years on the farm. He could handle medical cases of every kind, from flu and accidents to anaesthesia and delivering babies. He was on the go all day with his kit, treating patients. He didn't spend much time in the clinic, if only because within minutes of his arrival there'd be a dozen city kids trailing after him wanting their sick leaves signed.

Dr. Yang listened to her description of the symptoms and examined her briefly. Then he turned and said to Chen Xu, "It doesn't look much like she's ready to deliver. You see, the pregnancy lines on her abdomen are not very evident."

Chen Xu nodded dumbly.

Dr. Yang said, "You're both young; you don't understand these things. If you aren't sure when Xiao had her last period, we can't predict the time of birth very well. She's probably just tired herself out at work. A little rest and she'll be fine. The only thing we need to worry about is a miscarriage."

Chen Xu asked, "Should she go to the Farm hospital in town?"

"Can't say if they'd take her. If they didn't, you'd have to turn around and come back. All that bouncing around wouldn't do her any good."

Xiao Xiao remembered what that ride was like. The real surprise would be if the baby didn't come bouncing out half way there. And then there were the sheets at the hospital, the air... She closed her eyes for a moment and said, "If it's not coming yet. we won't go."

The doctor gladly gave her a packet of pain-killers and a three-day sick leave. Then he issued a few instructions and left. He was the most indispensable person on the farm.

Chen Xu sat down beside her and said, "I won't go to work today. I'll stay here with you."

"But, but you'll be docked for skipping work."

"Well, if I'm skipping work, so be it. I wouldn't be able to work with you on my mind anyway."

At noon, Chen Xu made her some gruel, but she took only a few sips, having neither the appetite nor the strength for more. A regular, recurrent ache kept coming on her from somewhere far away. In the midst of this drawn-out, unrelenting pain, she was haunted by an odd premonition, one that filled her with foreboding. If her child was going to arrive early, nothing could stop it. The real disaster would be that none of the things that Chen Xu's family was sending had arrived yet. All the food and everything else that the baby would need were somewhere between the Farm and Hangzhou. She simply could not imagine how they were going to get along if it should be born all of a sudden, before they were prepared for it. They didn't even have anything to wrap it up in. And then, if they couldn't make it to Jiamusi, if it was a cross birth...

She was afraid to go on thinking.

If only it wasn't going to be born now. What would they do if it was? When Lili had her baby they got a nurse. Well, it would be born anyway, sooner or later, and as long as it was, everything would be all right. But so many women died in childbirth...

"What are we going to do?" She moaned, in spite of herself.

"Do you feel like it's really time?" Chen Xu was a little curious.

"I can't tell."

"Well, then, how can I tell?" He scratched his head. "Anyway, all the people who work on the farm have their babies at home. If you're really going to have it, then you might as well go ahead."

"At home? How clever of you! What do you think I am, an old peasant? Just look how unsanitary this brick bed is, and we don't have any antiseptic..."

"Is it still hurting?" he asked, after a long time.

"It's a little better." She hoped it was.

"I don't see how you could be having it so soon." He was quite calm now, and trying to cheer her up. "Dr. Yang said you weren't. There are hundreds of kids in the grade school here, and practically every one of them was delivered by him, so he ought to know. What's to be afraid of? And besides, people don't have babies until their bellies are whopping big. But look at you. With your heavy coat on, no one

177

can even tell you're pregnant, so how could you be ready to have it so soon? Once your tummy is feeling better, we'll go into Jiamusi ahead of time. We can stay over at Bian's place. Everything will be okay..."

Xiao Xiao nodded. She thought that sounded safer.

She lay quietly for a while.

Chen Xu leaned against the heated wall, leafing through a pocket dictionary.

All of a sudden, something clawed at her stomach. And then something was rolling over inside her, tearing at her abdomen from inside, and then at her back.

The pain intensified savagely, each wave stronger than the last. Her whole body had caught fire; she was burning, boiling; a raging tornado rolled her up and swept her away.

She broke out in a cold sweat. Her shirt was soaking and clammy.

"Chen Xu!" She gasped. "Run! Get the doctor! I'm, I'm in a bad way..."

"Now, now. Try to relax. Do you want a drink of water?"

"It's coming, for sure, I can tell..." She groaned in spite of herself.

He dashed out.

It got dark. The house was cold and still. The ceiling seemed very low; it began to tilt, to revolve. The old heating wall, the bare brick bed, everything vanished into a world of dark shadows. There was a bird calling from the tree outside the window—was it a magpie or a crow? It sounded like a life about to begin, calling to her from far away.

She waited.

She struggled.

She fought back; then she surrendered. Agony, then exultation.

Several times she felt as though she were already dead. When one life came into being, another life had to pay the price: death and extinction. She bobbed like a capsized boat, floating in a hurricane, sinking ever so slowly beneath the waves.

A burst of cold air; the door was open. Chen Xu groped his way over to her, blubbering over and over, "Xiao Xiao, Xiao Xiao, are you all right?"

"The doctor?"

"I couldn't find him." He was wiping the frost off of his eyebrows with his sleeve. "I looked everywhere, but I couldn't find him. What are we going to do?"

All of a sudden she was very calm.

"Help me. My padded trousers."

Her trousers were freezing cold and soaked through. She wondered if this was what she had heard people call the bursting of her bag of waters.

Still holding her soaking trousers, Chen Xu crouched down on the floor, his head in his hands.

"Get up," said Xiao Xiao, weary but determined. "Go and look for the doctor again. You have to find him this time."

"What about you?"

"It may be a while longer," she said. It was a woman's instinct. She could do as every mother in the world did and rely on instinct to get through the most perilous moment in her life.

"Just wait. I'll be right back." He rubbed his eyes. He walked over to the door and then looked back. "See that you don't have it until the doctor gets here."

Xiao Xiao was too weary for jokes. If he had orders, he should give them to his child. Now the womb in which she had given the baby life had become her master. He had taken charge of his own fate and was coming into this world impatiently, heedlessly, unable to wait another minute. He would no longer obey his mother—if he was going to be a man. He was flailing away within the dark world that had nurtured him and kept him sealed in for nine months, pushing and beating his way out in search of the one road that led to light and to the world of men.

All the blood in her body seemed to be flowing downward.

A hot wave surged up and drowned her beneath it.

And suddenly the pain stopped and the creature within her body came miraculously twisting out. The flood gates opened with a roar; the black tunnel was flooded with light; sunlight burst forth; her heavy burden was lifted from her in an instant. She felt as light as a leaf, a bit of floss, a cloud, a drop of water. In so brief an instant, her bitter struggle was over. She was free.

By the time the doctor arrived at her bedside, the baby was entirely clear of her body. She was numb, completely empty. And yet her mind was clear, so clear that she felt she had become a different person.

"I never would have believed it, so quickly... So fast, and a first birth, at that. Very unusual..."

She could hear the low voice of the doctor, the snip of the scissors cutting the umbilical cord, the whimpering of the baby, all drifting slowly toward her from the crevices in the earth and the clouds above.

"It's a boy!" Chen Xu was shaking her. "Just like I said all along, a little man!"

She opened her eyes. There in the dim candlelight she could see something small and pink wrapped in a towel. With its tiny, wrinkled-up face, the eyes not yet fully open, it looked like a little old man, or a new-born kitten, a baby rat. She simply could not believe that this was her child. He looked more like a clumsy little animal of some kind. She found it hard to recognise any sign of her own flesh and blood in him. She turned away to avoid him, overcome by a sudden feeling almost of revulsion. Human beings, the world, she herself, none of it made any sense. One life had created another, one that had split off, evolved, and yet she herself was no longer the same. His existence would be separate from her own. It was like a kernal of grain, breaking through its husk and sprouting. And her own abdomen, her whole body, was no more than a husk, a temporary storehouse for that kernal. It was nothing at all like in the stories, where the first sight of her child was supposed to fill her with the joy of motherhood. There, on the bare brick bed, what she had given birth to instead was a feeling of alienation, of distance. There seemed to be something rather absurd in this little creature, so far as she was concerned in it.

He was squealing, just like any other baby. But he did not cry as boldly, as freely as the other baby boys she had heard. He sounded timid, cautious, not at all the way he had behaved while still in the womb. He seemed to have been frightened at birth by the cold, by the squalor of this little hut.

Why was it that new-born babies cried, rather than laughing? Xiao Xiao wondered. Everyone, rich or poor, petty or great, they had all come bawling into the world in the same way. Was life so closely bound up with all its sorrows that everyone proclaimed his loathing and despair at the instant of nativity?

"Congratulations, Comrade Xiao Xiao!" beamed Dr. Yang, as he came back in after washing his hands. He sounded as though she had been chosen a model worker or something. "The foetus was in a bad position, but just before birth, he turned himself around so that the delivery was perfect. Few first deliveries go so easily. Perhaps it has something to do with the way you've kept right on working. Anyway, there aren't that many difficult births among the women on our farm."

"How come it was born so suddenly?" Chen Xu was still puzzled.

180

"Must have been a miscarriage, eh?"

Dr. Yang chuckled. "A miscarriage? Can a miscarriage cry? He doesn't look premature either. Look how long and black his hair is."

Only now did Xiao Xiao notice that her baby had a shiny black head.

"Okay. I'm going now. It's your first experience as a mom and dad, but you'll catch on to it in time." He shouldered his omnipotent bag. "Say, what about the things the baby will need? Haven't you got anything ready? Don't worry, I'll have my wife come over in a little while with some baby clothes. She'll cook up a little rice gruel for you. Get plenty of rest during your lying-in month, and send for me if you have any problems."

He left in high spirits. Father of five daughters himself, he could hardly be impressed by what Xiao Xiao had just been through. Her having a baby amounted to no more than somebody's chicken laying another egg, another pumpkin on somebody's vine. She felt just a little hard done by.

Chen Xu made her some noodle soup with a few onions in it. He also lit the fire under the brick bed, to keep their son from freezing. The soya oil in the soup tasted a little raw, but Xiao Xiao finished it right off. She began to feel hungry, very hungry and also very tired.

"I'll go and register the birth tomorrow." Chen Xu was talking in a loud voice from the front room. She could hear him chuckling to himself. It was the first time he had laughed since Beanpole died.

What shall we name him, wondered Xiao Xiao. She had thought of many names, but they had all been for girls.

"We'll call him Li, Chen Li." Chen Xu stuck his head in and announced gravely.

"Li as in 'first light'? But he was born in the evening."

"Not that Li."

"Li as in plowing, 'Litian'?"

"Not that one either."

"Well, is it the Li of wise old Fan Li?"

"It's Li as in 'leave'." He walked in and stood in the centre of the room, quite full of himself. "I want him to get out of this hole as soon as he can." He bent down and planted a firm kiss on the baby's face.

Xiao Xiao was surprised. Her lips moved, but she did not know what to say. She turned and looked at the baby. Chen Li. Leave. Leave us? No, no. Leaves of grass across the plain, bloom and die in a single

181

year... Li as in eccentric, in anion...

All that night she could hear the baby's intermittent crying at the head of the bed (he always cried softly) and felt bathed in a new emotion. She was exhilarated one moment, restless the next, then depressed, then relaxed. Now that the hurricane had passed, the little island regained its calm, but she still could not close her eyes. She could not understand what she was thinking, and in fact she hadn't thought anything. Chen Xu had been snoring heavily for a long time already. He seemed to have accepted this gift of fate as a matter of course, calmly and philosophically. She leaned over and listened to the other faint breathing beside her, the tiny creature that had been part of her own body only a few hours before, marvelling at how he had broken in on the life that the two of them had just established together.

How could she have become someone's mother?

She was holding a doll with moveable eyes. When she put it down, the eyes closed. When she picked it up, the eyes opened.

When she pressed on its stomach, it cried.

She accidently dropped it on the ground. When she picked it up, the eyes would not move any more and the stomach did not make any more noise.

Chen Xu said, If it can't cry, that's fine with me. The racket was a bother.

Some people she did not recognise passed her door. They had jet black hair. There was a grade school boy with a bulging satchel on his back and a red scarf around his head. A gong sounded at the door of the well house. Perhaps someone was being paraded for criticism. Everyone ran outside for a look. They all had styes, and their eyes were swollen.

She put the baby under a cucumber frame, but he cried.

She put him in a basket, but he went on crying.

She put him in the vegetable cellar. He was still crying.

The root cellar was very long and sloped upward. She was getting tired from walking up it. The potatoes had sprouted and there were strings of small potatoes with clods of earth on them. She tried to dig them out and discovered they were little polliwogs. The polliwogs croaked like frogs and began calling out to her, Big Sister!

She slid down the slope.

All at once, Chen Xu jumped up in bed and reached over Xiao Xiao to touch the baby, muttering, "Why isn't he crying any more? Has he frozen to death? He must have frozen..."

He remembered to turn on the light. There was electricity late at night, and the light went on. Xiao Xiao could see a peaceful little pink sleeping face.

Did she really have a son now?

22

Xiao Xiao began to 'sit out her month'.

"To sit out your month, you just have to sit up there on the brick bed."

"You're not allowed to lie down or to get off the bed, you just sit up there for a month like a good girl."

In the space of three days, practically all of the womenfolk on the branch farm had come in their turn to visit the little cottage—old women, housewives, recent brides, young girls. They said, "Why don't you have a piece of red cloth on the outside door? If you put up a strip of red cloth, men won't come inside." They left themselves entirely out of this prohibition. They counted as 'hot and cold running neighbourliness'. They would snatch the baby up in their arms and pat him for a while, clucking. Then they would say, "What a nice fat baby."

"How lively he is."

"Looks like his mother."

"No! More like his dad! Just look at that forehead."

They were as happy as if the baby were their own, or belonged to someone in their own families. But Xiao Xiao did not even know most of them, had not even exchanged a word with some. Ordinarily they just went bustling noisily by along the highway in their blue or green scarves, carrying gunny sacks or hoes.

An old lady stood at the door shouting, "Hey, Neighbour! Come quick and have a look; one of the city kids has had a baby!"

Apparently, a city kid's baby might be different from those of the masses.

They came in little knots and clusters, taking it all in: mother and child, the bed, and the room, inside and out. Then they would cluck and comment on every last thing.

"Why is it so cold in here?"

"Betcha the fire under the bed don't burn right!"

"Have your old man fix it up. Kids can't take the cold."

184

"Don't worry if the bed gets a little hot. Babies don't mind the heat."

"Aiya! How come you don't have no more diapers than this?"

"Don't you have no eggs neither?"

"When I had my oldest, I ate five hundred eggs."

"I ate eight hundred."

"Millet and brown sugar, that's what'll do it."

"Look at the wide stitching on that quilt! When they do quilting down south, they put the stitches so far apart you'd think they were planting trees."

"Why hasn't she got nothing in the house?"

"Their moms and dads are so far away, don't you know, there's no one to take care of her during her month."

They buzzed away like a swarm of wasps, laughing merrily. Their bright, high-pitched laughter could be heard long after they went out the door.

Xiao Xiao scrambled under the covers and lay down. She had never heard of such a thing, sitting up all through a lying-in month. All the new mothers she had seen when she was a little girl down south had spent a whole month lying down, with a handkerchief wrapped around their foreheads.

No sooner had she tucked in the edges of the quilt than the outside door was pulled open and a blast of cold air blew in. A voice called out, "I brought you a little frozen meat, I'll leave it out here!" After a while, there was someone else. "Here's a dozen eggs. Eat them up." And someone else. "Here's some worn-out clothes; you'd better make diapers for the baby with them."

They neither knocked nor came inside; they just put down their things and left. Xiao Xiao sat up a little, but she could not see who they were. Anyway, they were women who had had babies of their own.

There was another noise at the door, and someone else came in. Xiao Xiao shouted at once, "Come on in!"

It was a tall, skinny, middle-aged woman with high cheekbones and a red face. She put two cabbages, a dozen eggs, a package of brown sugar, and a little pillow down on the brick bed, smiled at Xiao Xiao, and then exploded in noisy astonishment. "What are you doing lying down again?"

Xiao Xiao said nothing.

"If you lie down too much during your month you can ruin

your back, you know!" she fussed. "That's what everyone says around here, so you'd better be careful. It could last the rest of your life."

Xiao Xiao nodded, but lay there without moving.

Why was it that here in the north even a lying-in month was not the same as down south. Did people change according to the place or did places change according to people?

"And don't comb your hair during your month, either. It'll make your scalp hurt." She sat down on the edge of the bed. "And don't bathe, it'll make your bones hurt. Us women don't have an easy time of it. We have to look after our kids, and after grown-ups too. Chairman Mao tells us, 'Once the principal contradiction is grasped, if we lead the ox by the nose, all the other problems can be readily solved'."

She struck Xiao Xiao as quite an interesting woman. She seemed to have a little education, and she could talk.

The woman bent down, looked at the baby, and whispered, "Is he much trouble?"

"He, he's all right. If you give him some sugar water, he goes to sleep."

"Hasn't your milk come in yet?"

"No."

"It's on its way. Another day or two. The best thing would be to stew up some carp; that's the thing to bring on your milk."

Xiao Xiao thought of something she wanted to ask her about. "The baby has had some bowel movements. Why are they black?"

"Nothing to worry about," she chuckled. "That's womb shit. Once that black, gummy stuff is out, his insides are clean. Chairman Mao teaches us, 'New things always have to experience difficulties and setbacks as they grow'."

Xiao Xiao interrupted her. "Who are you?"

"I'm Xu the Storekeeper's wife, everybody here calls me Min." She stood up and dusted herself off. "I'd better go, but you be sure to call me if you have any problems. We live at the east end of the third row. Oh yes, hasn't Dr. Yang made out a chit for you, so you can buy eggs?"

"Yes, Chen Xu has gone over to the barn to get some."

"If you don't have enough, get some from us, hear?"

"I certainly will. Thank you very much, Aunt Min."

"Think nothing of it. Chairman Mao says, 'We hail from all corners of the country and have joined together for a common revolutionary objective.' My old Xu used to be a soldier, and I came up here from Jiangsu in '62. You're still young. Hang around here for a few years and you'll be one of us."

She tucked the pillow gently under the baby's head and added, "Let him lie down more; don't always be holding him. The people around here keep their babies sleeping on their backs, so they don't develop a bulge on the back of their heads. Well, when in Rome, eh? 'Policy and tactics are the lifeblood of the Party'..."

She finally left. Her pronunciation was a mixture of northern and southern, so it was hard to tell where she actually came from. Perhaps Xiao Xiao would be like her some day, mixed on this palette until she was completely changed.

It got dark, and the electricity was off. In the dusk, she heard Chen Xu push the door open, come inside, and throw his satchel full of cold angrily down on the brick bed.

"What's wrong? Did you buy some eggs?"

"The barn boss said they don't have any eggs, that the hens don't lay in the winter." Chen Xu clenched his teeth. "And then he said that if I was so smart, why didn't I take one home and try it myself. That motherfucker!"

He had taken up swearing. Xiao Xiao frowned and said, "Never mind. If there aren't any, well, we'll just do without."

"Shit! Those hicks, those local big shots. Their hearts have been eaten by dogs. Can't we even buy some for money? Who knows whose little nest he gave those eggs to. I saw them just yesterday."

"Perhaps they've all been sold."

"Sold? They're just giving us city people a hard time. It's chauvinism!" he snarled. "What am I going to give you to eat if there aren't any eggs?"

Xiao Xiao said, "Light a candle and have a look in the outside room."

Chen Xu stood in the outer room for a while, saying nothing. Then he came back inside and looked at the things on the brick bed. He muttered, "Where did all this come from?"

"I don't know their names. They're all locals. None of the city kids have come back yet."

The baby started to cry and wriggle around in his blanket. Xiao Xiao pulled on her clothes, sat up, and went to pick him up. The baby was soft and floppy, very awkward to hold. Every time she picked him up she was a little anxious.

"Changing his diaper?" Chen Xu looked up.

187

"Yes."

The outside door opened once again. There was a patter of little footsteps, and then a tiny form was standing in front of them, holding something in its arms.

"My mom and dad said to give this laying hen to Mrs. Xiao. You can either keep it for the eggs or just eat it."

The shadow on the wall had two little turned up pig-tails.

The hen was lying comfortably in her arms, craning its neck as it looked around the unfamiliar place. It seemed quite happy to have come.

Xiao Xiao recognised her as Liu the Brute's eldest daughter, Xiaoqin.

All of a sudden, the pigtails on the wall melted into a tangled thicket. She sniffed and wiped her eyes.

One day, after they had eaten dinner, Chen Xu put their bowls in the pan to soak without washing them and threw on his cotton cap. Then he tied on the latest of a long series of straw ropes and picked up two work baskets. He said, "I saw a tractor going over to the little open pit at Hegang to get coal this afternoon. There's sure to be some coal tonight. I'm going over to wait at the tractor crew garage, to see if I can get some more for us."

"You know, you really do look like a bandit going to pilfer some coal."

"That's what it is, pilfering coal." He wrinkled his nose in self-mockery. "How are we going to get any otherwise? In another few days, everybody will be back from the city."

"Did you get enough to eat?" asked Xiao Xiao.

He nodded, turned, and walked out, pulling the door firmly shut with one hand.

Xiao Xiao was never sure that he really was getting enough to eat. As soon as he had managed to whip together a meal, he had to carry water and chop firewood, then wash diapers. No sooner had he finished with the washing than he had to get another meal together.

The low-lying hay fields had been submerged during the autumn flooding, and then it had snowed early, so they could not walk in the fields. They had planned to wait for a hard freeze, when Chen Xu would go with some other people to cut reeds up at the reservoir, but then all the city kids had got their unexpected home leaves, so no one was left. During the break at New Years, Chen Xu had gone off by himself to one of the most distant fields and cut dozens of bundles of straw, but he could not carry them back. He finally managed to borrow a cart to go get them, but when he was still not home long after it got dark, Xiao Xiao had gone up the road to look for him. She found him sitting dumbly on the empty cart. The ox was busily grazing on the grass along the side of the road. It was so stubborn that no amount of whipping could get it to budge. It turned out to be hungry because it had not been fed after its day's work.

Their wood and kindling pile lay there like a little mound, not even as high as a chicken run. After a big snowfall, they had to scratch around forever just to come up with a little clutch of straw no bigger than a handful of chopsticks.

Chen Xu had been planning to go up to the reservoir to cut reeds again during the Spring Festival, but then there was Beanpole's suicide, and for days afterward he had just sat there silently without so much as touching his sickle.

Without firing, they could not heat their kettle, which was the quick and efficient way of boiling water for cooking. But it seemed as though they were forever short of fuel, and forever worried about it.

Luckily, the furnace for the heated wall was connected with the brick bed, so as long as they could come up with coal and firewood they could cook and keep warm. But each time they lit the stove, smoke would belch from the stoke hole instead, and in no time at all the whole room would be filled with it. They went over all the joints between the bricks, but they could not find where the smoke was getting out. Its invisible, intangible spirit went right on tormenting them just the same, making them cough until their throats were sore and itching.

She did not know where Chen Xu was getting coal and firewood; she only knew that in order to save coal he lit the stove again for each meal. Cooking took a long time, and meals never came at any particular hour. She never knew after one meal when the next one would be. "The firebox is like a tiger's maw. I throw in a whole shovelful of coal and it doesn't even cover the bottom," he grumbled in the outer room. But when he brought the bowls in and caught a glimpse of his son, his face would brighten and his brow relax, and he would say, "One tiger outside and another tiger in here."

Xiao Xiao had been born in the Year of the Tiger. Her appetite increased during her lying-in month. She could never get enough to eat, and even when she did, she was hungry again in no time, so hungry that she was embarrassed, because every time Chen Xu fixed her some millet porridge or an egg, he would sit by himself on the bench in the outer room gobbling down something or other, without her knowing what it was. She never heard him frying anything, but sometimes she saw soy sauce stains around his mouth. When she asked him he would say that he had only licked the top of the soy sauce bottle. One day while he was out, Xiao Xiao crept out of bed, opened the door, and took a look. On the counter in the outer room was a pan of cold hominy and a few roast potatoes soaking in soy sauce.

"Eat with me." After this, she thought of a counter-strategy.

"We each have different things, so we have to eat by turns," he said with a jolly smile, wiping his hands on his jacket.

"If you won't eat, neither will I."

"It will get cold."

"If it gets cold, too bad."

"Well, I'm not the new mother. Just think of it as eating for the baby," he coaxed her.

"No." She was filled with self-reproach, and her eyes flooded with tears.

"Hurry up and eat!" He got impatient, and his eyes flashed with anger.

He left. Out into the dark to check the fire, into the wind and snow in search of warmth.

The baby had fallen asleep. The little cottage recovered its calm. She lay there peacefully, listening to the wind that howled all day over the plain outside the window. An indefinable unease and frustration spread through her. How many more weeks were left? How many more hundreds of hours would she go on lying there, lying there to eat, to sleep, while the baby cried and Chen Xu rushed restlessly about, for what? The dark cottage was like a pen keeping her pinned alive to the brick bed. There was nothing wrong with her, but still she had to lie there.

It slowly began to get lighter in the room, so that the pale little face of the baby next to her and the string of many-coloured diapers hung up by the heated wall were visible. She rolled over and saw a half-moon outside the window, peering in at her. The moon's edge was very clear, as though it had been carefully cut in half with a knife and the other half thrown into outer space.

Could it be that the moon was the sun's child? The sun nourished it with its own light, raising one each month. In a year the sun had twelve children, and each went far away once it was grown up.

190

Was this fragile little thing really her flesh and blood? What would she raise him on? Those little eyes, that little nose, like her and yet not like her, like him and yet not like him, all mixed together so that it was no longer clear what was like her and what like him. Even though everything in the world could be divided up, it was hard to do so with a living being. He was like an anchor mooring them firmly to one another. And yet, day by day, each time the moon came up, the sun was already at its last gasp, that great, pitiful mother...

There seemed to be someone knocking at the outside door.

She listened carefully for a while, and indeed it was someone knocking. Who could it be? It was very rare for anyone to knock on a door around there.

"Come in," she shouted, as loud as she could.

Someone came quietly in, flashlight glowing. But he did not seem to know his way around the cottage and bumped into the water bucket in the outer room and then into the edge of the brick bed.

"It's me." He stood in the middle of the room and said in a very raw and colourless voice, "I came to look in on you."

She was wearing a cotton cap and a heavy padded jacket, just like a man, but Xiao Xiao could recognise the voice as Guo Chunmei's. At some point, she had stopped using their hometown dialect, as the southern kids did among themselves. Now she always talked like a northerner.

Xiao Xiao was taken aback. Guo Chunmei was the only one on the whole Branch Farm who had not gone home, but she had not come to visit once during the past few days.

"Have a seat," she said. She was not sure what to say. She pulled her coat over her as she sat up.

"I've just come back from giving a talk on 'study and application' at the provincial level. I didn't know that you..." Guo Chunmei put a package on the brick bed. "These crackers are for your baby."

It was on the tip of Xiao Xiao's tongue to say that the baby was too young to eat crackers, but she swallowed the words and said, "I haven't seen you in ages."

"The load gets heavier and heavier. This year I'm going to fatten up five hundred piglets."

"Was it only because of the pigs that you didn't go home?"

"Well, there are meetings, too, at Farm Headquaters, the District Office, and Regional Headquarters. So, I was too busy. One's family is a tiny concern compared to making revolution, you know!"

191

"Aren't you, aren't you homesick?"

"No. And if I am, I can overcome it." Guo Chunmei spoke very sternly. "Xiao Xiao, the main reason I came today was to discuss something with you. Say, don't you have a candle?"

"It's on the table; could you light it yourself?"

Guo Chunmei lit the candle. Xiao Xiao noticed that her face was bright red and her eyes were narrower than before. She really wasn't attractive, not even a little bit, to tell the truth. Her brows were so thick, and her clothes smelled of the pigpens.

Guo Chunmei glanced at the baby from a distance and asked, "What is his name?"

"Chen Li."

"'Li' as in plough the field, 'Lidi'?"

"Mm," she mumbled.

The baby started to cry. Just let him cry for a while, but don't change his diaper in front of her. The crying got louder. Ignore him, don't pick him up. But the crying didn't stop, and so she finally had to reach over and pick him up, like it or not. Under Guo Chunmei's watchful eyes, she felt like she was holding a red-hot coal.

"I want to discuss something with you," Guo Chunmei said again. "It's this. It seems to me that you should keep on with revolution now that you've married and had a baby. You absolutely mustn't give up on the remoulding of your world view. You mustn't give up on your study of political theory, it's the most important question of all. It really is!"

Xiao Xiao hung her head and mumbled that they had kept right on studying since their marriage. It was only just lately...

"You can't take a break for even one day." Guo Chunmei got upset, as though Xiao Xiao was likely to split in two at any moment on this account. "I brought you some books of study materials. They are all the latest things. You must catch up with the revolutionary trend of the Criticise Lin Biao Rectification, otherwise you could fall behind, become backward."

Criticise Lin Biao Rectification? Xiao Xiao opened her eyes wide in amazement. Something she hadn't heard of before. An outside world from which she was completely cut off.

Guo Chunmei pulled several books of new study materials out of her brown padded coat and handed them to Xiao Xiao. She stood up and said, "I'll be going. If you have any problems, you should rely more on the Organisation to solve them. Don't..."

Don't what? She didn't say. She paused at the door and gave Xiao Xiao a look full of significance. She added, "You must go on helping Chen Xu."

The outside door was thrown open with a bang. Something heavy fell on the floor with a thud, and Chen Xu shouted, gasping for breath, "I got some! Quite a lot!"

He barged into the room and just missed stepping on Guo Chunmei's foot.

Xiao Xiao was startled out her wits.

It was his cheeks, his lips, his teeth, his nose; he was jet black all over. His clothing and cap were black too, and covered with coal dust. Only the frost on the fringes of his cap was grey. In the dim candlelight, he looked like a big black bear who had just crawled out of a hollow tree.

She broke into a wide smile. She felt like crying.

"You have no idea how close it was. As soon as the cart stopped, people were jumping onto it from all sides. It was every man for himself. Good thing I'm big and strong. I shoved them all aside." He waved his arms around to demonstrate. "I've got to go back and make another trip. How's the boy?"

He moved closer to have a look at his son, but kept his distance so as not to get coal dust on him. He stretched out his neck and Xiao Xiao caught a whiff of alcohol.

Guo Chunmei spoke up, "Say, Chen Xu, There's something I've been wanting to ask you about."

Chen Xu glared at her over his shoulder and said coldly, "Oh, so it's you, eh? I thought it was one of the people from around here. What an honour."

Guo Chunmei forced a smile and said, "We're missing quite a few wooden troughs from the pigsties. I was wondering if, if you might have seen..."

"Nope!" Without waiting for her to finish her question, Chen Xu cut her off, speaking Hangzhou dialect. It was as though he had known well in advance what she was going to ask.

Guo Chunmei glanced toward the outer room and added, "I think they must have been stolen for firewood."

"Why don't you replace them with cement ones, then they'll be safe from thieves."

And with that he walked out and slammed the door.

Xiao Xiao felt a little ill at ease. She was on the point of saying something to lessen the tension when there was a noise at the front door and Aunt Min burst in, all in a tizzy and shouting as she came, "Hey, Xiao, your milk come yet?"

She had been by just the day before to show Xiao Xiao how to squeeze out the thick yellow colostrum. The coming of Xiao Xiao's milk had been her chief concern for the past few days.

"I'll be going," said Guo Chunmei, and she was out the door in a few steps before Xiao Xiao could reply.

"Isn't that girl the leader of the pig squad?" asked Aunt Min. "I hear she's quite a worker, gets as much done as five or six people, and then studies Chairman Mao's works once it gets dark. She can recite several hundred quotations from memory, where I can only do a hundred or so. I'm way behind her. Chairman Mao says, 'Modesty helps one go forward, whereas conceit makes one lag behind'. Well, how're your breasts doing?"

"Still swollen and tender, but there isn't much..."

"Let me have a look."

Aunt Min deftly pulled Xiao Xiao's shirt open with one hand and clucked in sudden amazement, "My! They're so big! Such big breasts, why don't they have any milk?"

Xiao Xiao blushed.

"Well!" Min gave her thighs a resounding slap. "I'll bet that your being upset has caused fire to ascend and make a blockage. That's no problem, get a few fish somewhere and stew up some fish soup. That'll bring in your milk for sure." She was pulling on a corner of her scarf. "Now, there's Bull, from your company. He's back from Hegang and just yesterday he was for borrowing some tackle from my Xu so he could go fishing up at the reservoir. I'll go have a word with him."

"Don't," begged Xiao Xiao, plucking at her dress. "I, I don't like fish. It's the smell. And besides, Bull..."

"What's the matter? He wouldn't refuse to help you out when you need it. Are you still thinking about those fights the first year you were here? They were just kids, bound to have a few run-ins. Don't give it another thought. You know, when people have been around a place for a long time they're bound to grow on one another, doesn't matter about southern or northern. They say he's taken a shine to a southern girl from the third company. What's to be shy about? Once you get angry and the fire rises, your milk can't come down. Just relax and get plenty of liquids. If you ask me, you'll have plenty of milk. When I was young and had my first little grabber, my oh my, my breasts were no bigger than this." She joined her hands in a circle to illustrate. "That's how tiny they were, but I still had plenty of milk. He could nurse to his heart's content. You can't expect everything to come easy. Chairman Mao teaches us..."

She paused, evidently at a loss for an apt quotation, and sighed as she leaned over to pat the baby. Then she asked, "You mentioned his name yesterday. Now what was it? I've forgotten again."

"Chen Li."

"Hmm. That's his official name. What about his baby name?"

"He, he doesn't have one."

"How 'bout my naming him? Call him, call him Dog's Leftover. How do you like that?"

Dog's Leftover? Puppy? Not Beanie, or Chipmunk?

"Oooh, Li'l Dog's Leftover!" She teased him. "Dog's Leftover, nobody wants you, you'll grow up big and strong!"

The baby opened his eyes and gazed silently up at the ceiling, lost in thought.

His eyes were big and round, transparent and calm like a pale blue bay. Even the most violent hurricane could raise no waves on it. There was an innate gravity and confidence in that pure, tranquil blue that always made Xiao Xiao uneasy. It seemed to shine with a look of worldly wisdom inconsistent with his infant face. When he rolled those little straw-coloured beads around, they overflowed with an unmistakable indifference and weariness born of repletion with all that human life could bring.

She knew that look well; she had seen his father in it.

But before, in the pile of Red Guard posters, on the stage before the crowds of thousands, his eyes had not been like this.

"Oooh, Li'l Dog's Leftover, eat your fill and take a nap." Aunt Min was still fussing happily over the baby. She reached over, and her hand fell on the study materials that Guo Chunmei had left.

"Well!" She shook her head in dismay, quite put out for a moment. "If you ask me why you've got no milk, it's from reading this stuff all day! You listen to me—you're not allowed to read during your lying-in month. You could ruin your eyes for ever."

"They're for the criticise, the criticise Lin Biao..." She reached for the books.

"I don't care who they criticise!" She picked the books up and threw them on the floor. "What is this stuff, don't you care whether your baby gets any milk? If I catch you reading the next time I come,

I'll throw the lot of them in the fire!"

And with this she steamed out.

Xiao Xiao was afraid to read any more, afraid to cry, afraid to lose her temper. She did her best to believe that if she could just follow all the rules, she could be just like all the other young mothers there and have copious streams of milk flowing from her swollen, tender breasts.

But days passed, and still the baby cried when he had finished nursing.

As he cried, he would open his little mouth and twist his white little neck around to look for something to the left, smacking his pink tongue and hunting anxiously. Finally, he would give up and twist around to the right, moaning plaintively and looking for that warm soft breast, for that wellspring of life.

It made her heart ache to watch. So she would pick him back up. He would clamp down hard on her nipple and refuse to let go of it again. He was like a little lizard, keeping his face pressed tight against her breasts, sucking viciously for the longest time. His little mouth was like a pump trying to drain her whole chest dry, sucking until her nipple got sore. If she moved even slightly, those tiny, tough little gums would follow after in a panic, clinging doggedly to her. If she was feeling patient, she would have to sit up for two hours to nurse him once, sitting there until her back and legs ached. She would get so tired that she would doze off, but as soon as her arms relaxed a shooting pain would drag her awake. If she was mean and pulled her nipple out of that pouting little mouth, a spell of agonised howling would follow, as though to tear the low roof off of their little cottage. He had right on his side and went on endlessly. She would pick him up again, and then put him back down.

And so it went, round and round without a break.

One was forever hungry, the other forever sleepy.

The more she worried about it, the less milk she had. Her milk was like water oozing drop by drop from a crevice in a cliff, each drop gathering for a long time before it fell. To bring in a pump simply used up the future supply in advance.

Chen Xu fed him sugar water, which he drank with gusto. But each time she changed his diaper he would go on crying. Their shipment of things from home was somewhere along the thousands of miles of rail line: how far away was it now?

Xiao Xiao often heard the baby crying as she slept. It was a dream, but she could not wake up. And when she did wake up, the baby would have worn itself out crying, would have cried itself hoarse, would have fallen sound asleep. And then she would wonder if the crying had only been a dream.

Chen Xu was busy at home and outside. His brown coat turned into a black coat, but his teeth turned brown, and his face as well. His hair grew long and his beard thick. He looked like a grey blur all over.

One morning he sat up as soon as it got light, threw his clothes on, and slipped into his shoes. He sat numbly on the edge of the bed for a while and then said, "I think I'll go into town today and see if I can buy some powdered milk. Do we... How much money is left?"

"Everyone says there's none for sale. There's only our, our last five dollars."

"Well, I'll give it a try. It's not going to arrive on our doorstep all by itself." He got the money out of the chest and put it in his pocket. "There's some wheat porridge in the pan. You can heat it up for yourself."

He tied the rope around his waist, kissed Xiao Xiao on the cheek, and left.

It was a crisp, cold day. The sunrise stained the frosty crystal tracery on the window like so many pieces of rainbow-coloured glass. That church in which their affection had first sprouted, how could it have been in a church? It had been a church. At the top of the stairs there was a round stained-glass window. It looked like a seven-coloured flower. That flower could grant seven wishes, but he had wasted them all. Only the last flower was left. What would the last wish be? How could it be the last one? Of course it was the last, the other six flowers had flown away. Could the last one have been the baby? No, that was her own secret. No, there weren't even any secrets any more. The biggest secret was that there were no secrets. Who said so? The last wish was for powdered milk. If only he wouldn't come home empty-handed. No, no that wasn't it, it was for spring, to watch the bamboo sprouts burst through their husks in a bamboo grove, to go to the botanical garden and smell the scent of magnolias, No, no, it was planting sunflowers, planting eggplants and red peppers... No, no, no, she had no wishes, no wishes at all. She was not thirsty or hungry or sore or tired or sleepy either; she was numb all over, her mind was blank. Lying on this bare, freezing brick bed, with her baby shrieking for the breast, how could she have any wishes of her own to speak of, how could she be qualified to wish? Lying-in months must certainly have suffocated people, it was just that no one said so, that was all.

The hut was stuffy and dark, it was smothering her. Whenever it occurred to her that she would have to spend another twenty days there in complete boredom before her month was up, she sank into deep despair. At times she would go wild with a kind of frantic energy. At others she would weep silently.

The winter cold was getting worse and worse. How terribly cold it was! All the little duckling could do was swim back and forth, trying to keep the water from freezing over completely. And yet his sphere of action contracted evening by evening. The water was freezing; people could hear the grinding and splitting of the ice blocks. The little duckling could only go on paddling his two feet to keep the water from freezing entirely, but finally he collapsed and lay still, frozen solid into the ice.

And after her lying-in month was over? Then what? After that, after that, she would be a mother in this little hut, an old woman, a...

She was swimming in a great river.

The river was swollen with water; it flowed slowly past the pile of fuel outside their door.

The water was milky white and steaming. There were several fountains on the surface, spraying water up into the air with a gurgle.

Chen Xu was lying on the bank, drinking from the river in huge gulps.

As he drank, the water level gradually dropped. He raised his head and said, This isn't water, it's milk.

I have a nanny goat; look out the window.

She looked outside, and indeed there was a goat standing on the snow, with a pair of bright red udders hanging all the way to the ground. The goat's milk was oozing steadily out and turning into a great river. The goat bleated as though calling for its mother. The baby was bleating too, like a little goat kid.

Chen Xu filled a bottle with milk and fed the baby from it. The baby smacked his lips and went on drinking happily until his little belly swelled up, blinking and smiling.

Look, he can smile. She started to smile too.

It's from drinking goats milk, said Chen Xu. I bought the goat from an old peasant. It was five dollars. There was no powdered milk in town, so I thought he'd better drink goats milk; it's good for him.

He won't turn into a goat, will he?

I don't think so. Foreigners drink cows milk and they don't turn into cows.

An old peasant dressed in ragged clothes and a worn fur jacket burst in their door, grabbed Chen Xu by the arm, and shouted, Hey, young fellow! You swindler! You cheated me out of my goat.

What's all this? What's all this? Instructor Yu walked up.

He swindled me out of my goat. He said my goat was sick and was going to die if it wasn't treated. He said he could cure it and then he led it away. The old peasant was sobbing. He said the name of some strange disease.

Is this true, Chen Xu? asked Instructor Yu.

Chen Xu ignored him and scooped some water out of the river with the milk bottle and drank it. The water gave off an overpowering stench of alcohol.

Take the goat away, ordered Instructor Yu. He convened a large criticism meeting at once and wrote out a banner—Criticise All Political Swindlers of the Liu Shaoqi Ilk.

The old peasant turned back and said, Look, General, he isn't Liu Shaoqi, he only swindled a nanny goat and drank a little milk, nothing too bad. Seeing how he's so hard up and his baby's got no milk to drink, I'll just sell him the goat and leave it at that.

No profiteering allowed! Instructor Yu kicked the goat.

Guo Chunmei led off shouting slogans: If We Don't Block the Capitalist Road, We'll Never be Able to Open Up the Road to Socialism!

Chen Xu roared with laughter.

Aunt Min shouted, Dog's Leftover got the runs. Call the doctor right away.

Doctor Yang came, listened to his chest, took his temperature, and said, Drinking goats milk is hard on his digestion. It has brought on inflammation of the intestine. He'll have to go to the Farm Hospital.

A tractor drove up and stopped in front of her. The driver stuck his head out and beckoned to her. Get in. Liu the Brute is having me take you.

It smelled like alcohol in the cab, and she started coughing. The driver drove the tractor like a drunk, swerving this way and that. She thought, It's because the driver is drunk, that's why the tractor is going like this. She took a more careful look at the driver, and he turned out to be Chen Xu.

Don't drink any more, please don't! she said.

We'll be home soon; don't worry. It wasn't wine I drank, it was fish broth. If you don't believe me, take a sniff.

She sniffed, and it was fish broth after all. It smelled delicious.

Where did the fish come from? she asked. If there's fish there'll be milk. If there's milk, we won't have to go to the hospital.

The fish were caught by Bull. He gave us half a sack full, said Chen Xu. I want to go learn how to fish from him.

The tractor stopped in front of their house. Big fat carp were piled up at their door, flopping around on the snow. One with red scales was gasping, opening and closing its mouth, saying, Please Granddad, won't you let me go? I'll grant your every wish!

A snow-white swan flew down and landed at her feet. Out of its bosom rolled a pure white egg.

23

They had made it through the coldest weeks of winter, but still the wind blew hard. It was tough and gristly now, with a little more give to it than before, no longer the vicious, rasping wind of midwinter, slicing and sawing at foreheads and necks. Instead, it kneaded and rubbed with broad, rough hands, while its blades cut to the bone.

The day after the nanny goat business, the Branch Farm messenger told Chen Xu that their shipment was at the station and that if he did not pick it up promptly the station would charge him a penalty. Chen Xu had already missed a couple of weeks' work while taking care of Xiao Xiao, and although Liu the Brute had given him a leave, his daily dollar twenty-five in pay had still been docked. He went to get an extension of his leave, but 'Susie J' would not let him go until he had written out a self-criticism. And so he spent half an hour writing himself up as 'deserving ten thousand deaths for cheating the poor and lower-middle peasants' and took it to the Branch Farm office. By this time, he had missed the morning tractor and had to walk out to the highway and hitch a ride to town on a horse cart carrying fodder.

The country along the road was streaked with dead weeds and unmelted snow, with here and there a stretch of black earth awakened by the wind and staring drearily at the blue sky. A few puffs of frozen cloud shivered along as though their one fear was that the slippery wind should melt all the worries that weighed upon their hearts. By the time the cart had gone a few miles, Chen Xu felt all the warmth in his body dissipating. His shoes were like an iron vise, squeezing so tight that his feet ached.

He curled up, folded his arms, and squinted out at the vast empty fields that stretched around him.

If their shipment had come just a little sooner, the goat business might never have happened. It wouldn't have. Why should anyone who was any good, anyone who was alive, anyone who was for real, have to rely on a goat for support? What had gotten into him? What had possessed him? It was only a nanny goat. A guy raises a goat, the goat raises his son; he's got something to feed the goat, why nothing to feed a human being? He wasn't up to being anybody's dad; the baby might as well just die, everything was such a mess. It was just as well the goat was taken away, otherwise when the boy grew up he'd only be able to bleat; make a good pedlar, crying his wares. The strange thing was that Xiao Xiao hadn't bawled him out at all. She had had a good cry, holding the baby in her arms, you could count that, and she had tossed and turned all night, but she had said nothing. All her words had been carried away by the goat. In fact, the nanny-goat had been more than willing to be a nurse—was there any difference between one kind of kid and another? These days people were living pretty much like goats anyway. All they could do was bleat. Sold? To whom? For how much? A priceless treasure painless sacrifice helpless quandary propertyless classes heedless of gods and men careless and thoughtless baseless charges gone back to the responseless bless the name of Amida Buddha...

He looked up and saw a solitary old oak tree rising over the snowy ground up ahead. It was an uncanny looking tree, the heavier boughs shooting this way and that, the smaller twigs writhing like vines. It was as if the big wooden observation tower on the Farm were thick with snakes, hissing and flicking their tongues, showing their fangs and tails. He remembered the time that he and Xiao Xiao had passed by there on their way to Hangzhou. That had definitely been in summer, and in the first morning light the bare old tree had stood there without a single shoot or leaf. The strange thing was that now, as he caught sight of it in the distance, it was covered with round brown leaves. They hung all over the boughs, the very image of vigorous and abundant life.

Haunted tree, are you really so untamed? You die in summer and come back to life in winter. Are you resolved to resist to the end? You create miracles, but your miracles will never create us.

As the horses' hooves swept past, the round leaves covering the tree flew up into the air and scattered in all directions, shooting like arrows up into the heavens and sinking to the earth like stones, raising a wind and whipping up the snow. Those leaves, no, wings, fluttered and squeaked and chattered.

It was a flock of sparrows. He spat on the ground.

Now, here was trickery for you. The haunted tree can lie why should only the haunted tree be unable to lie the haunted tree's lies were just more haunting. Or it could just be called playing a trick called a false appearance called pretending called a misunderstanding anyway it wasn't a lie. A lie was to protect oneself was when there was no alternative was when it could't be helped was a temporary escape was taking to the hills as a last resort. There has never been anyone who didn't lie I'd swear to it that goat was no more than a little joke how could it have been a lie? Lying has a definite aim a programme a plan has stages and is never acknowledged. If you were cheated you had it coming to you who told you to forget that sparrows rest on bare trees in winter, become leaves and then fly off on the wind. Who told you to forget that the haunted tree hasn't had leaves for more than a hundred years that's why it's called the haunted tree. There's a sign here a portent a fortune an omen! I know that this is its way of telling travellers whether their luck will be good or bad. Sparrows turn to leaves and then fly away you see something in it but even if you do no one can get out of the palm of its hand...

The whip cracked.

As the end of the whip whizzed through the air, a few bunches of green pine needles came drifting down. The cart was just going through a grove of pitch pines. The cartman was standing up on the cart, aiming his whip at a brown-coloured ball up in the pines. Another crack and the furry ball fell to the earth, rolled over several times on the snow, and disappeared into a clump of weeds.

"Shit! Got away." swore the cartman.

"Pine cone?" he asked, knowing that he was off the mark.

"Squirrel," grunted the cartman. "I get them on the paws, one with each crack; take 'em back for the kids to play with."

He turned back and saw that the haunted tree, like a dragon's paw, had already recovered its abundant foliage and looked just as it had before.

By the time he had lugged the heavy package back from town, it was almost dark. He pushed open the door. It was pitch dark inside the cottage. He reached in and pulled the light switch. Xiao Xiao was sitting motionless on the brick bed, like a statue, looking out the window. She heard the door open, but did not turn around.

"What's wrong?"

Silence.

"What's wrong?" He dropped the package and walked over to her.

The baby was awake, lying there with his eyes open, silently sucking on a corner of the quilt, as though he had something on his mind.

He tugged on her shoulder. It was wet and clammy. He looked into her eyes. They were bloodshot.

"What's wrong?"

"Nothing," she said dully.

"You've got something to say. I can see it in your eyes."

"How can you tell?"

"Because I've got something to say too."

"Then you speak first."

"All right. On one condition."

"What is it?"

"If you cry during your lying-in month, your eyes will hurt for the rest of your life."

"I wasn't crying. It was Chen Li."

"I've brought the shipment from home. Let him eat it all in two weeks."

She took a breath and opened her eyes wide.

"When he's eaten it all, the way will be clear."

"You mean that in two more weeks, Li will be a month old?"

"When he's a month old, he'll be able to ride the train."

"No matter how many days and nights it takes?"

"Of course not."

"And the train fare?"

"I'll borrow it. Gladly. I can pay it back a little each month."

"Will, will your mother take him?"

"Of course she will. Her first grandson, she'll love him to death."

"He, he's still too young."

"We can find a nurse in the country and send her some money each month."

Silence.

"Once we have him settled, we can come back to the farm. Without the baby dragging us down, things should be better. Otherwise we're done for. We'll turn into a couple of dotty old ladies. The crew of the prospecting team..."

Silence.

"If you're going to cry, I won't say any more."

She looked up slowly, her face covered with tears. She wiped them away with her sleeve and burst out, "How could you think of everything I did? Who told you? I've been thinking about it for days, but I was afraid to say anything. How could you think of it too? How could you be so cruel, to give him up, how could you...?"

She threw herself headlong into his arms and began to sob.

The haunted tree, it was the haunted tree that told me, that was it. It couldn't be wrong; it couldn't.

He crouched on the bed. He was too rough in brushing away her tears, and she moaned. He wiped his wet hand on his knee.

The baby had fallen asleep. The faint line of his brows and soft forehead contained within them a natural indifference and tranquility. It struck Chen Xu that he had no choice but to send the boy away.

24

Xiao Xiao was still not welcome. It seemed as though nothing at all had changed in that crowded little alley, except that the slogans on the walls along the lamp-lit street had been replaced a few times.

The one who was welcome was the latest addition to the Chen clan, the first grandson, Chen Zhongshun. As soon as he got off the train, Chen Li turned into a different person, a native of Hangzhou named Chen Zhongshun. It was, of course, not Chen Xu who had bestowed life on him, but Chen Xu's father, or his father's father's father. So, historically speaking, only his grandfather could undertake so fundamental a matter as giving him a name. Chen Li no longer existed. And, since he had already left that 'hole', he might as well be Zhongshun now. By the change of one word, state and family alike were given their due, tradition and reality both taken into account. There was, moreover, an element of making the past serve the present as well. Xiao Xiao smiled wryly.

The neighbours were all fit to be tied. They came to see him in an unbroken stream. A one-month old baby boy who had ridden the train for three days and four nights, across the Sungari River, out of Manchuria, across the Yellow River and the Yangtze, he was a genuine out-and-out rarity, the very biggest piece of news in Fan Alley. Why, just look! There's something to be said for going off to a village after all, if they come back with a grandson. Yeah, Heilongjiang can't be all that cold if they can still have babies there, we can stop worrying. Uh-oh. If we don't watch out, our two girls will be coming back fat. Then what? Hm, I told you so. You put a bunch of boys and girls together without their folks around, and they'll be getting in trouble...

Confronted with that teeming alley, Chen Zhongshun's serene little eyes were just as indifferent as ever.

Once the life-saving shipment of sugared milk powder had finally arrived on the Farm and he had acquiesced in this substitute for milk—beggars, after all, could not be choosers—his little face had got pinker and glossier by the day, and his crying had grown milder. He slept happily as the train rumbled past dozens of stations to the nap, making the gently swaying car a comfortable cradle. Now that the Spring Festival was past, trains running south were much less crowded than usual, and they could dry out his diapers on the seat backs. No one gave them any trouble. When their fellow travellers found out that the two of them were city kids from the South, coming back from the frozen Great Northern Wastes to bring home a rich little harvest from going 'up to the mountains and down to the villages', they all, no matter where they had come from, smiled at them indulgently and let them have seats out of the draft to sleep on.

He had come home peacefully and easily. The real mother of this baby who had once belonged to the Great Northern Wastes was the black earth itself.

But his young parents, who had been nursed on the milk of West Lake and the Qiantang River, would be bidding him farewell and going back to that black earth so far away.

Why was it always betrayal? Two mothers in a row. But they exchanged their roles. This retribution would cancel out all the faults and regrets on both sides. She felt suddenly free of a debt that had weighed upon her heart. Was she not exchanging herself for him? Perhaps it was fair this way.

In order for them to get back to the Farm on time, the baby's grandmother got someone to find a nurse right away.

It was drizzling the day they took the baby to the wet nurse's home in the outskirts of the city. It was February in the South, and in the space of a few days the willows had put forth a layer of tender shoots, veiling half the horizon. The wheat had leapt up to a height of six inches, glistening and green. Fuzzy little lavender flowers were squeezing their way out among the dark leaves of the broad bean vines, and foot-long silver carp were leaping with a splash into the air above their ponds.

I ask where an inn is to be found/ An oxherd points toward a village amid the distant apricot blossoms/ How could I ever forget the South/ The rivers in springtime green as indigo/ Spring wind—willow leaves in thousands/Six hundred million in China—all Emperor Shun and Yao/The exquisite look of misty hills in the veiling rain/ I come back home treading on blossoms, my horse's hooves fragrant/ Beautiful, not competing for spring/ Only calling that it is coming/ Perfect in light rouge or heavy powder...*

* These are lines taken randomly from poems written by different ancient Chinese poets and Mao Zedong.

"Watch out for the umbrella." Xiao Xiao nudged Chen Xu with one arm.

Wrapped up in his blankets, the baby nestled in the crook of her arm. He opened his eyes and looked up at the golden oil-cloth umbrella, his little face a rich light brown like a fresh orange. He kept his silence, calmly accepting whatever should be the disposition of his fate. The day they had left the Farm, Chen Xu had carried him as though he were a big wad of cotton, firmly secured under no less then three layers. The bus arrived at their corner packed tight as a cart-load of beancakes. She was genuinely concerned that the baby might suffocate. When they finally reached the little town and got off the bus, she turned back his blanket, and there he was, placidly sucking on a corner of it, eyes wide open and waiting as though nothing were happening.

They walked into a little village beside the highway.

The nurse was a village woman in her thirties with a somewhat sallow complexion. Her breasts bounced abundantly inside an oversized old jacket. Her son was already six, and her daughter had just turned one and was ready to be weaned, so she wanted to earn a little money for her family by taking a baby in to nurse while she still had her milk. She would get twenty dollars a month, hand five over to her production team, and still clear fifteen for herself. That wasn't bad compared to toiling for work-points in the team, so all the women with kids wanted to be wet nurses. They could earn work-points at the same time they were looking after the kitchen, the pig pen, and the chicken run. They went on eating every day, and the rice turned into milk, which then turned into fifteen dollars. It amounted to eating for free, to turning oneself into a mint, to growing a pair of piggy banks. Everyone did have their own way of getting by, in very truth. She looked clean and good-natured. She took the baby, unbuttoned her jacket, and clasped him to her bosom, saying over and over again, "He has such good features, he'll grow up to be an official for sure."

She started cooing at him, calling him A'zhong, Doggie, Li'l Threesie. It was as though he had already become her own baby boy. Was he really Doggie, or Dog's Leftover, or Zhongshun? Anyway, Chen Li was no more; he had lived for only thirty days. She kept them on for lunch: fried eggs with greens, and fried eggs with pickles. What about shoots from the bamboo grove? Snails from the pond? "You'll have to excuse us, we grow sweet potatoes on our private plot because there isn't enough grain, and we can't just help ourselves to public property from the pond whenever we feel like it." She smiled sheepishly.

After lunch, she saw them all the way back to the bus stop, carrying the baby. As the bus appeared in the distance, she licked her chapped lips and said, "Don't you worry about him. Your boy will grow on his own. When you come back next year he'll be able to call you mama."

Xiao Xiao blushed. Mama? And how could he call her mama? It had never crossed her mind that she could actually become someone's mama. She smiled gratefully at the nurse, staring involuntarily at her swelling breasts, the wellsprings of her baby's life. When he learned how to say mama, the first person he called that would not be she herself, but this woman who was raising him. He would recognise as his mother surely not her, but this woman. She had already stripped away her authority and her love. How vile those twenty dollars were. She envied the two damp stains on the front of that old shirt. What ugly yellow teeth!

She went on smiling gratefully. Without this nurse, she and her boy would be at the end of their rope.

"Would you like to hold him once more, Comrade Xiao? When the bus comes there won't be time. A'zhong, A'zhong, do you understand? Your mommy and daddy are going far, far away..."

She murmured at the baby, looking down at him. Then she held him out to Xiao Xiao.

Xiao Xiao instinctively retreated a step.

The baby had fallen asleep. His head lolled to one side, a picture of unconcern. He was breathing very lightly, his nostrils scarcely moving. He was without worries or concerns. He cared not the slightest where he was. His thin lips puckered for a moment. Such indifference. Such disdain. There was a wide space between his almost invisible brows. The world meant nothing to him. Only when Chen Xu gently pulled his blanket aside to kiss him did he open his eyes and glance around, revealing two sparkling little amber pearls. How terribly cold they were, like two frozen bubbles.

You're a bad mother.

I can't help it. I don't have any milk.

You're a bad mother.

I don't have any money.

You're a bad mother.

I...

You have me.

You're a burden. I don't want you.

209

I don't want you either.

The bus began honking its horn. The people waiting to board pushed forward. At the last moment, she turned and looked back at him. If only he would start to cry; it would mean that he can't do without me. But he paid no attention. He was fast asleep and showed no sign of saying farewell. He did not even look at her. She pushed her way resolutely onto the bus, hanging onto Chen Xu's coat for dear life. Mama! Don't you want me any more? She heard him shout. She wanted to jump off the bus and take him in her arms.

The doors closed. She smiled and waved to the wet nurse and the baby. She had thought that she would cry, but not a tear came. She was as calm as the pond by the road. A flowering crabapple tree faded into the fine misty rain. Saying goodbye was not at all so difficult as she had supposed, nor had she felt the so-called maternal grief that she had imagined. She was leaving very calmly; it was even something of a relief, as though she had only found the baby and now had finally returned him to his family. Why in her case had there been no trace of the final farewell scene so common in stories?

Chen Xu stared out the window. He had said practically nothing all morning.

The rain seemed to have stopped, but the fields were still shrouded in mist. When the bus stopped, they could hear the frogs croaking in the fields. Were those frog princesses in the water or on land?

The mist cleared a little; the damp road gleamed in the humid air. Not long before they reached the city she saw a tall jade magnolia whose pure white flowers had been swept to the ground by the rain and now lay scattered in the mud. A row of freshly felled old parasol trees lay tangled beside the road. For some reason, her eye was caught by a nondescript dark shape, a wad of black fluff in a fork of one tree. It was rolled over and mashed flat, with a corner sticking up like a nestling with its mouth open, chirping for food. It was a birds nest.

Suddenly she felt all hollow inside, so much so that she reached nervously out into the packed crowd of passengers for Chen Xu's arm. But she was surrounded by strangers. She hung her head. "Forgive me!" She wrenched herself around toward the back of the bus, but she could no longer see anything there.

25

She kept catching sight of something in the distance, walking toward her.

Dust filled the air, and nothing was clearly visible. The clang of a bell could be heard squeezing its way through the haze. It was a horse, but a strange horn grew from its head.

There was a tiny human form on the horse's back, wearing a brown woolen army cap and with a military overcoat over his shoulders. A long black beard was visible beneath the cap.

She asked who he was and where he came from.

He said that he was the new Party Secretary just transferred to their farm. He patted the wicker baskets slung over the horse's flanks. They held clothing, a wok lid, a chopping knife, a rice box, dried pepper, and garlic. He walked into the mess hall and lined up to buy a sponge cake, a sponge cake so big that it could not be held up even with both hands. He bent over it and nibbled away, smacking his lips. There was a crowd of rabbits under the eaves eating the dregs left over from making bean curd. He wiped his hands on the front of his jacket and his mouth on his sleeve, and whistled for his horse.

A tractor driver was just emptying a gunny sack of bean seed into the seeder.

Say, how much seed do you sow on this field, he shouted. An older worker with a pockmarked face was kneeling on the ground and noisily sharpening a knife.

The tractor was going around the field in circles. She held a spring-operated toy frog down with her hand.

Hey, how many seedlings are you keeping? He started swearing, standing arms akimbo out in the middle of the vast black fields. Hey you! Stop right where you are! You labour camp people plant like you were running a shell game!

She chased after him, stopped him, and pointed to the orchard, a large stand of crabapple trees with black clouds gathered around them. At the first puff of wind, black flowers fell fluttering to earth, drifted far into the distance and turned the sky grey.

It's blossom rot. He stamped his foot and bellowed at Instructor Yu, Why didn't you spray? I want to turn Half-way River into Flower Fruit Mountain, where the Magic Monkey lived!

Flower Fruit Mountain? Instructor Yu frowned, part of his face moving while the rest stayed still. Nowadays we don't go on pilgrimages to the Western Paradise for Buddhist scriptures like Monkey and his friends, we go to Dazhai, the model commune. Do you understand? If we start cheering for Flower Fruit Mountain today, doesn't it mean the return of an evil fog?

The wind in the blue sky sent the weather vane whipping around.

Yang the weatherman is the younger brother-in-law of the Branch Farm's former Party Secretary, she told the new Secretary, He stays home every day filling in observation data forms.

He what? His eyes opened wide. If that's your idea of a weather station, you might as well call it a weather guessing station! This damned Do-nothing Yang's due for a change of job! I'll put him on doo-doo duty, see whether he can weather that!

He walked into a large room filled with fat, grunting pigs. Over the door was a piece of paper reading, "Thousand Pig Forum."

Chen Xu handed some sweet and sour spareribs to Xiao Xiao with his chopsticks. The spareribs were fried a deep brown and had dark glistening drops of soy-coloured gravy hanging on them. They were perfectly crisp, and smelled so good that her nose itched. She took one bite, and then another before she had finished the first. The spare ribs stretched into the distance, where far, far away a herd of fat round pig trotters was thundering toward her.

I'll start by testing you with a few questions, said the little old man. How many days before a sow farrows are all the little piglets on their marks? You, the head of the production team, can you tell me?

Liu the Brute looked up drowsily, his cheeks wet with saliva. He answered, Is there a war on? I'm afraid the militia's rifles have got rusty.

The old man grunted and pointed to a chubby girl. You're the model pig-breeder, tell me, how thick should the bedding be when a sow farrows?

Guo Chunmei opened and closed her thick lips and then mumbled, About twenty centimeters.

She herself began shouting outside the window, Not twenty centimeters, thirty.

The old man's eyes twinkled, and he waved her inside.

The distant bank of fog rolled in again. At the centre, she could vaguely make out a little duckling of incomparable ugliness, waddling toward her, rolling a pure white swans egg under its thin flat feet, like a lotus bud wrapped up in its leaves. Then the egg split in two and a white cloud flew out, rising gracefully up into the sky.

It was a spring just like the year before.

The snow melted; the ice on the rivers broke up; the geese came back; the willows put out their shoots.

It was a spring completely unlike the year before.

The snow melted with a snicker, and as it melted it began to rumble and rampage through the arteries running across the black earth. The Half-way River happily threw open its mouth and wolfed down the blocks of ice, belching and swelling up as it bustled on its way. Flocks of geese filled the blue sky with all sorts of strange symbols, with numbers and words, and a new riddle in every cry. The willow shoots along the roads through the fields, barely containing the green in their throats, exploded first in strings of silver balls like silkworm cocoons, so bright they might have been mistaken for clouds on the horizon. The plain too burst forth from the grass roots in fluffy silver threads that caressed with such anxious affection that you felt as though their sharp little blades were growing inside your very heart and wished that you could reach inside and scratch them.

It seemed to Xiao Xiao as though spring on the farm had never stretched out so broadly, had never been so filled with life as it was this year, after she came back from taking the baby to Hangzhou. She was the first to shed her padded coat. Winter had been so heavy, after all. She tied a light blue scarf neatly over her head. She was not raising chickens or a pig; she did not even want her share of private plot land. She had brought back a little rectangular clock bought in Hangzhou. It ticked nervously along like an angel of death, hastening the two of them to join it on the heels of springtime. She could not let it leave her behind. She spread manure, worked on the pond banks, paced out the plots, transplanted seedlings, sowed spinach seed. If she had caught up with spring in the south she could certainly have lived with it there, but instead she had come so many thousands of miles back here to search for spring where the snow was melting.

They still had not seen the annual Sungari break-up. People said that the night before the break-up the ice boomed and roared as though

213

heaven and earth might collapse. And so they yearned to witness that awe-inspiring sight. But when they hurried to the river bank on the annual break-up day, black waves were surging down the river. The great battle was over and there was in fact not so much as a little white tooth left to see.

Such was the impatience of this springtide. She chased after it, but it always left her far behind. She could see its shape, but it had left her in the dust.

She had been assigned to make fertilizer pellets.

There was a big round grey dish mounted at an angle on a frame, looking like a home-made radar antenna. When the electricity was turned on, the dish revolved, and from the mixture of nitrogen, phosphorous, and potash—neither quite dry nor really wet—continuously shoveled into it, it rolled out wave after wave of peanut-sized pellets. When the operators were being conscientious and let it revolve a few extra times, the pellets came out a little smaller and smoother; when they were slack and did not let it revolve so long, the black pellets would come whisking out a little rougher and looser. Whatever their size and texture, they were rolled into shape in the dish, dumped out on the ground, gathered into baskets, carried away, and spread out to dry on the ground by the wall. After a day or so, the pellets began to dry out and lose a little of their dirty look, becoming as fluffy and tawny as peanut paste. Then they were sorted out in sieves, poured into sacks by grade, and put into the seeders. The big pellets were for beans, the small ones for wheat, for feeding the black earth so starved that its mouth watered.

Xiao Xiao liked gathering the little black pellets into baskets after they were formed and carrying them away. She piled them up over the brims, so that her pole creaked as she walked, the two ends swaying up and down as though faint with joy. She took pleasure in the breeze eddying around her ankles, the sway of her pole, her floating legs. And besides, the swinging motion under her blouse seemed more pronounced than usual, and the more her hips swayed to left and right the more light and graceful the pole became. She felt an inexpressable sense of delight at her long slender shadow in the setting sunlight, like a picture of someone from Xishuangbanna. Just look at those northern girls, they don't have any waists at all. She liked carrying loads on a pole.

"You one of the city kids from the south?" someone asked her. Their group leader had just called a rest break, and she always read during breaks.

She discovered that he had already been standing beside the home-made radar for a while, a little old man in black. He was studying the machine and the fertilizer with great interest. A swineherd? An old labour-camp inmate? She didn't care to pay attention to him. She felt a hint of inspiration for a poem coming on.

"A southerner knows how to carry a load with a shoulder pole. I can tell from the way you walk."

"What business is it of yours?" She did not even look up. "You just take care of your pigs. And another thing, don't step on my fertilizer pellets, either!"

"What are the proportions in the fertilizer?"

"So now you want a little for your vegetable garden, do you? Don't bother trying to make up to me!" She had lost her temper.

He smiled and walked away. One leg looked a little longer than the other, so he seemed to bounce up and down as he walked.

Her inspiration had vanished, and the dish had started to rumble around again. It was like a big clock. She picked up her carrying pole. Too bad it wasn't made of bamboo. It was solid and dug into her shoulder, so it was a good thing the fertilizer pellets weren't heavy. She could only keep her pretty posture, with her chest thrust forward, so long as the pole wasn't too heavy. Little pole, three foot three... like a wild goose... flying so free... Ai hai hai, yo hai hai, ya!... How mechanical and monotonous it was. She had worn a fixed path between the home-made radar and the drying yard. She could walk it with her eyes closed. When was the Branch Farm's broadcasting station going to play the little poem left behind after the rain storm? It's coming down, it's coming down, a little raindrop! As though it heard a bugle signaling the charge, come from up in the raven-black clouds. One squad after another, people go flying past, running to the threshing ground. The grain there has just been brought in... Run! Run! Figures flashing by, the thud of feet... It's coming down, it's coming down, a little drop of rain...

The big clock finally stopped its turning; quitting time had come. The odour of leeks and steamed bread came from over at the troop mess hall. Even the air was so hungry it grumbled. She went home. All of a sudden the loudspeakers on the power poles came on. She flushed. Those loudspeakers could be heard all over the farm.

From far away she could see Chen Xu taking the work basket out to dump their ashes.

"Did you get off work early today?" she asked, dusting off her clothes in the doorway with her scarf.

Chen Xu held out a hand, palm up, and said, with an ironic smile, "That's right; there wasn't a little drop of rain today, so we didn't need to cover the grain."

"Don't be sarcastic." She took the basket and went into the back yard to pick some giant radishes.

One corner of the garden was green. Cabbage and spinach grew densely over several plots. "Pease porridge sweet!" As soon as she walked into the garden, she could see Beanpole mopping his brow and looking up at the sun.

Chen Xu followed her, carrying half a bucket of water. He emptied it over the radish patch and squatted down behind her. Then he gave her pigtail a pull and said in a low voice, "Say, 'Mistress Poet of the Grain Just Brought In', do you know what kind of grain it was?"

"Well, cornmeal? Hominy?"

"Silly girl; it was grain that we had to buy back from the State."

"What's wrong with bought grain?"

"Pah! Our magnificent socialist state farm has to bring in grain from outside. What a stupid mess!"

"I, I wasn't praising bought grain."

"Praising the unselfish spirit of the poor and lower-middle peasants?" He wrinkled up his nose. That's all the grain we've got; if it gets rained on, it will mildew and go bad. Then what do we eat? What would happen if we didn't cover it up? That's what you call a farmer's instinct, it's typical peasant thinking."

His lips curled up in a sneer. He pulled the top off of a radish and then had to dig it out of the mud with his finger.

"All right. From now on I just won't write any more." She was a little huffy.

"Write all you like, just don't give people the creeps when they hear what you've written."

She tossed the radishes into her basket, turned abruptly away, and went back inside. Could he write poetry? She had to hurry to get dinner ready. The radishes she could cut up in thin slices for a salad. The main dish was fried soy sauce noodles.

While Xiao Xiao sliced the radishes, Chen Xu was in the inner room rolling out the noodles. He went on rolling for a while, and then spoke up. "That Li Yiren guy made his appearance today!"

"What Li Yiren?"

"The one who's come down from Harbin to be the Farm's Party Secretary."

"Did you see him?"

"See him? I talked with him for a good hour, beside the highway. I must have smoked five or six of his cigarettes, all cheap ones, 'Handshake' brand. You know, his collar is even dirtier than mine."

They said he had set up the first state farm in the country. After that he had been assigned to Manchurian Central—head of the Manchurian Central Bureau for Agricultural Land Reclamation. But it wasn't his fate to hold down a desk job. He still wanted to go run a farm. He had a wife, a doctor who didn't think two hundred every month was enough to spend and who would have died rather than leave Harbin. They had fought for years, and after they finally divorced, he had packed up his tattered bedroll and come to the Three Rivers Plain. He went around in his jeep to every farm and in the end, beside the Half-way River, he spat once and said, "This is the one!" They said that Halfway River State Farm was the most backward, infuriating shambles of any place under the Bureau's jurisdiction.

She was silent for a minute, and then asked, "How did you know he was coming today?"

"Catfish gave us his orders as soon as we got to work this morning. 'There's a big shot coming today, so everybody do a good job and don't make our troop look bad.' I figured something must be up, so once he left I changed places with someone working a strip next to the road and had Bubble stand lookout. It wasn't eight yet when he gave a shout that a jeep was coming down the highway. I drove the ox up onto the road, seeder and all. If the jeep had tried to get by, it would have either killed the ox or blown a tire."

"What were you trying to do?" She cried.

"What was I trying to do? I was letting him know right off that there's somebody at No. 5 named Chen Xu!" He gave up entirely on rolling noodles and came out into the front room, waving his flour-covered hands. "Listen! Sure enough, it worked like a charm. The jeep came screeching to a halt right in front of the ox. Before it was even completely stopped, the door opened, and a little old guy got out, really short, not even up to my shoulder, but with two sharp eyes. He glanced at the ox, at me, and then said quietly, 'What's up? Let's hear it'!"

"What did you say to him?" She asked, dropping her radish.

"I ambled over and said, 'Nothing special. If it was something personal I wouldn't talk about it here'. He stared at me. 'If it's nothing, what are you up to, just horsing around? I've got plenty of work of my own to do'. I laughed and said, 'I know all about that work of yours. If the Half-way River Farm keeps on the way it is, it'll never amount to anything'."

She started. "You said that to him?"

"That's what I said, and it stopped him in his tracks. He fished out a pack of cigarettes and gave me one, pointed to the ox and told me to get it off the road so it wouldn't interfere with traffic, and motioned to his driver to pull off the road. Then he sat down on the grass next to the ditch, struck a match, winked at me, and said, 'Okay, let's hear it'."

Now, don't get upset, just listen. I had worked out all my theory and facts ahead of time. 'Once the political line is determined, cadres are the decisive factor'. You try checking into things: Where on the Farm is there an office or a workshop that isn't packed tight with the cadres' kith and kin? Us city Youth call those places 'fish-boss factories' because they belong to the officials and bosses. How many cadres come down to the production front line to swing a pickaxe or work in the fields? And how many of them have really got the goods, for that matter? When they have a report or a denunciation to do, they have to get someone from the city to draft it for them. Who's educating who? I'd say that two thirds of them ought to be tossed out and replaced with new people—all they're good for is going back home and herding goats. Who does the State Farm really depend on? The vast majority of us city Youth are lacking any of the sense of responsibility that goes with being master of your situation. It's not just that we don't have it, we're not allowed to. The papers say we're the masters, but in fact we're just cheap labour. If you make educated people stay in a cultural desert, aren't you just turning city kids into old peasants? And another thing, the Farm is constantly developing pork production, but how many bits of pork do we see in a year? There's something fishy about those pigs, too. They never seem to produce any organs or any trotters, just a little bit of fat meat that gets stewed until it's the colour of starch noodles. And even at that, on a day when there's meat, the mess hall is thronged to the rafters bright and early, it's such a plus just to get an extra whiff of it.

He sounded quite pleased with himself. He grabbed a radish and took a loud bite out of it, spraying drops of water from the top onto Xiao Xiao's neck.

"What did he say?" She came to herself. "You're asking for

trouble."

"Well!" Chen shook his head. "He shook hands with me and kept saying, 'Good for you, young fellow. You've got a head on your shoulders. When I need something done, I'll come looking for you. After I've been here on No.5 for a while, we'll have another chat'. So, what do you say? I must have made a good impression on him, eh? He's a tiny little old guy, but really bold. Maybe Half-way River's finally got somebody in charge who knows his stuff."

Something occurred to her all of a sudden, and she interrupted him, raising her voice. "Was he wearing a black jacket, with bushy eyebrows and a little lame in one leg?"

"Well, perhaps," he mumbled, going back to the inside room to roll out noodles. "As for his legs, I didn't take a very good look..." He was not paying much attention, being still wrapped up in his own happy memories. His eyes, usually so apathetic and elusive, now shone with the lustre of a clear sky after rain.

26

"You've got a young city fellow here with a good head on his shoulders. Why haven't you given him something to do? I had a chat with him, and he puts the lot of you to shame!"

The old man was chain-smoking. His hair seemed to be on fire, streaked with black and grey.

"Who? Who are you talking about?" asked Susie J, eyelids drooping.

"His name is, well, let me see now... Oh yes, it's Chen Xu."

"Chen Xu? Hah!" The whole room broke out in mocking laughter, derisive laughter, the kind that cripples.

Liu the Brute was sitting on the edge of the brick bed, rubbing an itching heel. He put on a straight face and drawled, "That kid! He can talk okay, but when it comes to work, that's another story!"

Catfish patted the brown army cap on his head and cleared his throat. "That isn't where the real problem lies. The real problem lies with his class stand and the line he takes in his political thinking. It's clear that he attacked the rustication of urban youth as labour reform in disguise and that he has gone on inciting dissatisfaction with socialism among the young people even after having been placed in detention at Farm Headquarters."

The old man paced back and forth in the centre of the room, his brows knitted like two lumps of coal and his hair sticking straight up.

Susie J took a thick envelope and threw it down on the table with such a whack that the other papers jumped and a large red seal was set to bouncing back and forth. "He was in thick with that follower of Lin Biao's black line down in Hangzhou. What's his name? Yeah, Wang Ge, the one who's been arrested. We have to get him to confess what the connection between them was. We're just waiting until the spring sowing is out of the way!"

The old man hung his head with a sigh and walked out.

Chen Xu, who had been waiting outside for a long time, stepped forward and offered his hand. "Are you really going to stay a while,

Secretary Li? Did you mean it when you said you'd look me up and have a talk? I want to tell you what we've all been thinking."

The little old man looked up at him, his eyes blank. The lines on his forehead showed doubt piled upon doubt, as though he and Chen Xu had never had that talk beside the road. It had blown away like the smoke of their cigarettes. He simply nodded politely, turned his back, and walked away.

Chen Xu pulled himself together.

That thin little form walked off into the dusky distance, turning to enter a gate in the decrepit wall beneath the wire fencing.

He had nodded to him very politely. But then he hadn't said a word.

Half the sky was still covered by a rose-coloured sunset, and the grime on his collar still glistened in its light. He couldn't have failed to recognise him, not with those two sharp eyes.

Yes! Of course! Catfish had already been promoted to Deputy Chairman of the Branch Farm. Was he going to just sit there and watch the new boss take to someone who had been such a thorn in his own side?

The wind had suddenly turned against him, like a corpse lying across the road, drained of all blood. He stepped over it, scalp tingling. He stood facing into the wind for a while and then walked slowly back.

No, he didn't want to go home.

The setting sun finally vanished completely. Ever darker waves of blackness swept in from the horizon. It had closed its eye and carried off the very last faint ray of sunlight in his heart. Would his blood run green hereafter? Or blue? The sun was an eternal round period, setting in the west and rising in the east, over and over, forever adhering to its rule. So that's how it was. There had to be a reason for such indifference. Wang Ge? The Workers' Propaganda Team? That damned Catfish!

He believed in his own intuition, he believed in his own daydreams. He still dreamed very little when he was asleep, but his daydreams had steadily increased in number.

Chen Xu has a good head on his shoulders. Why haven't you given him something to do?

How bitterly he had struggled in the boundless ocean to grasp that straw, how tenaciously he had clung to even that one bush at the edge of the cliff. He couldn't be done for just like this, when the sun rose so boldly anew every day.

221

But...

Comrade Secretary, your arrival was the very last chance that remained to him. And perhaps it was also the only chance for you to revive your failed career. You could have got yourself a brave and capable steed, one that would have carried you through the forests and across the snowy plains all the way to Flower Fruit Mountain. You have probably never seen such a horse. All you have in your stables is tottering old nags, garbage good for nothing but breeding, farting, and eating soy bean cakes. You missed it, kicked it out, let it go. You'll be sorry; you'll be sorry for the rest of your life! And it will serve you fucking right!

He couldn't go back home, he couldn't. What would he say to her?

The night stretched out around him. The sun would never rise again.

He found himself standing at the door of the little hut by the company's threshing ground. The shifty light of a kerosene lamp showed through the tiny window.

A dark blurry shadow was moving on the filthy window shade.

He pushed the door open and went inside.

The shadow was sitting cross-legged on the brick bed with a white bowl at his feet. Puffy eyelids drooped like two empty clamshells. He lifted the bowl to his own mouth, slurped from it, and then held out a shaking arm. Without so much as looking to see who it was who had come in, he offered the bowl, muttering thickly, "Have a drink, have a drink..."

Chen Xu walked over, wiping his sweaty palms on his trousers, took the bowl, and threw back a large mouthful.

He almost jumped as his whole body caught fire, waves of flame surging through him. He choked and could not speak for a long time.

"Drink." The shadow pulled something dark and grimy from under his bedding and pressed it into his hand.

He held the thing under the oil lamp. It was a boiled egg, very strong smelling. He swallowed, rapped it on the edge of the brick bed, and peeled off the shell, revealing a tuft of pale yellow fuzz. It was a fertilised egg. Biting his lip, he stripped all the feathers off with a few pulls, tore away the unformed skull, and took a big bite.

"It's a rooster's egg, couldn't hatch." The shadow muttered. "Have a drink..."

222

The man spent his days drunk like this year in and year out. They called him Winejug Fan. When Liu the Brute saw him, he knew that he'd met his match. As long as he had wine, he needed no food. He got forty-three dollars pay and spent it all on wine, so he did not even have enough left to buy a train ticket back home.

Ordinarily, Chen Xu rarely spoke to him, if only because the sickening stink of alcohol he gave off could be smelled five miles away. Small wonder he was called Winejug Fan. Every time there was some kind of political movement, he would be trotted up on stage to hang his head and admit his guilt, snoring away right there on the platform. Once, he had actually mumbled a few words: "Under the archway, hop, hop, hop, See the big monkey, up on top." Susie J was beside himself, he was so furious. But not even having that pistol jabbed in his scrawny ribs could bring Fan around.

People said he had got in trouble for those very words. He was from Hebei. To mark the tenth anniversary of the founding of the People's Republic, his town had put up a memorial arch. He was just walking happily under this when the words came to him. They struck him as such a nicely turned phrase that, rather than leave well enough alone, he shouted them a second time at the top of his lungs. He was seized at once and turned over to the police. It was not until the cart in which he was being paraded through the town for criticism passed under the arch that he got a good look at it and saw that a picture of their Leader was mounted at the top. Just for that he had been sentenced to ten years as an active counter-revolutionary, and now he had spent more than a dozen years on the State Farm.

He had not gone home to that arch after his sentence was up. On the Farm, he got three meals a day and had wine to drink. In the winter, he caught meadow voles, and in the summer he set up a fish trap and hunted for sparrow eggs and the like, so he always had something to go with his wine. And as for what he had said while he was drunk, it was 'sterilized' once Susie J had led everyone through a few rounds of down-withs. As soon as the criticism rally was over and he came off stage, they marched him back to the threshing ground, to continue his job as technical advisor. Without him managing their technical services, the Farm's thousand acres or so of rice paddy might very well fail to produce anything but straw. So Winejug Fan occupied a status that was at once higher and lower than that of other people, but he got along well enough all the same. Someone teased him, "Say, Winejug, why don't you go back and visit your old lady?" He chuckled,

"I like wine better than a wife, gets me more confused."

"Drink..."

That bowl came shuddering toward Chen Xu again, giving off its cheap but fascinating warmth. A well sunk deep into the snow. A serene and balmy place.

He did not want to know who that shadow was. He simply felt the dark cold lingering in his heart and seeping into his bones, forming splinters of ice and blocking all his veins. He could hear blocks of ice creaking in his spine. He wanted to sink to the bottom of that well, that serene and balmy place.

Chen Xu drained the cup of wine in one gulp; perhaps he swallowed the bowl itself. His hair burst into flames, and the fire spread from the roots of his hair to his shoulder blades, his fingers, the soles of his feet. His blood rolled and boiled; a film of kerosene poured beneath his skin, hissing and burning. His joints relaxed; his teeth felt loose; the blocks of ice began to melt, oozing through his bones and echoing within his chest. He did not exist. He would not exist again. There was nothing but a deep well exhaling warmth, spraying torrents of fiery blood surging toward him, submerging him, and then forcing him on. Where was he?

"Have more drinks, don' worry..."

He stuck his head into the well and greedily opened his mouth. He would drink it dry.

Where was he? Did he no longer exist? But how could there be a world without him? Did he exist? If he did, why was there no world for him? Had he sunk beneath it? If he had, how was it that he was roaming so freely through space, making his way among the eternal stars, high above the mountain peaks of Earth, looking down on wretched, despicable mankind and bringing all its truth and falsity, its good and evil under his scrutiny? Why were this cottage, the whole plain shrinking to such a size that he could knead them in the palm of his hand? Wings spread from his body; even without wings he wandered through the clouds. He surpassed the universe. His mind was infinite, and so were his hands, so huge he could not see himself. He drove the winds, the thunder and the lightning, the rivers in their courses, the magma within the earth. He laughed aloud. This was what he had dreamed of. Even gravity would have no more effect on him. Ask the vast earth, Who governs rising and setting? A respectful sun rose from the well, flooding that damned hole with golden sulfur. Exhaling alcohol fumes, the sun earnestly massaged him, those drunken hands passing along his every troubled, suffering acupuncture point until he was practically bewitched. Then came forgetfulness, and after forgetfulness there was joy.

"Have more drinks, don' worry."
"I can't. I've got to work tomorrow."
"Tomorrow will take care of itself."

"Have another cup."
"I can't, my wife will be coming to look for me."

"Drink, empty it at one gulp."
"I, I have no more money. I've got to raise my kid."
"Your kid? He can grow up on water."
"Look Fan, how about lending me ten bucks?"

Since the evening when he had found that little bit of comfort in Winejug Fan's deep well, Chen Xu had discovered to his surprise that he had an extraordinary capacity for alcohol, an infinite thirst. He had not a moment's rest or satisfaction until that flaming lamp wick steeped in kerosene was roaming beneath his skin and he had stumbled into that strange realm suspended in mid-air.

Once he woke up to find himself lying in a puddle in the cart road, soaking wet. The frogs were croaking in his ears, and something hot was licking his forehead; the licking was what had wakened him. He sat bolt upright, and whatever it was backed off a few steps, barked once, and ran away with its tail between its legs. It was a dog. He lay on the river bank gagging and vomiting, the taste in his mouth bitter and salty by turns, so that he could not tell whether it was alcohol or tears. He had long since run out of tears, but he felt like crying all the same. He staggered on home and leaned against the door for a long time without going in.

Xiao Xiao would look at him with such disappointment, silent tears running down her cheeks. Are, are you drunk again? It was as though he had come back from committing suicide once again. He could not bear that disappointment.

If she had only done like the barn boss's wife, and set up a little table in the shade of the tree outside their door, so that when he came home after a hard day's work, as the sun was setting, she could fry up some eggs with peppers and pour a cup of wine for him, for her husband, none of this would have happened.

He was a man. He wanted to smoke, to talk big, to live like someone who really counted for something.

But she had turned their little cottage into a library. She did not want him associating with just anybody. She did not like the smell of tobacco or alcohol. She did not even like the smell of pork. Apparently, she was planning to become a Buddhist. They sent twenty dollars back every month for the baby, and twenty dollars was deducted to repay the loan for their trip south, which left only a third of their combined wages of sixty-four dollars a month. What else could they eat, once they had bought grain and oil? Pickles and soy sauce, soy sauce and pickles. She could treat such abstemious living as a matter of course, but he couldn't take it.

If he were to get a few people together and just barge into the village and grab a flock of chickens, even if they were seen, by the time the villagers had got some tools and turned up at the door, all those fat hens would already be bled and plucked and hung up in a pretty white row. "Stolen chickens? Have a look! You must be able to recognise which ones are yours!" Let them glare their hearts out.

Stealing a goose would be easier. Grab that long neck while the geese had their heads up eating elm leaves, snap it back, twist it into a knot, and tuck it under the wing, safe and sound without a peep. Carry the goose home inside his coat, and who would ever know? Cook up a whole pot, enough for meal after meal.

But he had never done it.

To begin with, Xiao Xiao's eyes would open wide and she would cry, "A goose! Where did it come from?"

I bought it. How much? What about the money? It's such a waste!

A present? Who from? We can't just take things from people for nothing. I'll go give them some money.

Stolen? Could he bring himself to say it? If you stole personal property you were a thief; public property, and it was looting. You worthless...

He knew that the emotional bond between him and Xiao Xiao had been frayed many times already. He had disappointed her too often. The fine young man that he had been when they first met had been too badly tarnished. Another unforeseen storm, and perhaps that bond would be sundered.

He kept remembering the business with the nanny goat back

during the winter while she was sitting out her month. Although she had not uttered a word of reproach, her lips had turned cold, and her arms as well, for days on end. And when his fingers, when the tip of his tongue touched that body, in which he had always found such ecstasy, he felt alone and set apart for the first time. In her distracted and indifferent embrace it suddenly seemed as though she had never been his, or perhaps that she had turned into someone different. He loved her; he was afraid of this coldness and reserve. If he had to choose between a goose and stark poverty, he would submit to the latter. She was the only thing in the world he treasured. He would not destroy his place in her heart.

And yet it was a submission that went against his nature. He would yield to her, and then lose his temper for no reason. He smashed things up and then went on bended knee to beg her forgiveness. He began getting out of the cottage to go somewhere else. But Beanpole was dead, and since Bubble had a girlfriend now, he was over at the girls' dorm hauling water and splitting firewood whenever he had a free moment. For the rest, there were only his poker and drinking buddies, and his enemies. After only three days on the Farm, Secretary Li had got a phone call summoning him back for a meeting at the District Office. He had forgotten all about Chen Xu and his talents. The only ones who remembered him were Catfish and Susie J.

And so he went on sneaking off to the threshing ground to drink at Fan's place. He told Xiao Xiao that he was on night shift, hauling bricks or working the coal pit overtime. He would get thoroughly drunk, collapse on Fan's brick bed, and sleep until dawn. Then he would go off to work with everyone else, still bleary-eyed, nipping into the woods for a nap when he got a chance. Sometimes he was so sick that he waited until he figured Xiao Xiao had left for work and then went home the long way around. When she finished work, she might ask him, Off work so early? But she wasn't the sort of woman to go around checking up on what kind of night shifts the company had or what they did. Not even in her dreams would it occur to her that he might skip work.

But the number of days he skipped work increased steadily, so that he not only didn't have money for wine, he didn't even get his full thirty-two dollars pay. What would he tell Xiao Xiao? What about his debts? His son? He didn't know. Sometimes he was drunk and sometimes he was sober. When he was drunk, he borrowed money from Fan. When he sobered up he vomited chopsuey in repayment.

When he was on the river bank he knew he would have to repay all the money he had borrowed, but once he was plunged into that well, he no longer knew where Fan's money came from.

Tomorrow, tomorrow, tomorrow was hanging from that son of a bitch's belt!

27

It was a clear, moonless night. He was drinking with Fan, who had got a nail in his foot a few days before. Fan had had a few days off to recuperate, but he was still none too quick on his feet. It was so quiet around his room you could hear the lizards on the walls. All of a sudden, Blackie set up an awful barking at the door. Fan slipped off the brick bed with remarkable agility and silently handed Chen Xu a two-tined mattock. A burst of alcohol fumes struck his ear. "Quick, go out and take a look. You're a fast runner. If it's someone stealing fertilizer, grab him, okay?"

He ran outdoors. It was black as pitch; he could not tell the sky from the ground. He swept his flash around and made out two people running and stumbling away toward the west. He let Blackie off his leash and soon caught up with them, swinging his mattock. He heard a yelp and something heavy fell to the ground. Someone flopped down and knelt at his feet. He turned on the flash. Two sacks of fertilizer.

He called Blackie off and barked, "Where you from?"

"Village over the west side, farm over there, don't have 'nough fertilizer, the production team sent, sent us..."

There were a few battles every year between the State Farm and the villagers, fights over land or water rights. The preceding summer, the peasants from one village had mowed almost two hundred acres of the Farm's grain. Someone had been killed, and then they came to the Farm with the coffin and staged a demonstration, demanding compensation. Once a suit got to the regional court, the Farm never won. You people on the State Farm eat public grain; you're a big operation and you've got iron rice bowls. You'll never starve. The consequence was that no one knew just how much pesticide and fertilizer was stolen or filched from the Farm by the village production teams each year. Anyway, if the Farm ran a deficit, it could rely on the State. Do you know what sort of deals the Farm officials made with the teams? When the Farm's tractors went to plough the peasants' fields for them, whose wallets got lined with the pork and the glutinous rice for wine-making, the bean curd and fodder that the village sent in return?

His fury erupted. He gave the mattock a yank and snarled, "Nothing doing! Come with me!"

The dark form moved a little, reaching for something inside its shirt.

"What are you up to?" He dodged away and aimed his flash full in the other man's face, then froze as the man pulled out a crumpled ten dollar bill.

"Look, mister, won't you let me off this one time? It ain't easy, farming ain't. The State Farm won't miss a couple of sacks of fertilizer. We got no place to buy any even with the money."

The ten dollar bill, so obviously made ready in advance, was stuffed into his hand. He stood stock still. The man vanished in a flurry of footsteps.

He flicked his flash on again. It was a ten dollar bill, much worn. On it were some filthy images of worker, peasant and soldier with fierce expressions on their faces.

He looked around at the dark fields and snorted.

"Be Vigilant for the New Direction in Class Struggle!"

"Mercilessly Criticise the Theory of the Extinction of Class Struggle!"

"Down with the Counter-Revolutionary Fan Shicai!"

"Make the Careerist and Plotter Chen Xu Come Clean!"

It was Guo Chunmei leading the shouted slogans. She had been putting on weight. Her eyes were sunk in folds of flesh. Keen arrows shot out of her throat one after another.

"Chen Xu has gravely compromised his class stand. He has been sucked in by a class enemy. He gets drunk with a farm worker. He is plotting secret counter-revolutionary activities."

He interrupted her. "Hey! Slow down a little. Do you know what a class enemy is? What's a farm worker? He's someone who's stayed on the farm to work! That's not the same as a labour-camp inmate. Don't mix up friend and foe like that!"

The crowd snickered.

She paid no attention to him, but threw her head back and went on reciting. "Finally, at the instigation of a class enemy, he has stolen public property and extorted money from the poor and lower-middle peasants. I want to warn Chen Xu most seriously: You are placing yourself in danger! You must rein in your horse before you go over the cliff!"

He gave her a sly look and drawled, "What's in danger around here isn't me, it's those five hundred pigs of yours. They're so hungry they're tearing all over the farm, chomping on our shit and licking up our piss. We don't have to clean out the latrines any more. I hope that our model pig breeder will invent a new feeding method so that when she goes off to lecture on her 'study and application' she won't have to call someone in to replace her. Let those pigs learn to be self-supporting and self-relying..."

A strange noise swept through the crowd.

"Faaaaaafffffoooooooppppsssss..."

Laughter shook the hall. People were whistling, pounding on the benches, tossing their caps in the air...

Susie J leapt to his feet, shaking with embarrassment and rage, and shouted, "What's so funny? A fart's just some air in your belly. If you aren't careful, out it slips. What are you laughing at? Anybody laughs is gonna get it!"

A long, brazen fart.

A few stars had squeezed their way out through a space in the clouds, but the earth remained pitch black. They would not shine on him. Their light came from centuries past.

He stamped his numb and aching feet and looked down at the damp ten dollar bill clenched in his palm. He gritted his teeth and stuck it in his pocket.

He went back to the hut, threw back his head, and drank off half a bottle of fiery 'Erguotou'* in one pull.

Fan limped in after him with a spade in his hand. He had been waiting for some time at the door.

"Get away?" Fan asked softly, furtive eyes full of suspicion. "How come there wasn't any noise?"

"Got away." Chen slumped back on the brick bed.

Blackie came in, wagging his tail, and put his front paws up on the little table.

"Get down!" Fan shoved the dog away, muttering, "This damn dog ain't worth two hoots. I got to get me a better one next spring. Yeah, like the one with the white paws I used to have. Now there was a dog, and you city kids went and ate it!"

"I'll pay you back!" Chen cried, "Honest I will!"

---

* A Chinese strong alcoholic beverage.

231

28

She was reading a book. There were bookmarks stuck in between many of the pages. When she took them out, she discovered that they were money, bills in every denomination from ten cents to ten dollars. Then there was an oval-shaped one with 'four dollars' written on it, a triangular one with 'three dollars', and a heart-shaped bill that said 'twenty dollars'. It occurred to her that she had never seen three, four, or twenty dollar bills before. She was puzzled, and took a more careful look. They had sheaves of grain and sickles on them, and crowds of workers, peasants, and soldiers. She tried rapping them, and they rang, like pieces of metal, so she felt reassured. She gathered them all up, put a rubber band around them, and packed them at the very bottom of her canvas bag.

She started counting the money up in her head. With this windfall, she could repay everything she had borrowed for her trip home and send an extra ten dollars to the baby, making a total of thirty. The baby would soon be six months old. To judge from the pictures, he had not grown much; probably the nurse did not have enough milk. If she could save a little more money, she would buy a sheet and two pillow cases. They had not got any more bedding since their marriage.

She went into the back yard to pick cucumbers.

Chen Xu handed her something wrapped up in a baby blanket. She took it, but when she looked, it wasn't their son, but a fat white gourd.

She took a sniff and then grabbed him.

You've been drinking again.

What? He put his arms around her.

Someone told me you're always drinking over at the threshing ground. And you were lying to me when you said you were on night shift. I know all about it.

Chen Xu laughed out loud and clutched her to him. Opening his mouth, he held it close to her face and exhaled. Take a sniff, he said. Is it wine? No, it's fermented glutinous rice.

She sniffed, and it did smell like fermented glutinous rice after all, sweet and vinegarish, a strong smell. Her mouth watered. She said, I want some of that too.

So Chen Xu went to draw water for making fermented glutinous rice, while she sat down to copy out an essay she had written. She was going to enter the literary competition held on the Farm to mark July 1, the anniversary of the founding of the Communist Party. The topic was a line from a poem by Chairman Mao, "Who is Dancing in the Sky Holding a Rainbow of Ribbons?" She had copied only a few lines when Chen Xu came back and told her that the well was still frozen over and that fermented glutinous rice couldn't be made with ice. She felt very let down. Chen Xu said, I'll copy your essay for you. I've got nothing else to do.

So Chen Xu copied out her manuscript. After a while he held it up and said it was done. She went over and took a look at it. Over the title he had written a different line from another of Chairman Mao's poms, "Several Flies are Bumping into the Wall." She exploded, threw it down, and shouted, What are you doing, changing my manuscript?

She borrowed a bicycle and went off to the post office to send money to the baby.

It had just rained, and the road was a quagmire of bumps and puddles. The six-inch ruts were filled with water and the road itself tilted steeply over until it formed a dark round tube just like a trick cyclist's ramp at the circus. Suspended in mid-air, she rode along at top speed, gasping for breath. She could just make out a ditch running next to the road up ahead, with a trickle of water gurgling down it. There was water on the road, too, with only a strip no wider than a piece of sugar cane left dry for her to cross over. She clenched her teeth and kept on riding, but suddenly she found herself on a high wire. The handlebars slipped, and her bike fell into the ditch. She went all the way under water, but it was soft and warm and felt good. She gave a hard push with her feet and stood up on the bottom of the ditch, putting her head above water. She could see her bicycle, also half-submerged. The banks of the ditch were completely bare. She tried to climb out, but she could not get up. As soon as she took a step, her foot would slide back down. This happened over and over, until she was exhausted. Then all of a sudden a little boat came floating down from upstream, with a pitch black awning over it that could be pulled out like a desk drawer. The toes of two bare feet gripped the two oars, one forward and one aft. A pair of arms like thick lotus stems

233

pulled her and her bicycle on board. She was dripping wet, and the chain of her bicycle came clattering off in coils like intestines. The little boat rowed slowly down a green stream covered with little yellow flowers. The channel grew narrower and narrower, filling with water weeds, until their way was blocked. The little boat turned around and rowed off down a different stream, but as it went, she saw the little yellow flowers bursting into bloom one by one, faster then the boat could move, until they had sealed off the entire surface of the river. She looked around, but the golden yellow water stretched out thick as paste in all directions, with no way for her to go. The boatman pushed the yellow flowers under water with a bamboo pole, but they bobbed right back up to the surface again. She went to help him pull up the flowers and noticed that he was wearing glasses. He was Zou Sizhu.

When Xiao Xiao woke up in the morning, her eyes were a little puffy and she felt drowsy. She was worn out from sleeping. She felt more tired than if she had not slept at all.

The spraying of the paddy fields was under way, so a day's work was even more tiring than usual. Chen Xu was on the weeding squad, and he too was so bone weary every morning he could hardly get up. He wolfed down a couple of bites of leftover rice and rushed out. She washed out the bowls, locked the door, and set off for work.

Before she had gone very far, she heard someone behind her calling her name. She looked back and saw it was Dr. Yang, carrying a leather satchel with a red cross on it. He was yawning as he walked.

"How's the baby doing?" he asked. "Have you had a letter?"

She nodded. "He's still in the country with the wet nurse. His grandparents go to see him often."

"Well, he may have been a little weak, but there was nothing wrong with him, so I wouldn't be concerned if he's on the thin side. My only worry is that what with growing up down south he may get too soft to take it when he comes back."

"Yes." She smiled.

"Have they taken his hundred-day pictures?"

"They, they haven't come yet."

"Make sure you give me one when they do, eh? He's the first baby I've delivered for you young people from down south."

Xiao Xiao nodded again and smiled. She was anxious to get to work.

"Uh, wait a moment." He stopped her, seeming oddly strained.

234

He hemmed and hawed. "Well, there's something I want to talk to you about—now be sure you don't take it personally."

He hitched up his bag, stopped walking, and thrust his hands under his armpits. He seemed to be avoiding her eyes on purpose. "Well, I guess I don't have to tell you that we're into the busy season now. Every year about this time there are mobs of people after me for sick leaves. Of course there are rules governing sick leaves. I can't give one unless there's a fever of at least 38° Centigrade."

She broke in on him. "Dr. Yang, I'm not asking for a sick leave."

"I don't mean you. It's Chen Xu." He sounded a little nervous. "He, well, he's had people hide hot water bottles under their clothes when they're having their temperature taken, and hold cigarette butts next to the thermometer. Really now! Do people really get fevers of 40° C and live through it? Do they think I fool that easy? Anyway, I'm telling you so that you can have a word with Chen Xu. Should a grown man with a son of his own to be up to such tricks?"

Xiao Xiao did not stay to hear him finish. Biting her lip, she took to her heels.

It was him. Only he could have done it. Dr. Yang would never accuse someone falsely. Chen Xu had not touched a book since they got back from Hangzhou. And ever since Secretary Li Yiren had gone back to the Farm Office, Chen Xu had been as listless as the cucumber vines in the garden after the season was over. The young people in the troop were no longer divided between northerners and southerners, but had gradually formed various 'factions' cutting across the lines between north and south and between boys and girls. They were now divided along lines of mutual interest, advantage, influence, or even degree of affinity with the officials. They were like fairy rings springing up in the fields after a rain, one ring surrounding another, and each small ring with a larger one around it. Chen Xu's group was made up almost entirely of people who had got on the wrong side of Director Yu. They slacked off at work, raised a ruckus in study periods, and got into mischief during breaks, all in opposition to Director Yu and Chief Sun. There had been another criticism session not long before, this one called to criticise Chen Xu for drinking with a farm worker, conduct that constituted a serious 'blurring of class lines'. But he had stood up and faced the stage quite nonchalantly, as though he had a speech to make, a very picture of heroic daring.

She had tried reasoning with him, but each time he either had some plausible story or else just grinned.

But she had never dreamed that he would put them up to cheating people, to tricking Dr. Yang.

He was probably just doing it as a joke. He didn't take anything seriously any more. He was probably just too tired. He never got a day off, out soaking in the paddy fields all day long. How could anyone take that? He hadn't done it on purpose. No, probably, probably...

She felt an indefinable ache inside, felt as though she were sliding rapidly down a black chute, impelled by some irresistable force. She could not tell just where she was, nor could she regain control. The chute tilted over until it formed a dark round tube, just like a trick cyclist's ramp at the circus. Suspended in mid air, she clenched her teeth and kept on riding, but suddenly she found herself on a high wire. If she stopped for an instant, she did not know where she would land.

She ate lunch in the fields and barely managed to last through to quitting time. She walked back home in a daze. She went inside, but did not feel up to cooking dinner, and so just sat numbly on the edge of the brick bed.

"What's this, feeling inspired or something?" Chen Xu walked in with a chuckle. His mud-soaked trousers were rolled up above his bare feet and there was a large wet spot on his back. He pulled some money out of his pocket and put it on the table. "Look, thirty-one dollars and fifty cents, my wages for April, handed over to my wife just as it was paid out. Count it! They issued pay at the company last night, but I didn't know about it."

Xiao Xiao looked at him dully.

"What, are you tired?" He patted her on the back. "All dragged out? Okay, I'll make dinner."

She could hear him going out to get straw for the fire, then putting the millet in the pan, adding water, lighting the fire. How should she begin?

Someone was knocking at the outside door. It sounded urgent. The door opened, and Chen Xu said something in a hushed voice to the visitor. She heard the other person raise his voice and say he was looking for Xiao Xiao. She went out just in time to see Chen Xu pushing him out the door. "Let's talk outside!" He sounded a little flustered.

Xiao Xiao walked over, getting a grip on herself.

She recognised him, a young guy in the company from Hegang. She had heard he was after a Hangzhou girl.

He looked down at the ground and stammered, "It's like this.

236

Last month I gave Chen Xu some money to get me a pair of Dacron slack from down south. But he still hasn't got them, and I've been thinking, if they're so hard to get, I won't buy them after all. Pay was issued yesterday, and I was thinking that, that the money..."

Look, thirty-one dollars and fifty cents, handed over to my wife just as it was paid out.

"How much?"

"Twenty."

She turned around, went back inside, got twenty dollars, and gave it to him with a smile. "I'm very sorry for the delay."

"Oh, that's okay." He backed up step by step, bowing his head even lower and clutching the money. He left as though in flight.

The kindling was crackling in the furnace. Part of the fire had burned as far as the stoke hole and was sending flames hissing up into the air. There was a big pile of straw next to the furnace door. Let it burn. If it catches fire, so much the better. One big fire and it would all be over. She stamped out the sparks and leaned weakly against door, shaking from head to foot.

The dingy ceiling, shrouded in cobwebs. How had she got stuck in such a dark, dead-end pit? Walking down into the Purple Grotto on Jade Emperor Mountain in Hangzhou, each level as black as the last, a sheer bottomless cliff with a railing around it. So, so this was how it was, this was what he was, this was what he could be, what he could become! Lies emerged from that pit full of corpses, that poisonous snake that she had never seen before. Was it a bamboo snake? The colour was like bamboo leaves.

"Is it true?" she asked.

"Yes," he answered.

"And the business with the thermometers, is that true too?"

"Yes."

The fire in the furnace had gone out. He sat down and added kindling, stirring the fire with the poker and blowing into the fire chamber.

"Why!" She put all her strength into the question.

"No reason!" He stood up, and smiled as though there were nothing wrong. "If you don't want to be a patsy you have to be a cheat!"

Whap! She raised her right hand and slapped him hard. She saw stars; they filled the room with a flash like lightning. She was stunned. She leaned against the wall, holding up her hand and shaking all over.

She looked at him in terror. What had she done now? He might hit her back. She turned and seized his arm from the side, hanging on for dear life.

He pushed her gently away, looking at her with narrowed eyes, as though he were meeting her for the first time, staring at her in silence. His face took on a livid deathly grey that struck terror in her heart. After this grim stare had lasted for a few seconds, she saw the door open and Chen Xu walk straight out.

A frog popped out of the water onto a lotus leaf and then hopped from the lotus leaf onto a mountain top.

There was a pond on top of the mountain, with a goldfish swimming around in it. The goldfish and the frog had identical eyes. She looked at her reflection in the pond and saw that she too had eyes just like the goldfish. She swam in the pond. There were cliffs on all sides. She could not swim away.

She was waiting for someone on the mountain top. She could see people down the mountain and hear their footsteps. Some people wearing red scarves were picking tea leaves. She picked very swiftly, using both hands at once. The others all began to shout that she was picking too fast. She detached one of her hands at the wrist and shouted back, It's a false hand, it's a false hand!

A mountain breeze was blowing. It was very cold. She curled up in a ball.

Dr. Yang made his way out of a cornfield with his medicine bag on his back. He was wearing thick glasses and shaking a thermometer. The mercury was jumping up and down. She gave it a shake and out popped a spring.

She awoke with a start and found that she had fallen asleep sprawled out on the edge of the brick bed. There was a large wet patch on her sleeve.

The outside door was open; the wind banged it against the wall.

The alarm clock on the table was ticking away. The hands pointed to a quarter to nine.

Everything that had just happened came back to her in a rush.

She remembered that he had walked out. She had never foreseen that she would get so angry. It was his fault. Why did he lie to people? He should come back and admit to her that he was wrong. If he came back, she would forgive him.

238

She had gone on waiting for him and then fallen asleep.

But now more than an hour had passed, and he still had not come back.

He must be really angry with her.

She had gone too far. She shouldn't have acted like that.

But he...

Where had he gone?

To the company dormitory? The threshing ground? The old man's house?

He had no place to go. But he had not come back.

Her mind was churning with remorse and self-reproach. That time her bicycle had gone into the ditch while she was on her way to send money to the baby, he had come to get her and carried her bicycle all the way back home for her. During her lying-in month, he had lived on potatoes soaked in soy sauce and hominy day after day.

She picked up the flashlight, pulled on a sweater, and walked outside.

The moon was bright, like an eye brimming with tears. It was so bright that all the shadows on it were clearly visible, like stubborn spots of mildew.

Some girls were walking toward her, chattering away.

One of them said, "The moon is so bright, you can gather kindling by it."

Another said, "It's so bright you can see to sew!"

And yet another said, "No one would dare steal anything with the moon so bright."

She walked faster. The moon itself had a shameful secret. It hid that half forever in darkness.

She knocked at the door of the men's dormitory, looking for Bubble, and asked if Chen Xu was there. Bubble was quite surprised and said he had not been around that evening. She also asked him if there was a night shift, and Bubble said there wasn't. He asked her what was up, but she changed the subject. She did not want people to know they'd had a fight, so she left in a hurry. She thought she'd go over to the threshing ground for a look, but the sight of the little path lined with wormwood stalks like dense swarming human shadows scared her a little. She walked back and forth a few times along the main road, but she was afraid to go on. She remembered hearing people say that back in the days when this had been a labour reform camp, people had frozen to death along that path every winter. Her flesh crawled.

The moonlight drifted over the vast green waves of lush grain in the fields along both sides of the road. The fields were a fond illusion filled with doubts and misgivings, empty and chill. She stood for a while at the side of the road, the slightly bitter and still somewhat unfamiliar tang of the crops on the night air bringing home to her just how strange and far away a place she was in, how weak and alone and comfortless she was.

And suddenly her eyes, her whole heart, were on the verge of tears. She just wanted to find him soon. If she could just find him, she would forgive him for everything.

A ray of hope appeared to her. She thought, He must have gone home already.

She hurried back home.

To save time, she took a short cut through the piles of firewood outside the houses. The moon was so bright that she could see every piece clearly.

She almost tripped over a bundle of kindling.

It was their own straw pile. There were a few bundles of sheepgrass scattered around.

All of a sudden, she heard a noise in between some bundles that were lying flat on the ground. It sounded like faint snoring.

Her hair stood on end, she was so startled. She swept her flash instinctively over the straw pile and saw a high, broad forehead glimmering in the moonlight.

She knelt down and put her arms slowly around him. She took his thick hair in her hands and gently cradled him in her arms. A great teardrop fell onto his forehead.

"It's my fault." she said.

"It was me." She buried her face in his chest and began to sob quietly.

29

The geese had come and gone, tracing out against the blue sky the V-shaped Chinese character for 'man' and the single straight brush stroke of 'one', monotonously, over and over again. The solution to the riddle of springtime held off until autumn and finally vanished amid sudden cold spells and frost that covered the earth with silver foil.

Only the leaves in the grove of oak trees at the eastern edge of the Branch Farm, blown all crimson by the autumn wind and fanned dry by the wings of the wild geese, stood out brightly in the rich morning sunlight, rustling like windchimes. Tugged and twisted this way and that by the winds, they fluttered on their boughs, but not a one of them would fall to the ground. Seen from a distance, lined with a thin film of newly formed ice, their flickering made the grove of oak trees look like a dancing bonfire, burning warm and bright.

She was taken by surprise. She just happened to be passing that way.

Autumn had come, and in the woods the leaves had turned yellow and brown. The wind swept them off to dance in the air. And so the duckling left.

Just as she reached the top of a ridge, her line of sight opened out, running along the edge of the oak grove to take in a broad stretch down below of golden straw, of soil left black by the autumn ploughing, then a green mass of pitch pine seedlings, and against the pure blue sky a bit of tawny cloud. Such was the beauty, the abundance of autumn. Had the grim scenes of autumns past, the murmuring of her heart, the sadness of her dreams, had they all been transmuted in that bonfire? She had never before seen leaves that turned red but did not fall, that kept their vigil over the snow-clad earth until the coming year.

How she wished she could slip into the oak grove to bask in the warmth of that scarlet fire. And yet she hurried past without stopping for even a moment. She had to hurry on to the big fields at the east side of the farm. Everybody on the Branch Farm was there, working to get the corn harvest in quickly. She was already late, because Director Yu had called her in before work especially to discuss the points she should keep in mind while writing her report. And then, just as she was about to set off for the fields, the sheet of red paper bearing the words 'Political Culture Room', which she had pasted up on the door of the little meeting room at the Company Office only two days before, had been blown down by the wind. She had found some paste to stick it back up, but that took time. No one had helped her, because the 'Political Culture Room' was now very definitely in her sole charge.

She touched the stiff notebook in her jacket pocket, the smooth fountain pen. What was she doing with a fountain pen? Taking a fountain pen into the fields? It made her feel that she had somehow become a little strange, a little unfamiliar to herself. It was the Culture Room. How was it that she had suddenly entered this place that she had scarcely dared dream of before?

The Political Culture Room had been set up the previous year, when the papers were full of the slogan 'Read the Six Books by Marx and Lenin'. A few bookshelves remained on the walls of the little meeting room, left over from some time in the past. Of course the works of Marx and Lenin were on hand, and there were also a few dust-covered novels, 'Furnace and Steel', 'Tracks in the Snowy Forest', 'Red Crag' and the like. Then there were long rows of duplicate volumes of 'Shajiabang' and 'Struggles in Hongnan Village', abundantly supplied by the bookstore in town, more than enough to give the impression of a reading room. But by this time it had already lost the plain honest name of reading room and could only be formally opened after the word 'political' had taken command of culture.

Xiao Xiao had gone to the Political Culture Room several times, searching patiently along its vacant shelves in the hope of finding something worth reading. She had dutifully browsed through the new books. If liking them was out of the question, she was equally afraid to despise them. Although they yielded no more flavour than chewing wax, they still elicited a kind of apprehensive respect. Each of the magazines, whether large format, such as 'Red Flag' or 'Study and Criticism', or small, such as 'Party Life', had a nail hole through its upper left-hand corner, through which a string tied to a nail on the wall had been threaded. For some reason, all their lower right-hand corners were curled up, so that they looked like cabbages cut open across the top.

When the Political Culture Room had first opened, quite a few people had come, but most of them just took a turn around it and left in giggles. The books still stood neat and tidy on the shelves. There was only one thick book standing up straight on the shelf, with an odd black streak running down the top of the pages. She took it out. It was a 'Barefoot Doctors' Manual'. Before she could flip through it, it fell open of its own accord, as though it were mounted on a spring, right at the place marked by the black streak. At the top of the page were the words: Chapter 8 — Personal Hygiene.

A tall girl from Harbin had been in charge of the Culture Room then. They often saw her as they were setting out for work in the morning, emptying the water from her wash basin. Later, she had disappeared without any warning. Someone said that she had gone to Qingdao and joined the Army.

After she left, the Culture Room was closed.

Xiao Xiao had been to sneak a look in the Culture Room door. It seemed to her as though yet another window in their life had been shut. She would have liked the Culture Room to be open every day, even if there was nothing in it.

After Secretary Li's first stay, Director Yu had called her in for a chat one day.

"The Political Culture Room is going to be reopened. After all, political work is the lifeline of all economic work. So, the Branch Farm's Revolutionary Committee has decided to have you take over this important revolutionary responsibility. Eh? Why? You should know the answer to that. It's because you have already struck roots on the Farm. To have struck roots makes you an example for the urban youth."

Struck roots? That was a new one! Only 'progressive models' used that phrase, in their 'study and application' reports. She had never dreamed that 'striking roots' could be used in connection with her. It didn't make much sense.

Yu went on talking at length, saying something to the effect that the Culture Room would be open every weekday evening and on Sundays, so every afternoon she would go to the post office at Branch Farm No. 7 in place of the postman to pick up the mail. In addition, she should write regular news reports for the Farm's central broadcasting station and the 'Three Rivers Daily', one report each week. She could use her working hours for writing them.

Running the Culture Room and serving as acting reporter and postman. It was the work previously done by three people.

But she was not about to haggle. She was simply stunned, simply excited; she simply nodded. She was astonished by this sudden inexplicable favour, even a little dazed by it. Everyone on the Farm was trying to get out of working in the fields by whatever means they could. The locals relied on personal connections; the outsiders on gifts. And she? She was the wife of Chen Xu, with whom Director Yu was so fed up. She was. What was going on?

Chen Xu frowned. "What's so special about taking care of a few books? If you've got any backbone, you won't do it! How do you know what Catfish has got up his sleeve?"

"Probably, probably it isn't Catfish," she objected haltingly. "I think it may be Secretary Li's idea. He's been in office for six months, and he's already 'streamlined administration' twice. All the 'local force' teachers at the high school have been replaced by young people from the cities."

He grunted, "If he's so fond of talent and has such insight, why hasn't he given me a job?"

Xiao Xiao found the attraction of the Culture Room irresistable. No matter how Chen Xu sneered, she started work there, started her participation in the official political study, filled with enthusiasm and caution. As she gently wiped the dust from each white-jacketed book, as she got together paper and ink and wrote in the words 'Political Culture Room' stroke by stroke, she felt for the very first time that she would truly belong to the Farm henceforth. The strange thing was that she had never felt that way before, not even the day they registered their marriage or the day her baby was born.

I think I should go out into the world, said the little duckling.

All right. Go on then, said the hen.

Today would be the first time since taking up her new job that she would be carrying out her duties as a reporter.

Once she had left that bonfire behind her, the brown cornfields lay ahead, the rows sparse, but dense with people.

This mass attack on the harvest had burst upon them with Secretary Li. He had assumed personal command of it. If he had not come back for a second stay, the corn planted in the big eastern fields would have had to wait until the following spring.

Director Yu had his own way of handling the visits of quality-check teams sent in from higher levels. He had the crops along the road harvested, had the mess hall prepare a few dishes, and then came up with a few bottles of good wine. In this way he had managed to muddle through each time by hook or by crook.

Then, to his surprise, Secretary Li arrived. Within three days, Li had been to see every field, even this remote bog. On the fourth day, he had brought the work forces of all the company together and led them personally on this war of annihilation. She had just heard Director Yu say that Secretary Li was going to adopt the responsibility system. Each worker would cut down stalks, strip the cobs, and pile up the stacks, after which the quality inspectors would check and accept the crop. Whether this would work or not they would see after it had been tried. Yu himself was going to Farm Headquarters for a meeting and would hear detailed reports on the situation after he got back.

She left the ox-cart road, crossed a patch of weeds, and approached the corn fields. In less than half a day, the corn had been cut almost as far as the eye could see, revealing the streaked brown fields. The workers had already shrunk to small black dots following the solid rows of stacked corn stalks into the distance. She walked along a ditch between the rows, her trouser legs snagged by cockleburs that had not been cut down. She squatted down to pull out the burrs and saw the parched yellow cobs lying in the furrows between the rows. They really were scrawny.

"When I first came to the Great Northern Wastes, the fish in the rivers and creeks were old ones, heaps of them... With one shot, I brought down a four hundred pound..."

There was a voice coming from the row of corn stalks nearest her. A crowd of people was sprawled around it, apparently taking a break. A little old man was buried in a mass of brown-coated city kids, caught up in a story he was telling.

"Well, there were lots of fish, and wolves, too. How many? Once it got dark, those green wolf eyes had us surrounded like the stars." He chuckled. "I'm not kidding you. Believe it or not; it's up to you. I loved hunting wolves. When I got one we'd fry up a pan of wolf meat to satisfy our appetites for something good to eat!"

Xiao Xiao could make out the gravelly voice with its Henan accent amid those bursts of laughter, but she had never dreamed that he would be entertaining everyone by telling stories. It was Secretary Li. There had never, ever before been an official at the Branch Farm who sat down in the fields.

"Back when we was clearing the land," A lanky figure stood up, rubbing his eyes and hitching up his trousers. It was Liu the Brute. He must have been awakened by the laughter, and now he was getting in on it. "Back when we was clearing the land, it was mosquitos and no-see-'ums we had a lot of."

Someone interrupted him. "How many would you say there were?"

"There was so many, so many that when you went to the privy your butt was bit all over before you could even squat down on the straw. If you wanted to take a crap, you had to climb a tree and squat in a fork between the branches"

More laughter, people laughing until their sides ached. Xiao Xiao smiled too. Someone noticed that she had come and dragged her over to sit with them. She sat down on a stack of corn stalks, but they dug painfully into her legs, and when she looked down and poked around in them, a pile of soda pop bottles appeared under the stalks.

Someone whispered in her ear, "Don't say anything. Secretary Li bought them. He's having a contest with everyone in gathering up the stalks, with pop as the prize. He's lost once, but he won't give up."

Xiao Xiao's eyes went round at the sight of the lively Party Secretary. His sober face, the skin rough as the bark of a tree, looked so straightforward and simple now, puffing happily on the cheap cigarettes offered by the city kids. His open smile suddenly moved her deeply.

"Hey! Secretary Li!"

There was a young guy with a bicycle on the cart road, his hands cupped around his mouth to make his voice carry. He was shouting as he walked along.

"Where's Secretary Li?"

Li jumped up from the pile of corn stalks.

"Over here!"

The young fellow broke into a run, following the rows in the direction of Li's voice.

"There's a phone call from Farm Headquarters. The Party Secretary from the Bureau is there. They want you to come back."

Li's expression changed. His face fell and he yelled at the top of his lungs. "Phone them back! Tell him that if his car can make it to Half-way River, it can get down here to the Branch Farm! Tell them that Li says if they want him they'll find him down here!"

He turned around, waved, and shouted, "Let's get back to work!"

And so the soda pop contest resumed. She remained standing on a ridge between the furrows, almost in a trance. Where would she begin her report? With the soda pop? The stories? They were beside the point. She bent down and idly chose a row, stripping off the cobs, thinking to herself that she should look for a chance to chat with some of the people working there.

While she was hesitating, she looked up and saw Secretary Li staring toward the rows of corn along the west side. After watching for a while, he hefted his sickle and took off in that direction, striding along like a shooting star.

There were a few people working a row on the west end of the field, going so quickly that they had left everyone else far behind.

Then Xiao Xiao realised that one tall figure among them moved very much like Chen Xu.

She followed.

Secretary Li walked up to the row, bent over, and poked around in the stalks, walking along as he did so. After he had covered some length of the row, he straightened up, his face grim. He sighed and hurried on.

"Say, fellow, you're making good time." He chuckled.

The other man straightened up and glanced at him coolly. It was Chen Xu.

"You're fast all right, but you're not doing a thorough job." He was still forcing a smile. "If you only aim for speed, that's no good, you know."

Chen Xu looked at him without saying a word.

As Xiao Xiao looked along his row at the piles of corn cobs, thinner than the other people's, she had already figured out what he was up to. As he cut the corn he was only stripping off a third of the corn cobs and leaving the other two thirds on the stalk. So he was going faster than anyone else.

Her face burned, and the soles of her feet felt sticky. Of all the times for this to happen! What about her report? Her first one. She felt like giving him a few good whacks with something.

"Go back and do it over," said Secretary Li quietly, "And you're not to do it this way again."

Chen Xu stood there without moving a muscle. He caught sight of Xiao Xiao out of the corner of his eye and snickered, "Do it over? Wouldn't that be a complete waste of labour?"

"What's that?"

"Have you looked to see if there are any grains under those husks?"

Chen Xu folded his arms and looked smug.

Secretary Li did not get angry at his impertinance. He just stood there a moment, then bent down, picked up a cob, and pulled away the husk.

The grains of corn were a pale yellow, shrivelled up and wrinkled, as scraggly as an old man's teeth.

"I suppose you've noticed," sneered Chen Xu, "That all the cobs are like this. Could they be used for food even if they were picked? Stop playing the fucking Eighth Route Army man fooling the Communist Party and treating us like a trained monkey show. Why didn't you find out first whether this marsh was suited for corn, whether it would grow stalks or cobs, and then come around issuing your orders? It's stupid leadership!"

"Chen Xu!" cried Xiao Xiao.

Secretary Li turned red and pale by turns. He clenched his teeth and pursed his lips, staring at Chen Xu but not interrupting him.

"Go on..."

Chen Xu began to grow vehement. "Look, this three-day mass campaign is a complete waste of effort! You can't do anything with corn like this except feed it to pigs. If you people are so smart, why didn't you send the stalks and cobs off to be ground up together for fodder? You could have saved us running around and kowtowing all over the place to buy feed once winter starts. Haven't the militia people been using that kind of mixed pig fodder for a long time? An ignorant old guerrilla leading the young guerrillas; it's the dumbest thing I ever heard of. All you understand is these human wave tactics. You're prying food out of people's mouths just so you can hit one of those targets in the slogans, 'Topping the National Agricultural Programme', 'Crossing the Yellow River'. You're just fooling yourselves and everyone else besides!" He gasped for breath and pointed out at the fields. "If you'd turned this marsh into fish ponds, we'd have been able to get a taste of fish. Oh no! you had to go taking grain as the main link so you could win a prize for learning from Dazhai. But nature just turns around and makes us pay the penalty. Since you're the Farm's Party Secretary, you might come down and do a little looking into what's actually going on here, find out for yourself how these local dictators are just paving roads to wealth and office for themselves with state property and the blood and sweat of us city people. Then you could talk!"

He was overwrought from his speech. He tugged his collar open, gasping for breath. The October sun had withdrawn its warmth from the wide fields, and the puffs of steam that burst from his thin lips swirled under the clear autumn sky.

Secretary Li smiled. It seemed to Xiao Xiao that there was something forced and bitter in that smile. He was keeping this obviously lop-sided conversation going with his last bit of patience. It was unbearable. Should she try to reason with Chen Xu? He had made a mess of everything. If she tried, things could get even worse, Why at a time like this did he have to display this sudden passion for truth-telling?

"Well, Chen Xu! You've got a very sharp tongue! I'm afraid I'd scarcely be up to a debate with you." He took a deep breath at last, and looked a good deal more relaxed. "We discussed things on the Farm once before, and we should find some time for another chat. I'll just listen and let you talk. How about it? I know you have lots of good ideas about the Farm..." He looked up, saw people starting to gather around, and spoke even more tactfully. "But for now I'm asking you to do your row over again the way I say. And do a thorough job of it this time!"

His voice would have driven nails.

Chen Xu paused for a moment and then threw his sickle to the ground, yelling, "Not me, mister!"

He turned and walked away, his trouser legs rustling against the corn stalks.

"Come back here!" shouted Li.

Chen Xu marched off without a backward glance.

30

A flock of geese flew over.

They honked noisily.

She could see a dark spot on the feathers of one of the geese. Its wings were very short and its legs stuck out behind it. There was a triangular patch attached to one foot.

It called to her as it swooped down to earth.

Wasn't this the little duckling, the Ugly Duckling? She wondered how it had turned into a goose. It was supposed to turn into a swan. Of course, the swan's egg had been broken long ago by Bull, so it could only turn into a goose. A goose was still better than a duck, though. It could take off and fly south for the winter.

The duckling was making indistinct noises. Sometimes it seemed to be calling her name, sometimes to be calling to its companions up in the sky. She looked up, but there were no swans in the sky, only clouds, drifting slowly along.

Still quacking her name, the duckling waddled up to her holding a letter in its flat bill. The envelope had a gilded image of the 'The Three Pools Reflecting the Moon' in West Lake. She opened it up, but there was nothing inside except a train ticket.

She threw the ticket as far as she could and ran away with all her might. All the books from the wooden shelves in the Culture Room began running after her. She looked back and saw a long white train, the cars made of thick books, the windows of thin ones. There was a black seal over the door. She pushed it aside and found written inside: "Chapter 8: Personal Hygiene."

She leafed noisily through the books, from one end of the train to the other. There were no words on the pages; every page was blank. Her heart trembled with apprehension. If there were no words on the pages, wasn't the Culture Room a sham?

And so she went looking for a pen, but the pen had fallen down onto the tracks. It was all black and wet down there, the pen standing erect like a human being as it sank...

Was it yesterday? The day before? What had happened? She ought to have said something to Secretary Li by way of apology. She felt that she had let him down, but she could not get the words out of her mouth. Her mind was all in a muddle. After Chen Xu had walked off the job, there was nothing for her but to be a good girl, to take over his row and go on silently binding the corn. She was depressed the whole day. All the happiness that the change in her job had brought her over the preceding few days vanished in a flash.

How could she write a report now? Her first assignment as a reporter, and it was all over!

It was pitch dark by the time they got off work. The weather forecast was for snow the next day, so Secretary Li had insisted on finishing field number seven. And what was more, they had actually finished it. Ordinarily, one of the big eastern fields would have required twice the work force. If the moon had been out, she would just as soon have gone on working in the fields. What could she say when she got home? She was glad to be getting off work late. It was actually getting harder and harder to while away the evening hours. She dawdled along, walking behind everyone else. As she passed the grove of oaks, she looked away. She was afraid that its indistinct flash of red would make her feel even worse.

Why wasn't the light on? As she approached the farm, she caught sight of the first row of family housing in the distance and realised that one space in that row of lighted windows was black. It aroused a sense of foreboding, like a squinting blind eye.

Her heart skipped a beat. It was their window.

The first night they had put in the lightbulb, all the windows had been lit up.

She hurried the last few paces and threw the door open. The air stank of alcohol, and there was a dark form curled up on the brick bed. She turned on the light and saw Chen Xu leaning against the heated wall in a daze, holding a bottle in his hand. A bowl in front in him held some of the garlic eggplant she had pickled just a few days before.

"Have you been drinking?" she gasped.

He grunted.

"Really? Have you been drinking?"

"Well, it's not like it was poison!"

She stood there dumbfounded, and all at once something dawned on her.

"So, this morning, out in the fields, all those things you said, was it because, because you were drunk? You must have been drunk. Did you get drunk in the fields?"

He threw back his head and laughed.

"Drunk? Me drunk? When have I ever been drunk? Did I look drunk to you? I would have had to be drunk to go on like an idiot, picking each and every cob. It just felt so good this morning, telling them everything that had been festering inside me!"

She looked doubtfully into his eyes. They glistened with excitement, but his eyelids drooped, calm and alert as usual. His eyes were as mysterious as a well, gathering water from the crevices in the earth on all sides. There were people who were incapable of getting drunk; they had no reaction to alcohol. Was he really not drunk?

"If you weren't drunk, why did you throw down your sickle and leave?"

"Now maybe you've got something to write about!" His face fell, and he grumbled, "It was so you could write your report and be a big success: 'Farm Party Secretary Helps Educate Backward Youth'."

She opened her eyes as wide as she could, to keep her tears from flowing out. She felt so wronged that for a moment she could think of nothing to say. She walked out into the front room without a word and found the stove cold and the pot empty. She was disappointed. Her stomach was rumbling.

"You mean you've been home all this time and haven't even made dinner?" she muttered.

"Dinner?" She heard him sneer in the inner room, followed by the sound of the bottle cap. A gurgling noise—he had taken another drink.

She felt impelled to go back inside.

He glared at her. "Make dinner? Me make dinner for you? You must be kidding! You've been sitting in an office all day. You're the big shot, you're the one who knows how to get things done. While I was taking them all on singlehanded, you just stood there and didn't so much as fart."

A chill scurried up from the soles of her feet. Her ears rang and she felt a pounding in her head. Her hands twitching, she swooped forward and snatched the bottle, screaming, "Stop drinking, you drunk!"

He leapt at her, clutching the neck of the bottle in one hand and grabbing her by the arm with the other. He yelled, "Any more out of you and..."

"Don't try to scare me!" She squeezed her eyes shut.

She heard a crash. Something flew past her ear and a cool spray touched her arm. The strong smell of alcohol filled the air. She opened her eyes and found the floor around her littered with pieces of wet broken glass. Chen Xu was standing with one foot up on the edge of the brick bed, his head lowered and sucking on one of his fingers. There were a few drops of red on the mat.

She felt like crying, weeping with great loud sobs and flowing tears. Shall I bandage it up for you? But she could not cry; she had no tears. Serves you right! She felt like going over and kicking the little table to pieces, breaking the windows. You could get drunk from the smell of alcohol, go crazy. And if you drank it, if...

Then she realized that someone was calling her name from the front room.

She jumped across the room as though she had received an electric shock, blocking the doorway. "What is it?" she shrieked in a blood-curdling voice. She'd say she had broken it by accident, she'd say...

"Director Yu wants you to come over to the company office," shouted the visitor. He didn't sound like he was coming in. She said she'd be right over, and he left.

She stood still in the front room for a moment, and then let out a deep breath. She picked up the broom and dustpan and swept up all the broken glass from the floor and the brick bed. Then she wiped off the mat. She washed her face in cold water, put on her scarf, and left without looking at him.

There was no moon. The black sky was low and thick. A fine, invisible rain swept past her face on the chill night wind. I like black. Black is the most permanent, the most penetrating, the truest colour. Something moved beside the road. She jumped and swept her flashlight in that direction. There in someone's garden stood a row of headless sunflowers, their bald stems swaying in the wind. There was a patch of tobacco stripped of leaves, the stalks bare of everything but their withered sprigs of seed, trembling and moaning in the dark, a reminder of the lonely cold of the autumn night. A night like this should be spent in a warm embrace, but she hadn't even had dinner.

Hunching her shoulders, she ran the last few paces and up the stairs of the office. She felt as though her very heart was about to start shaking.

Yu was sitting in his black leather chair, enjoying a cigarette, his expression enigmatic. Why was he back here after only one day? That report... He went on reading his newspaper for some while before looking up and noticing that she was there.

"Have a seat." He smiled politely. "I didn't ask you over for anything in particular. I just haven't had a chance for a chat with you since you were transferred here."

She tensed.

He cleared his throat.

"When the Farm Party Branch assigned you to work in the Political Culture Room, what was your understanding of the reason for it?"

"The leadership's concern for educated young people," she replied mechanically.

"And Chen Xu?"

"He, he was grateful too."

He flicked the ash off his cigarette against the edge of his desk.

"If the Farm Party Branch were going to subject Chen Xu to persecution, would we arrange a good job for his wife?"

"No. No, you wouldn't." She hung her head.

"You must be aware that Chen Xu's performance has not amounted to much since he came to the Farm. And then there's that stuff during the Cultural Revolution. How can we give him anything important to do? He has the ability, but his line of thinking is incorrect. Haven't we been helping him with our criticism all along? And how have we treated you? Haven't we treated you separately from Chen Xu?"

She stared at him in blank incomprehension. She hoped with all her heart to hear in those rolling eyes what he was driving at.

"It's a shame. He looks bright, but he keeps doing these crazy things. He just doesn't know right from wrong." His smile disappeared, and he leaned back heavily in his chair.

He sounded earnest and thoroughly distressed. His cigarette glowed and faded by turns between his fingers, the smoke swirling around him. They had already reached the brink; another step would hurl them into the abyss. What kind of trouble had Chen Xu gotten into behind her back? Could it be that row of corn that he didn't pick clean? Couldn't he do it over? "Director Yu!" Her lips trembled. She would say that Chen Xu had had an eye infection lately, so he couldn't see the plants clearly.

She had the impression that Yu had pulled open a drawer and taken out a thick letter. The writing on the envelope was very familiar, and so was the stamp, commemorating the soldiers on Zhenbao Island. Yes, yes, it was the complaint that Chen Xu had lodged with the Provincial Office for Educated Youth the previous autumn. It had been returned to the Farm. He had done his best in that letter to explain that he had had nothing to do with the Lin Biao line, but that there were problems in the way the Farm picked people for promotion.

"Problems? What problems? Which of them wasn't better than him? What's he got on his mind?" Yu finally lost his temper. His chair was rocking so hard it squeaked. "It seems to me he's just a careerist, maybe he's even out to take over the Party and seize power. You go home and think it over. If you want to go on working in the Culture Room, Chen Xu will have to knuckle under and admit his mistakes in front of the masses from the whole Farm, do a thorough self-criticism. Otherwise, he'll be sorry. You can take my word for it!"

There flickered before her eyes the bare headless sunflower stalks she had seen on her way over. She had no idea what Yu was saying.

31

It was raining. The road was a quagmire, the roof was leaking, and water was dripping from the ceiling.

She set up a plastic sheet over the bed to keep the water off.

After a while, the plastic began to leak too, and she discovered that it was actually a manila envelope. There was a colourful postage stamp on it.

She went outside. It was still raining. The whole sky was sealed over by a huge curtain of rain.

She walked for a long time, but then it turned out that she was still just wandering around underneath the manila envelope. There was writing on the envelope, and she went over to look at it. The envelope was high above her, and so she started climbing a mountain. The mountain was very steep. There were no steps, just rows of stacked corn stalks. It was a hard climb, but finally she reached the top and found herself standing at the edge of a sheer cliff. There were high mountains and narrow canyons all around her. She looked down. At the bottom of the cliff was a great churning dark reddish river. She wanted very much to fling herself down, but she was afraid.

She stood at the top of the cliff with sheer drops all around her and nowhere to go.

The sky was very low, and she could make out the writing on the envelope. It said, "What Kind of Person is Xiao Xiao?"

It was actually a big-character poster.

The big-character poster was crammed with words. She read right through it. At the top was a reference to ten great crimes with which she was charged, and a host of evil deeds.

All at once, a big-character poster had been pasted up on the cliff to her left: "Xiao Xiao Out of the Political Culture Room!" And on the cliff to her right was pasted another: "The Fake Model Settler Xiao Xiao". The posters were extremely long, reaching all the way from the tops of the cliffs down to the bottoms. And there were so many of them. Soon they covered all the mountains. She pushed her way through the crowds and read for a long time without finding out what her ten great crimes actually were. She pushed back and forth, and ran into Zou Sizhu, who was dashing about, drenched in sweat.

She asked him, I haven't seen you in ages; what are you doing?

He answered, I'm looking for my trunk of books.

Did you lose your books?

They were carried off by a thief. The trunk was heavy, and he thought it was grain.

Serves you right, she said. That's what you get for never coming to read in the Culture Room.

He shook his head and traced a circle with his hand.

Are you saying my books are worth nothing? she asked.

He nodded. I only read Hegel and Kant.

He wanted to leave, but she grabbed his jacket. Tell me, what should I do? You're my friend.

He suddenly caught on. He pulled a book from inside his jacket and flipped through it to find a particular page. Then, tapping each word with his finger, he read: A Supreme Directive—We never would have made it into Peking if it hadn't been for the Japs.

She interrupted him. I didn't ask you about that.

Then what are you asking me about?

She thought for a moment, but she could not recall what it was she was asking him. Anyway, it wasn't that. She took his arm and started walking, but the crowd was shoving this way and that, and soon she had lost track of him. She went on pushing her way back and forth through the crowd and then caught sight of him. She called out, and he looked around, but it was Chen Xu. Chen Xu said, Let's go right back. The leading official of Party Central answered my letter. He says my line is the correct one.

Chen Xu tried to kiss her, but she pushed him away. She noticed a foul smell on his hair. He reached out to embrace her, but she dodged him and ran down the mountain. She saw Yu Di with a clarinet slung over her back, singing as she stood at the top of a cliff. Some people were clapping. She was wearing a green army tunic with a turned down collar. The inner lapels were dotted in red on a white ground. It was very pretty. The sunlight glistened on her hair.

She asked Yu Di, What should I do?

Get a divorce, Yu Di said bluntly. Buy a pear and slice it in half with one cut and then you're set.

She went over to a little stand and bought a pear. The stand had only frozen pears, boxes and boxes of them. The pears were hard and black, like balls of lead. They could not be sliced. If they softened at all, they would melt and turn into bags of water. There was no way to slice them in two. She shook her head.

Yu Di was nibbling at the ice crystals on the frozen pear. A band of brightly dressed people playing drums and gongs came toward them. She asked Yu Di what they were doing. Yu Di said, It's a funeral. She looked at them carefully and saw that they had the 'double happiness' symbol on their chests. It was obviously a wedding party. Yu Di shook her head and said, Getting married is a funeral.

Yu Di started playing her clarinet, and pitch-black ink came flowing out of it. Xiao Xiao dipped her pen in the ink at once and began writing one big-character poster after another, cramming them with words.

She went to paste the posters up on the cliffs. A single-plank bridge led over to the opposite precipice. No sooner had she started across than she realised that Chen Xu was walking toward her from the opposite end. She waved, but he did not see her. Get off! she called. He did not listen to her. She tried to go back, but there was no place to put her feet, so she went forward. The plank creaked. She and Chen Xu walked toward each other, until they were face to face, but neither would make way for the other. A blast of air rose from the canyon, and the bridge began to sway. She tried to keep her balance, but lost her footing and plunged down headlong.

Her body gave a violent start and came down hard on the brick bed with a thud that even she could hear.

She awoke with a start.

It was just starting to get light in the room. An ambiguous dark grey had appeared in the window.

She must have been sweating; her shirt was damp. She felt hot and steamy, so she pulled back a corner of the quilt and let her arms rest outside.

She could feel Chen Xu gently tugging the quilt higher.

Was he awake? She curled up, doing what she could to get a little farther away from him, to avoid touching his rough, sweaty skin. They were still sleeping under the same quilt, since there was only one quilt for them to get under. The other quilt was their mattress. Their old single mattress had gone with 'Pole when he died.

After Chen Xu smashed the wine bottle, it had become more

awkward for the two of them to sleep under this same quilt. Actually, Xiao Xiao had long felt that the quilt was too small, just as she had long since stopped wanting Chen Xu to hold her in his arms all night as he had when they first moved in. She was forever aware of a mouldy smell that hung about the quilt. The night she came home after her talk with Director Yu, she had found Chen Xu sound asleep with his clothes on. She shook him awake and told him about the letter and that Yu wanted him to make a self-criticism before a general meeting of the Farm, and about the Culture Room and so forth. To her surprise, he blew up as soon as he heard.

If I'm going to make a self-criticism you make one too anyway I won't I wasn't wrong that was the truth. They aren't training successors they're training brown-nosers an out and out political fraud. I'm going to denounce them I'm going to expose them this damned hole it was after I got to Half-way River my luck turned sour it's some kind of localism chauvinism dogmatism bureaucratism it's such a mess it's every man for himself. I'm in the minority the truth is usually in the hands of the minority that haunted tree said so you don't believe me just ask it...

"If you don't do a self-criticism, what will I do?" She eyed him coolly. Did he really intend to have her buried in his tomb? If they were going to spend the rest of their lives there, they couldn't just go on making such a stupid mess of things.

"You?" He snorted. You think that Culture Room is such a great job you can have such a great future such a glorious career forget it I saw through this dump a long time ago there's no future in this damn hole people here talk bullshit who can understand bullshit who can talk bullshit...

"Don't act crazy just because you're drunk." She patted him on the back. "Let's go to sleep. We'll see about it tomorrow. Anyway, it looks like this is going to be tough."

He whipped back the quilt, tore off his clothes, and slipped into bed. Then he grabbed her and dragged her onto the bed, to himself. Go to bed! He chuckled, with a nasty leer. "You're my old woman; if you don't sleep with me, what do you do? Get off with the Culture Room!"

He clung to her mindlessly. She could smell the musty quilt, could smell his sweat. She was suffocating. She loathed the smell. He was like a frantic hunting dog, a dusky bat. His blood was seething, but her desire had not quickened in the slightest. In fact it suddenly fell to nothing. Finally, she exploded in fury and kicked him with both feet.

After that evening, Chen Xu did not touch her again.

Since they did not come to blows or have any more arguments, they could think everything through calmly from one end to the other in the indifferent silence. Xiao Xiao thought it over for several days and everything seemed clear to her. It was like that summer night when they had snuck back to Hangzhou. There on the dark highway, they had come to a fork in the road. They actually could see to the end of one branch, but even if they had gritted their teeth and followed it, all it led to was an abandoned village. Although the other road led off into the darkness, if they followed it to the end they might come to the main highway, to the railway.

The first time this thought occurred to her, as she lay sleepless late at night, she was shocked, even terrified, that it had come. With the greatest difficulty, she waited for her cold sweat to dry, and when her heart had regained its calm, she could hear the ticking of the little alarm clock. But his breathing flowed as smoothly as time itself, as though without a care in the world: it rose and fell easily, eternally untroubled. As she lay calmly listening to his breathing, tears rolled silently down her cheeks. She clenched her teeth and made up her mind. And then she drifted sadly off to sleep. But when she woke up the next morning, that hard back rose like a stone monument behind her, and she lost heart again. Her son's hundred-day pictures had come, an unfamiliar little face, the eyes still as calm and self-possessed as ever. Xiao Xiao hesitated at the crossroads. Sometimes there were eight roads meeting, rather than four, and there were even times when there was nothing but a black spot. She did not know which way to go. She wanted to talk to him, to put everything before him and ask him what she should do. He always knew what to do, after all. But the days went by and she still resisted, putting off that talk, even though they would have to have it sooner or later. It seemed she wanted very much to get along with him. That damned quilt!

She could feel him stir, reaching out with one hand and pulling up his foot so he could scratch an itch. He was awake.

"There's going to be a meeting of the branch farm tonight," she said abruptly.

"You know, you really could go have a talk with Secretary Li," she added.

Far off in the distance a rooster crowed.

"Thank you for your advice, but, at least so long as you don't turn me in, I plan to skip out," he answered at last.

She took a gasp of cold air. Skip out where? And tomorrow?

"We'll see about tomorrow when it comes. I'm just taking things one day at a time."

Her eyes burned and watered. No, he would never admit he was wrong. Anything he couldn't do he looked down on. That plank bridge. Would they go down together?

She rolled over.

The rooster crowed again. Dawn was pecking at their window.

She looked up at the ceiling. After a long time, she said coldly, "Before you take off, there's something I want to ask you."

The last sampan. Let me grab you. We'll go floating off together.

She actually wasn't sure how to begin her question. She realised that what she had in mind wasn't a quiz at all, but a contract, an explanation. She wanted to say that she understood and sympathized with all his misfortunes and sufferings, that she could forgive all of his faults, his indolence, his smoking, his drinking, his arrogance. The one thing she could not forgive was his lies. Wang Ge, the goat, the thermometers, the Dacron pants, she would not stand for any more tricks like that!

The words flowed from her mouth. "If I were to ask you now to never again tell me anything false, no matter what you'd done, not to lie to me, could you do it? Tell me."

"No, I couldn't!" The answer came at once, without reflection.

An abyss. A frozen pear spinning around on the ice.

"Why not?" She sat up. "Why couldn't you? This is what is destroying us, destroying everything most sacred to me. It's going to ruin both of us, both of us! You're a fool! You are! Why can't you ever tell me the truth?" She was so upset she buried her face in her hands and began to cry.

"I've never lied to you." She heard him say, as though nothing had happened.

Never lied to me? Never. He never had. It was true.

"Then why do you lie to other people?" She moaned through her sobs. "Is there something wrong with your brain? Don't you understand that lies are always exposed, and that things are even worse then, because people despise you?"

"I don't know," he said, as if to himself. "I don't know either. I never plan in advance to lie to people. It's just something that comes over me on the spot. I can't help it. It seems like you can't get anything done without lying." He dug the sleep out of his eyes and yawned.

She stopped crying and looked at him in wonder and despair.

"But that day in the cornfield, you told the whole truth, you said what no one else dared to say. Why was that?" He had things all backward. "I've discovered that when you tell lies, it's always about, about things..."

"Things?" He seemed on the point of laughing.

"What I mean is, well, something concrete. But about things that are emotional, or intellectual, it seems like, well..."

"Your discovery is most important." He gave her a sly wink. "Can't you take it a step farther and see that when I tell lies it's always other people I fool? I've never tried to fool myself."

Fool himself? What did fooling oneself mean? Fooling people seemed so complicated.

"I never fool myself." He seemed to take some satisfaction in it. "You've spent two years with me. You ought to understand that much. These days only a zombie could believe in people not telling lies. Everyone wants good food, good clothes, a good job; everyone wants to go back to the city; everyone hates this farm, but nobody says any of this. I'm the only one who dares. I have desires and feelings, I wouldn't be a man if I didn't. But for the sake of them I'm always having to tell a different sort of lie. And it's worth it! There are people who look like they never lie. But their hearts went false long ago. I want to live like a real human being, so I'm the one person I can't fool. If I started fooling myself, then I really would be finished. That must be what you mean by emotional, eh?"

She was fed up with listening to such nonsense. She sneered, "So you think that justifies you?"

"Of course it does!" He clenched his jaw savagely. "I've already been double-crossed and tricked enough by other people! I'm going to get my revenge! After Lin Biao went down that September, everyone else saw through the whole sham. You're the only one who didn't!"

"Shut up!" She cut him off. Her heart was pounding. She was incapable and weak; she would never be able to convince him. He was a diamond and she was glass. She threw her clothes on, got out of bed, and put on her shoes. She took her head in both hands and swept her hair back with all her might. Then she turned around and blurted, "I understand now. I never did before. You can't live the way I want you to, and I absolutely refuse to take the road you've chosen. I've done everything in my power, but you don't need me at all. I guess you still feel that I'm standing in the way of your freedom. We've stuck it out through two years together, but it looks like we can't keep on like this. And so..."

She swallowed, took a deep breath, and stopped. In the dull morning light his tousled hair and ashen face looked grim and cold. When his hair was this dry the sharpness of his cheekbones was hateful. How could he be like this! Say it now! If she didn't say it now she might lose the courage to speak.

"So, perhaps it would be better if, if we separated!"

He had made her say it.

He sat up a little, fished a crumpled cigarette out of his clothes, lit up, took a long drag, opened his mouth, and exhaled the smoke toward the ceiling.

He took one long puff after another, without saying a word.

If he had thrown down the cigarette, seized her tightly in his arms, and shouted, "Nonsense! I won't let you go! Let's start over again! I'll change, I'll change for sure!" She would have answered him with tears streaming down her face. "I won't leave. I was just trying to scare you. We won't separate!"

He stubbed the cigarette out on the heated wall, folded his arms behind his head, and said coolly, "All right then, we separate. I knew long ago it might come to this."

She stood paralyzed, then averted her face and said acidly, "Yes, that love of yours was probably just another little lie." She screamed, "It was fake!"

"As you like." He sat up and slowly got dressed. "Whatever you think, it's all the same to me. There's no other way for us. Oh, you'd better go and find out all about the procedures to follow. I'll go with you."

He had to try several times to do up his last button, and then it turned out to be on the wrong buttonhole, so he slowly unbuttoned it and then did it up again. He let out a deep breath at the same time.

32

The brick bed had cracked, and the room was filled with smoke, but they could not find where it was getting out. There was smoke everywhere.

Yellow false flowers were visible through the smoke, growing all over the floor. There was a white melon growing on each stalk. How could false flowers form fruit? she asked out loud. No one answered, and when she took a careful look she found that the white melons were just frozen pears. She got a knife and tried to cut one open, but it simply would not cut, no matter how she tried. She put the pear in the smoke to warm, and it softened almost at once. She cut it open, but it was just an empty husk with nothing inside. It all dawned on her. The fruit formed by a false flower was a false fruit.

Bull came by leading a horse. The horse was stumbling and limping, hanging its head wearily. After a few steps, it stopped and began to sneeze.

Bull said to Liu the Brute, The horse is tired.

Is it the horse that's tired, or is it you? growled Liu, hugging his bottle of wine.

Bull whipped the horse, but it would not move.

Bull laid into the horse's back, his whip whistling through the air, but even when it was struck, the horse would not move, and as the whip came at it again, it reared up on its hind legs, almost fully erect, and stayed that way as the whip fell. Its bay skin was lashed to ribbons and oozed blood all over.

Will you move or not? screamed Bull at the top of his lungs.

It let out a long neigh, without moving an inch.

The whip fell again, striking the roof of a house, which fell in with a loud crash. It struck a tree and pulled it up, roots and all. But the horse just stood there, blinking its eyes.

Stop beating it! She ran over and grabbed Bull's whip, but he pushed her away.

She stumbled and fell into a carrot field.

The carrot tops were a glossy green. She pulled up a carrot and took a bite. It was crisp and sweet. She pulled up an armful and carried them over to Bull so he could feed the horse.

The horse is hungry; don't beat it, she begged him.

She turned to look. The horse was lying on the ground, frothing at the mouth. It struggled a few times and then stretched out its legs and stopped moving.

Someone shouted, Bull has beaten a horse to death. Beating a horse to death is a crime.

Some people came and dragged Bull off to a criticism session.

It turned out to be a session called to criticise Bull. She breathed a sigh of relief. She and Chen Xu lay stock still in the grass, watching Bull stand on the distant stage, admitting his guilt. He looked very funny.

The autumn reeds were tall and thick. She and Chen Xu took one bundle after another and made a semi-circular windbreak with them and then lay down on the thick straw. The straw was nice and soft and fluffy. She lay with her head on Chen Xu's arm, looking up into the sky.

What are those, she asked Chen Xu, pointing up at some sparkling red fruit in the sky.

They're strawberries. Chen Xu smiled.

Is this Strawberry Glen?

Yes, it's Strawberry Glen.

Will you go pick me some strawberries?

Of course I will.

Be careful not to let anyone see you.

They won't. Anyway, we've both snuck out, so they won't be able to find us. And besides, with Bull for a target, they won't be looking for us.

The moon had come up, a shimmering blue moon. The green plains and the silver Half-way River both turned blue. Chen Xu came walking toward her, holding up a strawberry. It struck her that it was not a strawberry, but rather a blue star. You're trying to trick me, she cried. This is fake, it's a fake strawberry. I want real strawberries, like the ones we saw in Strawberry Glen that year.

I'm not trying to trick you, the moon is, chuckled Chen Xu. The moon is trying to trick you by lighting up the sky with its dark side, so the stars have turned to strawberries. Don't blame it on me; it's not my fault.

265

She walked away into the fields, looking for Strawberry Glen.

One day, after they had got off work and had their dinner, they washed their faces, changed into clean clothes, and went off together to the production brigade office to look for Yu Funian. The day after they had skipped out on the criticism session, they had waited on pins and needles for the axe to fall, but then they heard that a document had arrived from Party Central the night before, a real long one, and the criticism session had not come off. So they were stuck with having wasted several hours just lying in the fields. And now nothing had happened for several days. There was no knowing what Yu Funian was so busy with that he had no time to pay attention to them. Things were always in such a muddle on the Farm anyway. Since they were not being criticised for the time being, Chen Xu's idea was that they had better take advantage of the break to get the thing taken care of. He was always a bit cocky. Xiao Xiao did not object.

The new moon was a slender curve, very much like a large question mark. The new and old moons were parentheses, holding the stars between them. But the new moon was even more like a question mark, following them, only at arm's length.

They had been getting along a little better than before, the preceding two days. Since they would soon be going their separate ways, there was an atmosphere of something like hopeless calm at home. They both believed that this would be a final parting, and so they became more tolerant of one another.

A lamp was burning in the office, and there were two people playing chess.

"Is Director Yu here?" asked Xiao Xiao.

"Not yet."

They sat down on a bench to wait.

There was a poster on the wall, showing girl soldiers on patrol in a patch of reeds, rifles slung over their shoulders. Their thick lips and bushy eyebrows were just like...her!

Chen Xu nudged Xiao Xiao with his elbow and handed her a mimeographed document. The title read: "Matured Amid the Struggle Between Political Lines—A Report on 'Study and Application', by The Official Pace-setter in Studying the Works of Chairman Mao, Guo Chunmei."

He gestured with his lips and she saw a thick stack of the same kind of documents on the window ledge. They gave off the scent of fresh ink.

She picked up a copy and began leafing through it. The content was the same as the first one, with the addition of a report on the discovery of a 'plane feeding method'. This was simply to feed pigs in facing rows, which was both aesthetically pleasing and an efficient use of space.

People said that Guo Chunmei's selection as the province's Model Worker this time had been recommended by the Branch Farm, but that when the representatives of each branch farm had cast their ballots at Farm Headquarters, she had lost by two votes. Afterwards, the Farm's Political Work Unit had insisted on pushing her and assigned someone to help her recompile her dossier. Thus were 'models' nurtured.

"Look at this." Chen Xu made a funny face.

She followed his finger and found this passage:

> My growth in maturity over the past few years has certainly not been easy going. It has been the product of struggles against class enemies, backward elements among the masses, incorrect political lines, and leaders taking the capitalist road. Struggle is revolution, is victory.
>
> For example, there is an old troop leader on our Branch Farm. He helped prepare me to enter the Party, and I respect him, but I have gradually discovered his problems. He practises favouritism in employing people; he just keeps his head down and pulls his cart, without looking up to see which way the road is leading; he doesn't read anything. When I proposed that the Branch Farm should turn more pigs over to the State, to support world revolution, he absolutely refused. He said that the other branch farms weren't giving more, so what were we trying to prove. There wasn't a war on; if we had pigs we should slaughter them for food and put a little meat on the young people. I persisted in my view: revolution first and physical well-being after. In addition, I reported to the Branch Farm's Party Branch. He scuffed his shoes and yelled something nasty about 'never having seen a stingworm climb backward up a tree'. And he said he had gone out of his way to encourage me and now I was going out of mine to ruin him. Faced with this sort of obstruction and oppression, I once again turned to Chairman Mao's essay 'The Orientation of the Youth Movement'...

She sighed, feeling discouraged. Who could have thought that within two short years poor tongue-tied Guo Chunmei would have become so articulate, so bold. How fierce she was, how aggressive! They had come to the State Farm on the same train, and now Chunmei was going to meetings in the provincial capital, while she herself was waiting to file for divorce.

All of a sudden, the door opened, and Susie J came in with an army greatcoat draped over his shoulders. He glanced at them and said, with a brittle smile, "Well, well, if it isn't the two little geniuses of Farm No.5! Where did you two take yourselves off to the other night when the documents came down from Party Central?"

Chen Xu just sat there without saying a word. Xiao Xiao stood up. Her lips trembled, but no sound came out. It was only because she had not wanted to stay home and let them bother her that she had 'gone into hiding' with Chen Xu that evening. Now that they had agreed to separate, Chen Xu's flat refusal to carry out a self-criticism no longer concerned her. Otherwise their coming in to file an application would have been the sheerest fantasy. No matter how hard it was, she had to speak. She looked at Chen Xu, who remained expressionless.

"We..." she said, so faintly as to be almost inaudible, and then hung her head.

Susie J chuckled. "So, expecting again? Pretty hot stuff, eh? Having kids like you was laying eggs, one with every squawk. Look here, this won't do, there's no plan to it, you're already over..."

Chen Xu leapt to his feet and grabbed him by the collar.

"You watch your language! We've come to apply for a divorce!"

"Whawhawhat?"

Susie J was so startled that he backed up several steps, until he bumped into the window ledge. He stood there staring stupidly for several seconds before regaining his composure, his mouth agape and full of metal teeth. He blew his nose into his hand and wiped it off on the wall. Then he went back over to the black leather chair and sat down with a self-important flourish.

"Did I just hear you say that you, that you wanted a divorce?"

"Yes." Xiao Xiao's raised her voice.

"Which one of you," he drawled, "wants the divorce? Well, what I mean is, who was the first one to call it quits?"

"I was." Xiao Xiao's palms were sweating.

"Hm." He raised his voice, as though interrogating a criminal. "And why was that?"

Xiao Xiao bit her lip, not sure quite what to say next.

"Well, for example, has your husband been convicted of a crime?"

Xiao Xiao denied at once that he had.

"Well, then, has he been mistreating you?"

"No, not that either."

"Hm. All that leaves is that he can't have children. But you've already had one, eh?"

Xiao Xiao's face flushed. She just felt like running away.

"Well now, you say it isn't any of those, so why don't you tell me yourself what the reason is."

"It's because," Xiao Xiao stammered, "Because we, we don't think the same way."

He howled with laughter, his sharp chin twitching. "That's a new one! The two of you are living together, what does thinking have to do with it?"

Chen Xu stood up, grim faced, and said, "Cut the crap. Are you going to do it or not?"

Susie J put on a straight face and replied, "As soon as you don't have your kid around, you must have too much time on your hands, right? A divorce? You think it's easy to get a divorce? There are couples around here who've been at each others' throats for eight, ten years, smashed everything in the house and knocked out a dozen teeth, and they still haven't got a divorce! You..."

Just at this point, Yu Funian pushed open the door and came in. Sun Rujiang leapt to his feet, jumped to one side, and sat down on the edge of the table, relinquishing the black leather chair to Yu.

"I haven't heard of you guys having even one fight, and now you want a divorce?" He went on, spraying saliva right and left. "Never mind that everybody will be saying nasty things behind your backs, if I help you do it I'll be in the shit too, and my name will stink for eight generations. Let me give it to you straight: as long as I'm in charge of the official seal, everybody can forget about this divorce stuff."

Xiao Xiao's head was swimming. She had never dreamed that getting a divorce was so complicated. Perhaps they should write out an application, so they wouldn't have to listen to any more of such lectures.

Susie J winked, cleared his throat, and continued, "Have you got it now? Marriage isn't like kids playing house, getting on fine one minute and broken up the next. It looks to me like you got wind of the news that city kids will get home leaves next year, right? Well! Everybody knows that you don't get home leave once you're married, so if you get a divorce you get leaves too, right? Then, after you've had a trip south to see your folks, you can just move back in together, right? You got it all worked out real pretty; you southerners are real clever!"

Chen Xu glanced at him and said coolly, "It seems to me you ought to understand why we want a divorce even better than we do ourselves. A backward element like me, when I'm not doing time I'm being criticised or carrying out a self-criticism. How could a young revolutionary have any respect for me?"

Xiao Xiao's face felt hot. She snuck a quick glance at Yu Funian, who looked a little taken aback. He had never expected that Chen Xu would find an excuse to shift the problem onto him like this. Good for Chen Xu!

"Well, it's not like that at all," responded Yu Funian with a frown, after mulling it over for a little while. "Of course, what Sun here says is even farther off the mark!"

A ray of hope appeared in Xiao Xiao's heart.

Yu Funian suddenly became much more warm and understanding than usual. He sighed faintly and said, "Well, I've been so busy for the past few days I've neglected to look you two up for a chat. Something must have upset you, eh? You've read a lot, you're educated, so you're prone to emotional conflicts; it's just petty bourgeois sentimentality, that's all, only a little more pronounced. But never mind, it's quite normal for contradictions to occur between a husband and wife. Xiao Xiao has been doing a good job in the Culture Room lately, but if there's some difficulty, just say the word and we can switch you to another job. Chen Xu's problems are a little bigger, but so long as he accepts instruction and corrects his mistakes, he can still be a good comrade."

Why hadn't he brought up that letter again, or Chen Xu's self-criticism? Why another about-face? He wanted to give Chen Xu a scare, but he didn't expect to scare us both away. Now he's afraid he'll be accused of 'sabotage', the disappearance of his 'model settlers striking roots'.

"It seems to me that this is just the time, now that your child is away, to concentrate your energy and make revolution; next year you should be able to be named a 'Good Five Ways' household, you know."

Chen Xu interrupted him. "We came here to request a divorce, not to strike some kind of deal!"

Yu Funian's eyebrows shot up. He muttered to himself for a moment, and then said, "Well, let's leave it at this. You go home now and calm down a little. When you have a little time over the next few days, study Chairman Mao's essay 'On Contradictions'. You can't consider only your personal feelings. You have to take into account the whole movement to rusticate educated urban youth. You've already struck roots on the State Farm, you've set out to spend your lives together with the poor and lower-middle peasants. How can you turn back, give up on it half way? If you do that, what will the consequences be? What influence will it have? What will its effect on the educated urban youth be? These are the really important considerations. Personal affairs are minor, no matter how big they seem."

"We..." Xiao Xiao tried to explain.

"Now, I understand." Yu Funian patted her shoulder sympathetically. "They say that a husband and wife never stay angry overnight. Haven't you two always got along well?"

"You bet," Susie J chimed in. "When I first got here, they were getting along just swell. Is that like people looking to get a divorce? Who do you think you're kidding? You two get this straight: you really want a divorce you can start by not bloody sleeping on the same bed, by not bloody..."

"Sun!" Yu Funian silenced him with a shout.

Chen Xu yanked the door open with a bang and walked out.

Xiao Xiao hurried after him.

The next day, the news was all over the Farm that she and Chen Xu wanted a divorce, a fake divorce so that they could get home leaves. With everyone's guesses and embellishments added on to it, the story created a great stir. The looks they got from all sides were even more curious and contemptuous than before, when they had moved into the little cottage on their own. But now Xiao Xiao no longer had the courage to walk along as she had then, with her chest out and her head held high. She was caught up in a feeling of something like guilt. She went listlessly off to work, morose and taciturn.

The worst of it was that she did not really know how she and Chen Xu ought to get along while they were still living together. The tolerant atmosphere of the previous few days, when they were on the verge of a permanent separation, had been disturbed by the contempt with which they had been met. Even though they were both willing to get through their last days together on polite terms—one getting water and fuel, the other doing the washing and cooking—just as before, to wait without fighting or arguing for the Branch Farm Revolutionary Committee's final approval of their divorce—no one on the Farm would accept this. How could it be anything but a fake divorce when they were still getting along so peaceably?

They had to go to the mess hall to eat, first one, then the other, each one getting water individually and dusting one half of the brick bed. They divided their things up too, half at the head of the bed, the rest at the foot. The mattress went to Chen Xu to serve as a blanket, but then there was the problem of a mattress for him, and so he had to sleep on the mat. Even so, there were always people going out of their way to pass by their back window for a casual look inside. Xiao Xiao herself was confused as to who was divorcing whom. There was only one criterion for divorce, a quilt folded in half like a sleeping bag. Since there were people so anxious to look after their morals for them until their divorce, they dared not hang up their curtain any more.

This kind of life was harder to put up with than fights and arguments.

Xiao Xiao did not know what to do. If she had known in advance how much trouble getting a divorce was, she would have just given up the whole idea. But now that they had raised the issue, they were riding a tiger and could not get off.

First thing one morning, Chen Xu told her that after work that afternoon he was going to pack up his things and move over to the company dormitory. It looked like people wouldn't believe they really wanted a divorce unless they lived apart for a while.

Xiao Xiao nodded. "What about the mattress?" she added. The sky was dark; it looked like snow. He said that he could go sleep with Bubble. Did he really have no second thoughts? If he were to say...

She went off by herself to work. The Branch Farm's postmaster had come back from home leave, so she no longer had to go to the post office for mail every day. Director Yu had not mentioned her work in the Culture Room again since they had requested their divorce. Farm Headquarters had issued a set of study materials, and she had been busy the preceding few days putting them up along the walls. In the afternoon, just before she got off work, the postman brought her a letter.

Her heart skipped a beat. She hesitated a moment before tearing it open.

It was from her mother. The third letter, and she still hadn't written back. In the first letter, her mother had told her that her case had already been declared one of contradictions among the people. She wasn't teaching any more, but working in the school library, where at least she could write letters.

She had been waiting for two years, waiting for a letter from her mother, but she herself had still not written. Perhaps her mother still didn't know she was married, even now that she was about to get a divorce. If she wrote back, what would she say?

She read straight through the letter without stopping. The words were all blurry.

I'm just getting though life now, but without any grand ideals. All I have is a small personal article of faith. I want to go on living for the sake of my children, especially for my poor little Xiao Xiao. If she didn't have me, there would be no one in the world to love her so much. The whole meaning of my life is to allow Xiao Xiao to live happily. Today I'm sitting at the table in the library office for the first time to write to you.

This tiny little reading room is downstairs in what used to be the language teaching and research office. When you were in grade school, you often clambered up the narrow little stairway to come play in my office. From the window you could see the noisy playground of your school and the old camphor tree.

Everyone envies my job, because all I deal with is books and magazines. I don't have to put up with anyone's temper. People are always dreaming of freedom and equality. Actually, there are only a few thousand volumes in this little library; it's terribly limited. You could say that it's emaciated. There used to be so many good books, including the fairy tales that you liked slipping in to read so much you didn't want to come out. But they were all carted off by those impossible students and sold. The books that are left are covered with dust and in terrible condition, so I have to set myself to straightening them out and numbering them. And then I have to subscribe to the periodicals and order movie tickets. I'm so weary each day I can hardly drag myself home. All the same, I like this job very much. I get here bright and early and close myself in until after dark. Busy as I am, I'm always hoping to come across a good book for you to read some day when you come home. Yesterday, I happened on part of a tattered volume of Rolland's 'Jean Christophe'. I was really beside myself, I was so happy. I thought, if my little flower comes back, I will bring her into my reading room and let her read all the books and magazines she

273

wants. How happy she will be! The blossoms have already been shed from the osmanthus tree in the schoolyard, but there is still a rich fragrance on the branches. The osmanthus flowers have been shed three times since you left. The first two times I was still in custody, so I could only smell their fragrance in the distance. These flowers should be for Xiao Xiao, but she still hasn't come home. My dearest daughter, when will you be able to come back to your mother?

Last week I went to the country to see little Lili. (Don't be surprised. Your father and I know all about him. When the baby came down with scarlet fever, his grandmother came looking for us so we could go to the hospital to vouch for him. Of course your father was furious and wouldn't recognise him as a grandson. You know what his temper is like. But never mind. I'm here, so you needn't worry). He can smile and has two little teeth. He looks very much like you did when you were little. It made me miss you all the more...

Xiao Xiao stuffed the letter in her pocket and ran home like a woman possessed.

Chen Xu was just tying up his bags.

She leaned against the door frame, panting. Looking down at the floor, she said, "Don't leave. I, I want to go back to Hangzhou, back home, for a few months."

The cords on the bags came loose one by one.

"I think that, that if we are separated for some period of time, everyone will calm down, think it over..." She still hung her head, speaking a little incoherently. "This way, it's also an opportunity, for you..."

"An opportunity?" His lips curled into a slight sneer. "To make myself over? To test myself? Thank you ever so much."

She was a little irritated, but keeping her self control, she said, "Anyway, if we're separated for a while, it will count as... maintaining separate domiciles."

It took all her strength to speak those last three words.

"All right." Chen Xu tossed the cords all the way across the room and sat down on the edge of the bed. "I'll stay and you go. It's all the same; we just switch places." He took stock of her with a look. "But how do you plan to get a leave? Catfish is counting on you to be his model settler striking roots!"

I think I should go out into the world, said the little duckling.

All right, go on then! said the hen.

274

She bit her lip.

Chen Xu said, "Okay, write your mom and have her send a telegram, just saying the baby is sick. That'll do the trick for sure. Catfish is just now on his way out, and changing hands in the Culture Room kills two birds with one stone. What do you say? Maybe you'd better tell a lie too. These days..." Something occurred to him, and he broke off.

Her mother would probably not be willing to send a false telegram like that. Give it a try?

She stared blankly at him. She believed that he would not deceive her. Did she count as 'himself'?

A week later, the telegram from Hangzhou arrived, more promptly than she would have believed possible.

And sure enough, Yu Funian immediately granted her a one month emergency leave.

Xiao Xiao sold her watch to a young man in the company from Jiamusi and paid off what they owed from their previous trip to take the baby south. The money left over was just enough for a cheap through ticket from Half-way River to Hangzhou. She didn't want to sneak on the trains again.

33

Was this her home? Her home? It had been almost three years. It was like a dream.

There was a picture of the four of them stuck in the little mirror frame. The picture had been taken before her mother was placed under detention. The day she had left home for Heilongjiang, she had longed to take it out and carry it away with her. But now, after more than two years, it was still hanging up on the wall beside her mother's bed.

On the desk stood a china figurine with big eyes. She had dropped him once by accident and chipped his kneecap off. Her mother had taped it back on and covered it with a pencil sharpener in the shape of a violin. They called him the Poor Boy. He sat in the window year in and year out, playing the violin for them.

There were still a few wax plum twigs stuck in the old vase on top of the bookcase. The twigs were adorned with artificial wax plum blossoms that she had made years before by wrapping hot wax with yellow dye in it around her fingers. Now the faded petals were covered with dust, but they had not fallen.

On the pale blue wall were marks left when she had dusted it with a damp cloth. The trunk was covered with a linen cloth on which she had once sewn a round patch. Under the glass on the desk was a butterfly specimen she had brought back from a spring outing years before, the wings half blue and half purple.

It seemed as though she had never left. No, she never had left. The traces of her childhood were everywhere. Such traces were not memories called up anew, but scars branded on her heart, linked to every vein in her body.

This was home, the only home she truly acknowledged deep in her heart. She could not deny it. She had gone to the very ends of the earth, but at last she had to come back, back to the place where she had been born and raised.

Her first meeting with her mother, the prospect of which had troubled her all the way home, was finally past. Two years. She had left determined to have no regrets, but they had tugged constantly at her heartstrings all the same. Could she still feel remorse? After all, it had been she who had thrown away the umbrella that had protected her head for twenty years and run off with him to a land of wind and snow in spite of everything. She had vowed never to return.

But she had waited at the train station until dark and then lugged her heavy bag full of fresh potatoes through the cold autumn rain to knock, soaking wet, at the residence door. If her mother had come a moment later to open it, she might very well have lost forever the courage to knock. The beating of her heart sounded louder than the knocking at the door. The door opened, and she stood there stiffly, chin resting on her collar. In that instant, all the embarrassment, the remorse, the guilt, and the helplessness she had foreseen so many times on the train came welling up within her. The ugly duckling had run away, all its feathers pecked off by its fellows. She was a battered and bloodied survivor of a rout, wearily returning to her point of departure years before. Why did she want to come back?

Then she felt two warm hands struggling to free her from the heavy load on her back, a soft and fluffy towel wrapped lightly around her cold, wet neck and hair, stroking and rubbing her all over. The slender fingers diffused the familiar scent of soap. She buried her head in the rain-dampened towel and wept for joy. The lawn she had loved to play on as a child. When she looked up, she caught sight of the furrows on her mother's forehead, like the veins on the underside of a withered leaf.

Her mother had grown old. In the lamplight, silver strands shimmered in her black hair. But her eyes were still as clear as ever, like a pool of water capable of washing away all the dirt in the world.

It was for her mother's understanding and forgiveness that she had wanted to come home. Perhaps in all the world it was only members of the same family who could forgive one another. It was like a crab's pincers growing back after they had been broken or cut off. Family. Feifei, who had given her a candy wrapper as a momento when she left home, stood silently looking at her. Finally she went over to the pile of wet clothes by the door. Standing up carefully on her toes she asked, "How about a louse? Show me a louse. They say that when people come back from Heilongjiang..."

She was really sorry not to have brought back a louse for her little sister. She had never realised how intimate and important lice were. If she had brought a louse home with her, it too would have received a friendly welcome. It would have, because this was home.

She smelled the scent of sunlight on the bedding, heard the creak of the old bed frame, strung with coir rope. A brick bed was very hard; solid and rigid, but too hard! Only a place with a coir rope bed could be her home. And so she abandoned herself to rolling over in bed.

Her mother had said nothing more, only urged her to go to bed early; she herself would be going out to the front room very early to sleep on the wooden bed. Her mother said that since she had just spent three days and nights on a third-class train seat, she needn't wait up for her father to come home. He had to go to the street committee office every evening to look after investigators sent from all over the place to check up on people in trouble. Father! If you're going to stick with him, don't ever come back! I'm getting out, all right! If her mother had been at home then, they might never have had that fight. How was she going to bring it up, to tell them that she was considering a divorce? And then there was Chen Li. Shouldn't she go to his grandmother's to see him the next day?

She could not get to sleep. An evergreen privet tree outside the window threw the fluttering shadows of its leaves on the wall, painting a strange landscape of endlessly changing forms. The Zhoushan Islands? The Alps? A waterfall on the Amazon? The forests of Xishuangbanna? She had cherished endless dreams in those vague shapes so many years before, dreams of travelling to every unfamiliar corner of the world. There was no place she had not been in her imagination. And finally, at the age of nineteen, she had gone beyond this screen of clouds and travelled to her longed-for horizon, only to discover that she could really hardly take a single step after all. And now that she had come home, those islands and mountain ranges had vanished. All that was left was a rapidly twisting highway throwing her a huge curve just ahead.

Night after night she heard through her drowsiness the clump of galoshes coming in the door, followed by the crackle of a plastic raincoat.

"Is that you?" her mother asked softly.

"Someone else investigating him," said an anxious and irritable voice. "The people they send here on investigations are completely unreasonable. They insist that I blame the failure of our attempt to start a rebellion among the enemy troops on his sabotaging it. He had a hard enough time of it putting together enough money to get a dozen rifles for the uprising, and now they accuse him of plotting a counter-

278

revolutionary coup. It's ridiculous."

Over the preceding few days she had learned bit by bit from her mother that her father had previously been carrying coal at the railway yards, where he could make two dollars a day. But later on, more and more people started coming on various investigations, and each time, someone had to be sent to call him back from the coal yard. His pay was still coming from the neighbourhood administration, which felt that this was a poor bargain, so they had to have him transfered somewhere nearby to be a sheet metal worker. His wages fell to a dollar twenty, but her mother preferred the smaller income, as carrying coal along those high scaffoldings had been too dangerous. And as a metal worker he could repair pots and pans for the neighbours.

"What I just can't figure out is why they keep wanting me to testify that all the people I introduced for Party membership were spies or Trotskyists or traitors." He groaned as he took off his shoes. "Wasn't a single one of all those doctors and journalists and teachers I sent to the base areas any bloody good?"

Xiao Xiao had discovered long before, before leaving home, that her father's language had at some point come to be very oddly assorted. Into the midst of his educated speech he could drop some disconcerting bit of profanity.

"If I had just gone to the liberated area myself instead of getting mixed up in underground work, I wouldn't be in such a fix now!" He went on grumbling, sitting on the edge of her mother's bed. Then he lowered his voice and asked furtively, "How did it go with her today?"

"What do you mean, 'how did it go'?"

"Did she have anything to say about why she came running back from the State Farm?"

"Some people came by this evening."

"Well, why didn't you make a point of asking her after they left?"

"I, I was tired."

"You must talk to her about it tomorrow."

"Let's let her rest for a few days."

"We can't. Every day the real situation isn't clear is another day I can't stop worrying. You should put our position to her plainly. If she still won't admit that she was wrong, if she won't make a firm, final break with that bastard, she'll never have any future."

"All right, all right. Let's get some sleep. It's almost midnight."

Xiao Xiao closed her eyes tight. She felt a sudden pang. This

Chen Xu, hm! He was a reactionary student, he's got no political future. Had she decided to leave him for the sake of her own future? No, she had not. It was not at all so simple as that. Her real suffering lay in her still not knowing whether she had done something wrong. She did not even know if she still loved him. But she believed that he loved her; if he loved her, how could she have been deceived? She did not know whether she should simply throw him away like an old rag, or return him like a misfitted shoe. Or perhaps some rare and unrecognised ore? She just wanted to walk calmly away, to walk away and never hear another one of his lies. What about Chen Li? Ever since she had moved into this simple residence at the age of six, her whole education had been intended to make her a responsible, decent person. He had destroyed her ideals, not just her future.

She was definitely going to leave him. All the memories left behind in that room over the years had been calling upon her at every hour, every minute of the preceeding few days to return to her original track. But she had never foreseen how wide a gulf would have opened up in the understanding between herself and her father.

There was no one at home during the day, so she took on all the housework. Washing and making up the beds and mosquito netting, scrubbing all the pots and pans, shopping and cooking, a busy round from morning to night. She had to keep herself moving at all times, for as soon as she had a free moment, as soon as she came to rest for a second, Chen Xu would leap out from some corner, sneering at her.

I'll hide these books at my house; they'll be perfectly safe there. Why don't you put up a picture of yourself at home instead of those official portraits? I'll come this evening and teach you how to ride a bike.

Everyone seemed to be doing their best to avoid something. Her father looked morose all the time. He said nothing at the dinner table, and once he had finished eating he went out. Fortunately, he did not spend much time at home. Her mother always seemed to have something on her mind that she could not quite bring herself to say. Only Feifei was in good spirits. As soon as she got home each day, she would start telling stories about things at school that sounded as if they could only have happened in some comedy show. But when Xiao Xiao stopped laughing, she felt just as heavy-hearted as before.

Finally, one evening, as they were washing up together in the kitchen, her mother suddenly whispered, "Why haven't you gone to see the baby yet?"

"Chen Li?" She chose this reply on purpose. She did not want to use the word 'baby'; she still could not bring herself to say it. She did not know what it was, but something was keeping her, blocking her from going to see him. She ought to have gone as soon as she got off the train. She was afraid he would call her mama, and so she kept putting it off, until a week had passed. Avoiding her mother's gaze, she said casually, "Oh, I'm, I'm going tomorrow. Later..."

Should she say it? But once they were divorced, what about the baby? Perhaps this was the only reason that she was afraid to see him.

Her mother's reply was immediate. "Go tomorrow. Don't go back to the nurse's place in the country. Their brigade isn't allowing them to take in children any more, so Lili's grandmother took him back to her own house. Do, do you want me to go with you?"

She shook her head. She could not go to his house to see the baby. If they knew that she had come back, they might send the boy to her. People who loved their children were rarely able to bring themselves to go through with a divorce. So, should she say it? Can you take it, Mother? With a somewhat forced smile, she said, "What shall we do? I don't want to go to his house. I don't get along with his grandmother, but Lili..."

"Well then, you'd better let me go pick him up," responded her mother at once, as though she had thought it all out well in advance. "I can say that I'm taking him for his shots."

Xiao Xiao felt as though the needle had struck deep into her own flesh. She bit her lip hard. I can say? Can? Mother, when did you learn to tell lies too? She splashed the water in the basin around noisily and asked, hanging her head, "Where will you bring him? Here?"

"No, no." Her mother's eyes flashed. "To the park..."

In the Indian summer of a southern October, in the balmy midday light, it still seemed possible to smell the long vanished scent of osmanthus blossoms. The few perfectly ordinary lavender chrysanthemums left in the flower garden raised their proud heads. The flowers back in the meadows belonged to whoever picked them. Where had that little boat sailed away to, the one decorated with parasol tree seeds for sailors? Only the stubby clumps of Sudan grass still grew, thick with strings of sapphires. If he had been a, a daughter? While she waited for him, everything around her became completely unfamiliar.

When he appeared before her in her mother's arms, she was a little surprised. The forehead, the straight brows, the corners of his

281

mouth, he looked so much like Chen Xu. How could he have come to look like this in only six short months? She reached out to take him in her arms, but he twisted languidly away. He was wrapped up in a grimy old cotton jacket and looked very small, not much bigger than when she had left him. His little arms, lifted up to her mother's forehead, looked thin. If the rest of him had not grown, how had his features developed? She had never heard of such a thing, she mused. His face being so small, the eyes seemed unusually large, the foreign-looking eyelids drawn elegantly upward. Only the eyes were not like him. But that same look, always so vague and elusive, watched her with timid indifference. It was him all over.

"Say 'Mama'." Her mother was rocking him back and forth.

He stared at her, not making a sound.

She glanced all around, and her face flushed. She would leave while she had the chance, before he really recognised her. She seized his two little hands and held them to her chest. He pulled away. She did not know what else she could do to win him over. She did not recognise him either. The only baby she knew was one who let people order him about, a little wrapped-up kitten. She tried her hardest to smile at him. He showed no response. She did recognise him; his expression was exactly the same as his father's. If she kept him, it would be like keeping his father with her forever.

She began to feel impatient and glanced at the watch on her mother's wrist. Her mother pointed out a circular bench under a camphor tree, and they went over to it. When she reached over again and patted him, he turned away and ignored her. She remembered that she had a plastic balloon in her pocket that she had bought for him. She blew it up and held it up to him. He embraced it and put it to his face, nibbling at it.

"Doesn't he like to smile?" she asked.

"Apparently not," her mother replied. "He is a little blasé."

"Isn't he rather greedy?"

"Well, babies are like that. He's a little thin. The wet-nurse really didn't have all that much milk. Now that they've taken him home, he's eating baby food with milk powder in it, so he'll probably fatten up. You were weaned at seven months too. His grandparents do dote on him."

She sighed, though she could not have explained why. All at once she felt like kissing him, biting his glossy cheeks. She reached out again to take him in her arms, but he recoiled in fear and pushed his way into her mother's armpit. She was rather irritated. She picked him up and held him forcibly. He struggled a little and whimpered as though he were going to start crying. Her mother gave him a piece of candy. He grabbed it and stuffed it in his mouth, and this did calm him down. He sat awkwardly on her leg, absorbed in the piece of candy.

You're hopeless. She cursed him silently. If you'd just throw a good screaming tantrum, you'd at least seem like a man. Who do you really take after? She felt a wave of bitterness. Come on, call me mama, call me mama just once and I'll never leave you again. Her eyes filled with tears, she rocked him gently. How can I be a mama to you if you don't treat me like one? She kissed him ferociously on the nape of the neck. If you burst out crying, I'll never be able to let you go. She scraped the dirt out from between his fingers bit by bit and then pulled out a handkerchief and wiped his mouth. She held him tight, stroking his downy hair, her heart suddenly flooded with tenderness. If she raised him, he would play violin, he had such slender little hands. In fact he was entirely indifferent to what she did with him. She couldn't take him back to the frozen Great Northern Wastes. Did she want him? Or not? Want him? Or not? Or not or not or not want him or not or not or not or not or not want him want him want...

She felt something warm on her knee and leapt to her feet. A damp spot. "He's wet." Her mother smiled indulgently. She smiled too, feeling helpless. She did not know what to do and looked at her mother's watch. It seemed as though they had been there a long time. "Let's go back," she said to her mother. "I'll go with you and wait at the corner."

Their meeting had lasted all of forty minutes, and nothing at all had happened. But deep inside, she had been waiting all along to be inspired with some maternal feeling. She wondered how she could be so calm, as though she were looking at a friend's baby. She was a little disappointed in herself, and yet somehow she rejoiced when they got off the bus.

She waited at the entrance to the alley while her mother took Chen Li back to his grandmother. Then she and her mother walked home together.

The street lamps have come on, I'm going home with Mother. Down the long, narrow, meandering alleyways, the light of the setting sun on the walls transformed the bamboo stalks into magic wands, to keep her from falling into the dim space beyond Baoshu Hill. By the shore of the deep blue sea there lived an old man and his wife...

Finally she stopped below the stone bridge that she had crossed on her way to junior high school every day. Looking down at the dark, dirty water she blurted, "Mother, it looks like I'm going to divorce Chen Xu."

She had to say it eventually. What had quickened her decision? She did not know. She did not want to be a mother; Chen Li had grown his teeth even without a mother. It was especially that he looked so much like his father it made her flesh creep. Nowhere in the world did she have so much as a foothold for herself. How could she take on a baby not a year old?

Her mother sighed quietly. Just then a few yellowed leaves came floating down the black river. She stared after them as they floated into the distance, and then said, "I understand. You and Chen Xu just don't work the same way. I don't want to say bad things about him; he helped us out when we were in trouble. But he doesn't have character, he doesn't have will-power. He flows with the stream, and any obstruction or storm is liable to send him under. He can't take charge of his own destiny. You remember how many rafts there used to be were in this river, being poled upstream along the banks, step by step, toward their destinations. You shouldn't waste any more of your life on him."

Xiao Xiao clasped her mother's arm tight and rested her head on her shoulder. Thank you, Mother! Her tears ran down her cheeks, dropped onto the grey bridge, and then splashed into the grimy river.

34

Xiao Xiao began to relive the idle life she had known before she went to the countryside.

The modest teachers' residence, built at the time of the Great Leap, seemed the ultimate in comfort to her, now that she had returned from the frontier. There was no pile of straw for the stove, no brick bed to fire up, no pig pen or chicken coop, no latrine built over a sheer pit. Instead, there were coal stoves, hot water bottles, running water, bookshelves. Since the air was not as fresh as out on the open spaces, why then did it make her breathe so deeply and feel so free? She belonged in the city. She liked city life. Whenever she remembered the Farm, she felt ashamed of herself. Perhaps she had not yet been entirely remoulded; her three years there had been wasted.

And yet she really did delight in running water, which she used with the greatest of thrift. She scrubbed the floors with the laundry water, cleaned the toilet with water she had washed vegetables in; she even kept the water from washing her face for rinsing scrub rags. Her mother was puzzled by all this, and told her, "The armed struggles are over; they won't cut off our water any more."

"It's not that..." Xiao Xiao blushed, uncertain how to explain. That long well-rope sheathed in ice. When Chen Xu carried water he would accuse her of wasting it even if she were more careful than she was being now.

Xiao Xiao never went out except to buy food. Her teachers? Her fellow students? Her relatives? She didn't want to see any of them. The wheels of the train she had taken to the north had long since stretched her innocent, immaculate past out so long and thin that it had finally snapped. She just wanted to hide inside a crystal cocoon, to turn into a chrysalis, all its silver threads disgorged at last, and pass the winter in peace. But instead she was like a little bird on a desert island, unable to fly across the great wide sea and uncertain which direction to go. She was lonely and needed a friend to talk with. But the 'perfect student' upstairs, Du Qingqing, had gone off to settle in the countryside. She could hear Pingping next door, who had just started junior high, playing his violin, but never talking. Lili, the fourth grader across the way, was busy at her lessons under a fifteen watt bulb in her kitchen every night, reading 'earnestly instruct' as 'honestly in his truck' and 'weltanschauung' as 'weld and show him'. Their family had a black and white television, and the mother spent every evening watching it under a three watt fluorescent tube, while the father brought home lively fresh carp on his motorscooter. He was in a Workers' Propaganda Team.

The strange thing was that Xiao Xiao's father did have some guests and friends.

The people who came to see her father were of two kinds. First, there were the officials from the street and neighbourhood administrations, who all had stern faces like the KMT tax-collectors in the movies. They came to call him away to meetings. The others were men who worked with him. They were dressed in worn-out clothes and called her father's name from the doorway in loud raspy voices as they barged in, trailing the smell of tobacco and alcohol and talking in thick Hangzhou dialect peppered with obscenities. They knew plumbing, lighting, house repairs, pedalling cabs. The one thing they didn't know how to do was write letters, fill in applications, and the like. So they came to see her father. They had a way of sitting on clean bed sheets in their grimy, oily pants and kept on shifting their buttocks as though they were doing it on purpose. When they spat on the floor, it was as much as she could bear.

"They help me out a lot at work," said her father.

She had found out during the Cultural Revolution that they were all either ex-labour camp inmates or people who had been dismissed from their jobs on account of some scandal involving the opposite sex. They had settled like dregs to the lowest levels of society. She did not like them.

There was a bald guy called 'Eternal Ringworm' who could build a stove that both saved on coal and didn't smoke. It could be closed up overnight without the fire going out. The first time he saw Xiao Xiao, he boomed, "Well! Mrs. Xiao's little blood pressure fairy is back!"

Was she her mother's blood pressure fairy? This was how she first learned that her mother had been suffering from high blood pressure for years.

'Forever Ringworm' was a cheerful sort. Once, while he was out pedalling his three-wheeled cart, delivering something, he felt hungry, so he stopped in a little shop and bought twenty cents worth of pigs head meat to take home and have that night with his wine. He stuck it behind the seat of his cart, but as he continued on his way, his mouth began to water so badly he finally couldn't wait any longer. Resting on his pedals, he reached around and pulled out a piece. He went a ways farther, then had another. By the time he got home, the handlebars were covered with pork fat and all the meat had vanished without a trace. Apparently food meant a great deal to him, which is why when he met Xiao Xiao he winked at her and said, "Well, now that you're back, fill your belly good before you leave!" According to her mother, it was because, back during the lean years, he had called in sick and then gone down to the Qiantang flats to catch little crabs for his son to eat that he had been sent for labour reform.

He had another appetite, which was to collect all the wildest gossip current in Hangzhou and then tear over to their house to give a rip-roaring account of it. Hangzhou was abuzz with scandals; they swarmed thick as mosquitos. Now it was some sort of police strike, with traffic all snarled up and young toughs ganging up on a girl and ripping her clothes off; now it was a thief plundering a food store by some trick; now the collective suicide of a family of six; and then there were peasants and townspeople trading wives, and so forth. The sources of his news were as diverse as they were alert, and he recounted all this with an infectious glee. Of course, his enthusiasm was markedly diminished if eating was not somehow involved. His narrative genius dried up on the spot, the story being disposed of in a few words that left the impression that it was not so much simple as incomplete. Her father always suspected him of exaggerating things and asked very detailed questions, at which Ringworm would get impatient and reply, scratching one of the bare spots on his head, "Believe it or not, it's up to you. But is anything impossible nowadays?"

One night, past ten o'clock, he popped in their door, took a bright, shining knife out from under his umbrella, and laid it on the table.

"Here, I'll give this to you to cut up watermelon with. What do you say?"

Her father and mother cowered on the other side of the room, afraid to approach any closer.

He chuckled and told them that he had made the watermelon knife a few days before out of a piece of scrap steel from a factory. But someone had seen him and reported it, and the neighbourhood security people had called him in for a talk. They said that he was up to counter-revolutionary activities and ordered him to hand over his weapons. He had made a great show of excogitation and finally said, as though it had just dawned on him. "Oh yes, A knife! Yes, I've got one. I'll go get it." He had gone home and found a little knife made from a steel ruler to hand in and so managed to get off the hook. But it was no longer safe to keep this 'true blade' at home. When he got this far, he turned around and saw Feifei.

"Hey you! Don't you go off and tell anyone about this, hear? Just say it was bought at a shop somewhere, got it?"

"You're a liar!" Feifei was not impressed.

"If you don't lie, you'll starve." He rapped her smartly on the top of the head and went happily off, umbrella tucked under his arm.

There was just one man whose clothes were always tidy. Even the strip around the soles of his cloth shoes was always perfectly white. He was middle aged, wore glasses, and spoke with an air of distinction in a very pleasant baritone voice. "Is Mr. Xiao at home?" "Please tell your father that I shall come to call on him again tomorrow." "Here are the books that I borrowed last time, three volumes in all."

"Are you at the neighbourhood workshop too?" she asked once, being curious.

"Oh, no, no, I mean, yes..." For some reason he began to stammer and left in a state of confusion.

A scandal? She was sure of it. She decided not to chat with him again. When her father got home and saw the books, he was delighted. "Was Lu Zhui here?"

"Who's Lu Zhui?"

"The young man who was labelled a Rightist back when he was in university."

A Rightist? In addition to the ex-labour camp inmates, there were Rightists. Such were the people with whom her father associated. She hung her head and said nothing for a long time.

And Lu Zhui was not the only Rightist either. There was Aunt Mu, and Uncle Fang, Uncle Xu, and Uncle A'shan. If they weren't there to borrow money, it was to look for a place to stay over. Among these various Rightist visitors, the only one she liked was Uncle Fang. He was a tall man who wore glasses with clear plastic rims. He once pulled a small flat rock right out of his canvas knapsack and had her guess what the image on it was.

"A fossil!" She marvelled.

Fifty million year-old fish, seventy million year-old crustaceans, one hundred million year-old leaves, and every scale and muscle, every whisker and tail was distinctly imprinted on the stone, cast in the space between rocks. Relief carving? Rock painting? These were ageless. So the forms of life outlived life itself. Only by enduring hundreds of millions of years of pressure, buried under layers of rock, could immortality be gained. It was too cruel. History had been condensed onto a single little stone. And who would ever have discovered it save by some upheaval of the earth?

"Is it real?" she asked.

Uncle Fang chuckled. He said that his job had been just that, working in a museum, checking the authenticity of fossil specimens. Unfortunately, after he was declared a Rightist, the whole family had gone to live in a village in the country, so it was no longer his business to check whether the specimens were genuine or not.

When he sat down to drink with her father, he would start telling about the life they led in the countryside, how his two sons had gone fishing for soft-shelled turtles and come home with a straw sandal as their catch, how they had had to abandon their cat when food was short, but the cat had found its way back home and crawled into bed with them, how during a typhoon all five of them had clung like acrobats to ropes tied to the roof in order to keep it from blowing away. His stories had them in stitches. It sounded as though nothing could be more fun than going to live in a village.

Picking day lilies. Fairy rings. The white-footed dog in the shed by the vegetable plot. Collecting swans eggs. The snow queen's palace. The well and its windlass. If she were to tell about the Great Northern Wastes, it might sound like just as much fun, just as entrancing...

"You're telling lies!" She exploded at Uncle Fang. He was like a flattened-out fossil. She had learned long ago what life in the countryside was really like. If the village was so much fun, why was he always coming to borrow money?

There was no third kind of guest. Everyone who came to visit them was a hard luck case. No matter whether they were tidy or messy, gloomy or bubbly, she could always guess their backgrounds and why they had come. It was they who reminded her over and over just what the class status of her family was. She hated it.

Lu Zhui came to return another book. The book had a new dust jacket made of sturdy brown paper. She flipped through it. It was Alexei Tolstoy's 'Ordeal'. She had read it four or five years before. During the house raids, most of the books sealed inside the big wooden chest had been saved. And then there were the ones that Chen Xu had taken away and hidden for them.

He pushed his glasses higher up his nose and faltered, "You have so many books here. Who is your favourite author?"

"Fadeyev," she shot back.

He seemed quite surprised. "What about Dostoyevsky?"

She avoided his eyes. She did not want to tell him that whenever she read Dostoyevsky she was overcome by the fear of death. The writers she really liked were Pushkin and Sholokhov.

"His stuff is too obscure. How about you?"

"I like, well, Romain Rolland," he said quietly.

He must like Dostoyevsky. He hadn't told the truth either.

It was hard to keep their conversation going. There was always an invisible barrier between people. It was better to go back into one's own little kingdom, in search of a favourite teacher or an understanding friend. Xiao Xiao had always liked reading. Books brought her consolation and inspiration. But now she was almost afraid to read. Once she had entered the world inside a book, she herself vanished, and when she had fought her way back, her troubles were all worse than before. She was still afraid of being poisoned, of succumbing to a subtle influence. So books were like life, nothing ever seemed to match up the right way; large or small, it was always the same. Books were liars too!

She went with her mother to the reading room a few times. It had seemed so wonderful in her mother's letters, but when she saw it with her own eyes, it turned out to be just like the Political Culture Room on the Farm: the long rows of the same new books on the empty shelves, the magazines on the walls with their lower right corners dog-eared like water-lily pads, the black mark down the top of one thick, clean book, which fell open at the page reading 'Personal Hygiene'. The only difference was the damp, mouldy odour coming from between the shelves, like the silkworm room at her grandmother's. The books were all neatly numbered and labelled. To please her mother, she carefully selected Krupskaya's "Memories of Lenin" and took it home to read. She did not feel like reading the books that were available, and the ones she wanted to read were not available. What do you really want?

At dinner, her mother said, "When Xiao Xiao was little, she liked to write poems."

Feifei said, "No, she liked dancing most of all."

Her father said, "She's quick on the uptake. She'd make a first-rate reporter."

Mirages, castles in the air, every one. Soon her days of 'separate domicile' would be done, and she would go back to scrambling over the fields and ditches, grabbing steamed buns with bean paste in them like a good girl. She had written poems on the Farm. She had even written reports. Had it not been for his sneering and ridicule, perhaps she would have attained a certain standing in Half-way River. She was only at home to recover from her wounds so that, once she was sturdy enough, she could go back and be wounded all over again.

Yellow leaves covered the ground. A single goose flew anxiously over. The passage of geese, this was the most heart-breaking. And yet was it one she had known in bygone days? Had it come from Half-way River? Had it run away? Or was it on its way back? A light snow had fallen. Snowflakes danced in the air, for all the world like white feathers. When they fell into the palm, they turned into crystal drops of water. The snowfall had drifted through an early morning, but no sooner had the yellow leaves put on a layer of frost than the sun came out and it was gone without a trace. A dusting of white powder a moment ago, and now just a few damp spots. Snow in the south. Was snow a liar too?

Day after day, Xiao Xiao brooded; day after day, she went about in a daze, she reflected, she pondered. Her heart and mind were all tangled up. The more she tried to sort things out, the more confused they became; the more she turned them over in her head, the less sense they made. In her trouble and uncertainty, she sought help in the great books that she had read, but nowhere among the quotations from famous men that she had copied down in all those notebooks was there a single line that would come to her aid.

I think I should go out into the world, said the little duckling.

All right, go on then, said the hen.

One night she was awakened in the middle of the night by a dream. The wind, that damp night air found only in the South, was sighing as it shook the dense, broadleaved evergreen trees. The dim street lamps threw on the wall outside her window the shadows of the unfallen leaves. She lay there for ages, in a trance. There in the dark, her Alps had risen up once more among the shadows of the leaves. And then she suddenly understood that her soul was perhaps to wander forever in that great wide world. The only thing for her to do was to chase after that scattered flock of geese.

Fires were raging in Hangzhou. The flames were like snakes, slithering after her this way and that. She was trying to beat the fires out with a bundle of green pine boughs. There was dry straw everywhere. It was evidently somewhere out in the open pastures. Amid the stubble there was half an ear, covered with blood. 'Forever Ringworm' was croaking, A crime, a crime! It's a teacher's ear. He assigned homework to his students and they cut his ear off.

She asked him why he had come to the Great Northern Wastes. He said that the entire city of Hangzhou had moved. A transfer of southerners to the north.

Someone was knocking at the door. She went to answer it, and it was a young man. Who are you? she asked. Your father, he replied. She was astonished. How can you be my father? My mother isn't married yet. She's wearing a red hat and in jail. Her father said, We were comrades-in-arms, and you are part of our booty. She took a careful look at him. He was indeed in uniform, fanning himself with an army cap. Wiping the sweat from his brow, he said, We've reached the base area at last. He pulled a bunch of leaflets out of his satchel and tossed them into a mail box. He changed into a pair of work trousers and began teaching workmen how to read.

Her mother came home, riding in a small boat. There were fires burning on both banks. Her mother was empty-handed. Her grandmother asked, And where's your silk quilt? I gave it to someone, she replied. What about your trunk of clothes, your umbrella, and your necklace? They were burned in the big fire. Her mother carried Chen Li onto the boat and went off to the playground.

Chen Li had learned to dash along on a little bicycle, a puppy squeezing through burning hoops for fun.

Someone walked up and asked her in a loud voice, Who is that child?

She said, He's from my mother's brother's family. No, I mean my father's brother's family.

Mama, cried Chen Li, Look here.

And then she noticed Chen Xu sitting by the fire roasting soybeans. As he ate them, he recited:

> See the beans o'er burning beanstalks fry,
> And in their pods the little beansies cry,
> We've lived so long inside our beanpod nests,
> Why are we flying now to east and west?

That's wrong, she said. Who's wrong? he asked. You are. No,

you are. What have I done wrong? Why didn't you answer my letters? I didn't get them. Chen Li is always looking for his mother. You're lying, Chen Li is in Hangzhou. Hangzhou has moved to Heilongjiang. With all this snow and ice, the Liuhe Pagoda can't burn. You're trying to trick me. If you don't believe me go see for yourself.

Lu Zhui held out a slender arm and showed her his wrist watch. He said, This is a genuine Swiss watch. She shook her head. He went over to a bench beside the lake to read.

A line of bicycles approached from the distance, and several pretty girls jumped off, wearing lotus-coloured gossamer skirts. A girl covered Lu Zhui's eyes and giggled, Guess who.

The Seventh Fairy Maiden? Snow White? The teenage martyr Liu Hulan? A tough little Red Guard mama? The girl shook her head. He lost his temper, stood up, and shouted, I don't know you!

The girls fled and vanished without a trace. Lu Zhui covered his own eyes and stamped his feet, screaming with pain. She ran over and found his face bathed in tears and a film of brownish ointment covering his eyes and nose. She smelled balm, and her eyes watered. Just then, Lu Zhui shrieked at the top of his lungs, My Swiss watch is gone! Catch those dirty thieves!

She helped him chase them. There was a bicycle under the tree, but the tires were flat. There was a horse by the lake, but it had not been shod. There was a puffnik chugging away at the corner, but no driver. She got on and drove it herself, and it pitched and twisted its way down a steep slope...

35

Xiao Xiao decided to go back to the Farm after the Spring Festival.

She happened to let her mother know what she had in mind. All that night she could hear the creak of tossing and turning on the wooden bed in the front room. When she had left three years before, her mother had still been in the cow-shed. Anyone, herself, her mother, anyone at all, would see going back to that land of black earth as no different from being taken in chains to the execution ground. She could think of nothing to say that would comfort her mother. Her own heart was filled with something of the solemn resolve of one facing a fight to the death.

Her talks with her father were continuing. He had no time to spare for her future. Although she had explained to him more than once that it was only a matter of time before she and Chen Xu separated, he insisted on bringing the conversation around to their own sharp rupture three years before. He was unwilling to offer his forgiveness until she should appear before him in the garb of a penitent. Hardship had conferred on him prophetic foresight, and he had taken satisfaction in her finding herself betrayed in love. He placed his hopes in the prolongation of this satisfaction, which might to some degree mitigate all the injustice that he had suffered over the preceding twenty years. He wanted it recognised that after all possibility of any other recognition from anyone else had been lost, there still remained his wife and children. She was his life preserver. Her heart ached with sympathy for him; he seemed so pitiful, so pitiful that he compelled respect. And so when he doggedly repeated his verdicts, she finally compromised and nodded her head.

"He was a liar even then!"

"He never told you a word of truth!"

"He's a born liar!"

"He thinks that a family like ours was made to be cheated!"

"You ought to settle with him for everything since 1967!"

As she nodded, her heart was flooded with bitter tears. Tell a lie three times and it's true. Between him and her, and him, who had really lied? Perhaps Chen Xu too was always confronting this same inescapable scrutiny. She realised that she did not mean what she was saying, and yet it was her confession that brought lenience. Her father, could her father be considered part of herself? Was she actually lying to herself? Was this really a fair deal? To pay for a dead lie with a fresh new one?

She could not bear to spurn her mother's anxious looks and go back early; neither could she injure her father's self-esteem with a falsehood that might soon be unmasked. In the midst of her quandary, she remembered her uncle and his family living in 'Upper Sindhu', up in the hills behind Lingyin Temple. Some of the scenic areas around West Lake had been occupied during the Cultural Revolution, and her uncle's factory had been moved into the sealed-off Great Hall at Upper Sindhu. She had not been there. People said it was a green valley in the hills that kept its dress unchanged throughout the year.

West Lake had become very unfamiliar. She thought that perhaps it had forgotten her.

She got off the bus at Lingyin, walked past the screen wall with the faded words 'On the Verge of the Western Paradise' still just visible, and followed a new concrete road flanked on both sides by hills as it wound its way up through the lush green woods. The sunlight filtered down here and there, guiding her along the road like a butterfly. Sometimes there would be a flash of light among the trees, or she would hear the splash of falling water up ahead. It was a carefree stream singing in the secluded glen. She slid down to the bottom of the ravine, clinging to thick stalks of bamboo, stirred up the ice-cold water, and washed her face and hands in it. She ran onto the stone wisteria-covered bridge that arched over the stream, running across it one way and back the other. There was a osmanthus tree beside the bridge, spreading up into a high green crown overhead. When the osmanthus blossomed in the autumn, the flowers would fall into the stream, and the water itself would breathe this fragrance, whether it was used to brew tea or to do laundry. Could it be called Osmanthus Creek? She broke off a branch of osmanthus and plucked a tea leaf, holding it in her mouth and chewing it to extract the flavour, so bitter that she frowned even as she swallowed it all. There was no one on the winding road, only a tawny squirrel leaping from one treetop to another and then being swallowed up by the green. An old camphor tree, a patch of emerald bamboo, a stretch of tea fields, a hillside of horsetail pines, they stretched on in layer upon layer, a fresh and hazy green, so green that she too, like a tree...

"Hey!" she yelled up toward the mist-shrouded peaks.

"Hey!" the valley replied.

"Here I am!"

"I am..."

Nature. Lonely Xiao Xiao, your only friend.

Her uncle's house was beside a stone bridge close to the top of the mountain. On the bridge there was a little shop dangling over the stream, with the water gurgling down the mountain beneath it. At the near end of the bridge, there were a few stone pillars, the remnants of an old wall, with some barely visible inscriptions on them. Across the bridge, there was a stone gate on the right hand with a sign reading 'No.18, Long Life Road'. Once inside the gate, she lost all sense of direction in the series of nested rectangular halls and courtyards, all in the same style, ending in a square court in the centre.

Aside from a fascination with the 'Journey to the West', the old novel about the Magic Monkey and his trip to India with the monk Tripitaka in search of the sutras, her knowledge of Buddhism was a yawning void. Now she felt a kind of giddiness. There was something unearthly and mysterious about the hills here, the stream, the people. Had she not come to pay her respects out of a sense of reverence for the place? This was where the pilgrims had stayed in bygone years, no doubt about it. As she stood there musing, a little boy with big ears and a little girl with narrow eyes came running out of the house and took her by the hand. "Cousin Xiao! It's Cousin Xiao!" She stared; didn't she recognise them? They were her nephew and niece. And standing quietly to one side smiling, that was her uncle's wife.

According to her aunt, the three great temples built along the ascent of Sindhu Mountain had once been places filled with the smoke of joss-sticks. When the pilgrims of bygone days came to the great Treasure Hall at Lingyin, they had to climb the mountain as well, worshipping the Bodhisattvas at Lower, Middle, and Upper Sindhu on their way, or their devotion would not be reckoned sincere, nor their merit complete. But starting from the '60s, all three temple gates had been sealed, the aroma of incense had vanished, and the signs of various factories had been hung up. Her uncle's factory had been moved there, family and all. The temple grounds had gone to ruin, and the monks had dispersed no one knew where. Now, except for the empty hall, two huge camphor trees, and three ponds with their bridges, Upper Sindhu was nothing but a name. She recalled that as she was passing Middle Sindhu on her way up she had seen the sign of some revolutionary committee on the gate. The large gingko tree outside the gate had even been stripped of its bark. Could the factory people not even excuse a tree?

Her aunt shook her head emphatically. "Actually, it's not the factory people at all. It's..." She lowered her voice. "It's the peasants in the tea villages all around here. They believe that a place where the Bodhisattva has been retains magical powers to ward off evil. So, when they get sick, they come and strip bark from the trees in front of the temples and take it back home to steep in boiling water. By drinking it they can get the Bodhisattva's protection. It's the same at the gate to Upper Sindhu."

Could the Bodhisattvas not be toppled from power? The haunted tree, that soul of all the spirits that controlled every human fate... Might it protect her as well?

She went out for a walk by herself in search of peace of mind in this Buddhist retreat forgotten by the bustle of the dusty world. As she walked over the stone bridge in front of the temple, she saw the remains of incense sticks filling all the cracks between the stones. As she passed by the pond behind, she saw all the coins tossed in as a sign of devotion. She climbed up past one tea plantation after another, right to the top of the mountain. And from there, as evening was falling, she caught sight of the corner of one of the upturned eaves of the Great Hall, just visible through a mist-shrouded bamboo grove. Now she realised for the first time the mysterious power of the Buddha and the majesty of the gods. Once the Six Sources of sense impression were stilled, there would be no worldly desires, and without desires there would no longer be suffering. But he had said that he was a real human being only because he lived for the sake of his senses and his desires. It was so quiet in the hills, and the breeze, the pool, and the plants in the temple precinct were as serene as the Buddha himself. She sat all alone in a trance until dusk fell, waiting to receive some enlightenment and inspiration from the gods. But her mind grew more and more empty, as calm as a pool of still water.

At midday, if the weather was clear, she would go up to the top of the mountain with her niece and nephew to lie in the sun on top of a big black rock. Looking beyond the clouds, toward the mountains, they could see the Qiantang River like a silver needle, and West Lake like a mirror. Lying on the dry grass in the fields, they saw the thick clouds suspended over the horizon, sunk in a contemplation eternally unresolved. Sometimes they could find pine cones the size of chickens eggs, or a kind of prickly red berries called 'sugar cans'. Since they were sugar cans, of course they were as sweet as honey, and after eating a few their hands and mouths were all sticky. Sometimes, her nine year old niece A'hong would find a patch of shepherds purse growing alongside the tea fields. They would pick some to take home for her aunt make into wonton so fresh their eyes watered. The leaves of shepherds purse that A'hong gathered were so huge that they covered the bottom of the basket. When Xiao Xiao praised her, her brother A'hua, who was two years older, frowned and said, "Pooh! What's so great about that? Last time we took worm medicine, I turned out rafts of them, but she didn't produce a single one!"

A'hua and A'hong went to a grade school in Lingyin every morning and came back at noon. They never did any lessons, because there was no real homework. As soon as evening fell, A'hua would show a movie on the wall. He had a box of slides he had painted himself. He moved these around in the beam of a flashlight, mixing together characters from various 'revolutionary model Peking operas': Diao Deyi, Mountain Vulture, and the Japanese Commandant of the Gendarmerie. Xiao Xiao laughed so hard she collapsed on the bed, but when she praised him, his sister pouted and said, "Well, that's nothing special. He can't sing a single song. In singing class he just moves his lips while everybody else is singing."

Xiao Xiao laughed and laughed. She felt truly happy. In that moment it seemed as though there were still time to start everything afresh.

One afternoon, as she was coming back from washing vegetables in the stream, she saw her uncle angrily holding a feather duster in one hand and pulling on A'hong's pigtail with the other. He was bawling her out. "You went to jump a chain of rubber bands on your way back home, and then you told me it was your turn to do the classroom chores. I know all about it. Already telling lies at your age..."

A'hua was standing behind the door and said in a low voice, "She wasn't jumping a chain of rubber bands, honest she wasn't. I saw that she wasn't..."

"Get lost!" his father yelled. "You're cut from the same cloth. You see to the knot in your belt!"

Xiao Xiao knew that because the weather was so cold, A'hua

did not like to have bowel movements and just tried to hold it in. Every day he would make a false report, saying that he had already gone. So his father had to tie a complicated knot in his belt in order to check whether he had untied it or not.

She got her uncle to stop, and put her arms around A'hong. Getting out her handkerchief, she wiped away the little girl's tears. "Good girls don't tell fibs," she said.

Then she realised that A'hong had glanced at her with the strangest look in her eyes, and her face burned as though she had been stung by a wasp. Was she being oversensitive, or was it her guilty conscience? She blushed in front of the two children.

One day, a fat lady who lived nearby struck up a conversation with her.

"Back from Heilongjiang? How long you stay up there? Married yet?"

"Oh," she answered, feeling flustered, "How could, so early, how could I...?"

"Well," said the woman, suddenly seeing the light, "The peasants who grow tea around Sindhu Mountain here are doing very well indeed. From one village to another, a residence transfer would be simple..."

Xiao Xiao broke in, "I've come back on sick leave, it's arthritis..."

Who was she to be giving A'hua and A'hong lectures on morality? It was only that lies just flowed so naturally from her mouth, though she herself could not understand how. She was ashamed of herself. Even in this little mountain valley far from the bustle of the outside world, the phantom she so hated had secretly followed her.

All the happiness she had known since coming up into the hills abruptly vanished.

A few days before the Festival, it grew dark in the hills. It looked like snow. Her father and mother were coming up for a family New Years dinner, and she was helping her aunt get ready by going down to the stream to wash the fish.

As she was crossing the stone bridge, she saw someone leaning against the railing and staring down at the water, lost to the world. She went on down the steps and then looked back. He was still standing there motionless, his glasses on the point of sliding off his nose. She stopped. This was impossible! The high cheekbones, the thick glasses, the soft lock of hair lying on his forehead... But...

"Zou Sizhu," she gasped. But no sooner were the words out of her mouth than she whipped around and walked toward the stream.

She was seeing things. Not even she could believe that Zou Sizhu might turn up here.

But there were footsteps stumbling after her, anxious panting. He took her by the sleeve, his Adam's apple bobbing up and down, and said, "It, it's me. Don't worry."

The Farm really had given out passes for home leave. They'd all come home for New Years; he had come too. The first thing he had done after getting back was to come looking for her. Her mother had given him the address. There was no special reason, he stammered.

She went back to the house and got rid of the fish. Then she took him for a walk up the mountain. Her hands were shaking a little, and her legs felt weak. Chen Xu had not got a pass. She would take him climbing Chessboard Peak, the very highest one. Whoever came to see her on a day like this was her best friend.

"So, was it Chen Xu who had you come?" she asked abruptly.

"How could he?" Zou was quite taken aback. "I've scarcely seen so much as his face more than once or twice. He, he doesn't come to work much."

"Why?" Her heart sank.

He shook his head.

"Tell me, why doesn't he come to work?" She persisted. She had just realised that she was still anxious for news of him, that she still had him on her mind.

He stopped and rested his hands on his knees, gasping for breath, "I hear that he, well, that he's been gambling, that he lost more than he could pay and told people that he had an uncle high up in the government who could get people into the Army, to make up for the money, and, well, you can imagine how that turned out."

What was it that had broken? Bamboo? A ball? Leaves? Stones? The last shreds of her hope, her last little dream, broken, wiped out, turned to dust, for ever and ever.

"Now, don't be angry." He was a little apprehensive. "Anyway, aren't you, aren't you divorcing him? No one else on the Farm believes it, but I do."

"And why do you believe it?" she asked frostily. "You must have realised a long time ago that he was no good!"

"The distinction is hardly so simple as that!" He smiled. "A person can be good and bad at the same time. You know, when I first met him, back when he was in custody, I really looked up to him."

She hung her head and said in a low voice, "Yes, it was only

300

after he got to the Farm that he, that he began to slip. Once someone tells a first lie, he has to go on and tell a second, just to keep the lie going."

Zou Sizhu shook his head in disagreement.

"I think that those spectacular lies of Chen Xu's are a lot better than the hypocrisy of some people. I admit he has many bad traits, but he is really tiny compared to the powerful society he is up against, and those are the only defenses he has."

Xiao Xiao was shocked to hear Zou Sizhu say such a thing.

"In fact, telling lies and deceiving people are like the tongue in Aesop's fable," said Zou slowly, thinking it out as he spoke. "They're both good and bad, and it's hard to separate the two. Sometimes they are very good or very bad, and sometimes they are neither. For example, to keep knowledge of his true condition from someone who is gravely ill is good, but to get the confidence of the common people by empty promises is bad. To lie because you have to defend yourself against people who intend you harm is neither good nor bad. When peasants divide up their produce on the sly for the sake of subsistence, that's both good and bad. Lying is often presented in Chinese history as a matter of strategy or wisdom; as they say, all's fair in war. Deceiving people isn't always a farce. Weren't the ancients Diao Chan and Wang Zuo masters at lying? How do you explain that?"

She cut him off. In a tone filled with stinging distaste, she asked, "Then why don't you tell lies? Why are you always hiding inside your little snail shell, peering out at other people?"

He winced, and his face paled, as though she had touched a sore spot. The wisps of black hair over his forehead twisted this way and that. He stood still for a moment and then walked abruptly away.

Xiao Xiao hurried after him, unwilling to let the subject drop. She stared into his glasses, but in those dark lenses there was nothing left but tree trunks, moss, and withered leaves.

"Tell me, since you don't think he's bad, why are you in favour of our separating?"

Chill, damp fog was swirling up out of the valleys on all sides. Tea fields and bamboo groves faded gradually into the shrouding haze. Under the gloomy pines, a barely visible path reached up toward the peaks.

He sat down on a projecting rock, leaning over and pulling up bits of grass beside it. He cleared his throat once, and then a second time.

"I believed all along that the two of you would separate eventually, because your ideal worlds are so completely different. The kind of truth that Chen Xu wants can't help but look ugly to you, while the kind of purity and beauty that you want can't help but look false to him. He views the sea of humanity as dirty in a way that people can't cleanse. And I guess you believe that so long as you are clean yourself the world can't make you dirty. He attaches more importance to himself than to the world, while your spirit of self-sacrifice is just what has made you a furnishing for his tomb."

Xiao Xiao shuddered and grasped a tree.

What a cold fish. He's stripped the two of us down to nothing. But why didn't you tell me sooner. You've got something up your sleeve; you're after something. You wait until I've got into an impossible position, and then you come to shut the barn door after the cows have gone. All that reality and evil and truth and falsity of yours is just some kind of tongue-twister.

"So, are you saying that truth and goodness are incompatible after all?" she looked up and asked.

"This is a problem that touches on the central meaning of truth." He pushed his glasses back up his nose. "I have always wondered whether only what is beautiful can actually be true. Why is it that everyone says that lying is bad, and then goes on telling lies? There seems to be something preventing people from telling the truth. It's like animals developing camoflage for their self-preservation. People always have to disguise their true selves in order to satisfy the demands of society. I keep wondering, why can't we admit that evil is true also? Even the evil in human nature. You know, the most terrible thing in people is when they lie to themselves."

He stopped, and said nothing more. He was scraping the mud off his feet with a dead twig. The dimmer his glasses got, the paler his gaunt face looked in the dusk. He seemed to be perplexed by some huge problem, evident in the dark circles left beneath his eyes from lack of sleep.

They sat for a long time without speaking.

The wind blew, then stopped. Silence.

Why did you really come looking for me? To show your sympathy? To make Chen Xu's case for him? To demonstrate that you're smarter than I am? Or is it... That dream, why was he in it? The osmanthus tree in the moon. He didn't tell the truth either.

She stood up.

302

He stood up too.

They walked down the mountain.

Darkness fell. A pale voice roamed the tangled wood. She heard him saying that he had come looking for her to tell her that Guo Chunmei was very sick. She had rheumatoid arthritis and could not walk. They had sent her back to Hangzhou. She was in hospital. They might have to amputate. Some people from Hangzhou who had been on the Farm with her were planning to get together and go visit her. Even if they didn't usually get along, she wasn't going to be with them much longer and, after all, they had all been on the same farm together. He asked if she would go. He added that she shouldn't just stay at home and brood every day. If she wanted, he could take her to meet some people their age he had got to know during the Cultural Revolution. They had all come back home for New Years from everywhere under the sun and were lively and interesting people who had seen a lot. And he talked about books, and about things she might do. He suddenly had a great deal to say, but it came out all mixed up. When he should speak he had nothing to say; everything that he shouldn't say he had said already. What was with him? There was something a little loony in his incoherence.

She caught sight of the little shop on the bridge and stopped.

"Don't get carried away by your own words." She forced a smile. "Thank you for coming to see me. But now what I want to know even more is what to do about our boy when I go to get the divorce."

His glasses flashed in the darkness.

"It seems to me that neither of you is properly qualified to be a parent," he replied, without a moment's hesitation. "If it were me, I should refuse to let a child recognise me before I was able to win the recognition of society. It seems to me that, that the two of you should give the baby to someone who can educate him.

I never dreamed you were such a pessimist. How can you wax so eloquent about pulling oneself together, starting all over again? Your view of yourself is rotten to the core.

She froze where she was, trembling inside. She hunched up her shoulders and hugged herself. She was on her own. She pursed her lips. He held out his hand in farewell. It was a thin, delicate hand, even colder than hers. And those shoulders? That chest? Those lips? Chen Xu's hands always throbbed with warmth. She got free of his hand and said, "Let me know when you are going to visit Guo Chunmei. I'll go back to the Farm a couple of weeks after the Lunar New Year."

She was walking down the white corridor of a hospital. There were so many doors along the corridor, so many rooms. She would push a door open and go in, then come back out, never finding who she was looking for. She had forgotten whom she had come to visit. A doctor stuck his head out and called her name. The sign on the door read 'Curr. Tr.'. She told the doctor that she didn't want Current Trends, she wanted an Abortion by Curettage Treatment. The doctor shook his head and pushed her out.

She turned back and walked into another room, where she caught sight of Guo Chunmei. She called her name, but Chunmei paid no attention to her. She looked down at herself, but she was nowhere to be seen. She was positive that she was alive, but she had no form.

She saw Wei Hua carry in a big bundle of things. He bowed to Chunmei. I have good news to report: the Company's barley fields have surpassed the official target.

They embraced, but then Guo pushed him away and sobbed, Let me go back to the Farm. I belong to the Farm, alive or dead.

Wei Hua said, But you can return to Hangzhou on a medical discharge.

Guo Chunmei said, The Great Northern Wastes is where I want to die. If I really do die, you must take my ashes back there.

A doctor wearing a large mask over his mouth walked up and said, You're not going to die. With arthritis only the joints die. You can wear artificial legs.

She shouted, Can't you change a joint for me? We Chinese aren't even afraid of death. How could we be afraid of losing a joint?

She shut her eyes and appeared to have lost consciousness.

Wei Hua put his arms around her, shook her, asked her if she had anything more to say.

She burst into bits and snatches of song. It sounded like 'The East is Red', but also like 'The Red Guards on the Grasslands Have Seen Chairman Mao', or 'Sing a Song of the Hero Mai Xiande', or 'Learn From the Example of Lei Feng'...

People thronged the door and windows of the ward. Everyone was so deeply moved that they wept, their tears falling to the floor.

Guo Chunmei opened her eyes and caught sight of the red cross on the door. Staring at it, she cried, The Red Flag, the Red Flag!

Wei Hua said, No, that isn't the Red Flag, it's a wall.

She shouted, No, it's the Red Flag; let me kiss it. Wei Hua took off his jacket. He was wearing a red sweater under it and he brought this close to her face. Bubble tittered. Aunt Min sat down at her sewing machine. It began to whir, saying, Someone above vulgar interests, someone noble-minded, someone pure, someone of moral integrity, someone of value to the people, someone absolutely perfect.

36

As the puffnik turned onto the side road leading to Branch Farm No.5, Xiao Xiao took advantage of a large bump in the road to whip around and face away from the family quarters coming up on the west side of the road.

She did not want, she did not even dare, to see that row of cottages. That home, which she had set up with such difficulty and in which she had lived for a year and a half, had a brown wooden window that looked out on the road at an angle. The light would be extinguished from now on. She would not be going back there again.

The early spring wind howled over the plain. It sounded like a gigantic pain-wracked bird, frantically beating its wings as it followed in her tracks. She tugged on her scarf and shut her eyes tight. The cart wheels rolled unrelentingly over her heart. It felt as though the resolution she had nurtured so long in the balmy South was being extruded from her thread by thread and slowly softened. The little window still seemed more endearing than abhorrent to her, more loved than hateful. She was afraid of that giant bird. Might it tear her mind to shreds and scatter the pieces?

She had not written to him even once, so he would have no idea she was coming back now. If he saw her get off the cart and go directly to stay at the company quarters, he would understand everything.

She opened her eyes as the cottage flashed by, swept up in the brownish dust like a feather from that great bird as it took to the air. Anyway, she was past it. And yet, as she looked up ahead, there in front of her was a patch of unharvested corn beside the road. The withered stalks stood stiffly one by one, like a tuft of beard growing on the earth, stuck to the streaked fields from which the snow had not yet entirely melted. It was repulsive.

Someone snickered, snickered at the keeper of that private plot, who had left his autumn harvest out on these few rows right through the winter, as though he were storing cabbages. She felt a sharp pang. Although people up north were very sensitive to questions of face—

because she was present no one on the cart said anything too unpleasant—she still broke out in a cold sweat up and down her spine. It looked as though he really had given up, given up on their private plot, and given up once and for all the chance she had left him. So he was not counting on her to return to the Farm and make up with him. All her remnant illusions and hopes were routed under the rumbling of the wheels.

The truck came to a halt by the flagpole at the company office outside the wall. Stepping on a tire, she clambered down from the back. One of her legs had gone to sleep, and she felt just a little sick. She would have to return to the dormitory that she had left with no regrets a year and half before. Whether the Branch Farm officials granted their petition for a divorce or not, she would make her home there on the hundred-meter brick bed.

The dormitory itself was familiar, but the looks that met her were not. There was surprise, suspicion, and contempt in the air. The greetings were forced and the smiles, aloof. These little girls in the midst of their passions must have seen her as an unlucky symbol. Why was she coming back then, since she had moved her things so proudly from the brick bed without so much as a word that cold winter night, leaving behind the daily political study sessions, the reveille whistle, the water allotment, the lights-out, the military drills, and the dishwashing? It seemed as though she were eternally repeating the same sort of helpless penance, always having to go back to places that she had left. From Lotus Blossom Pool to the women's dormitory of Branch Farm No.5, another counterpoint. And what fate awaited her now that she had returned?

She put her bag on an empty place at the end of the bed in one corner of the room, intending to sleep there. She felt a sudden wave of panic. All her bedding was still at 'home', so she would have to go there to get it after all.

It was just quitting time, and the other girls were busy washing up. Some of them had a word or two for her, but no one expressed any welcome. None of them would be likely to offer to go bring her things back for her. Where would she sleep that night? She just sat there for a while, and then got up and walked out.

Footsteps chased after her, and a timid voice called her by name.

She turned around. It was a girl from Hegang named Xiaoying. Her older sister was a friend who had moved back to the city, much to Xiao Xiao's regret.

"Tonight, you, you'd better sleep with me," she stammered, blushing for some reason.

Xiao Xiao shook her head.

"Thank you, but it's okay. I have my own bedding," she said.

With a merry smile, those eyes, round like her own, handed her a big ripe tomato with seeds like rubies visible through its thin, glossy skin. This kind of tomato is absolutely delicious. Try it yourself if you don't believe me. I went to the garden to pick some, and when I had stuffed myself with them I peed in the tomato patch. She hurried away, for fear the tears suddenly welling up in her eyes should bring her the embarassment of feeling herself pitied.

She walked toward the family quarters.

That huge suffering bird was still on her track, struggling and moaning on the dusky horizon. Its wings were whipping up the defenceless dust and straw along the roadside and whirling them around her. On the distant horizon, the bleak sun looked like a rusty iron cup trembling in terror as the giant bird pecked at it.

Where the bus had just passed, on the slope at the western end of the last row of cottages, there where she had picked wild herbs beside the summer squash field the preceding spring, someone was standing in the last dim and weary traces of the sunlight.

He was standing perfectly still, gazing into a grove of willows not far away. There was almost no one on the road, just one ponderous empty ox cart lumbering back toward the Branch Farm.

He did not move. The only visible motion of that tall silhouette outlined against the dusk was his hair, tousled by the wind. She knew that he did not like to wear a hat. Only he would not be wearing a hat in such weather.

She walked toward him.

The same bitter taste welled up inside her once again. It was like a current of mud about to silt something up. Was he waiting for her or for someone else? It must be for her; except for her... No, if only he wasn't waiting for her or for anyone else, if only he wasn't waiting for anyone at all. She stood quietly behind him, holding her breath. No, none of it was that easy to cut off. The cottage, the straw pile, the vegetable garden. In those days, she had been a woman who could lift the heavy burdens of daily life and do it for many months on end. The wind tugged at her hair, roared all around her.

Then he looked around.

He stared at her, eyes wide with amazement.

She stammered, "I, I'm back, I came back to live at the Troop. I came to get my things and saw you here waiting for me."

"Waiting for you?" he countered, baring his teeth in a brittle smile. "What makes you think I was waiting for you? Why should I care whether you come back or not?"

He turned and strode off toward the end of the row of cottages, leaving her behind.

To have waited with such unwavering resolve was a secret for which a man's pride admitted of no equal exchange.

She followed him into the cottage, struck by the overpowering smell of tobacco. The floor was littered with cigarette butts. Thick black cobwebs clustered at the corners of the ceiling and hung down in grey foot-long threads, swaying overhead.

"What are you frowning at? Aren't you the one who likes the truth?" He kicked a cardboard box over to the wall with the tip of his shoe and spat on the floor. Then he sat down on the brick bed, pulling his feet up onto it with his shoes still on. He grabbed a paper packet and rolled himself a cigarette.

She looked at the shiny, grimy sleeve of his jacket and felt a wave of disgust.

"Well, when do we make our second trip to the office for a certificate?" he drawled. "After six months' separation, we probably have a chance this time."

She was twisting the corner of her scarf around her finger. Not a word of concern, of regret, not relenting even a little? He was too callous. Fallen lower yet. She should have seen through him long before.

Head held high, he puffed smoke toward the window. "Take whatever you want." Then he added, "The household stuff is worth a hundred dollars."

"Leave the money out of it!" Xiao Xiao exploded. "I've got a question for you. When did you come by an uncle high up in the army?"

But he did not so much as look up.

This made her so mad that her voice turned shrill. "The household stuff! You can keep the household stuff to pay for your gambling. That way you won't have to lie to people when you lose!"

But the little alarm clock was still ticking along. At least he had not gambled it away.

"Lie to people?" He snickered as though she had said something

309

hilarious. "Still harping on that, eh? I just can't figure out why you should be so touchy on that one point, so preoccupied with it. I think you're just getting yourself worked up."

"What did you say?" She bit her lip hard. Had all her earnest and well-intended admonitions, all those painful arguments been a complete waste of words? Had she not touched him in the slightest? Or was he simply stalking grandly off, refusing to admit he was wrong no matter what? "What do you mean I'm just getting myself worked up? Surely you understand that all along I've wanted to live an honest life. Of course I expected the same in my, in my husband."

"Oh, forget it." He shrugged. "Do you know what honesty is? Haven't I already told you that being a good person in this world is precisely the most false, perhaps even hypocritical..."

"So I suppose that makes you the honest one? You have the effrontery to..."

Quite unruffled, he rolled himself another cigarette, licked the edges of the paper, and said deliberately, "Why are you always harping on this 'you're a liar, you're a cheat' stuff? You'd think I had committed some enormous crime. Why don't you ask about how other people have lied to us? The times we live in, this political movement, this Farm, when have they ever told us the truth? Who is interrogating them? Who is accusing them? I'm not trying to get myself off the hook, and I'm also quite aware that lies are always exposed..."

She interrupted him. "Then why do you keep on making up one lie after another? I've been asking myself for a year, and I still can't figure you out."

"Why do you think?"

Could it be there is something psychologically wrong with you, that you can't control yourself, something abnormal...

The thought made her shiver, and she shook her head in silence.

"Do you want me to put it to you as clear as can be?" He cackled. "This is one hundred percent true. You can believe it or not; that's up to you. When I see someone believing one of my lies, I feel ecstatic. When I see something that I couldn't accomplish by telling the truth come about just like that because I've told a lie, I go wild with happiness. Those are the only times in my life that I am happy, and I could never overcome my desire for such happiness, no matter how I tried. No truth, no virtue, no matter how perfect, means anything if it cannot bring me that happiness. Especially when in the world we live in today it's only by lying that we can get even the basic respect that people

310

ought to have. Why don't you try asking yourself whether such a society deserves to get honesty and sincerity in return?"

"You think only of yourself," she said, exasperated beyond endurance. Her heart was pounding as though something were shaking and twisting it. It was horrifying, but she wanted him to go on all the same. "You're nothing but an egotist." She simply wished she could sink into the ground. "To think that I could be so naive as to fall in love with someone..." Someone with no shame at all. "Someone like you!"

He actually chuckled. His crafty eyes came boring through the smoky air, squeezing her chest. It had been dark for some time. He reached out and turned on the light.

"You see? Even you don't like this sort of truth. I reveal my inmost secrets to you and you treat them like poison." In the light, his mournful eyes looked somehow a little more honest. "You're forever saying how much you like the truth, but when I give you the truth about me, you can't take it for a minute. What you want is a good little sanctimonious phony me, a so-called nice, phony me. You just use the truth as a fig leaf, that's what you do!" He exploded with anger. "You're the hypocrite!"

She was stunned. Astonished. Infuriated. Ashamed. Weak. Silent as a cicada in winter. Was there really nothing more she could say to convince him?

The little rectangular alarm clock was still ticking away, walking into the distance somewhere. In its world alone was there no 'self'. But without any self, what was it for?

"But before, you said that you had never deceived me, and yet you still hid everything from me. Why?" she stammered. "If you really loved me..."

He leaned his head against the heated wall, his eyes half shut, looking much more calm. He said wearily, "As I said just now, if I had told you everything early on, you would probably have left me way back then. You might have rejected me as worthless. Because, because you still don't understand, you still don't have the strength to accept me. It was for the sake of our love that I concealed the truth from you and made myself out to be an angel, so that you would love me, so that you would give yourself up to me. But you will never be able to understand that my heart never deceived you. I did love you! You were the one and only person I could never have found pleasure in lying to. Isn't that enough? I loved you, from the very first moment we met. In order to preserve your innocence, I hid from you everything that was ugly; in order to keep you from becoming disappointed and disgusted with life, I faced the harsh truth all by myself. And above all, I never made you lie! Never! I let you stay in your own little kingdom, using my 'evil' to redeem your 'good', taking every care to keep your sincerity from being contaminated by this ugly world. How much more could you want of my love? Which of us has really paid the greater price for it?"

His voice fell. "You'd better go. I won't try to stop you. I realised long ago that this day might come. The day I told you the truth, everything would be over. Perhaps if I had told you a little earlier just what lies really amount to, you might have smartened up a little. I don't know of any better way. I am really happy to see that you are still as genuine as you think, to see you leave here, leave me, with all the self-confidence that was yours the first time I saw you. I may be very insignificant, but remember this: I have never deceived you, and in order not to deceive you I have probably deceived myself, and so I am suffering the consequences. But so long as you believe that I have not deceived you, I will be satisfied no matter what happens to me. I think of you as myself. If I haven't deceived you, then I haven't deceived myself, or deceived life. So why should life punish me? Evidently it doesn't like the truth, so we have both been deceived by it."

He turned his back on her. It was a hard, stern back, both petty and huge.

The light went out. Another power failure. Everything was pitch black.

Her mind had stopped working. She had lost the power to reason. A black and bottomless abyss, so black that not even fear and shock could be made out within it. Her heart was all black too. She had never seen herself clearly.

A huge black indistinct shape rose up on the wall. It seemed to have crawled out of her body, a monster from that summer night. He set a candle on the wooden edge at one end of the brick bed, and she stood up mechanically.

"I'd better be going," she said.

"If you need a hand, I can help you move one last time." As he spoke, he began rolling up the bedding.

She watched in silence as he divided the baggage on the brick bed into two parts. The green underquilt and the pink print quilt were once again returned to their rightful owners. A pair of chapped hands tied the rough hemp rope. Their brick bed broken up at last.

She took the rope and lifted the bedroll, steadying it with her other hand.

"Okay. You're on your own now." He moved out of her way.

She walked out, clutching her bedding. But she could not get out. It was too big and stuck in the doorway. Why hadn't he insisted on helping?

Behind her, he said abruptly, "One more thing."

She left the bed roll where it was, supporting it with her knee.

"What is it?"

Silence.

"Go ahead."

"Listen!" he growled through clenched teeth. "However you want to handle the divorce is fine with me. We can do it whenever you like. But the boy goes with me, and no two ways about it! Have you got that? He's mine!"

"I want..." The bedding was about to slip down.

"What do you want? If you really want a divorce, then give me the boy. That's all it takes, the boy! If you won't give him up, then don't blame me when the time comes and I..."

The bedroll slipped to the floor. All they owned. They had no property to dispute, only their son. Was he their common property? She took the bedroll in her arms and with one great heave staggered outside.

The fields were pale as death. A great round moon looked at her in sorrow and astonishment, as though wondering if it had mistaken the time and come hurrying over with its congratulations on the very day they were separating.

You are blackness too! And your light is a cheat! But do you know yourself?

Xiao Xiao stumbled along. She could not see her feet. She was only faintly aware that she still had not taken away her canvas suitcase.

She was walking through a vast forest, the thorny branches snagging her sleeves and leaving her pink shirt showing through the holes.

She remembered that in fact she did not have a pink shirt.

The forest was dense. Deep within it, olive-green fruit were barely visible, hanging one by one. From a distance, they looked like fresh stalks of asparagus-lettuce. When she walked closer, they looked like bananas from the side but like oval pear-apples when seen head-on. She had no idea what sort of fruit they were; she had never seen their like before. She pressed her nose to one and took a sniff. From its green streaks came a fragrance like cucumber or watermelon. Her mouth watered; she felt ravenous, and her stomach rumbled. She reached for the fruit, but then she noticed a black snake coiled around the branch, flicking its tongue. She recoiled a few steps, took the rubber band off the end of a braid, and tossed it at the snake like a quoit. The band landed right around the snake's neck, so that it was unable to strike. She jumped up, plucked the fruit, and gobbled it down. By the time it occurred to her that she ought to take one bite first and see what it tasted like, the whole fruit was already tucked away in her tummy. But in a flash it had no weight, and even she weighed nothing. She felt a pleasant cool sensation around her eyes. She seemed to be on the point of flying away, so amazingly strong had her arms and legs become.

She raced through the dense forest, dodging all obstacles long before she came to them.

She was frantically hammering a piece of molton iron. Before her hammer even touched the blank, the iron had taken shape.

She pulled up a huge tree. There was a torrent roaring down a mountain. She laid the tree across the stream and crossed over. She stepped on a leaf and crossed over the sea. She whipped up the waves with a branch of the tree until they splashed up into the sky. She lit a fire on the seabed and began roasting the ocean over its crackling flames, until the ocean had turned to a layer of salt.

A huge black shape swept across the sky, chasing after her and screaming, You stole that fruit, you spit it back out. You stole that fruit, you spit it back out.

I didn't know what kind of fruit it was I ate, she screamed. She stumbled and fell into a swamp. I didn't know what kind of fruit it was, she screamed even louder than before. She wanted to spit the fruit back out, but she could spit up nothing at all.

37

Spring came to the Great Northern Wastes riding on a donkey tethered to a millstone.

He had said so.

It was something that he had said. The donkey went round and round in circles with springtime on its back. It seemed to arrive, then it would go away again. The weather would seem to have warmed up, then it would get cold again. There would be a definite thaw, then a snowfall, and then a hard freeze. Winter was the donkey. It was blindfolded.

At last it got tired. It stopped to rest, and spring jumped down from its back. The earth oozed with the juices of happiness.

He had said so. What had he said? So many things, some forgotten and some remembered, but none with any meaning any more. Their letter of introduction had been issued; it said, 'conciliation unsuccessful; divorce by mutual consent'. Six words, and stamped with the seal of the Branch Farm. He and she would soon be going to Farm Headquarters to get it approved.

Just like springtime on its donkey, that letter of introduction had gone in countless circles around this little speck of land. That they were living apart was a fact. Their perfect marriage was bankrupt. But what about the glorious history of the first pair of city kids from the south to settle down on the State Farm? Was it to be simply cancelled at a stroke? That would be letting the little bastards off too easy. What if it was a phony divorce for the sake of home leaves? No hurry to give them an answer. What were the labour-reform officials doing to earn their keep? Couldn't they do some surveillance for a while? Ought to keep a close tail on them, see what sort of monkey business the two of them were up to with their pretended separation. They could divide up their bedding but still sneak into one bed, couldn't they?

And now, for the first time in her life, Xiao Xiao heard the expression *in flagrante delicto*. Chief Sun had used it at a meeting of the Company, attacking her without mentioning her by name.

315

Afterward someone had asked her if she understood what it meant. And she really did want to know what it was all about. She did not understand why she had to pay a price in disgrace on top of the pain of divorce.

The millstone came around and passed by once again. The next time it came around, the reins of hope were on the donkey's neck.

Then she noticed that the faces all around her were even more distant than before, even more chilly and impassive. The early spring wind cut to the bone, and it always blew from behind. Somewhere along the way, she had become a bad woman. The focus of censure had swung around to her. A few months before, she had been the object of sympathy and compassion, but all of a sudden, she and Chen Xu had completely changed places.

"She's the one who wants the divorce," they whispered.

"What a monster. Doesn't even want her baby any more."

And then, and then there was more, which she could not hear.

She had become a bad woman, since it was she who had asked for the divorce. And by having suffered rejection by such a bad woman, he became the good guy. He was the victim. They forgave all his past mistakes because a man was still a man, no matter how many mistakes he had made. No number of mistakes could justify a divorce.

She did not know to whom she could turn for help. It was an age without courts, without lawyers; there were only revolutionary committees. And the committee chairman's feelings were determined by a phone call from the farm chairman, or by the progress of spring ploughing, or by the fodder supply. What made things worse was that Branch Farm No.5 had no real chairman for its revolutionary committee just then. Yu Funian had been transferred to the District Office, near Hegang, to be Chairman of the Political Department. The newly appointed Branch Farm Chairman was Guo Aijun, who was still practising her walking in a Hangzhou hospital. That left Liu the Brute in charge for the time being. After he had spent an age trying to read the divorce report while holding it upside down, he said, eyes starting from his head, "Out of the question! Without his old woman, that kid Chen Xu will be even more impossible than ever! He needs someone to keep an eye on him!"

The millstone was pushed around and passed by once again. Spring was almost gone, but youth and hope still remained. Would it go on pushing its responsibility aside for ever?

In the depths of her despair, she had blocked Secretary Li's bicycle.

Please, stop!

And he had stopped. There were ice crystals in the air that day. His cap was wet and his lean face looked weary. He listened to her patiently, nodding from time to time. She seemed to see in his earnest look a belief that she was telling the truth. His kindness so encouraged and moved her that she opened her heart up to him almost as though he were a friend.

"They say that you and, and your wife couldn't get along. Did you get a divorce too? The two of you couldn't have, couldn't have come to blows right at first, could you? If there isn't a clean break, couldn't two people, well, just die?" She was hardly making sense.

He smiled faintly. He did not resent her touching his own sore spot at all. He even appeared to appreciate such frankness.

"All right," he said, "I'll have a talk with them."

The wheels turned and he rode on.

The millstone came around, and at last it stopped. Spring jumped down from the donkey's back and onto a fine horse. Or perhaps it was an ox. It made no difference. Even a snail could go forward.

And sure enough, he did have a talk with 'them'. And the result of that talk was the seal. People told her on the sly how an exultant Chief Sun had lectured Liu the Brute, "You see? Like I said long ago; let them divorce. That kid Chen Xu's old woman has run out on him. Serves him right! Now he'll have to stumble back to live with the Company like a good boy!"

Liu had walked silently away. Xiao Xiao knew that he was the one who was really sorry about their divorce. Whenever he caught sight of Xiao Xiao in the distance, he would turn aside and walk away. His face, which never smiled, now had the look of a yellowed leaf touched by frost. That light bulb he had got for them when they really needed it!

He had said, Spring comes riding on a donkey.

He had said, Autumn comes riding in a sleigh.

He had said, he had said, He loved her.

Whatever he had said, it no longer had any meaning. First thing the next day, they would ride over to the Farm Office to take care of the divorce procedure. Then they would separate, just as politely as you please. Perhaps she would not forget to say goodbye.

White silkworms were wriggling all over her bed. There was a breeze blowing in through the window, and the floor was covered with fallen white leaves. They turned out to be flakes of skin shed by the silkworms, drifting through the air like willow catkins.

She bent down and gathered up the catkins, but they turned out to be scraps of torn paper. She wanted to paste them back together, but they were in all sorts of irregular shapes and none of them would fit. As soon as she had one right, another would come loose. She worked so intently that she broke out in a sweat. Then two of the pieces surprised her by clicking together. She joined them, but then she found that the paste would not make them stick. She mixed up some starch on the stove, but it would not stick either; it was like water. She wiped some water on them and took them outside to freeze, but they would not even freeze. She brought them back inside to dry out on the fire, but they melted away, for in fact they had been snowflakes.

38

One morning, she put on her brown padded coat, tied on a scarf and a face mask, and put the letter of introduction into her brown satchel. She examined it one more time and then went off to the tractor barn to catch the trailer cart into town.

The two of them had agreed to meet there and go to Farm Headquarters together to take care of the divorce.

There was a layer of glistening frost on the sides of the cart. The people who were waiting had dragged along ropes, gunny sacks, and bricks and were sitting curled up on them, mutely wishing that the cart would leave. Someone greeted her, but she barely responded. She hung her head and looked at no one, for fear that more people would notice her. At last, the driver appeared. He yelled something at the people packed into the cart and then bantered for a while with the girls walking to work along the road. Finally he got into the cab. The tractor began to chug like an air-blower when the current is turned on.

She looked down the main road. He was not there. She stood up, but there was not so much as a shadow of anyone on the little path that led to the family quarters.

The tractor was revving up. It was about to leave.

Xiao Xiao took off her face mask. Her face was bathed in sweat, and her gloves were sticky. She couldn't go to Farm Headquarters by herself, in any case.

The cart gave a violent jerk, throwing everyone toward the back.

Clinging heedless of all else to the side of the cart, she stepped onto an angle iron at the back and jumped down. She heard people shouting in surprise behind her on the cart.

Without even waiting to recover her balance, she set off for the cottage at a run. Had he changed his mind? Why hadn't he come? He must have overslept. Anyway, he wouldn't be in time for that day's trip.

She shoved hard at the door. It was not bolted, and she went staggering inside.

The floor was covered with pieces of broken crockery and glass, strips of cloth, torn-up paper. An appalling heap of trash.

He himself was buried in this heap, crouched next to the brick bed, his head lolling on the wooden edge. He seemed to be asleep. There was an empty wine bottle at his feet. His throat made a rasping noise.

She walked over to him and shook his shoulder with all her might, but the piercing stench of alcohol made her turn her head away. She could make out broken dishes, torn-up bedding, and letters amid the trash on the floor. Even their humble little table was now a pile of kindling.

He was drunk. She let out a deep breath. It looked as though he too was suffering bitterly. She felt a slight sense of exhilaration. She had been longing to see something like this, to see him lose his male arrogance and show some weakness. It proved that the divorce was not a matter of indifference to him.

It was very stuffy in the cottage. The time had not yet come to open up the window, sealed against the harsh winter cold. The glass was covered with dust and grime. In the half-light, it was hard to make out the man curled up at her feet like a pile of rags. But he had been her husband, and he still was. She watched the tide of her love ebb little by little, revealing the dried-out river bed beneath, and realised just how helpless she now was.

Sitting anxiously on the edge of the brick bed, she suddenly felt terribly weary, as though she were cut off from the world. She could see nothing, remember nothing. She was all hollow inside, and everything outside her was hazy. Past and present, present and future, they all seemed to be separated by a gulf of such infinite extent that she felt puzzled once again at the thought of the months and years she had once spent in this little room. The passionate longing that once had burnt her almost to ashes had quietly vanished, gone into hiding in some shadowy corner, snickering at her. She wanted to burn again like that, a hundred, a thousand times. Why was she not a very sun? She would leave the heaven and the hell of this love far behind her now, to roam the earth and all of human society in search of a sheltered cove.

He stirred, muttering something. She came to herself, and went into the front room to ladle up some cool water, which she splashed on his face. She felt no sympathy for him at all, only loathing. By straining every muscle in her body, she managed to drag him up onto the brick bed.

He opened his eyes. They were bloodshot, confused and hurt as though he had just returned from another world. He made a wry smile, then knitted his brows, as though he did not recognise her at all, staring at her with an odd expression. Then, all of a sudden, he reached out and threw both arms around her, pulling her close to him. His strength was overpowering. He kept her arms pinned against her sides, so she could not move. She began to struggle, begging him softly to let her go. She grabbed him by the hair and fought back, to no effect whatever. He was like a raging bull elephant crashing out of the forest. His heavy panting rumbled like thunder before a storm. He all but ripped her collar open and thrust a hand far into her underclothes.

"No!" she shouted. She could not hear her own voice.

"No!" She could feel something cold rolling down from the corner of her eye. Her heart was breaking.

And yet that heavy body rolled over onto her all the same. She writhed back and forth, pushing at him, hitting him. She was exhausted.

"No," she said to herself. She clenched her teeth.

She knew that she could not talk him out of it. She could not spit out that fruit. She still yearned for those gentle caresses in the darkness, even if it were for the last time. Yes, she wanted him. She wanted a last taste of paradise beneath that broad chest he was her husband she still loved him longed for him she was used to him...

When he rolled clear of her, she felt as though she had escaped from under a mountain of ice and lay exposed stark naked on a snowfield. Vast, boundless, empty. Over and over, she shivered from the cold. He and she were like two unrelated boulders, like two hailstones fallen from the sky. All the world had returned to the ice age. And that Strawberry Glen, once ripe to bursting? There was nothing left of it but revulsion, emptiness, as though she had committed a sin.

He pulled half of a torn grey blanket up over his shoulders and sat there in a daze for a long time, staring straight at the wall in front of him. Then he mumbled something inaudible.

Come back!

The blanket slid from his shoulders, revealing a chest grown much thinner than a few months before. His teeth were chattering, and he shivered. He held out two freezing hands and seized her shoulders. A pair of eyes flashing blue with hatred snared her naked body.

"Come back, and we can start all over. We'll live the way you want."

She broke out in goosepimples, and the flesh on her face began to twitch. Perhaps this was the very assurance for which she had been waiting all along.

"Did you say something?" she asked.

He shook his head.

Please, Old Dad, won't you let me go? I'll grant your every wish.

She looked up and saw, deep within his wide-open eyes, the demon that had tormented her for so long, lying quietly to one side and licking its wounds. Here comes the wolf! It was staring at the gauze in her hand, trying in vain to transform it into a fog that would entice her into its depths.

She gently freed herself from his hands and picked up her scattered clothing piece by piece, silently pulling on her socks and snowboots, slowly doing up the laces.

"I'll never believe you again," she murmured.

He gazed sadly up at the ceiling, muttering to himself.

"Believe what? Like I said, you can go. Don't worry, from the first day you aren't my wife any more, nothing like this will happen."

In the dim and dust-laden air, there appeared on his face a look of pain and self-mockery that she had never seen before, a look of desolation so different from his usual arrogance as to make him seem another person. Her heart skipped a beat, and a sharp ache filled it. Perhaps she ought to kiss him once in farewell. She stood silently in the centre of the room, her body swaying as though buffeted by a blast of air.

"All right, you'd better go." His voice had turned cold and cruel once again. "I'll meet you tomorrow morning on the cart. Without fail."

She was making her way rapidly down a long corridor. There were innumerable doors on both sides, each with a narrow keyhole.

She opened the door of her own room.

There was a brick bed in the room, with a mat spread out on it. An enormous round pillar rose from the centre of the bed, right up beyond the roof. With a pillar like this, her house could never collapse, she thought.

She saw something flash by where the pillar made its exit. It looked like there was someone there.

She glanced down and found that she was stark naked.

There was a small lake outside the window, and she jumped into the water. A goldfish swam toward her, each bubble it spit out turning into a golden mushroom. A large net was tossed down right onto her head. She escaped onto the bank and saw in the sunlight that she was actually wearing a swimsuit. I'm swimming, she shouted.

39

"On, account, of, irreconcilable, differences, followed, by, six, months, separate, domicile, please, approve, divorce."

A skinny old man was sitting behind an office table, holding up the letter of introduction and reading it out in a halting voice. When he had finished, he squinted and looked them over sternly. He seemed delighted to have the case and very interested in them, very curious about them, so much so that his inspection went on for almost a minute, during which time his shifting eyes must surely have grown somewhat tired.

"Both city kids?" he asked.

She nodded.

"From Zhejiang?" He pronounced it 'Zhé Jiang'.

She nodded again.

"How long have you been married?"

"A year and a half."

"Any children?"

"Yes."

"And what is the nature of your irreconcilable differences?"

Xiao Xiao hung her head.

"You have a child, don't you? How can you be incompatible?"

He had reached an irrevocable verdict while his interrogation was still in progress.

"I asked you a question!" He stiffened.

Xiao Xiao stammered, "It's something, it's hard to explain, the Branch Farm knows about it; they agreed..."

"Well, then, have the Branch Farm take care of your divorce!" He was visibly angry. "Something that affects your whole life like this, are you just making a fuss for the fun of it?"

Chen Xu cleared his throat noisily and spoke up. "The differences are mainly my responsibility. My character is poor. I skip work a lot, I drink too much, I steal, I cheat; I've been in quite a lot of trouble. She just can't go on living with me. And I can't change my ways, so I've agreed to the divorce."

He was as calm and frank as if he were telling a story about someone else.

The 'Acting Judge' gaped in astonishment, his eyes taking the shape of olives stood on end. He was left speechless.

"Is, is that true? That stuff he just said?" It finally occurred to him to twist his head around and ask her.

Her eyes filled with tears for a moment, and she glanced gratefully at Chen Xu. He avoided her look. A real man. If only he could be so strict with himself all the time!

"Is he telling the truth?" The judge was getting a little impatient.

"Yes." Her voice was so quiet that only she could hear it. But what she wanted to answer was, No! Why didn't anyone ask them whether they loved each other? Why was it that people who had perhaps never known love themselves were sitting in judgement on their fate? She simply didn't know what she would do if they couldn't get the divorce.

Silence. The judge swung his legs back and forth, puffing on his cigarette, more and more shrouded in smoke.

Chen Xu stepped forward and tossed over a pack of 'Springtime' cigarettes. "Come on, Director, give us a break." He looked pained and troubled. He pointed at his chest and then his head. "I'm politically backward, and she's one of the revolutionary younger generation. The divorce is due to a change in class relations, a reflection of class struggle. You can't take that lightly; it has to do with which road we take in politics. The Supreme Directive says, 'There is absolutely no such thing in the world as love or hate without reason'."

"Hm." The judge stood up and yawned. Now that class struggle was involved... He grew alert and stern. He was bored.

He took out a key and unlocked a cabinet in the corner of the room. He poked around in it for a long time, looking for something, but with no success at all. At this point, someone pushed the door open and came in to ask him about something. He shouted, "Where're the divorce certificates that are supposed to be in here? Shit! Hasn't been any call for them the last eight hundred years."

"How about looking in the Political Work Office?" the other man suggested.

He was gone for a long time, but finally came back with a stack of papers. "File these in," he told them.

The remaining procedure was simple: sex, age, property, reason for divorce...

But when they got to the heading 'children', he asked with a snort, "Who gets the child?"

"I do," Chen Xu broke in.

"Do you agree?" he asked her.

She sensed that Chen Xu was throwing her an almost desperate look and dared not raise her eyes. If she nodded, it would mean losing Chen Li forever. If she shook her head, all that they had accomplished so far would be lost. He had lived up to his word. How can I be a mama to you if you don't treat me like one? Chen Li had grown his teeth even without a mother. He looked so much like his father that it made her flesh creep.

"Come on, what do you say?" A drop of ink was hanging on the tip of his pen.

"We agreed long ago that the child should be mine," snapped Chen Xu.

Such a cruel exchange. He had carried out his promise. Could she refuse to do her part?

When that drop of ink hit the paper, it would become law.

She cried, "If he remarries, the boy should be returned to me. He mustn't have a step-mother. Please, please put that in!"

"Remarry?" sneered Chen Xu. Then he barked, "And what if you remarry? I won't let him have a step-father!"

All the judge's sympathy was inclined to the man's side. He rapped on the table and announced imperiously, "The child goes to the husband. You don't have to come up with a penny for support, so why are you making such a fuss?"

And with this, he sternly picked up his pen and wrote, under the heading 'remarks': "The child belongs to the husband in all respects. The wife is not to interfere."

After this, he picked up the big seal, breathed on it, and brought it down on the paper with savage force.

Now she and Chen Xu each got a blood-red circle. Their names fell separately within the circles.

"All right. From now on, you go your way and he goes his. Dismissed!"

And with this pronouncement, he slumped listlessly back in his chair.

They walked out one after the other. Behind the stand of bare trees outside the door there hung another blood-red circle. The sun was setting. A day would soon be over. Did a red circle mean an end, or did it stand for a beginning? Was it empty or full? Was it a drop of blood or the sun?

Chen Xu walked away without a backward look.

She held the piece of paper covered in red seals between her fingers, gazing numbly after him as he disappeared into the distance. She had spent too much of her lifeblood for that piece of paper, and now that she had it, she still felt almost incapable of relief. Where had her nerves been stripped away? She remembered clearly their coming to register their marriage the day before. She would return to the Company by herself.

She was putting on an acrobatic show in a vacant lot. She squeezed through a flaming hoop. She squeezed through with all the agility of a hairless rabbit. And yet, for each hoop she got through there was another across her path. She began to get tired, but the flaming hoops were as endless as the wreaths in a National Day parade. She stood on a float, costumed like one of the Seven Fairy Maidens. The road was lined with leafless poplars.

She was looking for something on the ground. She remembered there was a path through the weeds. But she could not find that path, no matter how she looked.

It had started to rain. The ground was covered with cobblestones, glistening like the Milky Way. Chen Xu was standing on the other side of the river, holding an imitation leather suitcase. He could not get across, so he had to put the suitcase in the water and float it over. There was no water in the river, and the suitcase sank. There was only a little clock, ticking away. But when she scooped up the clock and held it to her ear, it was obviously a heart. The heart was not in Chen Xu's chest; how could it be beating where she was? She tried to call over to him, to tell him his heart was there. But the Milky Way was too broad, so he could not hear her at all. She could see him on the opposite bank, looking tall and handsome, but dressed in the patchwork cassock of a monk.

The rain got heavier, and the waters of the Milky Way began to rise. There was a road barely visible through the water, like a dyke along the Imperial Canal. A magpie brought her the suitcase in its beak, but she just could not manage to open it.

40

A pile of rubble.

She was buried under a pile of rubble, gasping for breath, her limbs heavy. She could not get free of the weight on her legs. She caught sight of a patch of clear blue sky shining with a kind of metallic glint through gaps in the rubble. She had never seen so blue a sky. She could not tell for certain whether it was the sky or the sea.

A huge lizard slithered in through the lighted gap in front of her. The odd thing was that it had no tail. Blood was dripping from where the tail should have been. Its beady little eyes stared at her. She was not frightened at all, and reached out to stroke its head. The lizard bent down and drank from a puddle, and then its tail began to grow, wagging like a dog's.

A crab climbed up out of the sea and cleared away part of the pile of rubble with its tough pincers. There turned out to be a patch of glossy green chives underneath. The crab began clipping the chives with its pincers, but as sooner as it cut off one clump another would grow up in its place. She said to the crab, Come on and help me. But no sooner did the crab turn over a rock than its pincers snapped off. She panicked. Then a new pair of pincers appeared with a click, right where the old one had broken off. The crab helped her move the stones away and she squeezed her way out. She took a deep breath and then snatched the crab by the sides of its shell, shouting, I'm going to eat you; then I'll be able to grow new pincers!

The crab was immobilised, but she could not think where she should go to steam it. She looked down and found that she was covered with wounds.

The sky was so blue, so utterly blue.

She did not know where she was. The place was unfamiliar. She looked around. The ceiling was high and dark, the windows large and low. The trunks were not left down on the brick beds, but were stacked in the centre of the room. The room was not large, but all the same it did not seem cramped. There were a dozen neat bedrolls spread out, with a wall not far beyond. Hanging on the wall were a chart and a few sheaves of grain and corn. The sun cast bright specks of light on the yellowing leaves. Hens could be heard clucking in the distance.

It was in a research team. She remembered. It was on Branch Farm No.7, several miles beyond No.5. She remembered. She was forever moving about, like a drifter. She had been on night duty with her friend Dakang the night before, checking and recording the progress of the sprouting experiments. She had this morning off. And she remembered that she had been formally transferred here from No.5. She stretched luxuriously. Trees died if they were moved, but people lived. By moving she could begin her new life and seek out her own path according to her inner ideals. From her first day on this branch farm she had felt a fresh enthusiasm for everything there.

Liu the Brute had walked into the girls' dorm one day around noon with an unlined leather jacket thrown over his shoulders. She had felt awkward around him ever since the divorce.

"No work today on account of the rain." He rolled himself a cigarette and sat down next to Xiao Xiao's bedroll.

Someone cracked a joke:

> "The rains of spring bring joy to all below;
>
> Rich and warm, across the land they Liu."

She looked away. She didn't know what to say to him.

"It's nothing special," he said in his kindliest tone, puffing on his cigarette. When it was finished, he ground it out under his shoe, cupped his hands around his mouth, turned to her, and whispered, "Now that you've been separated from him a little while, aren't you after transferring out to some other place?"

She shook her head. Where would she go? She didn't know anyone.

"It seems to me that you two can't help running into each other every time you turn around, and it'll always be awkward, it's never going to seem right. If you want to move somewhere else, I can go have a talk with Director Xu over at No.7. His wife and mine are sisters."

She had not felt that running into Chen Xu would be so hard on her, but other people, perhaps everyone else on the farm, seemed to find it unbearably awkward. Hadn't Aunt Min put it to her as nicely as she could that same day that if she moved somewhere else she might find it easier to get over her painful memories? Perhaps she herself would change as well.

And one month later she was in fact transferred to Farm No.7.

The day she left No.5, it was drizzling off and on. Thick layers of cloud had swept away the last traces of winter, and the wind was gentle and humid. The rain dripped with a noise like the pendulum of a clock, and the splash of wheels along the muddy road sounded like rain falling on a bamboo rainhat. A bamboo rainhat in tea-picking season. It never seemed like springtime unless there was rain. Only a spring in which rain could be heard dripping on a bamboo rainhat was a real springtime. Such weather was all too rare there in the North.

She was riding to No.7 on a horse-drawn hay cart. The cart moved along the road between freshly sown wheatfields, drops of water quivering on the tips of the stubble. Whether she looked back or up ahead toward her destination, the road vanished into the misty rain. It seemed almost as though she had left all the weight of her body behind at No.5, but after a while she felt that the crevices in her heart were still clogged with dirt. It seemed almost as though the raindrops had soaked the fluffy hay so thoroughly that it might sprout and start growing again along the way; and then it seemed they might slip away in a twinkling of an eye and go back up to hide above the thick layers of cloud reaching to the horizon.

She had passed her first few days after parting from Chen Xu in a state of uncertainty and depression. But oddly enough, it seemed a little easier to take than she had imagined. If you want to despair, you will. If you want to hope, then hope is possible. She believed that if she could just leave Chen Xu she might fulfill her regenerative power just as the lizard did.

Please Old Dad, won't you let me go? I'll grant your every wish.

The cart rattled past the lines marked in lime outside the quarantine station, the boundary of No.7. And all at once there were the herds of brown local cattle and bay horses grazing leisurely in the pastures, stretches of run-down fencing made of unmilled lumber, and a row of dilapidated thatched cottages. As the sky began to grow lighter, she could see that this little branch farm, which specialised in raising livestock, was like an oil painting that turned rough and crude when you walked closer to enjoy it.

Here she would search for a divorced woman named Xiao Xiao. In fact, it made no difference at all to her where she went looking. She had no idea where she might find herself again. Here she would make up for the time and the responsibilities she had forfeited during the few years just past. And then there was her reputation.

When she remembered all this, she stopped worrying about herself. She was delighted by this little farm surrounded by pastures and a reservoir, delighted by its quiet peace, almost cut off from the world. When the sun was shining and she looked out from the research team's little experimental plots toward the cluster of brown barns below the green hills, it looked just like a landscape by the Russian Itinerant painter Izaak Levitan she had seen in high school, or like an illustration from a Soviet novel. And in the morning, when hundreds of great bay horses came shooting out of the barns like balls of flame, raising clouds of red dust along the highway, she felt as at no other time how beautiful life still could be.

Some small red leafless flowers on the windowsill caught her eye. They looked a little like peach blossoms, with a touch of lavender amid the pink of their pretty petals, but with straight firm stems. Tartar scent? The first flowers of springtime in the north. She had been in the Great Northern Wastes for several years, but she had never managed to pick these earliest of wildflowers. How she had wanted to know what the azaleas of the north were like, and now they had appeared at last.

They must have been picked by Dakang, she guessed. Dakang, the big girl whose bedding, placed next to her own, was covered with a green checked plastic cloth. She had taken the girls back to the fields before dawn again. It was Dakang who had come running up to her, thick braid swinging, that rainy day when she got off the cart and stood there uncertainly, bags in hand. "Come with me!" Dakang's forehead was as broad as a runway. She was big all over—her eyes, her nose, mouth, front teeth, hands, feet. "People call me Dakang, 'Big Kang'." She flashed an easy-going smile. "I'm in charge of the research team. It was me who asked Director Xu for you!"

How open Dakang was, and how happy.

Her hands were busy all day long, and so was her mouth. As soon as there was a break, all ears were filled with her 'solo'.

"One time back during the 'Smash the Four Olds' campaign, my mom was spanking my little sister. My sister ran outside, shouting, 'Chairman Mao says we should struggle with words, not with weapons. And you a block warden, why don't you spend a little time studying the Sixteen Points?' My mom was so mad there was smoke coming out her ears. She chased her right out into the street, yelling, 'You little squirt! I'll whop you sixteen points' worth!' When the people outside heard that they thought she was such a reactionary old lady, they took her off to the police station. What's that? Something wrong with your ears? Even at the station my mom wouldn't back down. She gave them an earful besides. 'Do the Sixteen Points cover spanking my kid? You need to add another point then, that's what you need!'"

"...When I went home that time, my sister-in-law gave me a ticket to the show. When the actor was on stage, what a mouth! You wouldn't believe how big it was. It was so big you could see all the way into his belly. It was really something. But once he got to chatting with people off-stage, that mouth of his was clumsier than his feet!"

Around Dakang, life seemed to be made up of jokes and funny stories like these. Even illness, fights, and hard luck she managed to fill with a kind of happiness and amusement, for she had to be constantly dispelling them with all her might. And so in this tiny little isolated corner of the world Xiao Xiao felt for the first time that the daily life she was so sick of was no longer really so hard to get through.

Once night fell, things got even noisier in the girls' dorm, and it was always Dakang's voice that was loudest.

"Hey, looking in the mirror again? You're going to make it crack! You know what they say about modern movies? Chinese movies are newsreels, Korean movies are melodramas, Vietnamese movies are done with live ammunition, Albanian movies... Say, Xiao Xiao, tell us about your West Lake and the 'broken bridge'. Did it break from people walking on it? You southern kids, once you start eating the potato flour up here you get fat. Are you sure you can still fit into your clothes? Hey! Look here! What do you say? Wide pants; my mom got them ready for me way early. She says people swell up like bread once they start working on the farm."

Someone gave her a shove, chased her all around the dorm. Laughter swept Xiao Xiao this way and that like a whirlwind. Once she had had enough, Dakang would settle down all of a sudden and start reading in some book. But after a few pages she would be yawning and her eyes would glaze over. Rubbing her eyes, she'd have Xiao Xiao teach her a song. She tried learning to beat time, but no matter how much dust her big heavy hands raised, beating on the brick bed, she still could not keep the beat. "Those numbers in the score are like a pack of fleas!" She looked discouraged and fell back on her bedroll, face beaded with sweat. "'I'm from the class of '68, Just like Pigsy, that's my fate'. I've had it!" she would proclaim.

But if anyone got sick, she really turned to. Bringing over special food, boiling water, nothing was too much trouble for her. On Sundays, when Xiao Xiao was going to strip and wash her bedding, Dakang would push her back on the bed. "Go on, you just read your books and keep out of the way!" Before long, her gleaming sheets would be hanging up to dry on a cord strung between the elm trees in front of the door. Afterwards Dakang would curl up quietly on the bed with a ball of white yarn and begin crocheting. She would make a chrysanthemum, then work it into an exquisite pattern. When Xiao Xiao happened to look up to rest her eyes, she would find Dakang watching her with a merry smile.

Why are you always reading? Don't you get tired of it? What's the point in reading all those books? Looks to me like you're real high level. You're so smart, you must of made good grades in school. I was no good at all, really slow. But when I see people with some education, I'm really impressed. You got any problems, just squeak; I love to help out. Aren't you homesick? Don't you miss your baby? You're really tough. But I know you're sad. There's nothing you can do, so you just read all the time. When you're reading, you forget everything, right? I understand; I really do. You came to our farm to get away from him. The people around here are okay...

Tears welled up within her, enfolding her heart in gentle warmth. She looked over at Dakang and saw those two big affectionate eyes damp and downcast too.

"In the summer, we'll go picking chrysanthemums. You know, there's such a mess of them out by the southern pasture."

"After it rains in the fall, I'll take you mushrooming. There's hazelnut mushrooms and pine mushrooms and straw mushrooms and, let's see, oh, I must be getting old! And there's thunder mushrooms, too! One clap of thunder and they pop up slick as a whistle. But be sure you never touch a deadly mushroom! One bite and you're finished before you can stand up!"

And so Xiao Xiao longed for labour-weary summer, yearned for autumn and its bounty. Her heart was a hard, dry field, thirsting for a river, a wellspring. Having experienced solitude, she treasured fellowship all the more; having rejected love, all the more did she crave friendship. And these straightforward northern girls seemed more open-hearted and less designing than the clever girls from down south. So she actually felt more relaxed and at home in the research team and on Farm No.7, where everyone was from Jiamusi or Hegang, than she had on No.5. The people here were only interested in things they felt like being interested in, not like at No.5, where they always paid so much attention to other people's business.

Her tiny little Peach Blossom Spring.

She jumped up. She would go work in the fields too. She felt restless as soon as Dakang was not at her side.

41

A herd of great horses came galloping toward her, trampling the little experimental plot that she tended.

Jack Rabbit! Jack Rabbit! Come here!

Little Ears, you've got out of the stable again. Come back!

A whistle blew and the horses pricked up their ears. After listening for a moment, they shook their heads and went obediently away.

A little stablehand holding a whip was stroking their backs and murmuring, Little idiots, you know you're not supposed to eat the grain in people's fields!

Do your horses all have names? What's your name?

I'm Little Bump.

She looked at him and noticed that his face was deeply tanned. There was an upside down cooking pot on his back. Bump, Bump, she called his name, so you're a hunchback. Can a hunchback herd horses?

Sure. They say you should treat horses like gentlemen. You see Little Slyboots there? He's an old horse. He's got heart trouble and tracheitis. Dr. Chu treated him, so he recognises Dr. Chu. As soon as he feels sick, he starts coughing and goes over to the veterinary clinic on his own to wait for him.

And indeed she did see one horse ambling along behind the rest of the herd. After the stablehand had run up to the front, it looked all around and then began biting off great mouthfuls of the grain growing along the road. One horse stood transfixed in the middle of the road, staring at some pieces of paper blown about by the wind. All of a sudden, a red fox popped up beside the road and at once the horses stampeded, tearing off in all directions. She would block one, and another would get away. She yelled for Bump, and he pulled another whip from inside the pot on his back and gave it to her. She lashed at the horses, swinging her whip so hard that her arm began to ache. Finally, the horses ran obediently off toward a hillside, while she smashed the pot on Bump's back with one crack of her whip. Flying out of the pot came rafts of postage stamps...

"Good morning, Students."

The first time she heard that gentle voice, she felt warm all over, and her every pore relaxed. Good morning, teacher. How very long it had been since she had heard that greeting. Especially here.

She looked up. In front of her was a middle-aged woman with a baby tied on her back, the coarse cloth straps crossing over her chest. Her tousled hair was combed carelessly back, and her black trousers were smeared with kitchen grease. A peasant woman? She felt terribly let down and wondered if her ears had just played a trick on her.

"Good morning, students." The woman with the baby said again, walking up to Xiao Xiao. "Aren't you Xiao Xiao? she asked with a smile.

Dakang broke in. "Xiao, this is our agronomist, Su Fang."

It did not seem to her that a graduate of Northeastern Agricultural College who had come with her husband to settle on the farm should look like this. She should be wearing a white jacket, a pair of trousers with suspenders, and a broad straw hat. She was baffled as she looked at Su Fang, for it had never occurred to her that she could be as plain, from her dress to her smile, as a local peasant woman.

Mrs. Su carried her baby to the experimental plot with her, since there was no nursery on the Branch Farm. During rest breaks, she would undo her jacket and nurse the baby, a rather startling sight. But when she opened up her stiff black notebook and took notes on the experiments in fine and well-shaped strokes of her fountain pen on the white paper, that surprised Xiao Xiao as well.

April was over, and May had come. The experimental plots were a rich green. Mrs. Su carried her baby with her out and back every day, a little baby boy with big blue eyes, turned-up lashes, and a head of soft brown hair. He would lie peacefully in the shade of the trees beside the field, sucking his thumb while the sparrows hopped back and forth all around him, so happy that he kicked up his little feet. Mrs. Su turned up at the experimental plot reserve right on time every morning. She had been working on a strain of early ripening wheat for four years.

"After the spring sowing, we must be sure to put more effort into tamping the earth; the more it's tamped down the better the capillary action of the soil works, so the subsoil moisture rises faster."

She was like a skilled and effective teacher. It was a very faint scent, something that could be smelled, but not seen. It seemed as though she—Mrs. Su—had somehow been formed by folding a peasant woman and a professional up together. When she was whisking the insects away from her baby, asleep in the shade, she was the former; when tirelessly lecturing to the girls in the research team, the latter. Xiao Xiao could not make sense of it. How could someone turn out this way? Was Mrs. Su glad she had become like this or not? She herself had wanted to be a frog princess ever since she was little. This was probably what intellectuals were supposed to be like after they had been remoulded, possessed of this dual nature, skilled in both words and action. Father!

Whenever Xiao Xiao passed by the door of the veterinary clinic, she could see Mrs. Su's husband, Dr. Chu, a graduate of the Veterinary Medicine Department at Northeastern Agricultural. He would be bustling about the room in his face mask and rubberised apron, with his sleeves rolled all the way up his thin arms. The smell of bleaching powder and alcohol came from the clinic window, but there was a 'No Entry Except on Business' notice pasted up at the door, so all she could see inside were a huge horse and that tiny figure. Dr. Chu was the busiest, tiredest, thinnest man on the Branch Farm. According to Dakang, if it weren't for him, all the farm's livestock would have been used to stuff dumplings.

Mrs. Su took Xiao Xiao home with her, to a topsy-turvy little courtyard. There were chicken droppings all over the ground and the chopped-up firewood was soaking in water. The stove counter in the front room was a complete mess, like seeds spilled from a split pumpkin. In the inner room, a whole wall of tidy bookshelves had been set up by resting long boards across the far end of the brick bed. The floor was strewn with diapers, milk bottles, a whirligig drum, cracker boxes, and what not, And yet everything actually seemed to coexist without difficulty.

Ideals were stubborn, and so was reality. Which had compromised with which? And which had vanquished which? They were each as whole as they had been before, and yet each was half of a unified whole. Why hadn't he and she been able to do it? Had he been wrong or had she? Could love exist only by sucking the blood from ideals? If love obliterated ideals, then it wasn't love. Her heart skipped a beat. This cramped little cottage was familiar and homey, and at the same time alien and aloof.

"Come over anytime if there's something you want to read," said Mrs. Su.

She nodded and quickly took her leave. She was afraid of hurting the still unhealed and tender scab on her heart. But she began to have some idea how, in such an out-of-the-way place, so fertile and well-watered, there could be such a vigorous research team and so effective a veterinary clinic. The world was very large, so large that you could never have any way of knowing where you were, and yet it was also very small; even a little seedling plot, a tiny cubicle, could contain all the self-confidence and the hopes your soul possessed.

She felt that there was a faint understanding between her and Mrs.Su's cottage, one that spurred her unrelentingly on toward rebirth.

As spring turned to summer that year, the rain went right on falling without cease. One had only to look longingly toward a patch of blue sky for the dark clouds to sweep in on it. One rain followed another; the air seemed to be made of water. The earth was soaked to the consistency of loose beancurd dregs, its very bones and sinews softened. The run-off from the previous winter's heavy snow, added to the rains, formed pools of standing water on every low-lying piece of land. With the scattered stalks of dead grass rising above their surface, these looked rather like the reed marshes at spring thaw. No sooner did the seeding tractors leave the garage than they were mired in the mud, consigned to their stalls before they could even nibble away an edge of the fields. In the three years since Xiao Xiao had come to the Great Northern Wastes, she had never seen such vicious spring waterlogging.

The loudspeakers were repeating over and over again exhortations from Farm Headquarters to wrest a bumper harvest from the jaws of natural disaster. There had been consultations by telephone. Because traffic was cut off, no jeeps had made it through to them.

Everyone on the branch farm was called out to work, to go into fields knee-deep in water to sow the fodder corn. As the local adage put it, 'plant your seeds by the middle of June, or rue the day when fall comes too soon'. And Mrs. Su said that if they waited for the water to recede before sowing, they would miss the season.

The girls in the research team all shed their long johns, and even their boots, going barefoot as though they were transplanting paddy rice. Xiao Xiao was actually rather anxious to get started. She liked to vary her work continuously, and besides, this scattering of seed across the water, handful by handful, was fun, a little like feeding fish. She rolled her pant legs up over her knees and waded into the bone-chilling mud. She would show them all what she was made of. She wasn't the sort to get a divorce in order to leave the Farm! Go on in, grit your teeth, move ahead, the water creeping up, hang onto the wash basin heaped with seed. Her heart was in her throat, and yet her hands and feet tingled with warmth. Hot blood came spurting through the ice crust. The basin exerted a force that seemed to be pulling her toward the centre of the earth. The seeds longed to return to the soil. She would sow all her wishes with them. When she picked up one foot, the other would sink deeper. She had never before felt so strong. Each step left her basin emptier, but her mind more firm. She felt utterly at ease; she really liked the rain.

Dakang was not far ahead of her, digging out a 'furrow' with her hoe, turning back to glance at her and smile from time to time. The furrow was in fact no more than a groove scooped out of the mud. Dakang kept on splashing over, sending mud flying in all directions, to help Xiao Xiao load up with corn seed. She always threw herself into her work like this.

A crowd of young men came slogging up behind them.

They were laughing and having a grand time.

"Last year when we were sowing soy beans, we roasted some to eat in the field, and Guan Er wouldn't have anything to do with them. He kept saying that those bean seeds had a 90% sprouting rate, and that if we ate them we'd have beans growing out of our belly buttons."

"Hey, Guan Er! Your dad's name is Du, your mom's name is Yang, and your name is Du Yang. So you've got to take care of two families, right?"

"If this flooding keeps up, the fish will escape from the reservoir and we'll be able to pick them up in the fields!"

She listened to them absently. It had been so long since she had heard men's voices. Were they from Ningbo? Hangzhou?

Dakang came up close beside her and said in a low voice, "Don't pay any attention to them. Those are the little rowdies from the tractor crew. Director Xu packed them off to help out here since the machines can't work the fields, and they're miffed. Just look how they're throwing the seed around!"

She noticed that they were indeed moving very quickly, groups of two or three carelessly strewing their offerings all over the place, practically dumping whole basins full of seed into a single hole.

Soon they had reached the far end of the field.

"Hey, Radish! Radish!" Someone yelled, "Let's knock off early and go over to the reservoir and catch a couple of fish for dinner!"

"Radish has the knack when it comes to catching fish with his bare hands. Last time we went, he jumped in and dived under the sluice gate. He caught the first one by stopping up the sluice guard. Then he took that one between his teeth, caught one more in each hand, and came back to the surface. Three in one dive! What do you say to that?"

Someone wearing a grass-green raincoat gave it a resounding slap and yelled, "We'd best go right now. I'll show you guys how it's really done!"

"What'll we do with these seeds?"

Silence.

One of them looked around. When he saw Dakang glaring at them, he made a face and then turned back for a hushed consultation with the others. The one in the green raincoat shook his head. Their squad began to move forward, but for some reason they did not leave.

"They do what Radish says," said Dakang. "He's the one in the green raincoat. He's a work-team leader, but once summer comes, he takes them into the fields to steal watermelons. If he wasn't such a good worker, Director Xu would have sacked him a long time ago."

Radish? She was on the point of asking something, but someone was shouting for Dakang from the edge of the field. It sounded like Mrs. Su, telling her to go to the experimental plots. Luckily, the field they were working was not very large, so Dakang had already dug her furrow out all the way to the end. She gave a few instructions and left.

Xiao Xiao went on quietly sowing the rest of the seed in her basin, not stopping until she had reached the end of the furrow.

The damp legs of her trousers clung to her, raising little red spots when the wind blew. They were awfully wet and itchy. There was mud splashed on her neck and forehead, but she could neither wipe it off nor scrape it out, and her back ached so much she could not straighten up. She turned her wash basin over, set it on the ground, and sat down on it, gasping for breath. The sky was turning dark, and only a few people were left, scattered here and there across the fields. A few spotted magpies were hopping around in the willows beside the field, their snow white breasts standing out vividly in the gloom.

Then she noticed that the kids from the tractor crew had vanished after all.

An empty gunny sack had been dumped at the edge of the field.

She wondered what was going on.

There was a patch of foam on the muddy water not far from her. What about their seed? She walked over.

She could see a heap of dark yellow seed corn thrown into the black water.

They really had gone fishing. Run off like thieves. So this was their game, doing shoddy work, just faking it. She was furious. Those little gluttons had better watch out, or they'd get a bone in their throats. She looked all around, but everyone else was far away. Perhaps it was getting close to quitting time. She thought for a moment, then turned around and went back into the field, quietly picking up her basin. Then she went over to the pile of seeds and scooped them up into the basin, mud, water, and all. She hoisted it up, rested it on her hip, and walked into the field, one step at a time.

In any case, we can't just throw the seed away in the field like that, she said to herself. We'll be short of fodder. It wasn't to get off the farm that she had got her divorce. If she had never been married, she could have been a model worker. Of course her family background was a problem, but it was precisely because of her background that she ought to be remoulding herself all the more consciously. Something done with conscious purpose did not require recognition or publicity. Maybe someone would see what she was doing, but she did not care whether they did or not. She needed to satisfy her own conscience. She refused to cheat either the farm's land or herself. She could ask Mrs. Su whether false flowers were male or female.

She trod a furrow through the black mud, the water opening up and then quietly closing behind her. The mud was loose and slippery, but even though she was often on the point of sinking into it, there seemed always to be a strong hand beneath her feet, bearing her up, firm and solid.

She thought she heard the quitting-time whistle blow. It did not seem all that late. Turning up for work in bad weather was really just symbolic anyway. She glanced back at the patch of foam on the paddy and then carried her basin over to it once again. She thought she had better see to it that all those seeds ended up where they belonged. How she had hoped for a chance to do something like this as a sort of remedy for her soul. She wiped the sweat from her neck with a damp sleeve. Her wet, clammy shirt clung to her back. She looked back at the road again. People were still walking home. But Dakang wouldn't come back. She would have to finish sowing the seeds by herself.

She bent down and got to work. The worst of her fatigue was behind her, and her feet no longer felt stiff at all. She had enough strength left to spread the seeds evenly along the rows, and it filled her with joy to hear them rustling between her fingers and disappearing with a plop into the mud.

By the time the basin was finally empty once again, it was so dark that the two goldfish on the bottom of it were scarcely visible. God preserve you, golden fish! I don't want your reward. Go on back to the deep blue sea and swim freely about there just as you like. She looked up. She really felt like singing, but she could not make a sound. She started back, carrying her basin. She was beginning to feel hungry.

All of a sudden, her hair stood on end, and she froze right where she was.

A huge black shape stood not far away, staring steadily at her. The fields were deserted, and dusk lay heavy all around. She was frightened. She wanted to run away, but the mud clutched her like glue.

"It's me," said the shape, taking a step forward but not coming up to her.

The voice sounded high-pitched and childish, but a little choked up. She got a grip on herself and made out that it was someone wearing a faded army raincoat. Radish? Her temper erupted, and she shouted, "What are you doing here?"

"I..." He hung his head and stammered, "When we came back from fishing at the reservoir, we passed by here and, well, I wanted to see who it was who, who helped us out."

"Who it was? Does it really matter who it was?" She cut him off, turned on her heel and walked away. He had a lot of nerve coming to see!

He chased right after her. Mud splashed on her clothes. She jumped onto the road, but with one stride he had cut her off. Whipping the rainhat off his head, he almost pleaded with her. "Don't, don't get mad. I'm telling the truth. No one's ever been like this. Really, they'd just go tell the bosses. Why didn't you..."

Xiao Xiao finally got a good look at him. He had an unusually youthful face and a head that was a little too large for the rest of him. Through the rain, his round dark eyes flashed with a stubborn and mischievous good humour. His wet black hair was standing up, like the green brush of a southern rice paddy in March. The corners of the mouth were slightly turned up.

"I guessed it was you." He smiled.

Some nerve! Who recognises you?

"Don't you recognise me?" He sounded disappointed. "It was me who took you guys part way in the puffnik that night!"

Even a dog could learn to drive if you put a steamed bun on the steering column. Her eyes brightened. Yes, it was the kid who was raising the bird in his cab. How could he have grown so tall? We're going into town to buy books.

"I guessed right off it was you. I've seen you lots of times, when I'm driving past the experimental plots, always sitting under a tree and reading," he said earnestly. "People who like to read..." But he swallowed the rest.

Probably it was only people who liked to read who could be so dumb. Knowing mockery was evident in his eyes. Three years could change a person, and of course he had been only fifteen back then. "Don't you read?" she returned.

"Not much," he admitted, scratching his head. "Besides, there aren't any interesting books around."

Her stomach was grumbling; she was cold and tired. There were cool streaks on her face; it seemed to be drizzling. She suddenly felt a little let down. It was not on account of the labour she had put in, but what she had got when it was done. She quickened her pace. It was almost completely dark. There was only a faint glimmer of light from the grey puddles on the muddy road. How could he still remember her after three years? Obviously everyone on the Farm knew she was a divorced woman. What should she say to this kid?

"I'd only finished the sixth grade when the Cultural Revolution started." She heard the husky voice still following along after her.

"If you read, you have a chance to go to University. Aren't there worker, peasant, and soldier students nowadays?" She addressed him as an adult would a child.

He sighed, "University? Fat chance of that. I just wanted to, to join the Army."

"You didn't pass the physical?"

"No, it's, it's my Dad. They haven't let him go yet."

"What about your mother?"

"She left. She didn't want us any more. There was no one left at home except my grandma. Sometimes she'd crawl out of bed at two in the morning and go line up to buy meat, so that she could heat it up and make lard. She would give me every last bit of the dregs, but I

343

could never get enough to eat." The clump of his feet drew a little closer. "So I thought, there's no use in my going to school. Only in the Army could I learn something. The day before I left for the countryside, I went to see my Dad in the Municipal Committee's warehouse, where he was being held. There was a light way up in the air, hanging from that pitch black roof, so high up it seemed like the moon. My Dad didn't say anything at all, he just took this raincoat down from the wall and draped it over me. Don't you think he must have meant for me to go in the Army? It was raining the day they took him away, and so he was wearing this raincoat when he left. Later, in the cow-shed, it was his blanket. Whenever it rains, I remember my dad and wonder if he's cold."

He sniffed and said nothing more.

A mistreated little kid. You spent your childhood surrounded by nannies and cakes, and so the sudden disaster naturally threw you off your stride. It probably took a little trouble to make a fallen aristocrat like you grow up. You've done your level best to make yourself worldly-wise, but one slip-up and the truth is out—you're still decent and honest. You've just learned to play a few tricks on the soil; a rather inglorious little two-face.

The raindrops were getting bigger. She frowned. She wanted to say something to comfort him, but for a while she said nothing. "So, you have to tell me, why did you help us out by doing the sowing? And when no one was watching, at that?" He insisted on an answer, but he sounded just a little nervous. "I told you so much just now because you don't seem like other people. You make people feel like talking with you. There's plenty going on around here, but there's no one to talk to. Since you were transferred here, I've noticed how dedicated you are. Really, you don't have to be so, so conscientious."

She stopped.

"No reason at all." She interrupted him softly. "When I went back to work, I was in a daze. I just thought we shouldn't waste that seed. Now perhaps I understand it a little bit better. Perhaps it was just because, because I didn't want you guys to get away with putting one over on me!"

"Putting one over on you?" He cried.

She smiled apologetically. "Let me put it this way. Since I had seen you playing a trick on the land, if I had let you get away with it, you might as well have played the trick on me."

He stood motionless for a long time, the raindrops spattering on

344

his raincoat. The wind was gliding over her shoulder, but it could not stir her damp braid. It seemed as though a great deal of time had passed. Why didn't he say anything? The rain came sweeping over them like a wire brush. It looked like the tractor crew dormitory up ahead.

All of a sudden, he whipped off the raincoat and thrust it upon her. Without saying a word, he turned and ran away. In the darkness, the splash of his boots receded into the distance. The raincoat covered her completely. The clatter of a lute spread down from the top of her head, cutting her off from the cold wind and rain. She felt more alone than ever.

She could hear Dakang shouting in the distance. It sounded like her name. A flashlight was shining her way.

42

She was sitting in a large room with a huge sheet of white paper spread out in front of her. She could see the words 'Please use a pen name' written on the blackboard at the front.

She remembered that she was taking an examination. It was for entrance to a forestry college. But she was positive that she had meant to sign up for the Shanghai Dramatic Academy examination. She could not make the number on her examination permit match the one on her paper, and on top of that she did not know whether she had a pen name or not. Her fountain pen was a Hero 100. She wrote in the upper right-hand corner of her paper, 'Smile Among the Flowers' and then crossed it out. She wrote 'Clouds and Rivers are Surging' and then crossed that out. 'A Riot of Red Flags', and crossed it out. She wrote 'Store Grain Everywhere'.

The examination questions were:

1) Why is it said that the tricksters of the open road cannot out-trick the tricksters in government?

2) Why is it said that the First Emperor's native place was in Xiangtan?

3) Should we give home leaves to Confucius?

She could not think of any answers and sat there in a daze. When it occurred to her that if she could not get into university she would have to spend her whole life on the Farm she got so upset that she felt like crying. All of a sudden, a paper wad was tossed at her feet. She picked it up and saw tiny writing all over it. It was all answers, but she could not understand any of it. She looked up, and there was Zou Sizhu in the seat behind her. He made a face and held his hand against his lips, then blew her a kiss, and waved. She turned away and ignored him, tossing the paper wad back. Pen speeding across the page, she wrote, Give up an inch on socialism and capitalism gains a mile.

Secretary Li rapped on the desk with his pointer and asked in a loud voice, Who will go with me to repair the roads? Everyone who works on the roads will be recommended for university.

Only she and Zou Sizhu went with him. Their work proceeded at lightning speed, as though they were running the hundred-yard dash. She was actually using a 'Locomotive' spade. Secretary Li stuck up a sign beside the road. It read: Done in a Day.

A large truck drove down the road, loaded down with big wooden poles. Secretary Li blew his stack. You unload those right now! he roared. The settling-in of the city kids on the State Farm is approaching its climax. Leave the wood for them to make furniture with. Anyone who objects will be shot!

A tractor came lumbering up. The driver was chomping on a green radish. She gave him a book, but then he turned out to be Zou Sizhu, only without his glasses and with big strong arms. He said that he was going to Nenjiang as a public works labourer for twenty years. She saw him off, waving a bouquet of blue flowers.

"It's too far for you to keep making the trip back and forth. Really, you don't need to, to come so often. There's nothing..."

She was standing under the mountain clove tree in front of the girls' dormitory, speaking as gently as she knew how. The dim stars shone on his pale forehead. In daylight, fine lines were already visible on his brow. Could people really begin to age in their twenties? If the clove tree had a memory, it would know that this was not the first time she had spoken this way. And it would know too that he was not replying for the first time, but rather as usual, when he said, "Oh, it's not too far. It doesn't tire me out at all. It's just a short walk. I'm here almost as soon as I start. What wears me out is field work, mechanically doing the same thing over and over. But when we're talking, the time just flies by. You know, back at the Company, there are fewer and fewer people to talk with."

She could not tell when it had started, but each of the other girls on the farm now had her own secret. They kept them under their tongues to chew over by themselves in bed at night. Even Dakang was not laughing as much as she had before. Here on the lonely frontier, among this quiet circle in the midst of a wide world, Xiao Xiao found that her oldest, most understanding, and most trustworthy friend was Zou Sizhu.

Zou Sizhu had come to see himself as her natural protector early on. He looked in on her every week, even in bad weather, bringing her books and abstruse theories he had dug up somewhere or other, and occasionally some wildflowers he had come across. (But he never

347

brought anything to eat. He never mentioned anything having to do with food. He ate practically nothing.) Dakang said, If the guy with the glasses doesn't come Saturday, he's here first thing on Sunday.

She was glad he came. As soon as he arrived, she felt as though her backbone had been stiffened and the muscles in her back made stronger. For the moment, she had a goal, a firm footing. The various doubts, the questions that had been steeped from her in this sleepy and out of the way place now had a way dredged clear for their release. She had felt somewhat closer to him ever since their talk on Sindhu Mountain. The gates of her mind were thrown open, as though she had received a revelation. She especially liked to receive and be immersed in the limitless wisdom that flashed through his glasses with the tireless instruction and earnest advice that he offered her like an elder brother.

And yet she soon noticed that once he appeared, all the girls in the dorm slipped out one by one. Even Dakang, Dakang too...

Then it dawned on her. Did they think he was her boyfriend?

Her boyfriend? Her heart was dry and dead. She did not even blush. Everybody was hunting for a match—bringing water, binding kindling, giving eggs, catching rabbits, cooking up meals by themselves, whispering together. But when he came, he looked down on everyone, arguing in a loud voice and venting his spleen as though there were no one around.

"Have some melon seeds?"

"Eating those things is a waste of time!"

"I don't feel well today."

"Never mind, never mind, just bear it a while and you'll be better."

Her boyfriend?

She snapped at Dakang, "He is not!"

He wasn't? If he wasn't, what was he? All those wide-eyed, sidelong, drawn-out looks still went on piling up, even after she had denied it over and over again.

There was something odd about it, anyway.

Especially since he stayed so long when he came. He did not leave until late.

Especially since when she saw him out the door, he would always linger a while under the mountain clove tree. And then the flood of talk that had been flowing from his throat for hours was suddenly cut off by a kind of sluice gate, and he became as quiet as a mute. In the

348

darkness, his glasses would throw off flashes of light that were gone before they started. He stood there silently, as though he had something on his mind, but saying nothing. Then he would suddenly snap out of it and disappear into the heavy evening air with a wave and a simple "I'm going."

Someone noticed that when Xiao Xiao went to see him off, she could not seem to get back inside, and with this their conclusions were as good as confirmed.

Especially since he looked so visibly displeased and fled in dismay any time he came and found Radish on the scene. Radish called him 'Four Eyes', and if he bumped into him on pay day would insist on dragging him off to the canteen to treat him to a couple of bottles and then invite him over to the 'chicken coop'—the tractor crew dormitory—to play cards.

Zou Sizhu frowned and tugged at his glasses. "Do you know who invented the tractor?" he would ask. "Who wrote 'Queen of Spades'?"

A shake of that round head and a merry smile. "You know who invented the atom bomb, but you're scrabbling around in the dirt all the same! Why not scrape up some Hearts and come try your luck with the King?"

As soon as the two of them met, they were at it, neither willing to give in. In bed, Dakang muttered in Xiao Xiao's ear, "Zou Sizhu is too petty. Radish is five or six years younger than him. He doesn't need to take him so serious."

Xiao Xiao's face flushed hot. She wanted to say that Zou Sizhu didn't mean it that way. He wasn't jealous. He just didn't approve of Radish's heedless and easy-going attitude. He was dead set against such little aristocrats whether their luck was running good or bad. But she did not even believe in that explanation herself. Heaven only knew why the two of them got along so badly.

Ever since the evening Radish had whipped off the raincoat and thrust it upon her, only to arrive the next day in glowing spirits to retrieve his treasure, he had taken to dropping by the research team dormitory almost every evening around dinner time, mess kit in hand. Sometimes he was looking for something, or after something to eat. Sometimes he brought a few wild duck eggs or baked potatoes.

He seemed to have forgotten how unhappy he had been that time they met in the rain. He expressed his lively interest in food without the slightest reserve. Sometimes he told stories about hunting rabbits and dogs to eat; or he brought a menu and showed Xiao Xiao how to have a Barmecide feast by reciting the names of the dishes, as though they were really savouring the food. She laughed until her sides ached, in spite of herself. He showed her how to bake bits of corn bread on top of the stove, making them as crisp and tasty as cookies. They scratched going down, but they really did satisfy the appetite. In this easy-going mood, she felt all the blood vessels in her body tingle and her every nerve relax.

And Radish liked to laugh. When he laughed, dimples as big as almonds appeared on each cheek, washing away all cares and filling up with the happiness they had summoned. Wiping the oil from his satisfied lips and fishing a harmonica out of his pocket, he would play "Coming Home from Target Practice" and "I am a Soldier." His clear eyes flashed. Their blue sheen had hints of orange in it, not like Dakang's warm and open smile. His simplicity concealed a certain cunning, the complexity that settles out on someone who has left home at the age of fifteen to make his way on the road of adult life and has taken his share of tumbles along the way. The simplicity had probably won him trust, while the cunning had earned him respect. She had marvelled at how these two seemingly contradictory elements were united in his personality. Apparently it was just because of this that he had won over the young fellows in the tractor crew. They would not support anyone who was too serious or anyone who was not serious enough.

And so she told him stories, "Hamlet," "The Gadfly," "Spartacus." Her stories held him spellbound. Out of nowhere, he muttered to himself, "Are books really that interesting? Before you came here, the only stories we ever told over there at night were about how to sleep with girls." He borrowed books to take home, and then brought them back. Although he was embarassed to call her 'big sister', Xiao Xiao felt almost as though she had found a little brother. Even the kerosene lamp that had always smoked so badly turned bright and clear. All Radish had done was fit the wick into a thin steel casing.

When Zou Sizhu saw the lamp, he grunted. After that he never looked quite at ease.

Is there something bothering you, something bottled up in your heart that you find hard to talk about? Why don't you just come out with it? Under the faintly star-lit clove tree, they were separated by a curtain of night. They had drilled through to the last layer of stone between their hearts, but finally they could drill no further. I don't know why either. That Autumn Festival, I saw you in my dream; I prayed for you on the mountains of Lingyin. How I used to long for freedom and for your friendship. But after getting my freedom I became more stingy with it, and with my friendship too. My divorce had nothing to do with you. If you only don't make the mistake of thinking that it did, and if you have, why don't you ever admit it? What demon is it that obstructs you, what monster bites you tangles you up worries you you like making life too complicated too tiresome too strict too stiff more than I could have imagined I'm really the most uncomplicated person there could be I can't take this profundity of yours...

She felt apologetic under his unremitting gaze, unable to say out loud what she had said to herself a hundred times. Since early summer, all his attention had been focussed on reviewing for the year's university entrance examinations. Word had it that worker/peasant/soldier students would be chosen on the basis of their marks. He brought Xiao Xiao review outlines and reference books, set example questions for her, scored her work, explained things. He seemed even more interested in the university examinations than she was herself, as though he had placed all his hopes for the rest of his life on this single sampan drifting across the sea. It even began to seem to Xiao Xiao that he had a sort of crazy 'stake everything on a single throw' attitude toward the examinations. Was this perhaps their only chance to leave the Farm? Why did he have to be so desperate to drag her into it?

Have you got straight the relationship between subject and object that I explained to you last time? You should base your understanding on the definitions in the dictionary of philosophy I gave you. Don't consult just any old book. Then, there are such basic concepts as logical thinking, absolute truth, and dualism, all of which fall within the scope of general knowledge, so you should have a grasp of them whether they are on the exam or not. You can have a look at the "Dialectics of Nature" in the *Selected Works of Marx and Engels*, volume 3, pages 444 to 573. When I read something, I read the original source. As for the compositions, there is always one on singing "The East is Red," so you should put a little time into working something up in advance. The language section is sure to have a question on developing Lu Xun's spirit of thoroughly beating a dog who's already fallen into the water and fair play should be put into practice later on the great teacher must be on pins and needles in the next world at being used as a tool in political struggles it's too bad too bad...

These obscure theories kept her exhausted and confused. She

did not like all the dull examples and concepts and wished that she could relax a little and listen to some songs and jokes. But she knew she had to struggle to get into university. She wanted to acquire knowledge and skills that she could bring back to build up the frontier. She knew that she had no other opportunity to get ahead. She had to force herself, to oversee her review and memorisation of all these things that she seemed never to have studied or been taught. Books were unfamiliar to her, and so was her brain. She would rather have been doing a blackboard newspaper or writing radio scripts or something. She thought that she probably had no chance anyway. Could a person with her background get into university? She must be dreaming. She began to get tired of Zou Sizhu. She realised that the time she spent with him was really very tedious. He had passed his sobriety and reserve onto her, until she felt like crying from despair.

You know there's another way of catching fish? It's even easier than grabbing them in your bare hands. You get a warm mutton bone and put it in an old wash-basin. Then you cover the basin with a rag, leaving a hole in the middle. You tie a cord to the basin, hold the end in your hand, and toss the basin into a stream. Before half an hour is up you pull in the cord, take off the rag, and there you are! Half a basin full of carp, flopping all over the place. Really! I've caught them and they're really lively. Those fish are so dumb, as soon as they get a whiff of the mutton bone, they squeeze in through the hole, and then do they ever get to scrapping with each other!

Then take me fishing with you, will you? Radish, I was born in the year of the cat. Oh, no, I can't, I have to review my notes, there's still two weeks left.

In the middle of June, the wheat flowered; toward the end of the month, snowy potato flowers dyed the fields of the Great Northern Wastelands white. And then they heard that there wouldn't be any entrance exams after all, that the same procedures as the previous year would be continued. Overnight, blank examination papers had covered three and a half million square miles. Hailstones fell that morning as big as eggs, turning the experimental fields into a green pickle vat and punching holes in the lush pumpkin leaves. Even the surface of the reservoir, usually dead calm, was peppered by the hailstones. The iron gates of university would be shut tight henceforth, and all their dreams of higher education were pulverised.

When Zou Sizhu appeared before her, his ashen face almost frightened her out of her wits. His glasses had slid down his nose like a pair of grey tiles. His tanned scalp was visible through his dishevelled hair. He collapsed on the brick bed; he was ruined.

She gave him a cup of cool water.

Do you know Prince Myshkin have you read all of Dostoyevsky Idiot Crime and Punishment The Brothers Karamazov Vanity Fair Arch of Triumph whoever wrote them they're all hard-luck cases I could write them too Ordeal Old Goriot do you know why Martin Eden died was it a symbol that his honest soul could not get along with this false world it was his complete rejection of human life you don't understand me don't understand me a stupid bottled-up place can bury people alive...

She watched him in silence. She did not know how to comfort him. She did not like listening to his bitter complaints. If failure to get into university was enough to reduce him to such a state of despair, he was really too fragile. And in embracing such a yearning in the first place, he had been too simple. There was a dark patch directly below the little oil lamp. Dakang called it the 'lampdark'. Could the flame not illuminate itself? What she had been hoping he would tell her was not something in those books, but what she should do right there and then, even if it were to go have a fight with Radish.

Afterwards, he continued to come once a week, but when he came, he would just sit on the edge of the brick bed staring up at the rafters in a daze, without saying a word for the longest time.

One day she was walking back with Mrs. Su after they got off work. Summer was almost over, and only the pale blue wild chrysanthemums were left along the road, tinged with lavender by the sunset. Mrs. Su bent down and picked one, giving it to the baby on her back to play with as she asked Xiao Xiao with a smile, "Is Zou Sizhu still coming over all the time?"

She nodded.

"Whenever I see him, he reminds me of a boy I went to college with who looked a lot like him and had the best grades in our class." She gave Xiao Xiao a significant look. "He was very nice to me, but he just left me cold. When we were about to graduate, he wrote me a letter. I thought he was okay, but somehow I couldn't work up any feeling for him. Then one time we had a games day and I was in charge of first-aid. Chu came in with a sprained ankle, and I fell for him at first sight. Later I came here with him. You know, it's funny, but I think love is a little like those double-banger firecrackers: if it doesn't go off right away, it's less likely to catch the longer you wait."

Xiao Xiao had torn the flower in her hands to shreds. Tears crept into her eyes. Thank you, Mrs. Su. I could probably never have fallen in love with him, and the more time I spend with him the less likely it is. That dream on the moon belonged to night, but what I am longing for inside is sunlight. When Chen Xu burned me, the fire was real. Zou Sizhu is so damp he only smokes, and I am no bellows.

"It's too far for you to keep making the trip back and forth. Really, you don't need to come so often. There's nothing..."

And so she stood under the mountain clove tree in front of the girls' dormitory, speaking to him as gently as she knew how.

43

A black jeep came driving out of a grove of parasol trees. The doors were in back, a pair of them. They opened, and someone with short hair jumped out, someone very familiar. The newcomer grabbed her hand and asked, Don't you recognise me any more?

Everyone burst into applause, and some people shouted a slogan: Warmly Welcome the New Boss of Branch Farm No.7, Comrade Guo Aijun!

She thought to herself, Isn't Guo Aijun just Guo Chunmei? Isn't she in hospital in Hangzhou? Is she going to stay in the Great Northern Wastes even if it means dying here?

Guo Chunmei gave her legs a slap and said, Look! And as she spoke she broke into a run, as fast as a horse. Her legs were thin, with broad thick toenails, very much like a horse's legs.

Then she herself jumped on a horse and chased after Chunmei. Her horse was white. It ran as fast as the wind and caught up with all the other horses, which ran on after her. She sprinted up to the top of a steep mountain. When she looked back, all the horses behind her had disappeared. She felt the earth slowly revolving, felt herself slowly revolving as well. But Guo Chunmei was spinning around on her toes all by herself, like Wu Qionghua in the modern revolutionary ballet "Red Detachment of Women", turning dozens of circles in just a moment. She thought, Guo Chunmei must have batteries in her shoes.

There were slogans displayed everywhere: We Swear to Change the Face of the Earth With a Mass Campaign of a Hundred Days! People Plan for the Mass Campaign and Sweat Flows for a Victory!

Maroon and white poppies were blooming in the brick-lined flower patch in front of the dormitory. Guo Chunmei pulled all the flowers up and threw them down the latrine. There was a great mass of flowers abloom in the latrine, filling the air with their fragrance. Guo Chunmei went to use the latrine and let out a yelp. It turned out that she had been pricked by a poppy thorn. How could there be thorns on a poppy?

Branch Farm No.7 was in a tumult. Everything was being moved continuously from one room to another and then out onto the ground outside. Trunks were stacked up on the stoves, suitcases heaped on the fuel piles, wash basins sitting on people's heads. A loudspeaker was blaring, and Guo Chunmei's thick lips were visible inside it.

She herself was ceaselessly moving bricks; there was no end to them. She was carrying a load as high as a bamboo pole, so tired she could walk no farther. She felt like shying a brick at Guo Chunmei, but Chunmei was wearing a dark red shirt that turned bright green with each move, flickering so that she could not take good aim.

She saw a cow grazing. There were many green nails on the ground, and the cow opened its mouth and wolfed them down one after another. Guo Chunmei asked her if she had seen it eating class struggle, and she shook her head. A caterpillar was crawling backwards up a tree. She wanted to get away from it and tried to crush it with her foot, but it stung her through the sole of her shoe. It hurt.

Someone shouted for her to come to a political criticism session. She saw that it was whitewashed everywhere, that the murky root cellar was full of garbage, that there were trolley busses running on the branch farm road. A crane shelter had been set up beside the road and herons and the like were walking around near it. She thought she would go in and sit down, but she discovered that it was only a painting.

There was another shout for her to come to the criticism session. She walked into a huge and magnificent theatre with golden stars beyond count twinkling in the ceiling. Then everything went black. Power failure.

Just as the grain harvest was drawing near, a green Peking jeep came driving up past the dark green fields and stopped in front of the Branch Farm No.7 office. It was Chairman Yu Funian, fat as ever, personally escorting a new boss to No.7, Guo Aijun.

Her hair was cut very short, but she looked healthy, only a little thinner than before. As soon as she saw Xiao Xiao, she threw her arms around her and thumped her on the back in a show of particular warmth.

Xiao Xiao was astonished. She had never dreamed that Guo Aijun might actually return to the Great Northern Wastes as soon as she could crawl out of her hospital bed in Hangzhou. According to Dakang, Aijun had been assigned to their branch farm because her arthritis was too severe for her to work in paddy fields or push a feed cart any more. Dakang's tone suggested that she did not have much use for her.

When Aijun said that she wanted to live in the Research Team dormitory, Dakang's answer was 'no vacancy'. Aijun paid no attention to this and moved right in. No sooner had she moved in than she discovered the poppies growing in the flower patch in front of the dormitory. She tried to convince Dakang that she should get rid of them because they were a dangerous drug, but Dakang would not do it. So Aijun took matters into her own hands. She pulled up all the poppies, which had just begun to flower, and threw them down the latrine. Dakang had a big fight with Aijun over this and got so angry that she burst into tears.

Xiao Xiao tried to cheer her up. "Don't cry. It wouldn't do to let the people in charge think that the Research Team was growing opium."

Dakang pushed her hands away and snarled, "Isn't she lucky to have an old pal from home like you around! You didn't even try to stop her! For your information, opium is good for the runs!"

Dakang went to bed without any dinner, and went on moaning and murmuring even in her sleep. It was the first time that Xiao Xiao had ever seen Dakang cry, and it left her feeling very uncomfortable. She herself could not figure out why she had not tried to stop Guo Aijun from pulling up the flowers.

When she had seen Guo Aijun in the hospital in Hangzhou early that year, she had been deeply moved to witness Aijun's courage in enduring her illness, her unselfishness in the very face of death, her single-mindedness in her delirium, and her devotion to the Farm even when her life hung by a thread. That sight had shaken Xiao Xiao, had aroused and cleansed her. She had come to understand a Guo Aijun whom she had neither understood nor liked before. Once again she felt abashed in the face of this great and steadfast progressive model. Won't you do me a favour, Miss Mermaid? My old lady is giving me a hard time, she won't let me have any peace, old as I am. She needs a new wash-trough. And now Guo Aijun really had come back to the Farm in spite of her illness. At No.5, she really had given up a chance to go to university. Xiao Xiao felt more and more ashamed of herself. She did her best to chase the last remnants of her old impression of Guo Aijun out of her mind and turned her full attention to finding things in Aijun that she could love and admire. She realised that she and Aijun had only been kept apart by an unintended barrier to their open communion. If that obstacle had been Chen Xu, then it no longer existed. She wanted to enjoy Guo Chunmei's trust and friendship once again, wanted to make Guo Aijun understand that she wasn't at all the sort of person that people thought and said she was. They had come to the Farm aboard the same train. Why couldn't she accomplish everything that Chunmei had accomplished in those three years? Why couldn't she get what Chunmei had got? The more she couldn't do something, the more she wanted to do it. So, seen in the broader perspective, what was so important about Chunmei's destroying a few poppies?

A certain awkwardness arose between her and Dakang.

In fairness, it had to be admitted that there had been great changes at No.7 in the two short months since Guo Chunmei came. This was obvious at a glance to everyone, whether they were members of the Branch Farm itself, visitors from outside, or people from higher echelons.

All the buildings had been given a fresh coat of whitewash. Even the stables and cow barns had been left so white you would have thought someone was going to move in and start a family. Ground had been broken for a large heated cellar. There would be more cabbage and potatoes in the winter than people could eat. Two positively enormous blackboards had been set up at the door of the Branch Farm office, to be used for political essays, big character posters, Quotations, and the like. From a distance, the sight of all that red and green chalk was quite imposing. Screens had been put up on the windows of the young people's mess hall, white plastic tablecloths spread over the tables, and boxy wooden benches nailed together, so that no one need be tempted to sneak one home. On the wall at the entrance the following was painted in large red characters: People who wear their chopsticks down short, squeeze their wine jugs flat, and wear their chairs out with sitting in them are not much different from the New Tsars.

These words were there for the information of visiting officials. No matter what their rank, they never got special meals. Even Director Yu was treated the same way when he came, lining up in the mess hall along with the young people to buy his food. Everyone knew that Guo Aijun was a 'model citizen' cultivated by the Director of the Political Department at the District Office, Yu Funian. But if even he did not get special treatment, what could anyone say? This reform sent investigating bureaucrats high and low scurrying away in a huff. But Secretary Li praised Guo Aijun at a general meeting of cadres from the entire State Farm. In addition, the Farm's central broadcasting station produced a short item advocating that people learn from the Party Branch at No.7.

This broadcast reached No.7 just as all the young people were in the midst of moving their things around in the collective dormitory, rearranging their places according to a new scheme of Guo Aijun's. Dakang made a face at the loudspeaker on the telephone pole and muttered, "Showtime!"

Xiao Xiao could not resist asking her, "You're always calling one thing or another showtime; what do you mean by 'showtime'."

Dakang scowled. "You don't even understand what showtime means. It means to be hooked on putting on little shows just for people to see. Not real things, phoney ones! You think Boss Yu can't find another place to drink if he doesn't do it here?"

Xiao Xiao said nothing. She knew that she could not change Dakang's mind. Even Radish seemed to have it in for Guo Aijun. When they showed 'Song of Dragon River' on the farm, he sat through it eating green corn and joking. "This tireless heroine Jiang Shuiying looks an awful lot like Director Guo to me. Why call it the Dragon River style? It's just Heilongjiang, the Black Dragon River..."

Xiao Xiao glared at him. She wished they would stop making such fun of Guo Aijun. It was her arrival that had finally struck the resonant bell of this secluded little Peach Blossom Spring, had so enlivened this little backwater. It had broken the calm and quiet of this out-of-the-way place with the shriek of starting whistles, the blare of loudspeakers, and the singing before rallies, and filled life with excitement and anticipation. Xiao Xiao had discovered that she was not so fond of solitude after all. If those broken pincers only grew a little longer, they would just itch to reach out and wave.

After the summer solstice, the entire Three Rivers Plain began to show signs of drought. After falling to earth in the spring, the rains had evidently gone off for their own 'Linking-up' and not made it back on time. Since the beginning of summer, the clouds had dragged back and forth across the sky like squeezed-out wads of cotton, without ever shedding a drop of water. In fact, the rain had fallen so heavily all spring that by the time it finally ran dry, even the rains of summer and fall had been paid off in advance. When it came time for the wheat harvest, there was an unprecedented stretch of perfectly clear weather that lasted for a good two weeks. The sky was so clear that the parched heads of the wheat were sizzling and giving off sparks and the flat black earth was cracked in big squares like a tortoise's back. And so the combines and windrowers, which had crouched in their lairs during the spring sowing, all turned out and within a few days had brought almost three hundred acres of wheat to the threshing ground. The broadcasting station at Farm Headquarters read the item three times in one day, using a quote from one of Chairman Mao's poems in the title: 'A Thousand-yard Rope Ties up the Kraken and the Roc—Under the Leadership of the Party Branch, the Entire Crew of Branch Farm No.7 is First to Bring in the Wheat Harvest'.

Radish came by with his mess kit and asked, through a mouthful of summer squash, "And what about the yield?"

Xiao Xiao smiled. The yield was secondary, a bumper harvest wrested from the jaws of natural calamity. The important thing was people's consciousness. The summer hoeing, the grain harvest, capital construction, rectification... Every day, Guo Chunmei dragged her failing legs from the bean fields wet with dew to the stinking stables. She handled everything herself. She was everywhere. Sweat rolled down her forehead in streams. She had not been away to lecture on her 'study and application' once in two months. Patch after patch had been tacked onto the toes of her boots. She was so tired she groaned far into the night, and yet she was up and ready for action at the crack of dawn. One sturdy swallow bore all the weight of providing for the food and drink, the pissing, shitting, and sleeping of the several hundred people on the branch farm, and without so much as a flinch or a shudder.

Xiao Xiao sighed in admiration. After watching Guo Aijun for several months, she could not help looking up to her. When would she herself ever manage to catch up?

Guo Chunmei could not only work, talk, eat, and sleep, she could think too. Give her one end of a string and she would end by pulling it taut. A cow died all of a sudden, and she had Dr. Chu carry out an immediate autopsy. This resulted in the discovery of several nails in its stomach. The stockman was brought to the office for interrogation, and Chunmei had Xiao Xiao take notes.

Chunmei said, "These aren't simply nails; they are class struggle."

Dr. Chu was present, and spoke up, "It's not uncommon for cows to swallow nails while grazing. It's just carelessness on the part of the stockman, not sabotage."

Director Xu was squatting on the brick bed, puffing on his pipe. He said, "We don't have no classes around here. Everybody's a farm worker."

Guo Chunmei's face turned hard. She read aloud from a newspaper, "Repudiate the Theory of Extinction of Class Struggle."

When she had got half way through, Director Xu leapt to his feet, boiling mad. "I've never heard of a stingworm climbing back up a tree! If No.7 falls apart, who's going to answer for it? The tractor crew, the construction crew, the barn crew, the stock crew, if it weren't for me, they wouldn't do bugger-all for you! Where was your Party membership approved? At Farm Headquarters. And mine? By the Three Rivers Regional Committee. What rank do you hold? Do you expect me to ask one lump or two every time you say shit?"

With this, he spat on the floor and stormed out.

This outburst from Director Xu left Xiao Xiao's head swimming. As she sat there stunned, she heard Guo Aijun's voice, steady as a rock, saying, "There will be a criticism session tonight..."

She looked at Guo Chunmei in astonishment, but saw in her eyes not a drop of the tears of humiliation and rage she was afraid she would find there. They looked instead like a desert swirling with dust under the baking sun.

What sort of a Guo Chunmei was she, after all?

44

Brightly coloured goldfish were swimming about in a shallow cove. There was one black goldfish with a long mane like a lion and eyes that flashed like red lanterns. Another was drifting along with a wave now and then of its beautiful tail, which was as large and colourful as a butterfly. And there was a goldfish that was spitting out one dark green pearl after another and picking them up in its fins, which were like hands. A huge goldfish with purple markings came swimming toward her. It was almost the size of a whale and bore a palace with pillars of white marble on its broad, thick back. An old woman was standing on the shore, bowing to the goldfish and saying, I don't want to be a high-born lady any more, I want to be a mighty empress.

The school of goldfish swam away toward a large net and vanished with a wave of their tails as they passed through its meshes.

She found a pencil on the beach, but since she did not have a knife to sharpen it with she threw it away. Then she found a ball-point pen, but she could not get it to write, so she threw it away too. Then she found a writing brush, but she could not find an ink stone, so she could not grind ink. And so she threw away the writing brush. She wanted something to write a poem with.

Footstep came padding up to her. It was Guo Chunmei. Chunmei gave her a red crayon, and on her first try she wrote: A Great Transformation of the Half-way River No.7 Branch Farm Accomplished in a Hundred Days.

No sooner had she written it down than it was printed in a yellowing old newspaper. All the characters appeared in their traditional complicated forms, although she remembered that she did not know how to write them that way.

Dakang wadded the paper up in a ball, threw it on the ground, and stamped on it. She shouted, You pickspittle!

Radish pushed his way forward with a big smile and said, Miss Xiao can't write traditional characters. This must be a pre-Liberation newspaper. We weren't even born then.

She opened her eyes wide and read the paper. The article was indeed written in Classical Chinese, so she could not understand it at all. She said, It was revised by Director Yu. Guo Chunmei gave it to him to read yesterday!

Dakang nodded, having realised what had happened. She smiled and handed Xiao Xiao a handful of steamed green beans, saying, From now on, don't swallow a sickle unless you've got the crooked guts for it. It looked to me like even somebody had you sold out you wouldn't know where to get your money. Nowadays, No.7 has got a silly goose running things and pulling the wool over the eyes of her betters.

The goldfish came swimming toward her.

The day after the "Three Rivers Daily" carried the article "A Great Transformation of Half-way River No.7 Branch Farm Accomplished in a Hundred Days" by their correspondent on the Farm, Xiao Xiao had just got off work in the evening and was washing her face when she heard someone gasping for breath behind her and a familiar voice stammering, "This newspaper, did, did you write this?"

She was the only one left in the girls' dorm. They had all gone to dinner. She was moving slowly and had fallen behind. When she recognised his voice, she bent over and went on washing her face. Why all the fuss over one little article? Running two or three miles over here just to ask! She washed very meticulously, working some soap into her washcloth and scrubbing her neck, behind her ears, and even between her fingers. She deliberately took her time, just to make him wait. Who told him to come back today when he had been here only two days before! She spared no effort in her washing, until there was nothing left to wash. When she had dried her face with elaborate care, she opened her eyes and found a thin arm in front of her, woodenly holding out a folded up newspaper. There was no telling how long it had been there.

She could neither take the paper nor refuse to take it, so she turned away and started rubbing in cold cream. She could see Zou Sizhu in the mirror, walking back and forth, wringing his hands, his face puffed up like a fighting cock. His brows were knit into a black lump, and his thin lips were trembling. He shouted at her, "Tell me you didn't write this. I just can't believe that you did!"

She said nothing.

"I'm positive that you couldn't write such an article." he added.

She whipped around, snatched the paper away, and shouted, "I did write it, and so what if I did?"

He withered up before her eyes. He stumbled backward and sat down on the edge of the brick bed. All the blood drained from his face, which took on a shade even more livid than usual. He took hold of his glasses frames and, after a long while, murmured, "I can't understand how you could write something like, well, like this!"

Her offended dignity erupted. "How could I write it? Because it's the truth! Do you mean to tell me you haven't noticed the hundred-day transformation here? Her hard work has turned what used to be a crumby run-down outfit into something fresh and new. Why can't I write that up? Why shouldn't I? Why do you all have it in for her? Why does she bother you so much? You say she's a climber, that she's left the masses behind, this is wrong with her, that's wrong with her. But sick as she is, you have to admit she works hard night and day. Do you really think it's fair of you people to judge her hard work so unfairly? It was you who took me to the hospital to visit her last winter in Hangzhou. Didn't you notice when she was so delirious she mistook a red shirt for the red flag? It made me cry..."

He interrupted her with a snort of contempt. "It was precisely then that I realised that her mind had been remoulded beyond cure."

"Your reasons are always such empty abstractions." She spun angrily around and turned her back on him. "Look how much Guo Chunmei has done in the two months she's been here. Could you have accomplished what she has?"

"Let me put it to you bluntly. The things she has done are the very sort that I don't want to do, that I wouldn't be willing to do. They're just superficial gestures intended to make a good impression on her bosses; they can't solve the real problems. If the Farm goes on transforming itself along these lines, in a few years we'll be living on air." He pulled out a handkerchief and wiped the sweat from his brow. "We may not have any way to stop her or interfere with her, but for you to go ahead and publicise these empty frauds is a mistake on your part. When there's a good grain harvest in spite of the drought, is it scientific farming or is it some kind of agricultural shell game? If young people who've been to school strike roots in the countryside, are the untaught sons and daughters of the poor and lower-middle peasants going to put the satellites into orbit? A cow swallows a nail and dies, and so we seize on class struggle and end up killing someone, but it doesn't matter because the life of an ex-labour camp inmate isn't worth anything. I don't think she has any shameful hidden motives; she's just an idiot! What I can't figure out is why you're tagging along after her now, when you didn't have any use for her before. If you want progress, I've got nothing against that, only you should do it on the basis of the facts the world is the way it is it's not going to arrange itself according to your wishes. You used to think everything out for yourself but now you do everything in spite of what you think do you really know your own mind or don't you? It makes me so sad to see you doing it."

It's just because I used to think everything out for myself that I'm in the mess I'm in now. I haven't been that old weak and innocent me for a long time now. I'm going to support her even if I don't have any use for her. Who else can I support, if not her? Dakang is quite happy to make allowances for me and be done with it. And Radish too, he just laughs it off and doesn't hold it against me. It's only you who gets all worked up about it, as though I had committed some monstrous crime. If I want to write an essay, it's no business of yours.

Xiao Xiao threw her head back and screamed, "Don't you lecture me!"

He stared at her blankly and after a while walked slowly out the door.

Call him back. How could she be so mean? It might hurt his feelings. He was only being so blunt because he meant well, after all. Call him back.

She hurried after him. But in the doorway she almost crashed into Dakang, who was bouncing happily in, dinner in hand. "Mrs. Su wants you to go with her tomorrow to do a crop estimate," boomed Dakang. "Hurry up and eat them while they're hot, sugar tri-ankles!"

The way to the No.2 bean field led across the dam. After such a dry summer and fall, the reservoir was almost empty. It was muddy and shrunken, with sparse yellow weeds lying dead here and there along the cracked banks. Once past the run-down old night-watchman's shack, Xiao Xiao caught sight of a fire on the bare shore up ahead, staining the sky and water with scarlet. But the flames were not leaping up into the air. They lay flat and stretched out along the ground. When she walked closer, it turned out to be a large patch of red weeds, with rust coloured stems like bamboo runners covering the whole shore with their dense repulsive cobwebs.

"It's knotweed," said Su Fang in a low voice. "It's been growing like mad this year. It turns up as soon as there's a drought. After it freezes, we can use it for fuel. We rake it up by the cartload. It catches fire easily and burns for a long time."

She didn't want to know about fuel. She wasn't going to gather fuel any more. She would leave here eventually. In a dry year, instead of reeds there was this. Survival of the fittest.

They walked down from the reservoir and into the low-lying soy bean field. The long ridges reached to the horizon, but there were no beans in sight, only wave upon ragged wave of wormwood and ashweed, coming up to their shoulders. There were frequent bare patches on the yellow ground, like hairless scars exposed on top of someone's head. The sun shone listlessly through a pale overcast. Everything was withered. There was not so much as a mosquito or a meadow mouse in sight.

They worked their way blindly back and forth across the fields, their cuffs and socks full of prickly burrs and their shoes covered with dust.

Mrs. Su suddenly plumped down on a ridge and shook the dirt out of her boots. She took a deep breath and let it out.

"What's your estimate for this acreage?" ventured Xiao Xiao.

"There's going to be a serious shortage of fodder this winter and spring, never mind food grain." She threw up her hands. "The soil tends to cake up anyway after being waterlogged in the spring. How can the moisture content be maintained when no attention is paid to the fields during the summer? And now there's a stiff drought, and that isn't going to do the situation any good!"

Xiao Xiao could hear resentment in her voice, resentment of Guo Aijun's concentration of manpower on her 'hundred-day transformation'.

"So, wasn't she worried about a shortage of winter fodder?" asked Xiao Xiao, feeling puzzled.

Mrs. Su seemed to hesitate before replying. She never criticised people behind their backs. "Well, she was probably intending to open up virgin land to grow grain and to weed out some of the livestock on the Branch Farm." She looked very concerned. "Taking grain as the main link is the big thing now. I hear that when it comes time to work on water conservancy after the harvest, she is against repairing the dykes around the pastures and is holding out firmly for putting in a drainage canal."

"Well, what are we going to do?" She was getting anxious,

worried on Mrs. Su's behalf. "You, you'd better have a talk with her."

Su Fang shook her head. "She'd never listen to me. She just does whatever the people upstairs say. She won't even pay any attention to Director Xu or Secretary Li." She was picking the burrs off her calves one by one.

Didn't Mrs. Su like Guo Aijun either? Perhaps Aijun had only been able to attain recognition and success because she was like this. "Well, you'll have to think of something," she said earnestly.

Mrs. Su stood up. "Think of something? The only way we'll be able to scrape out a little fodder and put it aside when the time comes is if we underreport our crop estimate."

She strode off, raising a cloud of dust.

Xiao Xiao was thunderstruck. She could not believe her ears. As she thought over the implications, her heart began to race. So, was even Mrs. Su capable of telling lies? Keeping the truth from her superiors like this, a false report. Was it fraud to underreport rather than overreport? Not for one's own sake, but for, for what? She staggered after her. But Mrs. Su had been walking these fields for a dozen years, so Xiao Xiao had a hard time catching up.

"Mrs. Su, wait for me!" She panted. "There's something I want to ask you. I've been wondering about it for a long time, but I was embarrassed to ask. I was afraid you'd think it was strange."

Mrs. Su stopped. A pair of narrowed eyes, stung by the wind blowing over the fields, like an early autumn frost.

"What is it?" she asked.

"It, it's about false flowers, the false flowers on cucumbers and watermelons, and things. Are they actually the female flowers or the males? And why are they called false flowers? Everybody says something different."

The king has ass's ears. She suddenly felt completely at ease. Those false flowers had bothered her for such a long time, like a fish-bone stuck in her throat that she could neither swallow nor spit out. A ubiquitous monster. She felt greatly relieved already, just by asking her question.

"False flowers?" Mrs. Su shook her head. "I don't know. It's probably just a vernacular name. The term isn't used in botany." She thought it over for a moment. "But when people grow melons, they always pinch off the male flowers early on, in order to concentrate nutrients in the female flowers and make them mature earlier. From that, I'd say that false flowers may refer to the male flowers, which don't form fruit."

So was there no intermediate sex of flowers that was neither male nor female?

45

Nebulae covered the heavens; the red sun of the east and the green moon of the west shone together in the sky. Rows of black pennants fluttered in the wind, while a single purple beetle writhed on a vast expanse of earth. She walked closer, and the beetle turned out to be a bulldozer, whistling and roaring as it flew over the steep river dyke like an ancient swordsman leaping over walls and onto roofs, whirling around in a frenzy. She could see Radish working the control levers with one hand as he read a book clutched in the other. She waved at him, but he could not see her. She shouted for him to come down, but he could not hear her either. She thought, Didn't Yu Funian make it very clear that we were not allowed to repair the dykes, only to open drainage ditches? Isn't this mass campaign for water control turning into a rout? How would she write her report?

A jeep came driving by. She could see Director Yu and Guo Aijun inside. The jeep drove into a dark hole in the dyke, and water came gurgling out. She was going to stop up the hole but then she saw two legs inside, one wearing nylon stockings and the other silk. She hurried away, heart pounding. She jumped onto the bulldozer, and it began to bounce along as fast as a car, the motor purring away. She clutched the steering wheel and found that she was actually in a jeep, with grass-green seat cushions and doors. Radish said, Your class origin is beyond your control; your political road you can choose. How about drafting a public declaration by educated urban youth to strike roots and settle in the countryside? The District Office wants to get up a model. It didn't sound like Radish's voice to her, and when she looked up, it turned out to be Yu Funian, sitting right there in the jeep with her. She asked, Where are we going? Director Yu replied, You'll find out when we get there.

They walked into a large meeting hall. All the seats were filled by young people, big red flowers pinned on their chests. The odd thing was that they all had long root hairs growing from the soles of their shoes. Guo Chunmei was wearing a pair of bright red shoes embroidered with flowers, with the root hairs trailing out across the floor like water weeds, following her wherever she walked. Then a sudden gust of wind blew them up into the sky like the tail of a kite. Guo Aijun tried to grab the tail, but was knocked to the ground with a thud and turned into a peanut. She herself peeled off the shell, the white husk, and finally the red skin, and there was Guo Aijun curled up inside doing eye exercises. Once Aijun was finished in front, she did them in back. She was horrified to discover that Aijun had two faces like those in a Peking opera, one a dark red and wreathed in smiles, and the other an off white, sinister and treacherous. She was very frightened, but she saw that all the other young people in the hall had two faces too. If one face was speaking, the other mouth was firmly shut. If this side said, Fine, the other one said, No good. She was so frightened she curled up in a ball and asked, Who are you all? Someone with a heavy Manchurian accent said, We're all progressive models, of course. Only people with two faces get to be models, understand? Then she asked, If your mouths don't both say the same thing when you speak, then what? He shook his head and replied, How could that ever happen? One mouth is just for use here; the other is for when we get back home. Each has its place, of course. She remembered that she had only one face and sighed with relief.

The drought lasted into the winter that year. It did not snow until after the winter solstice, and then just enough to cover the ground.

The snow was very dry and fluffy, like chalk dust. It dropped off clothing at the slightest movement, leaving the surface clean and dry. And it was grainy too, like sand. It hurt when it touched people's faces and crunched underfoot. It was like shatter-proof crockery, keeping its crisp constitution and refusing to melt even when blown to powder. With the bold spirit of a northerner, it came to serve as loyal protector of the black earth all through the long winter, and did so in a manner that was almost peremptory, and yet friendly at the same time. It was not like the snow in the south, sighing over its fate as it melted with a sob into a pool of tears. It was tough and pliable, rolling itself into pearls high up in the cold eddies of the sky.

Halted in her tracks on her way back from work, Xiao Xiao stared at a few bits of crystal snow in her hand.

This was the nature of snow in the true north.

She was happy and moved, moved and a little sad. She did like the Great Northern Wastes after all. If she didn't, why did she like the snow there? Southern snow was warm, northern snow was cold; southern snow was gentle, northern snow was sturdy; southern snow was plain, northern snow was magnificent; southern snow no sooner fell than it melted, insubstantial as a dream, northern snow stayed until spring, a true story. And besides, southern snow was ordinary, northern snow was intense, so blazingly intense that it could even cause snow-blindness. She did not know which kind of snow was better suited to her. She gazed at the snow-covered ground as it flared up and suddenly fell dark. It seemed to her like a huge salt-pan, or a hospital... She was overcome with misgivings. She preferred coming back from work by herself, after everyone else, thinking things over in silence. It always made her upset to think of the future.

She walked toward the dormitory. Someone was pacing back and forth in the shadow of the eaves, hands tucked into his sleeves, cap strings straggling across his shoulders, and stamping his feet continually. She put down the shovel she had carried back on her shoulder from working on the drainage ditches and rubbed her eyes. Who was he looking for? She had a kind of premonition who he might be; there was something familiar about him. Never mind if it's a rat. Try it and you'll see how good it tastes. If you keep this chicken, by June it will be laying eggs. We are presenting you with this little table as a token of our best wishes.

"Bubble!" she cried. She thought her voice sounded a little flustered. Why had he come? Had he sent him? Could there be a letter? He mustn't get it out in front of anyone else. How was he doing? Perhaps Bubble just happened to be passing by. She smiled as best she could and asked, "Were you looking for me?"

"Yeah." He got out a pack of cigarettes.

"Let's go inside. It's cold out here," she said. It would be better if they didn't go in.

"It's not all that cold." He hunched up his shoulders, without looking at her. He pulled a match-box half open, flicked a match against it, and whipped it into the gap, so that the cigarette caught. He took a long drag. After a while, he said, "This is a nice place."

"It's not bad."

"Close to the reservoir, so you have fish to eat."

"It was dry this year. Lots of the fish died. "

"Have you got a horse to ride?"

"I've only ridden once. It was a very quiet horse belonging to one of the herdsmen. It wouldn't run even if I hit it. You couldn't really call it riding."

"You aren't herding horses?"

"No, I'm in the research team, developing better seeds, and things like that."

She realised that he did not have the slightest notion of her life there.

He said nothing, just puffed away on his cigarette. When it was finished, he threw it on the snow. There was a hiss as it went out. He looked at her and licked his lips, as though he had something to say but found it hard to speak.

"Have you eaten?" she asked. There was nothing else she could ask. She did not want to ask about anything. It was all done with now.

"Yes," he mumbled. He stuck his hands back into his coat sleeves, looked up at the sky, then back down at the ground. He showed no sign of being about to leave. It was getting dark, but a film of light remained on the snow, illuminating his hesitation.

"Chen Xu's bedding is all burnt. The fire under the bed got out of control." He began speaking very quickly. "But Susie J says that he fired the bed up too high and wants him to write a self-criticism before he'll give him ten dollars to replace it. Chen Xu's leaving for Hegang in a few days, to work in the coal mines."

"Why is he going to a place like that?"

"The wages are good, you know! There's a one dollar bonus for every day you spend down in the mine."

The wind came gliding over the snow and twined itself around her fingers.

Bubble was starting to stammer. "Chen Xu says he won't write a self-criticism. And he doesn't want to make up any more stories just to get some money. So, so he sent me to, to borrow some money from you. He needs twenty dollars to buy cotton wadding and make a quilt. He'll pay you back in a couple of months."

He got out another cigarette. The wind was blowing hard, and after striking several matches he had not managed to light it.

She was choked by the wind and could say nothing for a long time. As the wind passed, she turned away and asked, "Does he want it now?"

"If you could."

She walked inside, but stopped just as she reached the door and thought for a moment. Then she turned back and said to Bubble, "I've only got five dollars left. Could you come back and get it after I get paid? It's less than a week to payday, after all. Do you want to take the five dollars now?"

Bubble waved it away. "No, no, I'll come again. It's not very far, anyway."

He seemed very satisfied with her reply. He believed that she really only had five dollars left. She really did only have five dollars. And he believed that once they were paid she would certainly lend the money to Chen Xu. She would lend it to him. He would never have reached out to her if he were not in real trouble. Bubble turned and walked away, but looked back after a few steps and asked, "When should I come on payday?"

"After dinner will be fine," she replied.

She was very satisfied too, because even now he still trusted her.

Bubble was gone, a tiny figure far away across the snow. She let out a deep breath. She found that hearing news of Chen Xu left her as calm and indifferent as news of any ordinary friend. She had definitely ceased to love him already. She had.

It went on snowing lightly off and on for two days. On the third morning, after the weather cleared, the postman brought back from the post office a flour sack full of letters and papers that had been held up for days by the snow.

Xiao Xiao received a number of letters all at once. She picked the one in the manila envelope out first. Only her mother used that kind of envelope, and she wanted to read her mother's letter before any of the others.

Her glance skipped and dashed along like a starving rabbit in search of food, not missing so much as a blade of grass. It was happy and expectant. When the ground was covered with pine needles, there were succulent mushrooms below them. When the ground was covered with snow, there were red turnips below it. A hole in a pine tree lit up; it was a little squirrel bringing a pine torch. Flowers were blooming throughout the forest. The warmth of April had come ahead of time. Her eyes were all confused, her forehead flickered in the light. She was so happy she could scarcely breathe. It was her chance, come galloping from far away, just to see if she would be able to turn around and leap up on its back.

She was reading the following few lines over and over:

> ...We have also been concerned all along because your Uncle Qiwei has no children. We didn't know that he had

returned to Beijing from the cadre school until we got a letter from him not long ago. He's still working at the History Institute. Your Aunt Masha is back at the Petroleum Ministry, awaiting assignment. They say that a major oil refinery is being built on the outskirts of Beijing and that it urgently needs young workers. Your aunt is already seeing if she can arrange for you to be transferred there. As soon as there is any sign of success, she will wire you to come to Beijing to discuss the necessary arrangements. If you get a telegram from Beijing saying your aunt is seriously ill, ask for an emergency leave at once and go there without delay and without fail!

Mother and Father

There was nothing else in the way of explanation, no wasted words. It seemed as though they had had a kind of agreement with Xiao Xiao all along, that all the old high-sounding words about revolution, ideals, and building the frontier could be tossed holus bolus into the furnace of an oil refinery and cancelled with one stroke of a pen. It was as though they had never taught her to give her all to the State Farm. It was as though Xiao Xiao had to, was bound to, was certainly to leave the Farm.

In addition to her excitement at this undreamed turn of events, she also felt a sudden sense of shock, shock that her parents, who had always kept so scrupulously to what was expected of them, had actually bored a passage through solid rock, had learned something of the art of finding roundabout ways back to the city. She was also shocked to find that she herself had not hesitated a moment. She had accepted the arrangement happily and without the slightest resistance. A life preserver had floated over to her. Of course she would choose to go. She felt a faint blush cross her cheeks. She would definitely go. She could not reject such an opportunity. She was entirely powerless to overcome something so enticing. The hand in which she clutched the letter began to shake. Of course, because Chen Xu was here, sooner or later the two of them should make a complete break, never to meet again. She ran outside the dormitory. To be a worker was a big advance over being a peasant. The proletariat leads in all things. She walked across the fresh snow, leaving a ragged trail of footprints. Her aunt and uncle had always treated her like a daughter. If she didn't go, their feelings would be terribly hurt. She squatted down and made some marks on the snow with her finger tip. She did so unconscious of what she was writing, but when she stood up she could make out a few scrawled words: leave, leave, leave... She had not really intended to convince herself to stay.

She began to wait for the telegram, to long for it, to consider how she would go about asking for leave.

No one perceived the secret she carried in her heart. Not even Dakang knew. The human heart was such a strange thing. It truly belonged to you alone. Sour or sweet, sorrow or joy, they were all there for you alone to taste. It often concealed the true state of things from friend and foe alike, loyal only to you and fooling everyone else. And those other people's hearts were fooling you. No one could see anyone else.

She was constantly uneasy, filled with yearning, with anxiety, with secret concern. She was tangled up in feelings that she could not express, but which kept coming to knock at the gate of her heart. She had to fasten yet another lock on it, but they kept on squeezing their way in around the edges, snapping at her, twining around her. She scrutinised her heart, but the more she analysed it the more impervious to reason it became. These were unbearable, unendurable days. She had never before been so hard on herself.

The telegram arrived soon after, one long line:

Aunt seriously ill no one here urgently need your help await arrival Beijing Uncle.

After lunch, she took the telegram and went looking for Guo Chunmei. Chunmei never took a break at lunch time. She would be in the office reading documents or talking with someone she had called in to see her.

The office door was unlocked, and on the table lay a telegram: Xiao Xiao's aunt seriously ill entreat leadership approve two weeks emergency leave return Beijing attend aunt Xiao Qiwei.

Pulling a long face, Xiao Xiao handed her telegram to Guo Chunmei, who was just then munching on a steamed bun while she read the paper. Xiao Xiao sniffed and took out her handkerchief to dab at her eyes. She thought she really did look grief-stricken and anxious. And ridiculous.

Guo Chunmei read through the two telegrams several times without saying anything.

Director Xu came in with his coat thrown over his shoulders, glanced at the telegrams, and said, "Every family has some sickness or trouble one time or another. You'd best go."

Xiao Xiao blurted, "Can I use my home leave for 1974?"

"Certainly not," declared Guo Chunmei. "For one thing, there are still two days before New Years. For another, if we start giving home leaves at the very beginning of the year, people may object."

Xiao Xiao bit her lip, and then said, "Well then, I'd better request an emergency leave."

"An emergency leave can't exceed one month." Guo Chunmei looked at her. "Be sure to be back before the Spring Festival."

"Okay," mumbled Xiao Xiao.

Director Xu said, "If you see any good leather vests while you're in Beijing, pick one up for me. I'll get you the money right away."

Guo Chunmei pulled open a drawer, took out a seal, and began writing her a letter of introduction, saying as she wrote, "Director Yu phoned to ask about it again."

"About what?"

"That letter, of course!"

"What letter?"

"Have you forgotten? The open letter, the declaration to strike roots!" She glanced up with a look of reproach. She was unhappy with Xiao Xiao for having forgotten all about something so important.

Xiao Xiao smiled. "If I don't have time, you'd better write it. I wouldn't do a good job of it, anyway." She realised that she had found the perfect excuse to get out of drafting the letter. She was not all that willing to do it. She had never really considered striking roots herself.

Guo Chunmei tore the letter of introduction from the pad, read through it once more, and said, "In my opinion, of all the urban youth on the Branch Farm, on all the Half-way River State Farm, for that matter, you're the right one to do it. That report you did before on the hundred-day transformation was very vividly written and had a clear point of view. Director Yu spoke highly of you and said you were definitely the one to write up the public letter."

You numbskull, you fat-head! All you asked for was a wooden trunk. You're such a fool! How much treasure can a wooden trunk hold? Get out of here, you moron. Go back and pay your respects to that golden fish! Ask her for a log house.

"Do you want me to bring anything back for you?" Xiao Xiao interrupted her.

"Buy the Branch Farm some books on the movement to Criticise Confucianism and Praise Legalism," said Guo Chunmei firmly, adding, "Come back early if you can. You still have to draft the declaration. Use the time to visit some more model settlers and discuss things with them by way of preparation. While you're gone, pay close attention to how political trends are developing, so you can tell us all about them when you get back."

Xiao Xiao nodded over and over as she folded the letter of introduction up carefully, put it in her pocket, and took her leave. She felt like smiling in spite of herself. The crunch of her footsteps on the strip of untrodden snow alongside the road seemed to be tamping down one secret after another. She felt a kind of malicious delight. Somewhere or other she had scored Guo Chunmei off but good.

They paid out wages at the Company that night, one day early because of New Years. Xiao Xiao was in luck. Thirty-one dollars and fifty cents, enough for a hard seat ticket to Beijing, with something left over to buy a couple of boxes of wine-filled candies for her aunt and uncle when she got to Jiamusi station. She had her hands full that evening, what with packing her bags and various people coming to ask her to buy things on their behalf. Dakang wrapped up all her dirty clothes for her. Xiao Xiao kept her brow knitted, trying to hide her excitement under a furrowed forehead, lest anyone suspect the truth.

After she went to bed that night, she could not get to sleep for a long time. She rolled over once, and then again. She was afraid to stir any more, for fear of waking Dakang. But she heard Dakang's bedding moving over in her direction, and then a quiet sigh.

"Xiao, are you really coming back in a month?"

"Yes, really."

"You're really coming back?"

"What's wrong?"

"Nothing." Dakang rolled back over and murmured, "I'm just afraid that when you come back, you won't find me here."

"How come?" Xiao Xiao reached out and rapped on the back of her head. For more than a month, Dakang had been preoccupied with something. She laughed much less, as though something were troubling her. Xiao Xiao thought that she was probably unhappy at the way she herself had been getting along with Guo Chunmei, but she had not tried to talk her out of it. After the telegram came that day, Dakang had not said a single word. Go ahead and tell her about the Beijing business, tell only her. There were some joys that could only be called joyful if there was a friend to share them with. It's not as though it were underground Party work. And especially since if it hadn't been for Dakang things might have gone very differently over the preceding six months. But, she could not. Since she had concealed the truth from everyone else, she had to conceal her own thoughts from herself. Concealment to the end. There were some joys that would vanish if once declared.

There was a glimmer in the window. Was it dawn? No, it was light reflected off the snow. How desperately the snow shone, having been held down all winter long. It was so bright that it seemed the day need not dawn again, that it would not. She would leave the place at dawn. Would she leave it for ever? She did not know.

Early the next morning, as the tractor was passing the turn-off for No.5, she caught sight of knots of people setting off for work, their shoulders hunched up against the cold. Her breathing quickened and a cold chill struck the pit of her stomach—she remembered Bubble saying that he would come for the money on the 30th, after they were paid!

Twenty-four straight hours of excitement, hurry, distraction, and dreams, and she had forgotten all about it.

Really, truly, she had simply forgotten!

Running away? Her ears were ringing. Bubble and Chen Xu would be sure to think that she had stalled them on purpose, that she was thoughtless, that she had tricked them. How low! Them? Or her? Even if she could play tricks on anyone else, she absolutely should not let Chen Xu down. Jump off the cart and go back! There was certainly time to make up for what she had done, time to make amends for her mistake. The bare mat on the brick bed, the black and draughty coal-pit shed. All she had to do was rap on the roof of the cab and Guan Er would stop. If you get a telegram from Beijing, go there without delay and without fail! The next day would be New Years, and then there would be no trains for two days. If she turned back, wouldn't she miss out on her chance in Beijing? The proletariat leads in all things.

The cart wheels rolled noisily over the packed snow, under which countless secrets were surely buried. Liar. She had lied to him without meaning to. The first lie she had ever told him, and it came after they had separated. No, no, she had not done it on purpose. It was not a lie if it was not intentional. Someday she would be able to explain it to him in person. It could not be called a lie.

But if it could be called a lie, then it certainly was not the first. What about that telegram the previous year, when she went home to see the baby? The letter of introduction the day before? So confident, so at ease. And she wasn't only deceiving Liu the Brute, Chen Xu, and Guo Chunmei. There were Dakang, Mrs. Su, and Radish, as well.

The careening cart threw her this way and that. She allowed the wooden sides to pummel her body and yet she felt no pain. Whether she was frozen or just numb, there was nothing inside her but waves of wrenching nausea.

Do you really know your own mind or don't you?

Who was asking her? She asked herself.

It was Zou Sizhu. Yes, only he was capable of such an unflinching attitude toward himself, toward his own mind.

No! She had forgotten to say goodbye to him, too, just as she had forgotten about Bubble.

That savage, ancient haunted tree leapt up from the grey snow in a flash of black lightning, its branches writhing like the upraised claws of a dragon. It swept toward her with something like an unintelligible grunt. It might have been giving her some advice. Or perhaps a hint.

46

Was this Chang'an Boulevard? Was Chang'an Boulevard so narrow? And Tiananmen? How did Tiananmen get so low? And the Hall of Nationalities? How did it get so old? Was this really Beijing?

Xiao Xiao took a No.10 bus down broad Chang'an Boulevard. Her uncle lived in a lane off South Lishi Road. When she had come to Beijing during the time of Linking-up, she had stayed in a high school, with Red Guards from all over the country bedded down in every classroom. In those days, every building in Beijing had seemed taller and more imposing than now. They had been so beautiful and inspiring. There were red walls and red flags everywhere, and the sky over the great square in front of Tiananmen had been covered with red and golden dawns and sunsets. Had she grown up, or had they changed? In any event, this Beijing was suspiciously drab. How had it lost all its colour, all its life? It was more like an extinct volcano, all its warmth spewed out and reduced to weary lava stiffened in piles of grey walls and tiles, grey upon grey. Was her lucky break really somehow connected with this dreary grey?

She walked in past a heavy steel gate, went down a long corridor lined with rusty railings, and knocked softly at a door. A pair of large gentle hands embraced her and a smacking kiss was planted on her forehead. Her face flushing a bright pink, she cried, "Aunt Masha!"

Her aunt was tall and large of frame, with a resonant voice and a tendency to throw back her shoulders and laugh. When Xiao Xiao was little, Aunt Masha had come to Hangzhou with some delegation or other and Xiao Xiao had said, "I've seen you before." "Where?" asked her aunt, quite surprised. "Here!" She pointed to a picture of a Russian woman in a picture-book version of Ostrovsky's 'How the Steel was Tempered'. Aunt Masha looked just like the picture to her. Her aunt beamed and said to Xiao Xiao's mother, "What a clever little creature! You'd better give her to me and let her be my daughter!" Aunt Masha had given her lots of pretty pictures. Later, Xiao Xiao learned that her aunt really had come back from the Soviet Union. Of course she wasn't Russian, but she had studied there for five years. She was already thirty-seven when she married Xiao Xiao's uncle, so she had no children. Once the Cultural Revolution broke out, her aunt Masha became a 'foreign-connected counter-revolutionary element', her uncle became a 'reactionary academic authority of the capitalist class', and the daughter of their dreams flew far away.

"Weijia, our girl is back," called her aunt toward the inner room.

Uncle Qiwei came out in his slippers and took off his gold-rimmed glasses to have a good look at her. He was just the opposite of her aunt, a short, thin, taciturn Cantonese. "You'd better have a bath and change out of those clothes first," he said. "You should probably boil your clothes, your shoes, and your bag."

He had a mania for cleanliness. He would not touch anything after washing his hands and even opened doors with his foot. Had the years he spent in the cadre school not remoulded him? She gave herself a thorough scrubbing in the bathroom. She had been looking forward for ages to a vigorous clean-up like this, back when she could only get a hurried wash. Why hadn't they told her the news yet?

As Xiao Xiao came out from her bath, her aunt was just pouring something dark brown from a bright, oddly shaped silver pot into three little cups on the tea table. Then she added a sugar cube to each cup with a long thin spoon.

"I don't take sugar in my tea," said Xiao Xiao.

"This is coffee," said her aunt. "Take a sniff. Isn't it fragrant! An old schoolmate of mine gave it to me. You'll never find it on the market now."

"Aren't you working?" asked Xiao Xiao. To think that she couldn't even remember what coffee was.

"We still haven't been assigned work!" Her aunt cocked her head to one side and sneered. "People have to get new job assignments after they come back from cadre school. We're being practically spare-timed to death. Quick, drink it while it's hot!"

Xiao Xiao took a sip of the coffee. It was as black as soy sauce soup, and so bitter that she wrinkled up her face. Why not just call it medicine?

"What's wrong?" Her aunt raised her eyebrows.

"I..." She clenched her teeth and swallowed a mouthful. She just could not bring herself to say that she couldn't drink coffee. "I, I don't feel very well."

"Where does it hurt?" The two of them came and stood over

her.

Excuse me, but I can't digest such elegance. "I, I keep thinking about that telegram. I deceived my superiors. I've been upset about it all the way here." She hung her head, feeling sick at heart.

"You see? I told you so." Her uncle put down his cup and looked at her aunt. "I told you not to send the telegram so soon, but you had to go ahead and do it. And now look what's happened. Not only has the plan fallen through, but she's faked a..."

Xiao Xiao spat a mouthful of coffee back into her cup. Fallen through? It was all over.

But her aunt tossed her black hair and laughed, "Well, so what if it did? It doesn't matter! If it fell through, well, we can still think of something else, can't we, Xiao-xiao? And if you had to practise a little deception to get your leave, so what? They swindle ordinary people every day with one piece of hokum or another, and they don't lose any sleep over it."

"Quiet! Can't you be a little more quiet?" Her uncle stood up and went over to the window, bending down to make sure it was locked. But it was the dead of winter, so the windows were sealed tight, and they were on the second floor besides.

"What went wrong?" asked Xiao Xiao, on the verge of tears.

"Who knows?" Her aunt had lowered her voice, but it was still quite loud. "Everything was all set, a New Directive of '74, so we called you down in a hurry. But yesterday we got another wire, saying that no young people from state farms would be taken on. They went back on their word. It's crazy."

She did not get the wire out for Xiao Xiao to see.

Her uncle sighed. "It looks to me like that old fellow student of yours, the chief engineer in the Petroleum Ministry, doesn't have any real power. A 'Ninth Category', an intellectual, who studied in the Soviet Union..." He broke off.

Her aunt stroked Xiao Xiao's pigtails and massaged her shoulders, She laughed, "It's just as well if you don't go work in the refinery. Those places are dangerous. They can blow up at any moment, not like factories overseas. And an explosion would be awful, wouldn't it? I'll have another try, get someone to find a good place for you, and if that doesn't work, you can go to a chicken farm in the suburbs. Even that would be better than the Great Northern Wastes."

"You have to give people presents if you want them to do things for you," offered Xiao Xiao. "There was someone on our Farm who traded a truck load of coal for a residence transfer, and another who traded a tractor for..."

Her aunt shrugged and pulled open the wardrobe, taking out a lavender gauze scarf and draping it over Xiao Xiao's head. She clasped her hands, cocked her head to one side, and admired the effect. "My! How pretty my little girl is! Just like a little princess. If you ask me, you should spend these few days enjoying yourself in Beijing. We'll go to the Great Wall, the Summer Palace, wherever you haven't been." She seemed delighted that this unprecedented political movement and the oil refinery had given her back the daughter of whom she had dreamed so long.

Bubble, the fur vest, Anti-Confucius Anti-Lin Biao books, the Public Declaration.

Xiao Xiao's lips moved. "I, it was an emergency leave I got."

Her uncle said, "They dock your pay for an emergency leave, don't they?"

Her aunt raised her voice. "Well! What does that matter? I'll supply your pay. What point is there in hanging onto money these days, anyhow? The shops don't have anything you want. Let's have ourselves a real good time, eat and drink the money up."

The next day they took the train up to the Great Wall together, carrying along luncheon meat, tinned anchovies, and bread. Her aunt and uncle climbed half-way up and then said they could go no further, so Xiao Xiao had to go on to the highest beacon tower by herself. Unfortunately, the same grey blur lay outside the wall as inside, and it was freezing up there. She could not work up any enthusiasm. In the days of the Great Linking-up, the Red Guards atop the Wall had looked like a whole kingdom of ants carrying a centipede. How magnificent, how breathtaking that had been! She felt let down. The wind was blowing hard up on the wall. She waited around a little while and then came back down.

Her uncle glared at her. "You didn't write your name up there, did you? That's a stupid thing to do, a piece of mischief. Those Red... Hmm. Well, a real name is the one you leave in history."

She smiled. She had discovered that just because she was young, her uncle felt an extreme unease about her and a lack of confidence that he could not very well express directly, but which he kept on betraying all the same. Indeed, he seemed to frown on everything connected with the younger generation. "My name?" she replied in a loud voice. "I'm forever forgetting what my name is. Once winter comes, everyone is dressed up in brown coats and big boots, so we all look exactly the same and there is no telling who is who."

The grey wall behind her was like a huge fossil Tyrannosaurus from an age cut off and gone for ever. What she liked was a living Great Wall. It not only stood guard, but could also go on the attack. There was no such Great Wall.

The day after that, her aunt took her to the Moscow Restaurant for a Russian dinner.

They went up the little drive on the west side of the Sino-Soviet Friendship Palace (renamed the Beijing Exhibition Hall), but they did not find the Moscow Restaurant. Written over the revolving door was 'Beijing Restaurant'.

"Hardly the right name for it," fumed her aunt.

Although the name had been changed to Beijing Restaurant, the architecture and decor were still in the Russian style—the domed ceiling covered with carved snowflakes, dozens of round beige pillars decorated with a wave-like pattern, huge ceiling-to-floor windows (without curtains, for some unknown reason), parquetry floors in shades of brown, and long white tables. In the gentle light, the whole restaurant had a serene and comfortable atmosphere. Was it Anna Karenina, or War and Peace? The Cherry Orchid, or On the Eve? Xiao Xiao held her breath. She had never imagined that eating could be so serious. This was the first time she had been there .

Her aunt ordered two servings of ham salad, and one each of meat pie, baked prawns, and butter rolls. Finally, she added, "And we want two bowls of Ukrainian borsch."

The waitress was impassive. "All we have is tomato soup."

Her aunt looked up at her as though about to say something, but thought better of it and nodded her consent.

After the waitress had gone, Xiao Xiao said, "Perhaps tomato soup is borsch."

"Come now, how could borsch possibly be made from tomatoes?" Her aunt's brows shot up. "You need real Ukrainian beets, as red as..."

"As radishes?"

"How could they be like radishes?" Her aunt's astonishment was evident. "What I meant was like red agate or roses."

Xiao Xiao's ears burned. All her petty-bourgeois sentimentality, so ridiculed on the Farm, had been demolished by this half-baked, renamed restaurant in the capital. She had only read about these things in books. It was all so far removed from her. How sad it was. But how much she liked it there, if only because of the gleaming stainless steel tableware and the square platter heaped with salad. If they would just let her be a waitress and carry a tray! She did not like Western food all that much.

Her aunt cut the meat pie up with a knife and showed Xiao Xiao how to use her knife and fork without making noise, all the while grumbling that the food did not taste Russian at all, more like Cantonese dimsum. Brows knit, she laboured at chewing the meat pie. Out of nowhere, she asked Xiao Xiao, "Say, up where you live, aren't you right next to the Soviet border? Can't you get Russian food?"

Xiao Xiao shook her head. Her aunt's question sounded ridiculous to her. When they ate meat on the State Farm, it was stewed in big chunks with noodles. Who had any notion of Western food?

Her aunt put down her knife and fork and looked up toward the domed ceiling, pointing out the carved pillars. She said, "Look, Xiao Xiao. The wall lamps are at the tops of the pillars, behind a ledge, so the lightbulbs aren't visible from our seats. That's why the lighting is so elegant. One of the people who designed this place was a fellow student of mine in the Soviet Union."

"It must waste a lot of electricity, having the lights up so high." Xiao Xiao observed coolly.

Her aunt looked at her and shrugged her shoulders. They did not talk any more. Xiao Xiao did not understand Western food, and her aunt did not want to know about the Farm. When they had finished their rolls, they went home.

Her uncle was lying in his reclining chair reading a thick manuscript. When he saw them come in, he thrust it under his blanket. Xiao Xiao walked over and demanded, "What were you reading? Let me see it."

Her uncle offered her a nicely-bound copy of the Iliad, saying, "Here, why don't you read this. It's good."

Xiao Xiao pouted. "I want to read the book you're writing. I know it's something you're writing."

"Quiet! Not so loud!" Looking frightened, her uncle got up and dashed over to the window to make sure it was locked. Xiao Xiao took advantage of the opportunity to pull the manuscript out and take a firm grip on it. Flipping through it, she found some strange kind of script. On the first page it said, 'Stories From the Sutras'.

"You're writing Buddhist stories?" she asked, quite surprised.

"They're not written, they're translated." Her uncle still looked very worried. "And I'm not the translator. It's a, a professor. He asked me to help him out by reading through it."

"Are they interesting?"

"Well, I don't have anything else to do, in any case."

"What are they about? Tell me one." She was fascinated.

"Not so loud!" Her uncle sighed. "This sort of thing can't be published now. ... Well, all right. Go ahead and choose one."

She leafed at random through the pages until she came to one called "The Woodworker and the Painter," and then handed the manuscript to her uncle.

He glanced at her and asked, "Why this one?"

"It's the one I want!" she smirked.

Her uncle smoothed his hair down, cleared his throat, sat up and looked out the window one more time, and then began:

Well, once upon a time, in northern India, there was a craftsman who specialised in making things from wood. He was a man of the greatest skill. He made a wooden girl who was just as pretty and capable as a real woman, only she could not speak.

Now, in the south of India there lived an excellent painter. The woodworker invited him to dinner one day, and when the painter saw how fetchingly the wooden girl poured their wine and waited on them, he took a liking to her. The woodworker noticed this and said to the painter, It's getting late, and you can't easily get back home. Stay here tonight and I'll have the girl attend your couch...

"Why are you stopping?" asked Xiao Xiao.

Her uncle looked flustered and mumbled, "I'd better tell a different one. You're still a child, not married yet, so you don't know what attend..."

Xiao Xiao lowered her eyes. She hadn't told them that she had been married and divorced, and had a baby. She did not want to bring on a lot of questions. No, I haven't been a child for a long time.

"Go on, Xiao Xiao's already over twenty," said her aunt.

So her uncle continued with the story. It went something like this:

The painter and the wooden girl went into the bedroom, but she wouldn't approach him. The painter thought that she was bashful. He took her by the hand, and only then did he finally realise that she was made of wood. Embarrassed and irritated, he decided that since the woodworker had tricked him, he ought to pay him back. And so he painted a picture of himself on the wall, dressed in exactly the same clothes. Then he painted a rope tied around his neck, as though he had hanged himself. Finally, he painted flies and birds pecking at his mouth. Once the picture was done, he locked the door and hid under the bed.

"This is a good one," laughed Xiao Xiao's aunt. "Tricking each other just like people do nowadays."

"How about keeping your opinions to yourself?" Her uncle glared at his wife. "Just let me finish."

When it got light the next morning, the woodworker came out of his own room and went to look in on the painter. When he saw him hanging there, he was horrified. He broke down the door and rushed in to cut the rope. Thereupon, the painter crawled out from under the bed, and the woodworker realised what he had done. Now it was his turn to be embarrassed. The painter said, "You managed to fool me, and I managed to fool you, so now we are even." The two of them then sighed with regret, realising that they were no different from the run of men when it came to tricking each other.

"Is that all?" asked her aunt.

"Yep." Her uncle picked up the manuscript and lay back on his chair again.

"That's just what I meant," clucked her aunt. "Don't you think this is a real case of 'making the past serve the present'? Watch out, or people will say you're making insinuations about the government!"

"Why don't you say something, Xiao Xiao," said her uncle, looking around at her.

"It's like a parable," she said, after a while.

So, two thousand years ago people had been teasing and hoodwinking one another. It had been like this in a society two thousand years in the past, far away in India, under the caste system of a strange land. How similar the men of ancient times were to those of the present. Was there no eternally unchanging human nature? Was there a kind of human nature that was eternally unchanging? "But if we admit that evil is true also, even the evil in human nature..."

Her uncle's lips were moving, as though he were about to say something, but then he stopped. He had not really wanted to tell the story to Xiao Xiao. He probably knew that as soon as she heard it she would get the point.

Her aunt called from the other room, "Xiao, would you come give me a hand?"

She was moving a small green box out of the big locked closet. She had Xiao Xiao put it on the table and then took out a package of phonograph records. "Let's listen to a record. Don't pay any attention to your uncle's tired old stories." She carefully mounted the stylus, humming 'Katyusha' as she looked for something in the big pile of disks. "Is there something you would like to hear?" she asked Xiao Xiao.

Xiao Xiao shook her head. She had heard her mother say that Aunt Masha had a great number of records she had brought back from the Soviet Union. Hadn't she lost them during the Cultural Revolution? "Do you have Beethoven's 'Fate' symphony? I've never heard it." Her heart began to pound.

Her uncle tiptoed into the room and said nervously, "Be sure to keep it quiet." Then he walked back out to check that the door was locked and to tuck the window curtains in tight. Her aunt's face had taken on a youthful bloom, as though she were about to carry out some solemn rite.

When the music began, Xiao Xiao felt as though a pair of hands had given her a powerful shove. She shuddered and her heart contracted until she could hardly breathe. The battle drums thundered; it was a fight to the death.

"That's Fate knocking at the door," whispered her aunt.

Xiao Xiao buried her head in her palms, several strands of hair trailing over the back of her hands. She closed her eyes and let those splendid waves of sound sweep her off into the mountains, across the deserts and the seas.

A thick, heavy, closed door.

A snowstorm was battering the low, red-tiled house. The house was shaking. A black storm was howling, covering the earth. All nature trembled at that roar, fighting for its life. The storm was so powerful, raged so uncontrollably, that no one could oppose it on equal terms.

She collapsed on a lawn. The grass was green and tender, filled with longing for life. She was exhausted, covered with wounds, which she was licking gingerly.

Fire blazed up, engulfing the lawn in flames. She was looking for her own road through the fire. She rushed forward and then fell back. There was a red demon standing beside the road with a vicious smile. Beyond him lay a road. She was rolling over the flames to extinguish them in order to reach the road and escape. Pairs of hands reached out to her from the other side of the flames, but she just couldn't reach them. Someone was calling her name in the distance. She struggled to crawl ahead, raising herself up on her hands, standing up, standing up...

She was up, she stumbled, stood up again...

Her palms were soaking wet. She hugged her shoulders and began to sob.

The knocking at the door began again. This time the knocking was on a real door.

Was it really Fate? The three of them were dazed.

Knock, knock!

"Quick, cover the phonograph." Her uncle reacted. "Use the blanket!"

Her aunt threw a blanket over the machine as though she were smothering a fire.

Fate went on struggling under the blanket.

Her uncle pulled the plug.

Fate ran outside.

Xiao Xiao went to answer the door. She was very curious about Fate.

It was a scrawny old lady with a fistful of money. She chuckled and said, "Came for the yard-cleaning fee."

Her aunt burst out laughing.

Her uncle said, "You never come in. Come on in and rest a while!"

"Not this time." The old lady took the money and left.

Fate had not come in, it had gone to sweep the yard.

Xiao Xiao realised that it was best if Fate stayed inside the phonograph. It was enthralling so long as it was struggling inside. But in real life, people lost their heads as soon as it appeared, even if it only knocked at the door. Apparently Fate smiled too rarely, and too rare as well were people who could march out to vanquish an evil fate.

Xiao Xiao stole a glance at her aunt and uncle through narrowed eyes. They had regained their calm. As the soft music went on playing, her uncle held his tea cup, his head swaying slightly, a picture of serenity. Her aunt was leaning against the bedstead, chin resting on her arm and eyes wide open, like an attentive student listening to a lecture. They seemed to belong to a different world now, compared to their panic of a few minutes before. Perhaps they lived only in the world of the phonograph, enjoying the play of Fate and human life. But Xiao Xiao would have to go out that door and meet the cruel challenge of her fate.

The record went on spinning tirelessly, around and around without ever stopping. And yet the needle was quietly moving, following that fine black magic groove toward the depths at the centre. It too was forever going around in circles, but it never went back to its starting point. How marvellously it glided past that recurrent crossroad, climbing up to the summit of that fluid mountain.

This was the first time in all her twenty-four years that she had listened to a symphony. She thought that perhaps she had not really understood it. Nor could she remember any of the notes. And yet the music had called up all her memories and reflections on what she had been through in her life. She got to know Beethoven on the strength of her instincts and her experience of suffering. She hoped to carry him back from the grey city with her.

Xiao Xiao made friends with the records.

Her aunt studied her Russian every day as though sitting in Zen meditation.

When her uncle was not reading, he went out and found a neighbour to play chess with.

They went to the Zoo, to the Altar of Heaven. They loved her; they bought her chocolate and a woolen shirt. But her uncle liked talking about the sugar cane in Guangdong, and her aunt about the snow in Leningrad. Xiao Xiao wanted to tell them about the horses on the Farm, about the great marshes. As they sat visiting, chatting rather, after dinner, they all felt very tired. Music was thus the one friend the three of them had in common.

When Xiao Xiao was listening to the music, it seemed to her that the world could be spun around too. She made up her mind to forget the oil refinery business and to live her own life.

And so the days passed, relaxed and difficult at the same time. On the last day of her third week, she told her aunt that she was going back to the Farm.

Her uncle said, "We'll go have someone get you a ticket."

She had no money for a ticket. Money was evidently very important, for without it one's opinion did not count. She could tell because when her ticket came, she saw printed on the corner: Beijing-Hangzhou.

Well, she had overstayed her leave already. She'd spend two weeks in Hangzhou and then go back to the Farm. Might as well let it go on spinning. Each groove contained both a lucky opportunity and inescapable disaster.

When the train started, her aunt burst into tears. Xiao Xiao waved from the window for a long time, but she had no tears.

Farewell, Beijing, you dormant volcano. When will you erupt again?

One table after another. There were tables everywhere.

She struggled to move the tables out of her way, but a new batch kept blocking her exit.

There were stairs in front of her.

The stairs turned one corner after another, without coming to an end. At a corner of the stairs was a slide like an elephant's trunk. She slid down it.

She picked up a cradle. There was a doll in the cradle. Its eyes moved. They opened when it sat up and closed when it lay down.

She took the doll to a playground. The doll wanted to ride on a little tricycle, and rode it very fast. The doll smiled and gurgled. Liu Yin walked up and asked, Who is this?

She said, This is my sister-in-law's baby.

Liu Yin continued, Who is your sister-in-law?

She said, A golden fish.

Liu Yin said, So she must be a little goldfish! I'll take her for an X-ray and we'll see if she is a goldfish or not.

They walked into a pitch dark room. There was a huge emerald machine inside. She put the doll on the sheet of glass, which looked like a movie screen. She could see a pointed fish's skull quite clearly inside the doll's round head. And there was a complete fish's skeleton too. So she put the doll back into the deep blue sea. Once the doll had leapt into the water it did indeed turn into a fish. It looked like one of the big blue fish in the Jade Spring in Hangzhou. Before swimming away with a flap of its tail, it looked back and cried, Mama!

A tractor was turning up one red lotus root after another. Dakang was following behind the tractor, bent over and planting seeds, murmuring all the while:

Two stalks from each hole we dig,
One for the ox and one for the pig.

She looked into the holes in one of the lotus roots.

Inside one hole, Guo Chunmei, her hair in disarray, was painting a mask. The figure on the mask was even fatter than Guo, with thicker

391

lips and a flatter nose. She said, What are you painting such an ugly mask for?

Inside another hole, Zou Sizhu was burning books. He burned one page at a time, swallowing the ashes and licking his glasses. She said, you're sick. He said, You're right. It's all the people who don't think they are sick who really are. She asked, What about me? He reached out and embraced her. You're sick too. She ran away.

She ran into the last tube-shaped hole in the lotus root, the one that had no one in it. It was bright inside. As she squeezed out the other end, she found herself entwined in silver lotus fibres, like a silkworm. She saw a little boy playing under an oak tree. He had an assault rifle and was spraying bullets in her direction. She screamed, Don't shoot me, I'm your mother.

The little boy ran up to her, cocked his head to one side, and said, You're my mother? Do you have any milk?

She pulled up her dress, revealing two swollen breasts, from which milk was flowing in streams like silk from a silkworm. She took the little boy on the train with her. As it set off for the snowy mountains, its wheels screamed in agony; but as it passed by the green rice fields, they said, so happy so happy so happy...

47

In all her five years in the Great Northern Wastes, Xiao Xiao had never seen such a wind.

Heaven and earth alike were completely brown, a huge brown whirlpool, clutching at you, squeezing you. You became a grain of sand, a scrap of paper, tossed up into the air and then whirled back down to earth. The wailing of banshees, the vicious quarrels of the stars, the roar of the oceans, and the groaning of the rusty axis of the earth merged in this lunatic chorus. Rage, joy, destruction, death—the sun had been snuffed out, the moon split in two, the heavens ripped to shreds, and you as well, and the wind itself. The wind was blowing so hard that even it could not tell in which direction, while for the sake of standing witness for yourself you pushed on through the interstices in grit falling like a torrential downpour, your eyes held open by force of will alone, able to make out only the dim shapes of barns, houses, carts, trees—shapes that vanished with the vagaries of the wind.

It took Xiao Xiao a full half-hour to make her way over the few hundred yards from the long-distance bus stop at the turn-off back to the Branch Farm dormitory. The road was indistinct and deserted. There was not so much as a ghost to be seen, as though they had all been blown away by the wind.

Her whole body, her hair, her clothing, the spaces between her teeth, her shoes, everything was coated with dust stirred up by this emissary of springtide. She had been gone for two months. When she left, everything was still frozen. But now that she was back she caught the fragrant scent of sunlight on the roaring wind. The walking was difficult, and yet she felt relaxed and happy.

How are you, Springtime?

You have returned, and so have I!

She walked into the Research Team dormitory. The fire was out and no one was around. It was chilly. She sat down at her own bunk. Dust lay so thick on the edge of the brick bed a finger drawn across it came up grey. She noticed that the place next to hers was empty.

Dakang's bedding was gone.

Her eyes swept anxiously over all the baggage on the two brick beds. She knew Dakang's plastic cloth with the pale green checks, on which Radish had once played a game of chess. But that cloth was nowhere to be seen. And Dakang's blue painted chest, her chipped, flowered wash basin, and even the square mirror she had hung on the wall, they had all disappeared.

She broke out in gooseflesh.

She pulled herself together, put down her things, and ran outside.

The first person she thought of looking for was Mrs. Su.

But Su Fang would never be home at that hour.

The research lab next door to the decrepit old Branch Farm office was locked up.

The accounting office, the clinic, the broadcasting station, they were all locked up.

There wasn't even any smoke coming from the mess hall chimney. The breathing of the wind had suppressed all other breathing.

She ran to the veterinary clinic to look for Dr. Chu.

The horses, at least, had not been blown away to heaven. Dr. Chu was crouched under a horse, working away, his hands in transparent gloves. She rushed in and called his name several times before he looked up. He did not seem at all surprised to see her and chuckled, "Oh, did you come back to join the big campaign?"

"What big campaign?"

"The water conservancy campaign!" He said with a faint smile. He stood up, walked over to the window, and rapped on the glass. "No, the Battle for the Dragon King's Temple!"

She looked out the window, but it was all grey outside and she could not see a thing.

"Digging a drainage ditch to reclaim more land?" she asked anxiously.

"No, they're dyking the Half-way River," answered Dr. Chu.

She was a little surprised. She remembered that Guo Chunmei had been committed to increasing grain production.

As Dr. Chu poured some white liquid into a bottle, he went on, "It's a decision of the Farm's Party Committee. Secretary Li insists that No. 7 should concentrate on raising stock, and that means the dykes have to be strengthened and pasture land opened up. Guo Aijun can't refuse to carry out the Party Committee's decisions, so she has had to leave the drainage ditch half finished and take the squads down to

394

work on the dykes." He sighed. "But it's obvious that with spring sowing about to start, there won't be enough machines and manpower to go around. It looks to me as though we won't make it, big campaign or no. If it's only half done when the spring floods come down, we'll be completely..."

"Has everyone on the Branch Farm gone?"

"Everyone who's able to go. I said to Director Guo, I'm sorry, but one lost colt means three thousand dollars." As he spoke, he bent over and continued his work.

She ran out the door without saying goodbye. She had decided to go straight to the work site. Mrs. Su and Dakang were sure to be there.

The wind blew her this way and that. She took off her scarf and retied it so that it covered her whole head and face. She looked like a masked bandit. The scarf was white, so the fields and sky became a vague white blur as she looked out through it.

She had the wind behind her. It pushed her along, sent her on her way.

She raced along, speeding like a cloud. She had become the wind, and the wind had become her.

She could hear the faint chatter of voices.

She opened her eyes wide and saw clusters of light green and dark blue coats on the yellowing meadow, and as many grimy heads. In addition, there was a low, narrow mound of earth stretching toward the two sides of the meadow like a dead, shrivelled-up snake. Red flags were stuck all over the mound, flapping in the wind. At one moment they curled up like red whips, at the next, they turned into fiery red birds. Something seemed to explode with every crack. It was nerve-wracking.

There was some loose straw piled on the stretch of the mound nearest her. No, it was a few long-bearded clods of dirt. No, to be precise, it was a pile of brown sods.

Each sod was about the size of a small table. Dense grass roots wrapped themselves around the solid dirt, and above the dirt itself was a large mass of limp dead grass. Crystals of ice shimmered in the frozen soil.

There were not many people working. Some were wrapped up tight in their coats and sitting on the earth mound with their backs to the wind, their eyes shut almost as if they were asleep. There were also some people clustered around a grey bulldozer not far away. Under the chatter of the engine came the sound of an argument.

She walked over.

She saw Radish standing with one foot up on the bulldozer's tread and a grimy glove in one hand. He was he snarling over his shoulder, "Anyway, I've never heard of abandoning the machines and having tractor drivers get down and carry sods!"

Someone facing away from Xiao Xiao, covered with dirt and wearing a green army cap, was saying slowly and patiently, as though trying to coax a child, "But they didn't have tractors back when they first opened up the land here, did they? If you, the acting team-leader, won't do it, then all the comrades from the tractor team will walk off the job, and there won't be enough manpower left. You have to take the overall situation into account."

Xiao Xiao recognised Guo Chunmei's voice. She had her hair tucked up under her cap like a tomboy.

But Radish cut her off. "Not enough manpower? It will serve you right if there isn't! Who told you to leave the bulldozers out of it and go scrabbling with your paws?"

Guo Chunmei was a picture of stern resolve, "This is an important matter of the correct political line. It's the fundamental question of whether shovels can defeat bulldozers and men win against machines. The Party Branch Committee has decided on a general mobilization of the Branch Farm to carry sods. This is something with profound political significance!"

The veins stood out on Radish's neck like caterpillers. He shouted, "Your sods are too loose; they're not worth shit! The first time the water hits them they'll collapse!"

Was this Radish? The Radish who had poured the bean seeds out on the ground? When had he become so conscientious? Perhaps he was going to give up his tractor driver's job just because he didn't want to carry those dirty, prickly sods. She could not figure out what was going on. She had overstayed her leave by too long.

A warm dry hand took her by the wrist. Xiao Xiao looked around and saw that it was Mrs. Su. Her face was covered with dirt, leaving only her eyes white. Su Fang took her aside and asked in a low voice, "Did you just get back today?"

Xiao Xiao nodded, and asked right off what was going on.

Su Fang practically glued her mouth to Xiao Xiao's ear and said, "She's been criticised. Secretary Li wouldn't agree to opening up any more land for grain, and she took it badly. She was in the dumps the past few days, but then that Political Department Director from the District Office came. I don't know where she came up with such an order. All our manpower concentrated on building a dyke, a show of some kind of human wave tactics, human will overcoming nature..."

The Political Department. Director Yu? Why was she so obedient to him?

Radish's high-pitched voice was audible again: "Cut the crap! If you bring on the bulldozers we can handle the whole thing and promise to be in time for spring ploughing!"

Guo Chunmei snapped, "A decision of the Party Branch is not subject to change. You do it whether you like it or not!"

Radish burst out laughing and replied, "All right, do it yourself, then!"

He strode off like a shooting star. Several of the others followed him.

They soon disappeared into the dust.

Guo Chunmei snatched up a spade and began digging with all her might.

Xiao Xiao held onto her scarf. She really wished she could call him back. This was 'individualistic heroism'! But at the same time she secretly admired him for daring to embarrass Guo Chunmei in front of everyone. She avoided Guo's gaze and walked away with Mrs. Su, who looked worried.

It occurred to Xiao Xiao that she hadn't seen Dakang anywhere.

"Where's Dakang?" she asked.

"Gone."

"What do you mean, 'gone'?"

"Gone back to Hegang."

"Gone back? Why?"

"The mine."

"To work?"

"No, it was to, to get married."

"Who did she marry?"

"A miner. She can start as a dependant and after a while get a regular job." Mrs. Su was quite calm.

Xiao Xiao stared straight ahead in a daze. She just could not believe it. How could someone as happy-go-lucky as Dakang just go off without a word and get married? She was throwing away the experimental fields she had been planting for five or six years. And besides, they said that girls only married miners when they could see no other way out.

I'm just afraid that when you come back, you won't find me here, murmured Dakang, rolling over.

So, had Dakang been serious about what she said the night before Xiao Xiao left for Beijing? Had she known then that she would be leaving? Had arrangements for Dakang already been made by her family even then? Dakang, why didn't you tell me the truth? But then, you ran off to your refinery in Beijing, phony telegram in hand, so you didn't tell her the truth either, did you? And besides, was Dakang's reluctance to speak that night because of the distance that had grown up between them? No, everybody had secrets they couldn't tell anyone.

Xiao Xiao could not explain Dakang's action, nor could she explain her own. Tangled and uncertain as her thoughts had been before, they were now blown into complete confusion by the wind. It seemed that her return to the Farm this time had only confirmed just how weak, how empty, and how unsettled her mind really was.

48

After the wind had raged for a few days, it finally grew tired and burrowed under the earth to catch its breath. The sky cleared and the tracks of rubber tires, cows' hooves, and shoes of every kind appeared in the sheltered spots where snow remained on the ground.

Xiao Xiao went to the dyke every day to carry sods. The men were laying the rough and uneven sods like bricks to form a dyke more than two yards thick. The dry weeds and dirt raised red welts on her neck. Sweat washed the dirt down under her collar, where it itched and burned unbearably. She put all her strength and stamina into carrying sods every day, until she had worked herself to the point of collapse. Radish had not turned up again since the day he stormed off. Where had he gone? All she could do was throw in her lot with the dyke, live or die, like a good girl, not knowing whether to laugh or to cry as she fought this decisive battle against bulldozers with the spade in her hand. The bulldozer crouched on the sidelines with a silent sneer, openly gloating as it watched with sleepy headlamp eyes the dyke advancing at a snail's pace. Only Guo Chunmei went on day after day brandishing those beefy arms of hers and running back and forth without ever seeming to grow tired. Xiao Xiao could see the scratches on her shoulders, her clenched teeth, and she could hear the ugly things that weary people were saying behind her back. Brown-nose! But perhaps Guo Chunmei actually didn't hear what they were saying. Even if she did hear, she would never turn around. Xiao Xiao was growing fainter and fainter at heart, for it seemed to her that she would never manage to become like Guo Chunmei.

One day Director Yu came down to the battlefield, riding in a green Beijing jeep. He shovelled a couple of spadefuls of dirt and then brushed off his clothes and took Guo Chunmei aside for a long talk. Xiao Xiao happened to look over that way and saw Chunmei nodding constantly. She had her sleeves rolled up to the elbow and looked very energetic. Finally she stopped nodding, as Director Yu had disappeared with a slam of his jeep door. The jeep bounced away up the dirt road, raising a cloud of dust, into which Guo Chunmei smiled and waved.

As they were getting off work, Guo Chunmei walked over to Xiao Xiao and said in a low voice, "Don't come to work tomorrow. Stay home and write a political essay."

Xiao Xiao glanced at her with a quizzical expression.

"It should criticise the theory of exclusive reliance on productive forces and firmly uphold that of the primacy of the element of human effort. So, for example, how a single dyke has brought out in a concrete way the struggle between two political lines."

Xiao Xiao kept silent.

Guo Chunmei went on, "Director Yu was here today and stressed once again the importance of this struggle."

Director Yu. Why is it always Director Yu? You don't know what everyone is saying about you.

She mumbled a vague, "Okay."

"Think it over before you decide." Guo Chunmei smiled tolerantly. The ox cart was waiting for them beside the road, already filled with people. Once they got on, Guo said nothing more, like the sober branch farm boss she was.

The cart lumbered along under the scarlet sunset, where a frozen Milky Way squeezed through the magnificent sea of stars. It was like a translucent layer of eggwhite, scouring pieces out of the pink and violet clouds and brimming over the grain-golden haze; it was confusing, unsettling. This was where Radish had turned and run away that rainy evening.

After dinner, Xiao Xiao put some water on the stove for her laundry. It was still light out, and so she thought she would go back over to the 'chicken coop' and see if Radish had come back yet. All the way there she was thinking about how she might persuade him to stop slacking off.

From the windows of the 'chicken coop', she could hear the sound of people playing a drinking-game called 'guess-fingers'.

"Gimme five, five, five!"

"There they are!"

She could see his round face turned to one side, bright red. There was a frenzied look in those round eyes. With a rough gesture, he yanked his hand out from his armpit.

Gambling? She leaned against the wall. She was disgusted. She had been hurt somewhere. She wanted to leave, but everything was blurred before her eyes. It couldn't be, it couldn't be him; she rubbed her eyes.

"They said you were back, but I still didn't believe..."

A merry voice popped out behind her. She jumped, and before it could come to a halt the voice fell with a thump.

"Hey! What's wrong?"

She looked at his drunken face, his thick swollen neck, and snorted, "What's wrong with you!"

"I..." Confronted with her stern gaze, he wilted in confusion like a child caught out in some mischief. "I..." He rubbed his head. "I don't know what it is, but, but I've been feeling low; it was that day, in the fields. I just went over to No.5 and played around for a few days. Then I bought a bottle of good liquor and came back." He looked up at her. "They've been teaching me..."

She could not remember any of the things she had worked out to say to him while she was on her way over. Now she knew what people meant when they referred to 'resenting iron for not turning into steel'. Chen Xu hadn't been iron; he was a piece of granite, and granite couldn't be made into steel. But Radish was iron, a piece of pure ore. He shouldn't burn himself out in alcohol for nothing. She felt sorry for him, a kid with no one to look after him. Her voice a compound of anger and concern, she shouted, "Instead of going to work, you just hang around here and skylark. You're going to make a mess of your life!"

He hesitated, then straightened up and faltered, "It, it was her who wouldn't let us work. I'm a tractor driver."

"Don't tell me about her, or what she did! Do you work for her sake? We're shorthanded as it is, and unless we get the dyke repaired, our summer pasture will be flooded again." She was wringing her hands in anger. The backs of her hands were rough and she rubbed them until they hurt.

He said nothing more. His glance fell on her hands, and he winced slightly. He stood there for a while without saying anything, pushing the sand under his feet around with the toe of his shoe. Then he burst out, "Oh, I forgot to tell you. Zou Sizhu, the guy from No.5, seems there's something wrong with him."

"Something wrong?"

"I saw him running his hands along the walls as he walked. They say he hasn't slept for seven days and seven nights, and sleeping pills don't do any good. Aren't you, aren't you going to go see him?"

Zou Sizhu. I didn't say goodbye when I left, and now that I'm back... How could it happen? What upset him? Of course it couldn't be because I... It was the university entrance exams.

"Are, are you mad at me? I..." He asked anxiously.

"Go on home." She shook her head. Her mind was about to snap. She felt like going off by herself and having a good cry. She turned and walked away.

The sky had darkened, but it was not black. It was still blue, dark blue, sapphire, royal blue, heartbreakingly blue, like the seashore at low tide. Once he cast his net into the sea, but all he hauled in was a net full of mud. He cast the net again, but when he hauled it in, it was full of seaweed. The sea had swallowed all those shreds of sunset and hung a dim crescent beacon above the reef.

Someone walked toward her with a lighted flashlight.

"It's me, Guo Chunmei." The voice walked closer. "I guessed that you had gone to the tractor crew. What's up? Has Radish come back?"

"Nothing special," she answered. She didn't want to go into it. When could she go see Zou Sizhu?

"Shall we go for a stroll? We really haven't had a good chat since you got back. It's a good thing there aren't any meetings tonight." Guo Chunmei sounded very sincere.

Was it because she had overstayed her leave? Was it the manuscript? Between their minds there lay a river, and then a mountain.

"I've been at No.7 for almost six months, and it seems to me that you've made a lot of progress since you were at No.5." In the azure-grey dusk, the sparkle of Guo Chunmei's eyes was barely visible. It was hard to tell if her smile, which had once been so open and frank, was there or not. "So why haven't you applied to join the Youth League?"

Xiao Xiao gave guarded smile. Would you accept me? I gave up that fantasy as soon as I was old enough to join.

"The Branch Farm's Party group has been considering what to do now that Dakang has gone back to town and there is no one in charge of the research team. I think that if you were to take on the job you could definitely handle it. On top of that, the higher levels are now asking every organization at the grass-roots to set up a theory group. My own opinion is that you could head that as well."

Xiao Xiao gulped. She felt hot all over. So this was what Chunmei... It was strange that she had held her peace and said nothing about Beijing. In all the five years that Xiao Xiao had spent in the

Great Northern Wastes, neither the Organization nor Guo Chunmei had ever shown such trust and confidence in her. What were they up to now?

It was pitch dark. The wind rustled all around her. Guo Chunmei flicked on the flashlight and swept it in a circle.

"Haven't you always liked reading and writing? This is a rare opportunity for you to get some practice. You can write political essays or theoretical pieces and send them off to be published in the 'Reclamation Journal'. Oh yes, and that public declaration to strike roots that I mentioned to you before you went to Beijing; I, well, I did draft something for it, but it's not much good. How about revising it for me?" Guo Chunmei pulled a crackling wad of paper out of her tunic pocket and pressed it into Xiao Xiao's hand without allowing her to make any excuses.

Xiao Xiao wanted to say that she couldn't do it. Why couldn't she? It wasn't writing, just revising. Revising was only a little bit higher. She clutched the piece of paper. She wanted to see just what was on it. Guo Chunmei gave her arm a friendly squeeze. Xiao Xiao broke out in gooseflesh all over.

"Well then, let's settle on this. The theory group will meet tomorrow. I think that the essay about the dyke, the one criticising the theory of exclusive reliance on productive forces, I mean, can be your group's first bombshell!"

It was her who wouldn't let us work. I'm a tractor driver.

"Say, Xiao Xiao. Why don't you answer me? Director Yu just phoned again to ask about this. The topic was his suggestion."

So that was it.

"Director Yu is behind this all the way!" added Guo Chunmei.

"Director Yu? What's the connection between us and Director Yu?" she shouted. Her feelings had finally got the better of her. She was sick of it.

Guo Chunmei was quite taken aback. "Director Yu has always looked after us so well."

"After us?" Once she got started, Xiao Xiao could not control herself. "After us? Or just after you?" She sped up angrily and left Guo Chunmei far behind her.

That strange dream, the jeep driving into a dark hole in the dyke, the two legs in the hole, one wearing a nylon stocking, the other silk; she was disgusted. She didn't want to listen to Guo Chunmei going on about Director Yu. It was her nightmare come true, confirmation of the rumours. "Don't drag me into it!" she shouted.

Guo Chunmei's voice caught up with her. "Don't tell me," she said, "Don't tell me that even you believe all those, those stories?"

Xiao Xiao stopped. In the darkness she was astonished to hear that voice suddenly sound so wretched. Chunmei knew what she meant. She froze.

"Do you really believe them?" asked Chunmei, as though if she did it would hurt her more than the rumours themselves.

Xiao Xiao stammered, "Well, why do you do everything he says, and why does he, well, why does he treat you so differently from everyone else?" Everything goes your way; what accounts for your meteoric rise? "Everybody is talking about it. I couldn't believe it myself at first."

The moon turned away in disdain, the stars frowned. A dark shape sank slowly before her eyes, like a ship foundering on a reef. It was like a hallucination—she could hear quiet sobbing.

"I haven't done anything." The voice on the ground said between sobs. "Really I haven't. If you don't believe me, we can go to the hospital and..."

Xiao Xiao felt a little uncomfortable. It was a lie! She knew there was nothing to those damned stories; she didn't believe anything at all. But she hadn't meant to go poking into other people's secrets. Why did she pay so much attention to this sort of gossip?

"Well, if you haven't, that's that." Xiao Xiao walked over to her. "They were just making it up. You'd better just ignore it."

She touched Guo Chunmei's shoulders in the darkness. They were shaking. Xiao Xiao's hands rose and fell with them. It was a real human body, not a shadow, nor a sinking ship, nor merely a voice. She leaned over to support Chunmei, and although she could not see her face, she felt cold tears on her hands. Xiao Xiao was suddenly overcome by a strange feeling of sympathy and remorse. Not since the night when Wei Hua was hurt in the fight had she ever seen tears in Guo Chunmei's eyes.

"Don't cry, don't cry," she said, crouching down.

Guo Chunmei went on and on, choking back sobs and clinging to Xiao Xiao's hands. It was as though she had an enormous wrong inside her that had to come out in the form of tears, and yet she could not cry out loud. After some time, she looked up and faltered, "I've never done anything like that, really I haven't. There is a reason why Director Yu treats me well. But it isn't, it isn't what you're all saying. I

404

know you won't believe me, but I'll tell you the truth. I know that you're fair. You mustn't tell anyone else, you absolutely must not, not anyone."

Xiao Xiao nodded at once. Her heart skipped a beat. She felt so eager that she was light-headed. She really did want to know everyone's secrets. Everyone's. If Guo Chunmei was really going to tell her the 'truth', she could hardly wait.

The black shadow in front of her pushed Xiao Xiao's hands away and began her story.

You know about my brother Guo Chunjun, the one who died with the militia fighting the fire. He was in the very first group that came up to Heilongjiang to support the frontier in '68. But at that time our family status was... Well, how can I put it? My Dad was an accountant in a factory, but before Liberation he had been in, in the KMT Youth. You know how it is; the children of someone with a historical black mark against him can't go to serve on the front line against revisionism. But at the time there weren't many properly qualified people eager to sign up. My brother was very anxious. He said that if he was going it would have to be to the front line. So he wrote a letter in blood and sent it to the Shangcheng District Party Committee. The recruiting people from the Heilongjiang militia had set up offices at each district committee. Yu Funian happened to be a secretary at the one in Shangcheng District. After he read the letter, he told my brother that if he could get one hundred city kids to sign up, Yu would make an exception for him on the ground of unusual circumstances. My brother got in touch with some of his fellow students and, well, lots of people at school looked up to him, so more than a hundred people signed on. It got into the papers and made quite a stir. Yu Funian was publicly praised by the militia command because of it.

Don't take such a long way 'round. Just what is it that's so hard for you to come out with?

Now, at that time, you collected your own dossier from school and took it to the District Committee, because it was up to the officials from Heilongjiang to decide who would be accepted. When my brother handed his file over to Yu Funian, Yu said, No hurry; why don't you hang onto it for a few days. My brother couldn't sleep that night, and the next day he finally opened up the dossier and, and rubbed out the part about our father's past.

You make it sound so nice. Isn't it obvious that he was putting you up to altering your dossiers? Just to get credit for taking a few more people back with him. How low could a person get!

Not long after my brother left, he wrote home and said that everyone in the team whose background wasn't very good had been put in a special squad and sent off to clear new land several hundred miles from the frontier. He was very depressed and said he had been duped and made into cheap labour. And afterwards he sacrificed his life in fighting that fire.

I know about that fire. It was completely out of control, but the commander ordered truckloads of city kids sent to the scene anyway. The wind shifted, the fire changed direction, and not one of them escaped.

After he fell in action, he was posthumously declared a martyr.

He was lucky to have fallen in action. Otherwise he would have had to pay sooner or later for altering his dossier.

Because of the enormous losses caused by the fire, the officials in that unit were reprimanded and transferred out. Yu Funian just happened to be transferred here to Half-way River, Branch No.5. When he saw my file, he called me in for a talk. Perhaps his conscience was bothering him. He comforted me, and said he hadn't taken proper care of my brother and regretted it very much. He wanted to make up for it.

He was afraid you'd finger him! He was afraid you would spread his despicable story around, that you'd tell people how he took advantage of your brother.

But I know that his conscience isn't troubling him all that much, he's just using me. To tell the truth, I saw through him a long time ago. He's from Anhui; he's not about to hang around Heilongjiang all his life. Just before my brother left, my father had Yu over to our house for dinner and happened to mention that we had an uncle in Anhui who had become chairman of a district revolutionary committee. Yu has remembered that. He wants to use that connection to get his whole family back to Anhui in a few years.

A woman's chastity, her reputation; they will always be her most precious possession. In order to keep it, in order to justify herself, she had no choice, no choice but to give up her most painful secret. So this was how it was.

"But, but why are you..?" Why was she afraid of him? "Why don't you leave?" Xiao Xiao found the breath to ask.

Guo Chunmei had stopped crying. She stood up.

"My dossier was the same as my brother's. Going to university, looking for work, going back to the city, wherever I went they'd just get rid of me if I didn't fix it up, and if they ever found out what I'd done, I'd be finished. So of course I had no choice. Because my brother had altered his, I had no choice but to do the same, and that's why I had to sign up to come to this farm where no one knew me, instead of going with the people from my school. Anyway, so long as Director Yu is here, he can help me. I've thought it all over. As southern kids up here without any relatives or anyone in government to rely on, our only hope is to win the confidence of the leadership. I'm lucky, after all, so long as I am useful to him. As a matter of fact, I don't have any ambitions for myself, I do just want to build up the Great Northern Wastes. I only finished the seventh grade; I'm no good at school, but I could make a good branch farm boss. It's true, I really like the North, I like..."

She was getting excited, and a little flustered. There seemed to be something that in her confusion she could not bring herself to mention, something on the tip of her tongue. Xiao Xiao was suddenly moved, she felt her heart tremble within her, welling up and reaching out. This was a Guo Chunmei she had never seen before. She had never dreamed that Chunmei would bare her soul in the dark. It was not only things that gave off light that could be seen in the dark. Only the darkness visible in the dark was real.

"Then, then you're not afraid that I..." You aren't afraid that I'll look down on you because of this? "You're not afraid that I won't understand?"

"No. You had the courage to leave someone like Chen Xu, and that shows... Well, don't you know how afraid I am of people interpreting my relationship with Director Yu that way. I can't stand it. I despise people like that. I really like the North, and it's because, because the first person I ever loved, the very first, he's here. I've realised that you can only love this place if you love someone who comes from here. It's true. No matter what, I can't forget him."

"Him?"

"Wei Hua."

"Hasn't he moved back to Hegang? How are you two going to manage it?" Xiao Xiao was puzzled to find that she was not all that surprised.

"I don't know." Guo Chunmei shook her head sadly and looked blankly up at the sky. "If I work hard, perhaps, I may be promoted. The District Office is not far from Hegang, you know."

Tears came to Xiao Xiao's eyes. Her ears roared, and suddenly it all came clear. Chunmei had spoken the truth from the bottom of her heart. Chunmei too had something true to say. The truth had a mysterious power of its own to break down the walls between human hearts, even walls that had stood for ages. It could throw great soaring bridges across the seas, across the stars themselves.

"Well, now I've got it all off my chest." Guo Chunmei heaved a deep sigh. "Now that you know the truth, I feel a lot easier. My reputation won't be so tarnished that even jumping into the Yellow River wouldn't wash me clean. Except about my father's past, I've never lied to anyone. I really want someone to understand that. There aren't many of us from Hangzhou on this farm, so you have to help me."

The king has asses ears.

In fact, had she and her brother not been so determined to come build and protect the frontier, no matter what happened to them, that first lie would never have been told. And if it hadn't been for that first lie, all the misfortune, all the shame, and all the remorse that came after might never have occurred. There was nothing wrong in Chunmei's wanting to come to Heilongjiang. Whatever her father had belonged to, she hadn't done anything wrong herself. Nor was she at fault because her brother had altered his dossier, or because she loved Wei Hua. So who then was the Guo Chunmei that people so detested and hated? Perhaps it was someone whom even Chunmei herself did not know. How pitiful, how frail she now seemed.

"Let's go." said Xiao Xiao. And in that instant she forgave Guo Chunmei. She would help her.

49

A few days later, Xiao Xiao had the essay written. Because work at the job site was so exhausting, formation of the Theory Study Group had been put off for a while, and she had no choice but to draft the essay by herself. Of course this sort of thing was very easy to write. One had only to find a newspaper, copy one sentence here and another there, adjust the opening and the conclusion, and it was all set. The title ran "A Single Dyke, and Two Political Lines." It denounced the reactionary theory of 'productive forces' and its reliance on machines for production. After she finished writing the essay, it struck her as a little insubstantial and she felt diffident about it. But when she took it over and showed it to Guo Chunmei, Chunmei was quite satisfied and only had her add the point that the battle of the workers from Branch Farm No.7 on the Half-way River dyke was a great demonstration of the fruits of uniting criticism and practice. When Xiao Xiao had revised it, Guo Chunmei had her make an extra copy and then added red seals to both before putting them in envelopes and sending them off to the Farm's broadcast station and the "Three Rivers Daily."

Xiao Xiao took the opportunity to return to Guo Chunmei the public declaration to strike roots. She told her that it was very plainly written and sincerely felt, and that she had found nothing in it to revise.

With these two chores taken care of, she heaved a sigh of relief.

Then she hurried back to work, back to carrying sods.

There was something odd going on at the job site. People were in the midst of a heated discussion, ironic smiles and sneers flickering across their chapped lips. Someone had pushed a layer of fresh, dry black earth right up onto a stretch of the dyke stacked with sods a few days before. The dyke was higher, and broad tread marks were visible on the ground. It was obviously the work of a bulldozer, but the bulldozer sat there drowsing in its usual place, and there was not a whiff of exhaust on the warm breeze.

I'm a tractor driver. She remembered how discouraged and uncertain Radish had seemed when they talked a few evenings before.

She had a hunch what was going on and trusted her intuition.

She was not inclined to say anything. She had learned to be good.

Nor did Guo Chunmei have anything to say. She just took the lead in getting down to work, as though nothing had happened.

After the political study session in the evening, Guo Chunmei walked up to Xiao Xiao, flashlight in hand, and said, "Come on down with me for a look."

She knew that Guo Chunmei was going down to the dyke.

A few thin clouds were roving the fields on the evening wind. The wind was like a big fleecy sack stuffed full of things. It seemed as though a few green seedlings might slip out of it at any time.

They did not talk. They had talked too much the other evening.

They could hear a rumbling noise coming from the direction of the dyke while they were still far away. The roughness of the road made walking difficult, and their shoes filled with dirt. Sure enough, as they approached, they could see a great grey monster thrusting soil up onto the dyke, snow-white beams of light shooting yards ahead out of its staring eyes. When they had walked a little closer, they could see a round face in the cab, lips pinched, face tense, jaw clenched, driving the huge machine. It whipped around and ploughed into the steep bank, rearing up as though it were hanging on a cliff. The angle was close to forty-five degrees, and it made one's head swim to see the 'dozer evidently on the verge of flipping over. But he looked as though he were absorbed in some sort of game, charging up and backing down, scraping the dirt up higher and higher.

Good for you! He had found a way to help with the job without compromising his principles. Xiao Xiao instinctively raised both hands, cupped them around her mouth, and shouted. Of course the motor was too loud for him to hear her, and besides, the headlamps had not lit up the place where they were standing.

Guo Chunmei took hold of her arm.

"Let's go back."

"Why? Have him get out so we can ask him..."

"No, that isn't necessary. Let him get on with it." Guo Chunmei shook her head firmly.

Xiao Xiao glanced at Chunmei, puzzled that she seemed neither irritated nor surprised. She had apparently only gone down to the dyke to check on a 'horn blow at midnight', a little like the old Landlord Skinflint Zhou in the story of Gao Yubao, stirring up the roosters to make them crow in the middle of this night and get the workers up early. She seemed to have no intention whatever of putting a stop to his work. In fact, with Radish working like this, progress on the dyke would be much faster. But then the essay she had drafted would no longer be based on the facts. Xiao Xiao stalked back angrily. She felt a little awkward. Perhaps this was the direct result of her own grand attempt in the eloquent persuasion of Radish!

But Guo Chunmei was quite indifferent to this whole question. Making the best of a mistake was evidently another aspect of the art of leadership. That political essay had been read over the Farm's public address system almost at once. The embarrassing thing was that no one had said anything about it, just as though they had not heard it. Even Mrs.Su hadn't mentioned it.

Everyone went right on carrying sods day after day.

The sod dyke grew longer and longer.

And the part that had been covered with earth and strengthened grew longer day by day as well.

Everyone took it as a matter of course and just went on as though they were working on an assembly line.

Guo Chunmei had her plan all worked out in advance. Except for the night she had broken down in front of Xiao Xiao, she never betrayed any emotion at all. When Xiao Xiao watched her in broad daylight, she began to wonder if the person who had collapsed in her arms and made that tearful confession had only been a ghost in a dream. If she hadn't been a ghost, if she had only been the plain, dull, ordinary person she normally was, why did she have this mysterious power to tame Xiao Xiao, to make her waver, to make a person of Xiao Xiao's haughty independence into one she could control, could send to do her bidding, could make do without objection the things that this person called Guo Chunmei made her do?

Xiao Xiao could not understand what had come over her.

One evening, Guo Chunmei said to her, "Director Yu just phoned. That declaration to strike roots is going to be published in the 'Land Reclamation News'."

Xiao Xiao grunted.

Chunmei went on, "Director Yu feels that not quite enough people have signed it."

What did that have to do with Xiao Xiao? It was Chunmei herself who had been rushing hither and yon for days contacting so many progressive models on the nearby branch farms to get their signatures.

"Director Yu pointed out that we're the sponsoring unit here at No.7, but I'm the only one to have signed. That's not enough, not strong enough." Guo Chunmei smiled.

Xiao Xiao tensed. "Sure it's enough. It's only cadres who are young people themselves whose signatures carry enough weight for something like this."

Guo Chunmei was the only real youth cadre on No.7. Of course Xiao Xiao herself wouldn't sign, and one might have scraped every corner of the branch farm without finding anyone else who was suitable.

"You'd better get Dr. Chu and Mrs. Su the agronomist to sign," said Xiao Xiao, as a joke. "They've already struck roots."

Guo Chunmei tossed her head, not at all amused. "They aren't educated urban youth. It ought to be someone from the masses if it's going to be effective. Otherwise people will just say that the youth cadres have to strike roots anyway, since they've got responsible jobs."

Xiao Xiao avoided her eyes and stammered, "I think, I think it would best be limited to cadres."

"What about Luo Xinhuai?" suggested Chunmei, out of a clear blue sky.

"Radish?" She was astonished.

"It seems to me that Luo Xinhuai's word carries a lot of weight with the boys, and besides, he's the acting leader of the tractor crew, so he can be counted as either cadre or masses. I hear he's made up his mind not to leave for university. Is that right?"

Xiao Xiao gave a noncommittal nod. He wanted to go in the Army, but certainly not to stay on the Farm. But she didn't say so. It had just dawned on her that Guo Chunmei had never thought of asking for her signature. So far as Chunmei was concerned, she probably didn't even qualify to sign. Although she couldn't help feeling somehow insulted, it was an enormous load off her mind.

"Well, as for Radish, I have no idea whether he would be willing to sign or not," she said.

Guo Chunmei's reply was immediate, "Why don't you go try having a talk with him and see? Everyone says you have a lot of influence over him."

"But, he hasn't been carrying sods these past few days. Doesn't that count as skipping work? It could have a very bad influence if it isn't..." She ventured, unable to flatly refuse.

Guo Chunmei leafed through a newspaper lying on the brick bed and said with a shrewd smile, "Of course not. Director Yu says that we should direct our fire at those old guys who are taking the capitalist road. As for the younger people, we should do our utmost to twist them all into our rope."

Liu the Brute, Director Xu, Secretary Li. I never saw a stingworm climb back up a tree. Have you changed overnight all the regulations kept on the Farm these past few years?

In her confusion, she heard Guo Chunmei continue, "Luo Xinhuai must come home from the job site early every morning. You might wait for him along the way. Tell him that if he signs, he can still be allowed to go later, if he wants to leave. Do you understand?"

And with this, she rolled up a copy of Red Flag and left.

Xiao Xiao shuddered. Did she understand? No, she didn't. No, she did.

The chilly morning wind broke through the great gates of night, blowing the light of dawn inside and coating the black meadows with a ghostly white. The trees, the buildings, the sky itself, all took on a pale grey colour in the uncertain light, so pale that it seemed incapable of hiding anything. Squeezed along the horizon, the crumpled grey clouds had a stern and anxious look.

Xiao Xiao walked slowly along the dirt road. Her face was frozen stiff. She tied her scarf on tight. April mornings bore the last footprints of winter.

She must have gone over it in her head a thousand times, how she would talk him around. Why shouldn't he take this opportunity to change his situation, especially now while Guo Chunmei needed him?

She heard a deep rumbling in the distance. That monster was scrambling up through the thin grey fog. The ground shook, and so did she, deep inside. A frightened grey rat dashed across the road, and a ball of flame shot up and vanished at once. It was a reflection on the window of the cab. Had the morning sun stuck out its tongue? It rolled in with all its dignity, flattening the dim morning light.

She waved.

The engine stuttered. The machine came slowly to a halt.

She could see him clearly inside the distant cab. He had grown a thick moustache, of all things. He leaned out of the window and shouted, "What are you..."

"I haven't seen hide nor hair of you for days." She looked up and forced a smile. "I was afraid you'd got drunk and passed out on the dyke."

"Come on, now." He slammed the cab door and hopped down. "After that time, I never..."

"Okay. These are for you." She stuffed a package under his jacket. It was some sausage she had brought back from home. "You must feel like something good to eat. You're as thin as a rake."

He held the package up to his nose and took a sniff, swallowed, and smiled.

"Still smiling? You're playing the Landlord Zhou the Skinflint every night," she said.

"You mean Luo the Skinflint. No, just plain Radish Skin," he chuckled.

She laughed too. After a moment, her face fell and she looked serious.

"Say, why didn't you even tell me what you were up to? What you're doing is great."

He crinkled up his nose and grunted. In that distinctive Wenzhou accent of his, he said, "I was just afraid of spoiling the revolutionary friendship between you two, that's all. Aren't you 'helping each other, a fine Red couple'?"

"Don't joke about it, okay?"

"No, really, when anybody else overstays a leave by a month, they have to do three months of self-criticism, at the very least, before they're in the clear. But look at you." He did not seem to be joking.

"Well, you too. Guo Chunmei hasn't docked your pay for skipping work."

"That's because I haven't actually skipped work. I'm on night shift." He chuckled. "She's docking my night-shift bonus, though!" He yawned. "But if you hadn't given me such a bawling out that evening, I figure I just would have cut out from work for a couple of weeks and gone to Jiamusi to take it easy. Honest." He rubbed his eyes. "Anyway, I've finally come to the end of my night shift work now. You can tell her that Mrs. Su says we'll start sowing the wheat day after tomorrow, so I'll be taking the machine back. We can't stick with her sod dyke to the finish."

She has written a public declaration to strike roots.

"What are you standing there for? It's bloody cold! Let's go back to the farm together in the 'dozer!" He hunched up his shoulders.

Lots of people have signed it.

"Hop in. I'm dead tired. I'm going back to get some sleep."

You sign too, Okay? She clambered awkwardly into the cab.

Confronted with those weary, bloodshot eyes, she could not remember a word of what she had planned to say. Next to such a great big guy, cold as ice and fiery hot all at once, she suddenly felt very tiny. Her lips moved. The signature is just for show, you can still leave if you sign. She pursed her lips and pressed her tongue against her teeth. The motor was deafening. He was shouting something, but she could not hear him. She could not get the words out of her mouth. If she did, she might be sorry for ever after; she might get his contempt in return. He went on yelling, in the best of spirits. She hung her head and noticed a paper box under the seat. It seemed to be making a chirping noise. The cab was very warm. It was like a hothouse, protecting his heart and keeping it from harm. She just could not say it, no matter what. If she did, she might forfeit his trust forever. She wanted to pick the box up and have a look at the little bird, but the truck was bouncing around so much she could not get hold of it.

"It's an egg." She finally managed to make out what he was shouting. He sounded very pleased about it.

The tractor began to slow down, and the dormitory appeared up ahead.

"Do you still want to join the Army, Radish?" she shouted with all her might.

He nodded emphatically.

"So you definitely want to go?"

He nodded again.

When the truck had barely come to a halt, he bent over, picked up the box, and opened it up so she could take a look. There was a pool of dark yellow liquid and some pieces of speckled egg shell. It was broken. The snow-white swans egg. Why was it broken again? He blanched, looking old and drawn. He threw the box out the window and asked, out of nowhere, "Have you been to see Four Eyes?"

She was quite thrown off. Zou Sizhu? She had been so busy that she had forgotten all about him, so busy she had gone completely blank. Of course she remembered that she wanted to go see him, but she hadn't had a single day off.

"I'll go today," she replied. Odd, that Zou Sizhu had stuck in his mind.

"Anything else?" he asked.

She shook her head and squeezed out of the cab. Couldn't she even try just mentioning the declaration? She waved to him. A puff of black smoke burst from the exhaust pipe, the treads spun around, and

415

the bulldozer was gone. The exhaust dirtied the clean air all around, casting the golden view to the east behind him and his machine.

When Xiao Xiao got back to the dormitory, she found Guo Chunmei combing her hair. Chunmei was always the first one up in the morning.

"Well, how did your talk go?" Chunmei asked quietly.

If she said that Radish was unwilling to sign, Guo Chunmei was sure to be angry and hold it against him, and that would do Radish no good. She could not bear to do that. If she said that she hadn't spoken to him at all, Guo Chunmei might think she had gone back on her word, or that she had something against the declaration to strike roots, or that Radish had ridiculed her. Guo Chunmei would never believe that she had not said anything to him about signing. No one ever believed the truth. Guo Chunmei might secretly despise her. If she couldn't even talk someone like Radish around, she must not be good for much. She yawned and mumbled, while her mouth was still open, "He wants me to sign for him. His handwriting is poor."

She said it very casually, as though it were true. It even shocked her, and even she believed it. Guo Chunmei thought it over a moment, put down her comb, nodded, and said, "Well then, you'd better sign."

And so Xiao Xiao followed Guo Chunmei to the little office, watching silently as Chunmei took a stack of neatly written pages out of a locked drawer. On the top sheet was inscribed: A Declaration of Intention to Strike Roots on the State Farm and Make Revolution All Our Lives—An Open Letter Addressed to All Educated Urban Youth. Guo Chunmei said, Okay, Here's a pen.

"I've got one." She took out the ball-point pen she carried on her. On the last page she saw that Guo Chunmei had already signed in her vigorous, masculine hand. She bit her lip and scrawled the words 'Luo Xinhuai'. No one knew what Luo Xinhuai's handwriting looked like. Her hand was shaking a little. "Is it going to be published?" she asked.

"I don't know." Guo Chunmei's face was impassive.

Once it was published, that would be that, and Radish would just have to accept it there wasn't anything so special about it anyway she could put the blame on Guo Chunmei...

"You'd better take it to the District Office today and give it to Director Yu yourself," said Chunmei in a tone that admitted of no hesitation. "If we mail it, there's always a chance it could get lost." Ever since their talk that night, Guo Chunmei had been taking every

416

opportunity to show her special trust in Xiao Xiao. Was she taking special precautions as well?

"Today?" She was definitely going to go see Zou Sizhu that day; she couldn't put it off any longer. "Better make it tomorrow!" she replied. "I've got a bit of a stomach ache today."

The windows rattled, pelted by smoke and dust. The wind was picking up.

"I'll go tomorrow, for sure!" she repeated. She had no intention of refusing this assignment.

I don't want to be a mighty empress any more, I want to rule the seas. That way I can live out on the open sea, where the golden fish can serve me and I can have her do my bidding.

The windstorm bound the rays of the rising sun to the horizon and with its monstrous broom swept the faint colour of dawn from the sky. The storm had filled the air and covered the land with the dust that it carried, but it remained unconcerned. It whirled and roared, and the earth itself whirled and roared with it. And yet it seemed to Xiao Xiao that the storm would not blow into her breast again, nor could it move her. Her heart was cold and hard. If the storm had a heart it must be the same.

She decided that she would go to No.5 to see Zou Sizhu after work that afternoon. She would have to walk, since she couldn't ride a bicycle in such a wind.

50

Evening was falling, and the wind had not let up at all. Xiao Xiao was walking against the wind. When she had walked almost a mile from Branch Farm No. 7, she caught sight of a Beijing jeep barely visible on the road ahead of her, hopping along like a locust. Her spirits perked up. If it was Director Yu's car, she could give him the public declaration to take back and save herself the trip.

But as the car drew closer, it did not look to her like chubby Director Yu inside. The jeep slowed down as it passed her and then suddenly screeched to a halt a few yards beyond. The door opened, and a white head leaned out. He squinted. "Is that you, Comrade Xiao Xiao?"

"Yes!" She ran over to the car and took those two thin old hands firmly in her own. "Secretary Li!" she cried. Her palms were sweating. If only he hadn't heard that broadcast she had written about the river dyking. She could find nothing to say.

"Going to No. 5?" he asked, with a twinkle in his eye.

She nodded.

"How's the dyke going?" he asked, getting out of the car.

"Pretty well," she answered. "It's at least a couple of miles long now."

"Well, the length isn't the main thing. It's how well it holds that counts." He squinted again and looked out across the level fields. "I hear you people have come up with a way to build the dyke by hand using sods, so I thought I'd come out and have a look. It's so dry this year, I'm afraid the sods may not hold."

She nodded. She realised that she herself was not really concerned about the dyke at all. But he was. He was the master of the little kingdom of Half-way River. That essay criticising... If only they didn't publish it! He made her ashamed of herself. He was the highest ranking official she had ever encountered who was a decent human being.

"In the fall, in the fall there may be another big campaign, to fix it once and for all." For some reason she wanted to reassure the old man all of a sudden.

He smiled at her. His look was mild, but concern and anxiety showed clearly in the depths of those brown eyes, like a deep well so drawn upon that it had run dry. His white hair was tousled by the wind. Year by year the spring winds had blown the spirit from his hair, gathering its healthy gloss into the black soil beneath his feet. They had torn the bloom of his youth to shreds and returned it year by year to the green plains. Now the white of winter was in view. He was old.

He heaved a sigh.

"Ah yes, in the fall. So many things are waiting for us. But I, well, I won't be around Half-way River then."

Her eyes opened wide.

"I'm going to the Xing'an Mountains. They're setting up the new headquarters for an alpine farm," he said calmly. "The transfer order has come down. Today, well, perhaps this is the last time..."

Her eyes filled with tears. No, she murmured to herself. No, you mustn't go. If you go her sense of guilt will never be redeemed. "The Xing'an Mountains? It's very cold there," she said.

"Well, be seeing you!" He held out his small, tough hand. "Keep at it." He gave her a significant smile. "If I'm by here again, I'll stop in and see you all."

A vast cloud of dust shrouded the green car. The setting sun had long since been blown away by the wind. The sky was dark, and she could see nothing around her. Perhaps the wind would blow the sun back again the next day, but perhaps she would never see him again.

When Xiao Xiao walked into the men's dormitory where Zou Sizhu lived, she discovered that the one big hall had been subdivided into a series of small rooms. A long passage had been left under the windows on the north side. In the darkness she could see nothing but the heaps of cinders scraped out of each of the fireboxes. She asked someone who was emptying a stove where Zou Sizhu lived. He gave her an odd look and shouted into a room, "Hey! Isn't Four-eyes being sent back to Hangzhou? Has he left yet?" He didn't look very old. He was probably a city kid recently arrived from Harbin, so he didn't recognise her. Someone answered from inside the room, and he pointed toward a small room down at the end of the hall.

She knocked on the door, but there was no answer. She knocked again, but still no one came to open it. The door was well ajar, and a faint light showed inside. She looked in and saw someone with very long hair bent over and playing with a deck of cards. He divided the cards into a number of piles in front of him. Then he started picking up cards one by one. After a short time, he stirred the cards all up, heaped them into a pile, and began shuffling them gingerly, as though they were almost too hot to touch. He went on shuffling them for a long time, mumbling something to himself. When the cards were finally all shuffled, he started in playing just as before.

She was puzzled by what she saw. In the dim lamplight, his high cheekbones looked exactly like Zou Sizhu's. But he was not wearing glasses. And besides, his furtive motions as he shuffled the cards were quite unlike anything she had seen Zou do before.

Oh, I forgot to tell you. That Zou Sizhu from No.5, seems there's something wrong with him.

Her heart skipped a beat. She hesitated for a moment, and then gently pushed the door open and went inside.

"Zou Sizhu!" she called to him from a distance of several yards.

He slowly raised his head. It was him. Even with his face ashen and puffy, his eyes sunken, and his old bookish manner gone without a trace, he was still himself. Of course, he looked more like a shadow of himself. He stared at her intently, his eyes dull and unfocussed, as though he were in a trance. After he had looked at her for a while, he raised his hands and formed them into two cylinders, which he put to his eyes like a pair of binoculars. He swivelled around as though he were looking for something. Then his tongue moved, and he said, "It's you; you've come?"

Her heart fluttered; she was a little frightened. "I came to see you. I heard you were sick."

"I'm not sick!" He interrupted her, slowly shaking his head. His head seemed very heavy and hard to move. "I'm not sick. The doctor. He says. It's the people who don't think they are sick who are really sick. That's. Ab. So. Lute. Crap!"

The brick bed was cold, the bedding a grimy black. The room was dank and had an unpleasant smell. How long had he been sick?

"Why didn't you have someone bring me a letter? I, I would have come to look after you," she said, on the verge of tears.

"You?" He shook his head again and smiled sadly. "Haven't you been in Beijing? When you phoned from Beijing, the wind was blowing so hard that I couldn't tell what you said. But I did get your telegram."

What phone call? What telegram? Was he really that upset by my going to Beijing last winter without telling him? Perhaps it would have been better if I had come to see him sooner.

"The telegram?" she asked.

"Sure, here it is." He opened his blue tunic and pulled a crumpled piece of paper from a pocket of the shirt he was wearing under his sweater. But he hung onto it tightly and would not give it to her. He giggled. "When I found out you had passed the entrance examination for the Chinese Department at Beijing University, I was so happy I couldn't sleep. If you get in by examination, then you aren't counted a worker/peasant/soldier student, right? When I remembered that you had passed without wearing glasses, I thought, why should I wear them? That's what happened last time. I failed the physical because I wore glasses and my vision wasn't good enough."

Getting into university again! That university business the summer before had been too much for him. It had built up silently inside and finally made him ill. So it wasn't anything she had done after all, was it? He spoke slowly and methodically, without shouting or acting crazy, perhaps just because his nerves were completely exhausted. That was probably a telegram envelope he had picked up somewhere in temporary satisfaction of his inner longing. Zou Sizhu! Who would have thought that you could suffer so much, that your mind might be so fragile!

"Are you sleeping well now?" She tried to sound as casual as she could. "I often have trouble sleeping too."

He shook his head. "What's the point of sleeping? It's a complete waste and a mess. Last time they issued acceptance notices for university, I overslept. Last month they took me to a research institute. It was all white there, and I noticed that none of the people there slept. Actually, they invited me to stay and work there, but I thought there was no point in my going by myself after you had gone to Beijing. So, I insisted on coming back here. Before I did, they gave me a smallpox shot. It hurt so much I thought I was going to die. Now everybody's talking about keeping an eye on the Stinking Ninths, the Intellectuals. But it seemed to me that the people in that research institute were as thick as ants, all wearing blue work clothes."

Her heart shrank within her. She shuddered. All the blood in her veins reversed its course; her very bones froze. He had been sent to that hospital in Beian. Anyone who went there got a psychiatric death sentence. He was probably going to be sent right back to Hangzhou on a medical discharge, back to Hangzhou, back to Hangzhou.

"Say, how's Beijing U.?" he asked all of a sudden. "Do you get lectures from Wen Yiduo?"

She did not know whether to laugh or to cry. Wen Yiduo had been shot by the KMT in '45. "How's your appetite?" She changed the subject.

"Do you think I look like a cop or like a tiger? Why is everyone afraid of me? No one comes to talk with me."

"You seem to be in fine spirits."

"Of course I am. My cards are going to connect soon."

"Connect with what?"

"I'll be saved if I can just catch that turtle." He took the deck of cards up in his long thin hands and began to shuffle it again. He shuffled it for a while and then put it down. He sighed, "But I've been playing for so many days, and the turtle keeps hidden in the bottom of the deck where I can't see it. But it keeps on laying turtle eggs though, inky black, like a cuttlefish."

He could not even carry on a conversation. His reason, his knowledge, they were all tangled up. Is this really you, Zou Sizhu? It's hard to believe. Why did you have to become like this? How could you? What is causing you such pain, shackling you, killing you? If I had come a few days sooner, perhaps you wouldn't have come to this. But even if I had, I still wouldn't have been any help to you. I don't understand what you are thinking; you must be thinking about far too much.

He got a tube of toothpaste out of his trunk and held it out to her.

"Have a bite?"

She was taken by surprise; just as she was going to reach out and take it, he put the tube in his mouth and squeezed a large gob over his bared teeth. He clicked his tongue and made a face.

"It's good, really delicious. I have some every day; my insides are very clean."

She stood up abruptly and said in a loud voice, "Let me help you pack up your things! You're going back to Hangzhou University tomorrow. Why aren't you packed up yet?"

"No!" He blocked her with his foot. "Don't. Don't. It's not necessary. I'm going to leave all my things here as a momento for the Great Northern Wastes. After all, the North has supported me for five years, and not badly, either. I'll leave everything to it for fertilizer. I've already got too much of a load to take home by myself. I have to carry someone on my back."

She could not understand what he was saying.

"Look! Come here!" He beckoned to her conspiratorily. "Come here, I want to tell you something."

She took a few steps toward him, but still kept her distance.

He lowered his voice. Without their thick glasses, his eyes were sunk deep in their sockets and dull as withered leaves.

"It seems like there's always someone following right behind me. It's true, it's been going on for a long time. No matter where I go or what I do, he's always right there."

Her flesh crawled.

"You don't believe me? If you don't believe me you're just near-sighted. When I look at you, it's as though you aren't the person you used to be, but someone else, someone I don't know. And yet I know that this one is you and that one is me. That me looks a little bit like me, and he's about my age. But just as you are about to catch sight of him, he disappears, so you get a good look at him, but he's following me just the same, and I can't stand it. Sometimes he lies on the top of my head, sometimes he crouches inside my heart, sometimes he creeps into my joints, my blood, my insides. He can take any size or shape, but he always sticks close to me."

"Is he a shadow?" she ventured.

"No, no, he's a person."

"A ghost?"

"No, no, he's a person. I'm telling you, it's a person. It seems like, it seems like I'm not a single me; there seem to be two of me, two of me folded up together. If you go east, he goes west; if you go south, he goes north, always just the opposite from you. It's true, I'm not fooling you, and I couldn't fool myself." Then he grew very excited and began babbling, spraying saliva high and low. "I hate him. I want to get rid of him, chase him away, but he won't go. He keeps on talking to me in the middle of the night, making me sing. I think he must be a demon. I want to kill him, to rid the world of a public menace. I've rubbed my back against a tree to scrape him off, I've crawled into a haystack to suffocate him, I've eaten dichlorvos to poison him, I've cut him off with scissors, burned him with matches, but he's like the Monkey King, no matter how you try to kill him, he won't die. They say I'm crazy."

He threw his head back and burst out laughing, just like a frog, his Adam's apple taut and bobbing like a bullfrog's throat. He laughed until her heart was in shreds. It looked like he was in a bad way.

He fell silent, his eyes starting from his head. He stood up on tiptoe and pointed toward a corner of the room. "Hey! There! There! I see him! Catch him quick!" He dashed across the room, clutching at the air, tripped, and crashed down onto the brick bed with a ringing thud. He leapt back up. "There he is! He'll stay with me until I die! He can't die until I do! Catch him quick!" He shrieked in despair, picked up the deck of cards, raised them high in the air, and scattered them with a single toss of his hand. The black and white cards fell like snow, like ashes, all over the brick bed and the floor. "Catch him." He collapsed onto the card-strewn bed, twitching feebly, his lips moving and ringed with white foam. He had finally worn himself out; his head hung over onto the edge of the bed, eyes shut.

He had scared her almost out of her wits. She would have wept, but found no tears. Only after some time had passed did it occur to her to go ask for some cold water in one of the rooms next door. She dipped a washcloth into this and spread it over his forehead. Then she ladled some up in the cup on his wooden chest and slowly dripped it onto his lips. The water seeped down his cheek and into his straggly brown beard.

Her head ached as though it would split.

She crouched down and picked the cards up one by one. The white surfaces were covered with dirty fingerprints. One side was white, one was black. The face was the card, the back was not. Two of me folded up together; if you are going east, it is going west. She thought she had better find someone in charge of his company and ask just how they were getting him to the train the next day. She could come and help him. The next day? The public declaration. At least she should see him as far as Jiamusi. There was no way out for him but to go home to Hangzhou on a medical discharge. She wrung out the washcloth and wiped his face and hands for him. His long black fingernails scratched the back of her hands, leaving a faint smart. The draft blowing in around the window frame was mussing his dry brown hair. A wisp of it lay across his pale brow, soothing that overworked brain. She noticed for the first time, now that his thick glasses were gone, that his deeply sunken eyes were fringed with long, black lashes that curved gently downward, almost bashfully, giving his lean face a pretty, elegant look. She realised that he had never before looked so beautifully refined and gentle. Her heart went out to him. It was all too .

424

late. Was this to be another final parting?

She was running with the wind, and the wind bore her up higher and higher. Her feet left the surface of the earth. The square fields, marked off by the rows of trees planted between them as windbreaks, looked like poker cards ranged side by side. White clouds wound about her and turned into a long trailing skirt. She drifted along with the wind until huge pillars and a lofty palace came into view. Gleaming stone steps led down from a marble terrace to a fountain standing in a lawn. In the centre of the fountain a stream of pearls was flowing like water from the mouth of a large fish. Strains of exquisite music were wafted toward her, and angels with long wings were dancing to it.

What is this place? she shouted.

A beautiful goddess, one of the statues flanking the palace gates, replied, This is Heaven.

She recognised her as Athena, the goddess of wisdom. So the wind had blown her all the way to Greece. Was this an ancient Greek temple? She also recognised Artemis, the goddess of the moon; Eros, the god of love; Apollo, the god of the sun; and Zeus, the father of all the gods. They smiled pleasantly and invited her to rest and enjoy herself in Heaven.

She saw people strolling here and there around the fountain and on the lawns. People were dancing, reciting poems, drinking under the trees, and embracing and kissing among the flower beds. In the sunlight, a pure breeze brought the heavy scent of flowers. The trees and the lawns were a rich, moist irridescent green, and the milk-white pillars were veiled in drifting mist. Pearl necklaces glimmered on peoples' necks. Heaven did indeed live up to its reputation, it was so happy and entrancing a place. She felt herself fortunate beyond the power of words to describe.

Then, she noticed that one fat woman in a long purple gown had another gown on her back, an orange one. She wondered at this. Then she saw a man wearing a cloth shoe on one foot and a sandal on the other. She was astonished. As she walked along, she met an old man with a white beard. As he turned toward her, a second face appeared on the back of his head, this one with a long black beard. She was frightened and turned back, but she found that everyone around her had two faces. If one was smiling, the other was weeping; if the eyes in one face were open, those in the other were closed. And there were people kissing each other with the faces in back. In her terror, she shouted, What is this place?

This is Heaven. The goddess Athena glided toward her with a smile. She noticed that the goddess too had two faces. The other face was ugly, with a large mouth and long teeth. She thought to herself, No wonder Athena is so smart; she's actually grown two brains.

The goddess was gaily sowing seeds on the lawn.

In just a moment, little golden yellow flowers were blooming all over the grass.

She wanted to pick a few to take back, but when she bent down she discovered that the flowers were made of paper.

False flowers! She jumped away from them.

You're mistaken. The goddess Athena, who was wearing one of the flowers on her breast, shook her head. You're mistaken. These aren't called false flowers.

Then what are false flowers? She shouted the question, and her voice echoed across the vast courts of Heaven.

The only false flowers are the ones that form fruit, replied Athena.

Why? Why are the flowers false if they form fruit? She was becoming more and more confused. Is it really neither the male flowers nor the female, nor even those that are neither male nor female?

Of course not. Athena smiled mysteriously. Aren't the flowers that form fruit the parents of the false flowers? With these words, Athena floated away.

She wanted to go with Athena but she was stopped by a little girl with her hair cut short. I don't want to be a two-face; I don't want to be a two-face, sobbed the little girl, hanging onto her dress. Won't you help me, Ma'am?

She could see that the little girl's teeth were pure white and brilliant as pearls. But the face behind her was terribly ugly, with a mouthful of black teeth. She could not bear to let the little girl suffer, so she gathered a few clouds and began to scrub the black teeth, but no matter how she scrubbed, she could not get them white. She kept on scrubbing until her arms ached. She gave up; she knew there was no way to change anything. Since there were two-faced people in Heaven, there were probably some in Hell, too. All of a sudden she thought of herself and broke out in a cold sweat. She wanted to look around and see herself from behind, but she couldn't do it. She wanted to find a ladder and climb down from Heaven, but the foggy clouds were drifting so thickly she could not see where she was walking. All of a sudden, she stepped into a hole and fell from the sky like a shooting star.

426

51

The first thing the next morning, Xiao Xiao took the tractor into town to catch the train for the District Office, taking the public declaration with her. She made a point of getting off as they passed No.5, so she could see Zou Sizhu again. If he was really leaving that day, she could get a train from Jiamusi to Hegang so long as she made the noon train to Jiamusi. There was no sign of life when she walked into the dark, tumble-down hallway. The door at the end of the hall was wide open, and his baggage was still piled up next to the wall, just where it had been the day before. The room was empty; Zou Sizhu was gone. A wave of apprehension passed over her. Only the toothbrush and toothpaste were missing from the top of his wooden trunk, and also the deck of cards. I'm leaving these things to the Great Northern Wastes as a remembrance. She just stood there for a while, then numbly lifted the lid of the trunk. Didn't he take his trove of books? She shuddered—the trunk was filled with shreds of paper, shreds not much bigger than peanuts. They lay there quietly, the whole trunkful.

There, there, I see him, grab him!

She slammed the trunk shut and walked out.

She heard someone poking a fire somewhere behind her and a shout: "The loony's gone back to Hangzhou. They took him away!"

She walked along in a daze. She couldn't catch up with him. One was going north, the other south. The chilly south, the freezing north, they were both cold, anyway. The leaves were in shreds, the clouds were in shreds, the spindrift on the waves was in shreds, strands of hair were in shreds. Everything was in shreds. He can't die until I do. He can't die until he does, he can't fall to shreds until he does. But her heart had been torn to shreds and then put back together. Only here in this frozen land could she put herself back together, like water forming ice and snow during a big freeze.

The wind had picked up.

It was past four when Xiao Xiao got to the District Office, and she did not find Yu Funian there. They said he had gone to the Regional Headquarters in Jiamusi that morning. She left her material in the mail room, spent the night in the District Office reception centre, and caught the early bus the next morning for Hegang. She would have to change to the train for Half-way River there. It would take her most of the day. She was not prepared to wait for Yu to come back. She had hoped all along that he would not be there. She had to hurry back to the Farm. Things were just getting busy in the research team.

She got off the long distance bus on Hegang Old Street. The bus stop was quite close to the train station. She did not feel like wandering around the shops. She was planning to catch the 11:45 train and she did not have any money to spend, having sent half her previous month's wages for the baby. And besides, the wind was blowing so hard. The air in a colliery town is black, and so are the snowdrifts. He was mining coal here; he would never mine his way to springtime. She went into the waiting room to get out of the wind, but was driven right back out by the stench inside. Then she went to the ticket office, where it was actually much quieter. It looked as though almost no one was buying a ticket, probably because the train was usually a little late.

There was still an hour before the scheduled departure time. She had nothing to do, no place to sit, so she stood leaning against a window, turning things over in her mind. The window glass was filthy, so smeared with dust on the outside that nothing could be seen through it.

Under another window not far away, someone was standing and reading a newspaper.

She glanced over and noticed that he was reading the day's "Three Rivers Daily."

She took another look and noticed that the page facing her had a bold headline, "A Single Dyke—Two Political Lines."

Blood rushed to her head. She leaned forward and moved closer to get a better look. He turned and looked at her quizzically.

The paper dropped.

She looked up at him.

"It's you," he said softly.

"Chen Xu." Her lips moved.

He was wearing a tattered green jacket, with black wadding visible at the neck. His chest was grimy. A new but dirty dogskin cap was clutched under his arm, so his long, uncombed hair was visible, hanging down to his ears. He seemed to have changed very little, having neither

428

lost weight nor gained. But his cheeks were clean-shaven and he looked a little livelier than before. She studied him calmly, as though he were just an acquaintance.

"I was just admiring your work." He seemed to be responding at last, with that offhand manner she knew so well. He held the paper up and said, "You know, you really can write."

If there was anything in the world that she most wished would not happen, it was perhaps that he should see that newspaper. But he had just happened to walk by a newsstand.

"How did you know I wrote it?" Her displeasure was evident.

"Hey, don't be so modest! False modesty is nothing but hypocrisy." He cleared his throat. "Your talent along these lines has been evident ever since you started out in the Political Culture Room. It would have been a pretty waste of a year and a half sharing a bed with you if I couldn't even recognise an article you wrote!"

"Don't be so nasty." She was a little irritated. The old feeling for him that she had gone on supposing she might feel if they happened to meet again had vanished without a trace. "If you have an opinion, just say what you think." She wondered how she could get away from him.

"I know you don't like to listen to anything that isn't true." He nodded complacently. "So of course I'll say what I think. It's an amazing coincidence that we should have run into each other here today. I doubt we're likely to encounter one another again in this life. You're rising up to heaven and I'm sinking into the earth, each of us going his own way. So I'd be letting you down if I didn't tell you this."

He took out a pack of cigarettes, lit up, and took a drag.

"What I have to say couldn't be more simple. It's this: it looks to me now as though your talent for telling lies has long since surpassed mine!"

Something struck her in the head. She saw stars and broke into a cold sweat. Could you come back and get it after I get paid. A dark shape snickered in a corner. Her mouth was dry.

"No," she stammered, trying to explain, "I didn't mean to, that time you wanted to borrow money, I, I was really going to lend it to you, but, but then I got a telegram from home all of a sudden..."

He burst out laughing, the ash flying from his cigarette. She could not see why he should laugh.

"Borrow money? You think I'd borrow money from you? What a joke! That was a bet that Bubble made with me. He said that you'd never, ever make up a lie. But even if you did, it wouldn't fool me. Do you think an old swindler like me couldn't tell whether you were lying or not? Anyway, wouldn't care if you did fool me. I don't get all upset about it like you do. That's because," he paused, threw back his head, and blew a smoke ring into the grimy air, "Because fooling people and getting fooled is just part of life. We go on fooling each other back and forth and it all works out even in the end, just like I told you long ago. What do you say? I'd make a pretty good prophet, wouldn't I?"

"I haven't cheated anybody," she insisted. "Don't talk as though we were the same."

"Far be it from me, I assure you!" A sneer flickered across his lips. "Of course we aren't the same. With a flick of your pen that 'hundred-day transformation on Branch Farm No.7' crap covers the earth. All you have to do is close your eyes and say 'a single dyke— two political lines' and all the crows turn into magpies. How many thousands and thousands of readers have you cheated by thoughtlessly painting these phony pictures, by repeating all those lies? And now you're going to be praised and promoted and given big jobs for it. Shit! Don't you try to tell me you've never cheated anyone, that you've never learned how to lie! You've made it real big as a liar!"

Xiao Xiao was terrified. He had been following her in the dark, watching her, keeping track of her. The monster! If he knew, if he knew about the signature on that public declaration... She gaped, unable to speak.

"As for me," He threw his cigarette on the ground and stubbed it out with his foot, grinding away at it until it was completely pulverised. "I got in trouble for cheating people, condemned beyond redemption— and you know why I did it then, too. Now our situations are precisely the opposite of one another, and it's too bad, but we're going to end up in exactly opposite ways as well."

Silence. An ear-splitting blast from a train's whistle. The ceiling vibrated.

Exactly opposite? Perhaps. No, she hadn't cheated anyone. That was her job, her duty, her ideal, her...

He raised his arm and glanced at his watch.

"I came up out of the shaft especially to meet Bull." He sounded a little more calm. "He got two years for beating that horse to death. Now that his term is up and he's out of Tangyuan, he phoned me. He doesn't want to go back home. He wants to go down into the mines and earn some money. The train's a little late."

430

She stared at him wide-eyed. Bull? That broken swans egg. What was this? Were they friends now? When had they come together? He had forgiven him. Was it because of that sack of fish during her lying-in month? Friendship was both simple and substantial. Love was substantial, but at the same time, it was complicated. That swans egg was gone forever, but the swans returned every year. The most terrible thing in people is when they lie to themselves. The truth always happened on me, but I never happened on the truth. She was puzzled and confused.

"So, are you planning to just stay here, in the mines?" she asked. Why didn't the train come? She didn't understand why she was still standing there.

He shook his head and lit another cigarette.

"Take me for an idiot? You pour a little ink over your tobacco and smoke it for a month or so and it starts to show up as a shadow on your lungs. As soon as you get a medical discharge, you can head back home. At least I've got enough brains to pull the wool over a doctor's eyes."

She shivered.

"Don't get upset. People who can express whatever so-called evil they think of aren't the worst kind." He stared at her with his cold and piercing eyes. "Who's more honest, the bastard who admits he's no good or the hypocrites who think they're so above it all? You can't make your selfish desires, your inner distractions let's call them, go away just by refusing to admit to them! They won't disappear just because you want them to!"

When I look at you it's as though you aren't the person you used to be, but someone else, someone I don't know, and yet I know this one is you.

She did not want to listen to him make a speech. The train still had not come. She hesitated a moment and said, "Did you know that Zou Sizhu's had a nervous breakdown?"

"A nervous breakdown?" He seemed entirely unmoved, and puckered his lips. "Do you know if he's really crazy? All kinds of people are getting medical discharges by faking insanity. I..."

"You're heartless!" She broke in on him in exasperation. "If there's one person in the world who could never pretend anything, it's Zou Sizhu!"

He chuckled and gave her a sly wink.

"He can't pretend? Did he ever tell you he was in love with you?"

431

No he hadn't, never. And even if he had loved her, he must have stopped long ago. He was disappointed in her.

Chen Xu went on, as though he knew everything there was to know. "I knew he always wanted to get close to you, only he didn't dare think of it, let alone say anything. When he saw for himself that we had settled down on the Farm, he realised that if he didn't get into that university, if he didn't get off the Farm, it would all just be a daydream. Repression is a kind of pretence too. If you want to pretend you have to repress yourself, and the real surprise is when someone who's repressed doesn't go nuts. The difference between him and me, if you really want to know, is this. When I saw how the world works and that there wasn't anything I could do about it, I decided to fight fire with fire. Because the only way to beat those bastards is to be even worse than they are. But Zou Sizhu..."

Her eardrums were about to explode, her very scalp...

"But that Zou Sizhu was obviously sinking into a mudhole, and he knew it all along, but he went on trying to pretend he was pure and noble. No wonder he was suffering!" He pressed on, "Those bookworms think too much and then come up with these screwball ideas to torture themselves with. So I don't think you can really figure out whether he was actually crazy or just faking it. Lots of the old philosophers were nuts, you know."

If he kept on talking, she was going to go crazy herself.

"But there's really nothing wrong in that. It's just the way people are, true and false, good and bad, all mixed up together. If me and my kind ever got back on top, if they put me in charge, I'd work a real revolution on all this modern morality crap. I'd have everyone turn loose their so-called demons and give them time and space to get into trouble every day. Nobody would be surprised or scared of other people's demons any more, and no one would feel weighed down any more just from carrying their own demons around. And besides, none of the demons would develop a hatred of humanity because of having been bottled up inside too long. The only result of their slaughtering one another would be self-destruction. When they were worn out, they could rest. And when they were resting, perhaps the world would be at peace. Of course, a peaceful world is boring, not much better than being dead. So peace is always temporary. But at least people wouldn't have to go on lying and pretending. Their selfish desires could be released by a kind a spillway. Don't you think that would fit better with human nature?"

"Please stop!" Xiao Xiao felt her anger welling up inside, the veins standing out on her neck. How easily, how lightly he let himself off. What nerve he had, making up this demonology junk just to account for his own weakness and failure! He would never convince her. She would never act like that. She would find the truth for herself. And she could find it. "Goodbye!" she said brusquely. She turned and rushed off without a backward glance.

She did not know how she got back to Farm No.7. The wind went on howling around her, and it was dark out. She was filled with disgust the whole way. How many thousands and thousands of readers have you cheated by thoughtlessly painting these phony pictures, by repeating all those lies? And now you're going to be praised and promoted and given big jobs for it. Shit! You've made it real big as a liar! Those words swirled around in her stomach, her veins, stabbing right to her marrow like red-hot needles, like a keen knife cutting her skin away strip by strip until there was none left. If he had known about Radish's signature on that public declaration... He had seen through her long ago. He was the only person who could see through her!

She kept on walking, oblivious to everything. She seemed to be walking across a spongy marsh, her feet sinking farther and farther down into it. She struggled. The wind ripped at her, she ripped at the wind. The fields stretched out wide around her. She wandered through an uncertain void. She could not fill the void; it would swallow her up. She realised that her heart was actually empty; her brain was empty, like a fallow field, like a stretch of ground that had never been cultivated. But there was someone she did not recognise following her. Just as she was about to catch sight of him, he would disappear. It's as though I'm not one me, there seem to be two of me. He is inside me and I am inside him. She was terrified. She knelt down on the ground. Now your talent for telling lies has long since surpassed mine. She gulped down the wind and spat it back out. The wind is like a net, the net of heaven has a wide mesh. The most terrible thing in people is when they lie to themselves. From this it seemed that people had two selves, and the problem was that they never recognised each other. She had no doubt been lied to by her other self.

She ran as though for her very life. She wanted to catch up to the wind, to run before it. Anything to keep that almost visible character who kept hounding her from catching up! The wind was crimson, it had turned an icy crimson from coursing through her veins, a fiery crimson from passing through the sun. The sun was about to set, and the wind might turn cold, but also black. Black was his favourite colour. She did not know what colour she liked, but she would never like black. She had spent too short a time in this many-coloured world; more of her time would remain in blackness. If only she could like all colours except black! The wind was swirling around, swirling into a rainbow, a rainbow-coloured ring. She had never seen such a many-coloured wind. An exquisite, radiant wind. The sun would set in a moment, and it would be a new and unfamiliar sun that would rise the next day. The next day's sun would bring her no rainbow-coloured wind, it would not forgive her. She had to find Radish.

She saw Guan Er in front of the tractor shed, carrying a bucket. Before she could ask, he said gruffly, "Radish isn't here!"

"Where, where has he gone? I just got back," she implored.

"There's been a fire on the dyke." Guan Er pointed off to the west. "The dyke has burned to ashes. The firefighters have come back, but I didn't see him."

Xiao Xiao turned and ran toward the dyke. Sweat ran off her forehead and got into her eyes. She kept on running. She wanted to find Radish, to tell him the truth. She might feel better if she got it off her chest.

Far off on the dyke, wisps of dark smoke were curling up under the setting sun. The smoke was scattered on the wind, a swirl of black ash like a swarm of moths or flies.

She could smell burning.

The dyke that everyone had been sweating and toiling to construct for almost a month looked like a long snake with a broken back, lying paralysed on the bank of the river. The burned sods had collapsed in a soft heap. Now that the fire was out, the old earth bank, looking too fragile to touch, was revealed, like the bones inside a rotten coffin. It was not water that had destroyed the dyke, but fire. She was almost paralysed by the sight. A cigarette? Wildfire? No one had told her.

There was a pale grey human form sitting motionless on a mound of earth at the base of the dyke.

"Radish!" she called. Why was he feeling so bad? It should be Guo Chunmei sitting there.

He just sat there, making no sound.

"Radish, it's me." She stood behind him. "Listen to me."

He seemed to grunt softly.

"Do you still want to leave? To go in the army or something?" she ventured.

He nodded.

"What about university? Guo Chunmei says..."

He broke in. "What does Guo Chunmei say?"

"She says that, that," She still could not get the words out of her mouth. "She says that if you sign the public declaration to strike roots, she'll let you go."

He sneered. "If I go, I won't need her help."

She hesitated a moment, for his sake, and for her own. "But, I think, I think that if you just sign it, it won't mean any..."

He stood up and turned to face her.

"You mean I should put on a little act for appearances' sake?" He seemed surprised. He paused, and then declared, "No, I won't do that."

She avoided his flashing eyes. She lacked the courage to look him in the eye. Her own eyes felt sore and weak in that strong light. She knew that if she did not speak she would lose the chance forever. She would lose herself and his friendship. She bit her lips and then burst out, "I've already signed for you!"

"You're joking, aren't you?" Doubt and self-reassurance flickered across his face. He even grinned. "You're joking. You're not the type. If you hadn't come to No.7 this year, I don't know what sort of trouble I might have gotten into. I'll never forget what you said to me in the cornfields that day in the rain."

"No!" shrieked Xiao Xiao, "It's true! It's true! I'm telling the truth!"

It was as though he had been struck by lightning. He stood still, his arms shaking. After a long while, he raised his eyes and looked at her. She would never forget the look of cold disdain that flashed across those youthful eyes, around which fine lines had just begun to appear, eyes that had once sparkled with genuine respect for her. It was a look that in a single instant plunged the whole world beneath a cold black sea. A layer of ice closed over her heart forever. She trembled.

"Where is that thing now?" he demanded.

She told him it had already been sent to the District Office. She wanted him to understand that the thing was done. She realised that she had not really understood him. He strode abruptly off.

She ran ahead and blocked his way.

"What are you going to do?"

435

"I'm going to the office to strike off my name. If I don't, how will I face people once it's published?" He spoke calmly. She saw a file of great silver geese fly over in those sky blue eyes.

Was this the first flock of geese to return from the south? Had springtime come?

He brushed free of her arms and she let them fall to her side.

The wind tossed the strings of his leather cap, blowing them out behind him. Against the wind, over a dozen miles to town. She stood there watching his faded denim jacket vanishing into the wind-tossed dust. Perhaps she had really counted on his making up for her mistake all along, for his own sake and for hers. The sun was just setting behind their backs. He had no rainbow coloured wind. His wind was white.

The horizontal light of the setting sun drew her solitary shadow out long and pale across the green and tangled plain. He had gone. And he had gone. And he too had gone. She had gone. She would go sooner or later, somewhere high up. Only she was left; and the fine black powder filling the sky and covering the earth.

How many times had the world crumbled into ruin? Was it reborn from the shreds?

It was like the dyke, scattered by the wind, the ruined, obliterated dyke.

It was the wind, bereft forever of its warmth and of its tears.

A cruel wind that would never again bear those rainbow dreams away with it on its travels.

It was getting dark. She walked alone across the plain. How far had he gone? She knew that she could never again go back to where she had been before.

436

图书在版编目(CIP)数据

隐形伴侣:英文/张抗抗著;(美)白润德(Bryant, D.)译。
-北京:新世界出版社,1996.1
ISBN 7-80005-299-0

Ⅰ.隐…
Ⅱ.①张…②白…
Ⅲ.长篇小说-中国-当代-英文
Ⅳ.I247.5

隐 形 伴 侣

张抗抗　著

*

新世界出版社出版
(北京百万庄路 24 号)
北京大学印刷厂印刷
中国国际图书贸易总公司发行
(中国北京车公庄西路 35 号)
北京邮政信箱第 399 号　邮政编码 100044
1996 年(英文)第一版
ISBN 7-80005-299-0
05400
10-E-3052P